SCISSORS, PAPER, STONE

SCISSORS, PAPER, STONE

a novel by

Martha K. Davis

Winner
Quill
Prose Award

Red Hen Press | *Pasadena, CA*

Book design by Selena Trager

Library of Congress Cataloging-in-Publication Data
Names: Davis, Martha K, 1961–author.
Title: Scissors, paper, stone: a novel by Martha K. Davis.
Description: Pasadena, CA: Red Hen Press, [2018]
Identifiers: LCCN 2017051800 | ISBN 9781597090469 (tradepaper) | ISBN
    9781597092487 (ebook)
Subjects: LCSH: Brothers and sisters—Fiction. | Families—Fiction. |
    Domestic fiction.
Classification: LCC PS3604.A97256 S35 2018 | DDC 813/.6—dc23
LC record available at https://lccn.loc.gov/2017051800

The National Endowment for the Arts, the Los Angeles County Arts Commission, the Ahmanson Foundation, the Dwight Stuart Youth Fund, the Max
Factor Family Foundation, the Pasadena Tournament of Roses Foundation,
the Pasadena Arts & Culture Commission and the City of Pasadena Cultural
Affairs Division, the City of Los Angeles Department of Cultural Affairs, the
Audrey & Sydney Irmas Charitable Foundation, the Kinder Morgan Foundation, the Allergan Foundation, the Riordan Foundation, and the Amazon Lit-
erary Partnership partially support Red Hen Press.

   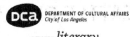

First Edition
Published by Red Hen Press
www.redhen.org

For Pat, without whom . . .

And in memory of
Edward S. Davis, Jr.
1963–1990

PART ONE

1964–1982

*Listen, whatever it is you try
to do with your life, nothing will ever dazzle you
like the dreams of your body.*

—MARY OLIVER

CHAPTER I

Catherine

Spring 1964

I HAD NEVER WANTED MY own family. The older I grew, the less I could tolerate the one I came from. Once when I was fourteen and my brother Andy was ten, we followed the stream at the bottom of our hill, climbing over low stone walls and balancing on trees fallen into the water before jumping to the opposite bank. We wanted to find out how far we could go before we encountered a barn, a road, someone's house. It was all woods, occasionally a pasture with a few horses flicking their tails. As we walked, we imagined that we were ten years older, exploring a part of the world where no one had ever been. I decided I would carry a jackknife, a compass, and *The Voyage of the Dawn Treader*, which my mother had bought me the day before when it finally arrived in the bookstore. Andy said he would bring matches to light campfires and a can of bug spray. It would be possible to survive by eating the plants, drinking the stream's clear water. We had been walking for over an hour before I realized I was actually running away, or at least investigating how it could be done.

As if he knew what I was thinking, Andy said, "Let's go home, Cathy. I'm tired."

Straddling two stones in the middle of the stream, I looked back at him. His hair was plastered to his forehead by sweat; his PF Flyers were soaked. We had been having fun splashing in the water and guessing what we would find up ahead. He jumped to a flat rock, leapt to solid ground, and started walking back, his head down. I saw then that when I left home for real, I would have to go further than downstream, and I could take nothing with me, not even Andy.

Twelve years later, I had escaped to the other coast. I lived with my husband and my new daughter in a house that Jonathan and I had built ourselves, and I was surprised to discover I had never been happier in my life.

Jonathan and I had been married four years before we felt ready to consider becoming parents. In the first years of our marriage, he had dedicated most of his waking hours to writing for the *San Francisco Chronicle*, working his way up to junior reporter for the City Desk, and we had both become involved in the civil rights movement, which in the Bay Area mostly meant marching to end job discrimination and raising money for voter registration in the South. When Jonathan rolled over in bed one morning and said, "Cath, let's adopt our child from Korea," I knew immediately it was the right thing to do. During the Korean War I had been in my early teens; I remembered listening to radio newscasts reporting on the Korean children who were orphaned and later those who were abandoned because their fathers were American soldiers. At school one of my teachers brought in newspaper clippings, and our class put together packages of toothbrushes and socks to send to those children overseas. I had seen their faces, read their stories. They had been real to me, like faraway younger cousins.

We waited until the adoption process was set in motion to inform my family and Jonathan's. Then I was glad that we lived three thousand miles away. Over the phone, my mother accused me of depriving her of her own grandchild, a direct descendent. When I pointed out that Robert and his wife Nora had already given her three, she told me I was being contrary and started to cry. My father blamed me for upsetting her, adding, "There's no use in trying to talk sense into you."

My sister Susie never returned the phone messages we left with other girls in her dorm. Weeks later she insisted she had never received them. I called Andy at his college too. On the phone he didn't say much. He seemed distracted, and although he congratulated Jonathan and me, I felt disappointed hanging up, wanting more. Robert and Nora, on the other hand, told us we were being absurd. Why would we adopt a child when we could have one of our own? It wasn't natural. Robert dismissed all the reasons we gave him, calling us bleeding-heart liberals. Finally Jonathan told Robert that it wasn't any of their business; if they didn't want to support us, we wouldn't talk about it with them anymore.

By then I could no longer be rational about the subject. After a certain point I could give no more logical reasons, no considered answers. Day after interminable day, we waited for the home study, then for approval by the agency, then to hear when our daughter would come to us. I became incapable of smiling at the children I saw downtown waiting with their mothers at the bus depot to go into the city or spinning a yo-yo on its string as they climbed a steep street on their way home after school. None of those children were mine. In the supermarket, the sight of a woman with a child in the seat of her grocery cart could reduce me to tears. I wanted to be a mother, and I wanted my daughter to be the scrunch-faced newborn whose picture we had picked out at the adoption agency. If someone had told me even a year before that I would feel so covetous, so obsessed, I would have laughed outright.

The night Jonathan and I waited for the plane carrying Min from Korea, there were five other couples at the gate looking equally as anxious as we felt. We all clustered in front of the big window, squinting up at the dark sky. We were trying to see past the spotlights to the airplane where our children were—where the children who were soon to be ours were. One woman had knitted baby booties and a little sweater for the child she was waiting for. She clung to them as if holding them tighter might hurry the plane's arrival, bring it down safely. Other couples carried baby blankets, bottles, dolls. I tried to be casual as I looked over their provisions, the offerings they had brought to welcome their children into their lives. I couldn't help comparing my blanket to theirs, trying to assess my worthiness as a mother. I had waited so long for this day, wanted this child so badly. I couldn't believe, after the months of interviews and endless waiting, that the moment had finally come.

Harriet, our social worker from the agency, patted my shoulder and wandered down the corridor in search of a water fountain. Jonathan looked at his watch again for what seemed like the fiftieth time. The plane was over an hour late, delayed by bad weather and lengthy stopovers. He shuffled through the papers he carried in his hand, some of them written in English, some of them in Korean: the visa, the adoption agency's home study certifying us suitable parents, the interim adoption court order, the official documents from the orphanage in Korea, other documents that Harriet had told us we'd need. One of them slipped from Jonathan's grasp and wafted down to the floor. He stooped and picked it up hurriedly, then went through the order of the papers, inserting the errant document in its place, counting the total number one more time. He looked up at me and gave me a wan smile. I couldn't smile back. I felt as brittle as glass. I had never been as nervous as I was that night.

Suddenly I felt a surge of fear and had to sit down in one of the padded chairs. I didn't know what I had gotten myself into. I was damp with sweat and my heart was thudding against my chest. Who was I to think I could be a mother? Especially to a child who, three months before, had been born to another woman, a complete stranger, in a country utterly unknown to me. I looked up at Jonathan, relieved that Harriet wasn't there. I was afraid that if she saw my terror, she would rescind her decision to allow us to be parents to Min.

Jonathan was looking out the window, past the other couples crowded against the glass. "The plane's here," he said in a curiously neutral tone. Then he looked down and saw my face. He moved nearer and put his arm around my shoulder, hugging me close against him. This was it.

I had never been so aware of change at the exact moment it became real. For all three of us, there was no turning back. I couldn't remember wanting anything this much. I leaned my head against Jonathan's stomach. I started to cry. My tears soaked into his flannel shirt.

"I love you, Catherine," Jonathan told me, squeezing my shoulder.

It only made me cry harder.

Andy came to visit us three months later, during his spring vacation. It was his senior year; in the fall he would study law at Vanderbilt. I was proud of him for having been accepted but baffled as to why he had chosen law school. I'd always imagined he would have a career as a marine biologist or a forest ranger, some kind of hands-on research job that would feed his incessant curiosity and his natural restlessness.

We spent Andy's first day with us in San Francisco, showing him the tourist sites. The day was warm after the fog burned off. Jonathan and I traded carrying Min as we climbed the steep steps from the Embarcadero up to Coit Tower, passing terraced gardens and rows of colorful Victorians on our way. Inside the building, Andy went up to the windy tower to see the views, while Jonathan and I stayed downstairs to show Min the historical murals of the area painted on the walls, pointing out to her the political and cultural references. She slept through most of it, but we were enjoying ourselves too much to care.

On the long way down the spiraling road, I took Min from Jonathan while Andy walked faster and faster ahead of us until he was running and shouting, "I can't stop! The brakes are gone!" I laughed, feeling Min settle her head against me and watching my brother disappear around a corner, his loafers slapping the road. Jonathan said something under his breath. I knew Jonathan thought Andy was immature, but he had only seen him with me. Andy and I slipped back into the memory of our shared childhood when we were around each other; it was one of the pleasures of being sister and brother.

To get Jonathan to smile, I reached out my hand and took his, swinging our arms between us. "He used to do that when we went skiing. We'd all gather at the top of the chairlift and set off, practicing our snowplows and stem christies to zigzag carefully down the mountain. Then Andy would come barreling past us, straight down, shouting, 'The brakes are gone!' My father called him a damn fool, but he never wiped out." It didn't sound particularly amusing once I explained it. "I guess you had to be there," I told Jonathan. But he smiled and swung our hands higher, until they reached the zenith of their arc and broke apart.

We took a ride on the Hyde Street cable car, but the clanging of the bell made Min cry, so we jumped off and walked to North Beach for lunch at Caffe Trieste. We were having dessert, Min in my lap, when I heard a voice ask, "Is she yours?"

I looked up from feeding Min a small spoonful of strawberry gelato. An older couple stood in front of our table, gaping at my daughter. I nodded but didn't answer. I was already tired of other people's reactions.

The woman smiled slightly. "How marvelous of you. Imagine what her life would have been like. She's a very lucky girl."

"Actually, we think we're the lucky ones," I said and went back to feeding Min. Out of the corner of my eye, I saw the woman's husband nudge her. They moved away and left the restaurant.

"Arrogant bastards," Jonathan said. I looked up at him. He was staring angrily after the couple. Andy was looking out the window.

I realized that Jonathan had rarely been in public with Min before. This was apparently the first time he had been subjected to other people's unsolicited opinions of what we had done. "You'll get used to it," I told him, conscious of how completely I had adapted to the changes Min had brought into my life.

I glanced at Andy again, who had turned his attention to the unlit votive candle in its glass cup on the table. He pressed his finger down against the wax, leaving a shallow impression. As soon as the subject had turned to Min, he had removed himself from the conversation. I felt hurt, realizing he hadn't shown much interest in my daughter ever since I had introduced her to him the day before. He had been polite, peering into her face and commenting on how small she was. I knew he liked the idea of eventually becoming a father himself, but I also knew he was uncomfortable around actual babies, so I hadn't tried to make him hold her. I had thought he just needed to get used to being around a small child. But it was a full day later, and still he practically ignored her, as if she weren't almost always attached to me, riding my hip or sleeping on my shoulder or giggling in my arms. Maybe he felt left out somehow, though he must have known the entire week was planned around him. Watching my brother inspect the candle, I wrote it off as insecurity, simple lack of experience. Being around Min would be good for him, I decided. He would see how Jonathan and I interacted with her, and he would start to love her as we did.

I leaned forward, holding Min securely, and pressed my index finger in the candle wax too, leaving my print beside his. "Do you want another ice cream?" I asked my brother, knowing he would never turn down a second dessert. And I had to admit I enjoyed watching him eat it. I had always taken pride in my ability to make him happy.

During the week, while Jonathan was in the city, I drove Andy to the redwood forest of Muir Woods, the beaches and trails of Point Reyes, the vineyards of Napa Valley. I strapped Min into her car chair in the back seat, where she seemed happy enough as long as we didn't ignore her for too long. One afternoon Andy and Min and I took a long walk at Tennessee Valley. We hiked up into the headlands, past stands of eucalyptus trees, following a narrow trail through the tall grasses. The sage plants gave off their tangy scent as we brushed past. At the top we turned onto the coast trail toward Muir Beach. Andy stopped every few minutes to look out to sea, following the flights of gulls as they dipped and soared. The wind carried the scent of a wood fire from the north. Eventually we sat on a large boulder, sharing a Hershey's chocolate bar. I took the Hike-

A-Poose off my back and held Min for a while, who was getting fussy
from staring at the landscape behind me for too long.

Before we turned around, Andy walked down and stood at the edge
of the cliffs. Far below him, waves smashed against the rocks, sending
up a spray of foam. I hung back, afraid of erosion and the unpredictable
winds. The ocean air sharpened my senses. I was aware of everything at
once: the rumble of water rushing back into the sea; Andy standing in
his windbreaker the way our father stood, with his legs apart and his
hands in the pockets of his khaki pants; the solid weight of Min's small
body as I held her against me; my own sense of completeness at that
moment. The three people I loved most in the world were with me in my
daily life. I wanted to hold on to that feeling, make it last. Andy could
surely find work as an attorney in San Francisco. It was easy to imagine
the future: Andy and I sitting back in deep canvas chairs on the deck of
his ocean-front house while Min and Jonathan took a walk down the
beach; later, after making us hamburgers on the grill, Andy telling Min
the story of his first visit to us, back when he was still in college and she
wasn't even crawling yet.

In front of me, Andy lowered his head and kicked a small stone over
the edge of the cliff with his topsider. Then he turned and walked toward
us, jutting his chin out briefly to draw my attention to Min. Perhaps
it was the salty breeze or the luxury of stillness after being jounced by
my walking that had pacified Min. Her head rested on my shoulder, her
mouth open and drooling onto my sweater as she slept. I put my hand
up and stroked her dark thatch of hair, awed all over again by her utter
vulnerability. When I looked up, Andy was walking back down the path.

We took a different trail back, further inland, and eventually came to
a fire road where we walked side by side along the ruts. I inhaled the scent
of wild oregano. Andy told me he was nervous about going to Vanderbilt
in the fall. He had heard that law school was tough, but, more than that,
he was afraid he would give in to the pressure of everyone's expectations.
All his friends, and especially our parents, assumed he would become

a Wall Street attorney, whereas he was interested in starting a private
practice in a small town. "I don't want to represent insurance companies.
I want to help ordinary people and have a normal life."

I listened, letting him talk. My brother touched my arm and pointed
into the distance, to the rise of the next hill. A large, long-legged bird
rose up and took wing, stroking powerfully out toward the ocean. "Is
that an egret?" Andy asked, his voice hushed.

"No, a heron."

We watched it turn south along the shore before resuming our walk.
Min wriggled sleepily against my back in the Hike-A-Poose, making little wet noises in her throat.

"I just don't know if I can hold on for the next three years," he said.
"What if I end up going the corporate route? It would be easier."

"But you're stronger than that, Andy. Not every law student loses his
bearings."

"Will you tell me that in a couple of years?"

"Yes," I said, glancing up at him, "of course I will. Any time."

Andy smiled. "You live too far away, Cathy, you know that?"

The road had turned to the sea again, and we walked on the ridge
of a hill where the tall brown grass was sparser, fields falling away on
either side of us. "You could live here too," I said. "They have lawyers in
California."

Andy laughed. "Depends on who you ask, I guess."

"Why? Are Mom and Pop still saying I dropped off the map?"

He didn't answer.

"It doesn't matter," I reassured him, even though we both knew it was
a lie. In our parents' opinion, I couldn't even manage to do properly the
one thing that was expected of me: marry a man with prospects and have
lots of our own babies. But Andy wasn't spared their judgments either;
they wanted him to follow in the footsteps of his brother. Robert, being
the oldest boy, was my father's model child. He had a lucrative career in

banking and a growing family. Sometimes I couldn't believe Robert was my own brother. I couldn't imagine anyone more different from me.

We were silent for some time. In my head I listened to our father repeat one of his most frequent warnings. "Planning: you have to take care of the future so it will take care of you." I wondered if Andy was hearing him too.

"Do you remember the time Pop wouldn't let you go on that overnight fishing trip with him and Robert and me?" Andy asked. "And you said you were old enough, and he said that wasn't the point, and you said what was the point, and he said it was a boys-only outing. And you said that wasn't fair, and you started to cry, and he said that was exactly why it was going to stay a boys-only trip."

I smiled in spite of the bitterness that memory still called up. "Yes. And I remember you stayed home with me."

He didn't say anything. I looked at him again, at his thick, frowning eyebrows and the hair curling on his forehead that my friends used to tell me was cute. "You're a good person, Andy. You won't lose that."

We walked in silence for a while. When we got to a long, straight, downhill stretch of the road, he burst out, "I'll race you," and took off ahead of me.

"I can't, Andy," I called out to him, "I've got Min." I could hear her waking up, feel her shifting weight against my back. He raised a hand, waving as he raced himself to the bottom of the hill.

Back in the house, after I fed Min, Andy sat on the closed toilet seat while I gave her a bath. I could tell by his restlessness that he was irritated every time I interrupted our conversation by crying out "Good girl!" and "Who does Mommy love best?" Min pushed and grabbed for the rubber toys floating in the warm water, not much interested in helping me as I scrubbed her with a washcloth. Kneeling on the linoleum by the side of the bathtub, I let her try to pull my glasses off. She was fascinated that week with their large brown plastic frames, but she couldn't understand how to separate them from my face. When I was satisfied that she was clean, I lifted her from the draining tub and sat her between my legs on the bathmat. After toweling dry her slippery-wet, almond-toned body, I hugged her, rubbing my cheek lightly against her velvety one, which made her laugh. Then she raised her arms to my neck, wanting to be picked up again. I was consumed by this child, by her round cheeks and huge black eyes half-hidden beneath her lids, her open-mouthed laughter and silent, serious gaze, her ten little toes perfectly lined up, her child's sweet breath, even her great need of me. Her clinginess moved me tremendously. I was ready to cover her in kisses, give her whatever she wanted, throw myself between her and the whole world if it would help her believe I would never give her up.

"You haven't answered me," Andy said, following behind as I carried Min into her room.

"What were we talking about?" I asked, putting out a clean diaper and laying Min down on it before fastening the pins.

"Never mind," Andy said. I pulled Min's rubber pants up while she tried to chew her toes. The front door slammed. "Jonathan's home," my brother announced before leaving the room. I heard the plywood floor creak and then the muted tones of my husband's and my brother's voices as I eased Min into her footie pajamas and settled her in her crib, kissing her goodnight and humming to her until she fell asleep.

Sitting in her darkened room, listening to her soft snoring, a wave of exhaustion poured over me. I wanted to crawl into bed myself. I would cook up a quick meal, nothing elaborate, something with fresh vegetables. I would ask Jonathan and Andy to set the dining room table this time.

When I came into the front room, the two of them were sitting in the living room area with glasses of beer. The wood stove had been lit and was already blunting the edge of the evening's chill. Andy's gift to us, *Meet the Beatles*, was on the record player turned low. As I crossed the long room, its walls crowded with our books, I half-listened to Jonathan working himself up again about the moral corruption of the country's political process. Andy was leaning forward, his elbows resting on his knees, his brows pulled together in a frown; it was the same look of intent concentration his face took on when my father used to lecture us, and it meant he was no longer listening. I stopped behind Jonathan's armchair and rested my hand on his shoulder. He glanced up at me and covered my hand with his. The last song ended. The needle whispered in its groove and then the record player's arm whirred and clicked off. I thought I heard Min upstairs, but as I listened, the house gave back only silence.

The day before Andy's departure, Jonathan came home early and took Min from me, kissing her nose and then kissing my forehead. I told him dinner was in the oven and that I wanted to take Andy to Limantour to watch the sun set into the ocean. Except for the drive to the airport, it would be the last time we would see each other alone for at least a year, probably longer.

The afternoon was blustery but dry and clear. We headed down the beach toward the cliffs, away from the wind. The sand was littered with large chunks of driftwood and tangles of dark purple seaweed.

"Remember how scared of seaweed you used to be?" Andy asked. I nodded and kicked at the damp, sandy strands with my tennis sneaker.

He bent to pick up a clump of it. "Here, I brought you a necklace," he said, draping it around my neck.

"Don't, it's cold," I protested, pulling the wet, slimy thing off and throwing it to the side. A shiver rippled through my body. Andy had always enjoyed teasing me. But we were adults now; it wasn't fun anymore. He smiled at me, delighted with himself, and put his arm around my shoulder. I remembered that he would be leaving tomorrow. We walked in silence, our steps synchronizing.

"So are you going up to Rhinebeck or straight back to school tomorrow?" I asked. The breeze was chilly despite my wool shawl, but Andy's sheltering arm kept me warm.

"No, I'll go see Mom and Pop for a night," he answered. "They'll want to hear how you're doing, and if Jon's going to go back to college and get a real job."

"That's not very funny."

I felt him shrug. We walked on, the ocean hissing to our left. Undoubtedly, they would want to hear that Jonathan and I were having trouble; it would make them feel self-righteous, even though they had come to like Jonathan. I thought about the silences in our family, how our parents' expectations of us had been made clear without anyone having to talk about them, and how resentful that had made me feel. There was nothing to push against, and yet my whole body seemed to ache from the effort. I decided to bring up the subject that had been bothering me all week.

"Andy?"

"Shoot." He took his arm from around my shoulder and stuffed his hands in his pockets.

I glanced at his face; his eyes were on the sand ahead. Still, it was hard to begin. "During the whole time you've been here, you've never once touched Min or addressed her directly. I know you think she's just a baby, but you act like she isn't there. Or like you don't think she's a real person."

He didn't say anything.

"She's my daughter, Andy. Why do you keep ignoring her?"

Andy started to speak, then hesitated. "Go on," I said. "We've always been honest with each other."

"You say she's your daughter, but she's not *my* family. You just present her to me and expect me to love her."

"Yes, I do," I said. He had known I wanted to adopt children ever since one of my vacations home from college. We were taking a walk down by the stream, the fall leaves crunching under our feet. We were talking about our parents and how differently we would raise a family. I said that if I ever had kids, I didn't want to bring more children into the world when there were already so many without homes. I had known this about myself for years. And I was dating Jonathan, who cared even less than I did about having a biological child. I had thought *all* men were attached to the idea of progeny, of creating another version of themselves to carry on after they were gone. At the stream, Andy had listened carefully, nodding as he kicked at piles of leaves and the stumps of dead birch trees; he had agreed with everything I said. He had even told me he admired my strong convictions. I had thought he of all my family understood Jonathan's and my decision. I had thought he was happy for me.

Andy's shoulders were hunched forward, as if he were cold. He glanced out over the ocean. The fat yellow sun floated, radiant, above the dark, frothing sea. In another half hour it would be gone, extinguished by the water, the sky etched with coral light like trails of smoke.

He wouldn't look at me as he spoke. "Look, if you had to adopt, which you didn't, why didn't you at least adopt a white kid? There are loads available. I checked. American kids need homes too."

"What does that have to do with it?" I asked, not yet understanding.

"Cathy, I've got nothing against Orientals, but you can never even pretend that she's your own. At least a little white girl might look like you."

I stopped short. My little brother was talking like this? Andy? I felt as though he had just smashed a rock into the back of my head, leaving me breathless and stupid. Of course I was aware of Min's racial difference; it was part of our reason for adopting her. But Andy was ashamed of it, and somehow that kept him from seeing her as legitimately my daughter. He kept walking a few steps, then realized I had stopped and looked back.

"Jesus, Andy." There was nothing more I could think of to say. I tried to breathe, tried to quell my rising panic.

He furrowed his brow. "You asked me."

"Well, I didn't want to know *that*," I answered, suddenly furious, walking past him farther down the beach. He caught up with me. "For your information," I went on, "I don't want to pretend *anything*, Andy. Min is Korean. We adopted her. I don't want it to be a secret."

"I'm not—"

"Don't interrupt me. Min will always know that she was adopted from another country. Jonathan and I will tell her everything we can about where she came from and why she's with us. That doesn't mean she's any less my daughter than Robert's kids are his."

"Look, you said you wanted to know my feelings. And I feel that she's not part of you. She can't be, Cathy. Anyone can tell you that just by looking at her. You're born into family, and family is born to you."

He was shouting, and I realized I had been too. I wondered dimly what we were doing; we never fought like this. We had always defended each other.

Andy and I had reached the end of the beach where the cliffs jutted into the ocean, blocking our way. We turned around and began walking back. Andy kicked at the sand with each step. The wind blew my hair across my face. Wearily, I disentangled it from my glasses. I swept it behind my ears and stuffed it underneath the edge of my shawl.

"No, Andy, that's the whole point. Family is who you choose. I chose Jonathan. And I chose Min."

"Terrific. So where does that leave me?"

"Oh, Andy, where do you think?"

What did he imagine, that creating a new family meant I was shedding my old one the way snakes left behind a worn-out skin? Why couldn't he change too? I was tired of taking care of him, tired of his insistence that he still needed me to lead the way. All that energy was with Min now. I stopped walking and turned toward him, peering up into his face. He stared at the ground. His jaw was clenched; I could see a muscle spasm in his cheek. I was trying very hard not to cry.

"You have to accept Min eventually," I told him. The muscle jumped, subsided. "You have no choice."

Andy gave the sand one more kick for good measure, then turned and walked down to the edge of the water, his hands still in his pockets. Just like Pop, I thought. Just walk away. I stood where I was, immobile. I had wanted to be able to change, to escape the ingrained behaviors that moved, as if through our blood, from one generation to the next. Would I pass onto Min a particular trait? How to tear down the people you love most; the lonely mastery of how to stand alone? I didn't want to think anymore about the forms of inheritance.

The sun had set without our noticing. The horizon looked like a bruised peach. Above us the sky stretched wide, a canopy of deepening purple. The wind was still up, and chillier. I wrapped my arms around myself and watched Andy below me. Near his feet the ocean was relatively calm, lapping in small waves. I felt numb, unreal. He ran his hand through his hair. As I started to walk down to him, he turned around to look for me.

"Look," he said, pointing down as the sea washed away again.

"What? I can't see."

He stepped forward and stooped to pick up something half buried in the sodden sand. He held it out to me on his palm. It was a starfish, all five of its arms intact. I touched it, stroking a bristly arm. It was soft, although it didn't move. I thought it might still be alive.

"Shouldn't we throw it back in?" I asked.

"It's too late," Andy said. "They can grow back a missing arm, but they still dry out from exposure. Do you want it?"

I shivered. "No, you keep it, unless you have a million already."

"I've only seen them on the ocean floor. Finders keepers?"

He closed his fingers over the starfish as if he had a right to it, as if it were already his. I imagined it stranded among his possessions, on a bureau or coffee table, brittle and exotic and alone.

Maybe he was right to question my adopting Min, but not for the reasons he had given me. "Sure," I agreed, looking out at the darkening sea. "Finders keepers."

Andy's plane left early the next morning. We were out of the house by the time Jonathan got up to take his shower. This time I brought Min in the

Chevy with us to the airport. My brother and I didn't speak during the drive down. There was nothing left to say.

At the boarding gate we sat silently, waiting for the plane to come in from Honolulu. I was sure he wouldn't leave without making some effort at reconciliation. I knew him that well, at least. I sat Min on my lap and let her play with my colored glass beads, taking them from around my neck and giving them to her when she pulled too hard. Andy bought a pack of Wrigley's gum. He pulled open the string at the end and offered me a stick. I took it without looking up. The sweet minty flavor flooded my mouth, reminding me of a time when we were much younger and nothing was as painful as this silence.

Then he was leaving, moving slowly toward the open door with the other passengers, kicking his overnight bag along the floor ahead of him. I stood with him, holding Min on my hip with both arms, alert to any hint of agitation in her as she gazed out at the large airplane. One of the stewardesses took Andy's ticket, returned the boarding pass. "Only passengers beyond this point," she told me. I had to say something. I couldn't bear to have him leave like this.

"Would you at least kiss her goodbye?" I asked Andy. "You're her uncle."

"Why did you call her Min?" he asked.

I was relieved by the question, thinking he had begun to accept her. It was the first time he had referred to her by name.

"Because that's what her mother called her in the note she was found with. Min-Jung."

"You see?" he said, smiling and wagging his finger at me. "You said 'her mother.' She's not really yours."

"Oh, grow up, will you?" I snapped, more loudly than I intended. I saw him flinch. Then he turned away, picked up his bag, and walked out onto the tarmac toward the waiting plane.

As soon as he was gone, I wondered what had happened. I felt disoriented, confused, as though I had been set down in a strange city. Then I understood that nothing had happened; Andy had left without making any effort to apologize, without even saying goodbye. I felt the sharp sting of tears fill my eyes.

The last of the passengers boarded the plane. The stairs were rolled away and the door sealed tight. A thought occurred to me. What if Andy didn't come to his senses after all? What if he never understood what he had done, never took the first step toward reconciliation? How could I talk to him then? I couldn't. I couldn't have anything to do with him. I closed my eyes, trying to shut out that unimaginable possibility. It terrified me. But the seconds kept going by, and I couldn't forgive what had happened between us on my own.

I watched the plane bearing my brother roll away, slowly moving out of sight. Min pointed out the window, uttering an unintelligible comment. "Yes, that was your Uncle Andy," I told her, combing my fingers through her thick black hair. "I don't think we'll be seeing him again for a long time." A tear fell on her hair, and I combed it in. What would happen if Min and I ever fought like this, when she was older? Andy would have said I could never be certain that some day she wouldn't walk away forever, because I wasn't her first mother, her real mother.

But he had walked away from me. So what did that prove about the bonds of blood?

Outside, the runway was empty. The sky was empty too, a flat gray. I watched for a long time. I held Min against me, breathing in her sweet baby smell.

CHAPTER 2

Catherine

Summer 1968

SOMETHING WAS WRONG WITH ME. I felt it as soon as Jonathan slowed the rental car and turned left into my parents' driveway, the twin beams of the headlights making a slow sweep in front of us. My parents had left the front door light on, and in its feeble glow the house loomed up large and solid and unchanged. The sight of it like that enraged me. It should have been burned to the ground or wiped out by a tornado. But the house stood as it always had, as if everything was still the same as it had been when I was a child. I wanted to put my fist through the windshield. Frightened, I clamped my hands together between my legs. I turned around to check on Min in the back seat. She was still asleep, curled up, her head resting on her polka-dotted plastic raincoat.

"She's okay," I said to Jonathan.

He glanced at me but said nothing as he inched the car over the crunching gravel and parked by the garage. In the suddenly silent darkness we opened our doors and stood, stretching.

"I'll carry her in," he offered.

"No," I said quickly, "I will." I knew it was ridiculous, but I was afraid Jonathan might drop her.

The next morning, the call of crows dragged me out of a restless sleep. Sunlight lay hot on my back. The side of my face was pressed into the pillow. I felt paralyzed, unable even to open my eyes. I was still half in my dream: completely alone, treading water in the darkness, afraid of touching something I couldn't see. I could feel the cold of the water, the fear of slithery seaweed wrapping around my legs.

Wanting reassurance, I reached out my hand and discovered that I was alone in the bed. Jonathan had already gotten up. I opened my eyes and stared at the space in the sheets where he had been. Why hadn't he woken me? He knew how anxious I was about visiting my parents after all this time. I needed him. Why hadn't he stayed close by this first morning? Where had he gone?

I rolled over on my back and lay looking at the room I had grown up in: the water stains on the floral wallpaper, the ornate, hand-carved bureau, the holes in the back of the door where my shoe rack had been screwed in. In the far corner, my old Raggedy Ann doll sat propped up on a three-legged stool. Without my glasses, I saw her face as a pale circle, unable to distinguish her eyes or mouth. I had loved that doll when I was very young, dragging her with me everywhere until Andy had come along, better than any doll to hold and then to play with.

Andy. I squinted, trying to make Raggedy Ann's face come into focus. I knew exactly how long it had been. Four years and eight days. Four goddamn years since you went out sailing knowing a storm was coming in. And before that, almost five months of silence. Not even a letter. And then you died. What was wrong with you? How could you have been so stupid?

Suddenly I was exhausted, flattened by inertia. There was no point in questioning Andy. He couldn't answer me, no matter how many times I asked him. I closed my eyes, too tired to keep them open. The air in the room was stifling. After his death I had decided not to dwell on the subject of my brother. I lay weighed down in the bed, defeated by gravity.

A crow called again. I heard the *flut-flut* of wings outside the near window. I opened my eyes. I was still in the family house, built a century before by my great-grandfather. The desk by the near window was still painted a sober gray. A row of my hardcover books was still lined up along the back, against the wall. Everything in the room was the same, practically untouched since I had left for college almost thirteen years before. Each object was familiar, but they seemed to me to be the props of someone else's childhood. They had nothing to do with me. Lying in the hot sunlight, I stared at the blur of blue and green beyond the far window. It had been a mistake to come back. I tried hard to remember why we had. Min. Of course. We wanted Min to know she had family besides only Jonathan and me. We also wanted my family to know we had succeeded in all the ways they had expected us to fail.

I wondered if Min would like to have Raggedy Ann to keep her company in her room downstairs. Maybe I could bring the books back to Mill Valley for her to read when she got older. She was starting to be curious about my and Jonathan's pasts. She might want some memento of my own childhood, a means of putting herself into my history. I pictured her sitting cross-legged in the armchair at home, mesmerized by my old illustrated copies of the Dr. Dolittle books. When I had been given them, I had read them straight through, then immediately started over, reading them aloud to Andy.

No, I thought, rolling onto my side, trying to press out the tightness in my chest. Why would Min want some ratty old books, a second-hand doll? I watched a swirl of dust motes orbit each other in a shaft of sunlight. I could smell them, or maybe that was the musty smell of the rug, or the odor of the house itself as it aged and slowly decayed. The remnants of my past would stay behind, I decided, with this house. Min's childhood belonged to the West Coast, and I belonged there with her.

Eventually I sat up, swinging my feet down to the floor. The green floorboards were mercifully cool. I had no idea what time it was. My head felt thick, balloony, unattached to my body. I reached for my glasses on the night table, blinking as the room took on edges. I found my nightgown still folded at the bottom of my suitcase and pulled it on over my head. In the hallway, the doors to the bedrooms where Robert and his family were staying were all open. I kept my eyes on the hall carpet until

I reached the bathroom and pulled the chain for the light over the sink. I couldn't look into Andy's old room, afraid of seeing it stripped bare of all his possessions, devoid of his personality. Yet if it had been kept intact, I couldn't have borne that either.

Back in my bedroom, I dressed quickly, starting to sweat. Another headache was coming on. I was tired of my headaches. They made me want to cry, and I refused to cry. I remembered I'd had headaches the last couple of trips home too. At Andy's funeral four years before I had thought I would scream from the pressure inside. The rest of my family seemed controlled and contained, greeting mourners after the service graciously. And at Christmas later that year, the last time we had visited, I had left Min and Jonathan to go upstairs and lie down, trying to shut out the family's voices singing carols below. How could they sing? When Jonathan had come up to find out what was wrong, I told him I had a splitting headache. He said he did too from hearing Andy this and Andy that ever since we had arrived. I understood then that I was right not to have told him about my quarrel with Andy. I remembered that in the months before Andy's death, Jonathan had never asked me why I didn't call my brother anymore. Now I didn't have the headaches so frequently. Jonathan had suggested that I see a doctor, but I didn't need to. I was getting them under control.

I rummaged through the shorts and blouses in my suitcase for my bottle of Excedrin and swallowed three without water. As I brushed my tangled hair, I glimpsed myself in the mirror above the bureau. Dark streaks had formed under my eyes. I looked pale and unhappy. Jetlag, I thought. That's why I feel so rotten. All I need are a few days by the pool. I tied my hair back with an elastic band and escaped the airless room.

Coming down the creaking, narrow stairs, I breathed in the welcome odor of fresh-ground coffee. The piercing shrieks of children's voices came from the dining room, making me wince. It seemed to me there had always been children yelling somewhere in the house; admittedly, I had been one of them, though the older I had grown, the more I had wanted to find a quiet place to be alone. I wondered again where Jonathan was. I had wanted to come down to breakfast with him, collecting Min on the way, the three of us entering the dining room together. What could he have thought was more important? In the hall I opened the door to the small room Min was staying in, which my mother still called the maid's room though it had been a storage closet during my entire lifetime. The bed was empty. The sheet and light blanket were neatly pulled up to cover the pillow. Her book, *Harold and the Purple Crayon*, was lying open on a chair beside the bed, waiting for her.

I found my daughter sitting quietly at the dining room table with her three noisy cousins and Nora, my sister-in-law. Through the French doors behind her I could see the gnarled, bushy trees in the orchard spaced evenly up the slope of the field. Min's juice glass was almost empty, perched on the tablecloth in front of her. I knew she wanted more but was too shy to ask. As soon as she saw me, she slipped down from her chair and came over, putting her hand in mine and turning back to the table with a look of satisfaction. She's on equal footing with her cousins now, I thought; her mother is here too. Nora's three weren't paying much attention. The youngest, Gerard, was kicking his sister under the table, and she was in turn hitting him on the arm with her fist. "You're a pest," she informed him.

I felt a tug on my hand. I looked down at Min's upturned face. Her hair stuck out on one side instead of falling neatly in straight bangs and past her ears as it usually did. She had put her red- and yellow-striped shorts on backwards, but otherwise she had managed to dress herself in the clothes I had laid out the night before. I let go of her hand and crouched down in front of her. Wetting my fingertips on my tongue, I started to smooth down the strands of her hair. Immediately she grabbed my hand away from her head. "Mommy," she said sternly.

"Okay, okay," I said, putting my hands up in the air to show I was giving up.

I heard my name being called. At the table, Nora and I exchanged kisses, smiling the wide smiles of in-laws who have a vague fondness for each other. She asked her children if they remembered me. Only Trish, who must have been almost ten, managed a doubtful yes. Min had sidled up behind me and stood close by, near Trish's chair. She seemed fascinated by the older girl's long blonde braid.

Trish twisted around, her hands clutching the back of her chair. "My mother says you came from Korea. That's next to China. People talk funny there."

"Why?" Min asked.

"I don't know," Trish shrugged. "Say something in your language."

"English *is* Min's language," I snapped. I was seething. "She's as American as you are. She's my daughter." *You're wrong, Andy,* I added in my head, *Min is as much my child as Nora's kids are hers.* I was afraid Trish would contradict me, or worse, her mother would, but instead they stared at me, a little stunned, it seemed, by my vehemence.

"No one said she wasn't American," Nora told me.

You have to accept her, I thought. But the argument wasn't over. How could it be?

I said, "Trish seems to believe that my daughter is foreign."

"Oh, Catherine, Trish is only ten years old, she doesn't understand that you adopted Min before she learned to talk."

"Maybe you should have told her."

I turned back to my daughter. The two girls were exchanging a long stare. I took her hand again. "Let's go get more orange juice," I said gently, reaching for her glass on the table. My fury had passed. Min's gaze lingered on Trish as we moved away.

My mother was in the kitchen standing at the stove, her apron tied over her cotton skirt. She poured beaten eggs into a pan. Bacon sizzled and popped in another. The anticipation of its salty chewiness made my mouth water. In the strong summer light, I could see the gray sprinkled in her short, wavy brown hair. The skin on her face was beginning to sag around her pale blue eyes and her chin. I felt as though I had never stood this close to my mother before; in the three and a half years I had been away, she had grown old, and I couldn't remember what she had looked like young.

She glanced down at Min, then up at me standing beside her. "Min was up early," she said, sliding her spatula through the liquid eggs. My daughter was peering up at the collection of antique kitchen utensils hanging from pegs on the wall above the stove. "When I came down, she was outside on the patio studying the insect population between the flagstones."

"Weren't you sleepy this morning?" I asked Min. She looked up at me, her large black eyes very solemn, and shook her head. She didn't like to speak around people she didn't know. I hoped that within five days, by the end of our trip, she would be as voluble as she usually was at home. I wanted her to like my side of the family, even if I had my own mixed feelings about them. I wanted her to enjoy this visit, even if I couldn't.

"Where's Jonathan?" I asked my mother.

"He went with Robert and your father down to the stream to go over the plans for the new house. Coffee's ready," my mother added, nodding her head toward the percolator on a back burner.

"The new house?" I asked, confused. "What do you need—"

"Ask Nora if she'd like a cup, will you?"

"Nora, coffee's ready," I called into the dining room.

"Thanks," she called back.

My mother scowled at me. One of the rules in the house had always been no shouting between rooms. Before she could say anything, I filled Min's juice glass and gave it back to my daughter. She took it in both hands. I knelt to retie her sneaker, pulling one long lace from under her slight weight. "There. Now I'll get coffee, and I'll meet you back at the table." She nodded. "Min?" I looked into her face, concerned. I hadn't seen her beautiful smile all morning. "Do you want to smile for your mommy?"

"I don't feel like it," she said seriously, lifting her chin a little. I watched her until she shuffled through the kitchen door, taking small sips from her full glass.

Behind me my mother flipped the bacon and put bread in the toaster, brisk and efficient. I stood up, wanting coffee, wanting my headache to go away. Already this day was not going well. My mother moved past me toward the ice box, not looking up as I stepped back out of her way. We were alone together for the first time in almost four years, and neither one of us had anything to say. The odd thing, I realized, was how normal this seemed to me. I took a mug out of the cabinet. It said "LOVE" in big, loopy, brightly colored letters. Above that, a flower bloomed into a woman's face. I bet Susie gave this to them, I thought, she's a big Peter Max fan. I couldn't imagine them choosing it for themselves. The vibrant colors and the exuberance of the lettering reminded me of the crayon drawings and finger paintings that I, and then Andy, and then Susie, had brought home from school. My mother had always reacted the same way, glancing at them once and saying, "Put it away now, it's time for your nap."

I poured steaming coffee from the pot and drank it black, holding the mug between both hands the way Min had. As I stood at the counter looking outside over the valley at the distant hills, I remembered Jonathan telling me the night before, as we were undressing for bed, that he and Robert and my father would be getting up early to walk out the boundaries of a second, smaller house my father had gotten it into his head to build. I had been too exhausted to register what he was saying. I gulped down the coffee and poured some more. I could imagine them down at the stream measuring out their long strides, thrusting sticks into the yielding ground. They would look thoughtful as they stretched a measuring tape along the perimeter, one calling out the numbers, another nodding and jotting them down. Min would have enjoyed the expedition. She might have counted out the lengths of her own feet, putting heel to toe, balancing herself with outstretched arms. She might have learned something about the importance of taking measurements or why it was always men who were expected to do these jobs. Why hadn't Jonathan insisted Min come along, since she was already up? My father might have listened to Jonathan.

"Where is Susie?" my mother complained. "She promised me she would arrive by breakfast."

"She probably forgot to set her alarm," I answered.

My mother frowned at me, as if Susie's tardiness were my fault, then turned back to the stove. "By the way, your father and I are going on a cruise to the Caribbean this winter."

"That'll be nice," I said. Before I could stop it, the image of Andy's hand slipping from the capsized sailboat, his head sinking below the choppy ocean waves, was so clear it was as if I had been there witnessing him drown. I blinked, opening my eyes to the scrubbed white walls of my mother's kitchen. I stared at her lined face, refusing to think about something that wasn't real. There was no point. I would not think of Andy during this visit, even here where my memories of him were strongest. Turning her back to me, my mother opened the silverware drawer and counted out forks and knives. Without thinking I reached out and rested my hand on her shoulder. She startled at my touch, whirling around.

"Goodness, Catherine. Here, take these out to the table." She dumped the collection of silver into my hands and went back to her cooking.

In the dining room, Gerard was showing Min a scab on his leg. They inspected it together, heads bent, touching its edges. I laid out the place settings. The two children started counting their bug bites, giggling. She was making a friend. I was relieved. Then I looked up and saw my brother Robert on the lawn striding toward the patio, his face eager. He can't wait to burst in and tell us one of his long-winded stories, I thought. I returned to the kitchen to help my mother soak some of the grease from the bacon with paper towels and pull a heavy stack of plates from the cupboard. I knew I was hiding, but I didn't care.

Through the window above the sink I watched my father and my husband as they climbed up the hill toward the house, my father with some effort. His legs were spindly and pale, as if this were the first day all summer that he had worn shorts. Otherwise he looked younger than a man of fifty-six. His hair was still thick and dark, his posture very erect. Jonathan kept up easily as he described something, blocking off portions of the air in front of him with his hands. Beside my father, Jonathan looked short and stocky, almost pudgy. His hair was the longest it had ever been, and he had grown a beard in the last few months, which I liked. It made him appear a little dangerous, a little unpredictable. It reminded me of how he had been when I fell in love with him.

When I met Jonathan, I had wanted to get as far away from my parents as I possibly could. I wanted to get married, but not to the sort of man they had in mind for me. I wanted to live unconventionally. Jonathan had been a radical—to the degree that such a thing was possible in 1958—when I met him during my junior year of college. He was a Democrat, and he had never finished college, both of which made him unsuitable in my parents' eyes. He rarely spoke to his own family and was curt to the point of rudeness with mine. Secretly, I was delighted. I believed he could offer me the two things I had been looking for my entire life: freedom and adventure.

But in time Jonathan had grown to like my family, my parents most of all. After our move to California, we would fly back east and spend long weekends with them. He said he felt embraced in a way he had never felt wanted by his own mother and father. He enjoyed their esoteric discussions during which no one yelled at anyone else, and he liked what he viewed as their permissiveness. He couldn't recognize that they were actually indifferent, at least to everything that mattered. He didn't see how they demanded polite behavior over honesty. He admired them for everything I did not. I tried to explain how often, growing up, I had sat at the dining table hoping that my father or mother would focus on me for a short time, ask me about school or my friends, recognize something clever I had said. We had all wanted that. Robert had received it to some extent, being the favored child. But mostly my parents existed in a world of their own, speaking to each other about things we knew nothing about and expecting us to either listen or conduct our own separate, intelligent conversation. I finally realized that Jonathan had been won over by my parents. This outraged me; it was the last thing I had bargained for when I married him.

I watched my husband and my father pace across the lawn, deep in conversation. They glanced at each other, smiling and nodding in agreement. My whole life I had yearned to talk with my father with that much engagement, that much passion. I carried the platter of bacon into the dining room and set it down in the middle of the table. Porter and Gerard immediately grabbed for it. Min watched us all. From across the table I caught her eye and smiled at her. She flashed me a lightning-quick grin, then it vanished and her gaze passed on to Robert.

When they came inside and joined us, my father nodded at me and sat in his chair at the head of the table. Jonathan kissed me on the forehead. I was relieved to have him back. But I couldn't be sure it wasn't temporary. After an absence of three and a half years, we hadn't even been here a day and he had gone over to the other side. I pulled him toward me, an arm around his waist, breathing in his familiar aftershave and the piney scent his clothes had picked up.

After the meal, Nora and my mother cleared the dishes while Nora's kids scuttled out of the house, racing each other down the hill. Jonathan asked Min if she'd like to go with them, but she shook her head.

"Shall we all take a walk?" he asked, standing up and pushing his chair against the table. He spoke loudly enough to include my father in his invitation. "Min, I know you want to see the pool."

Min looked up at me. "Mommy, can we, please?"

I watched my father leave the room, apparently not much interested in spending time with us, his daughter and granddaughter. I heard the front door close. "Why don't you go?" I said to Jonathan. Min and he came around the table, and I stroked his arm, catching his hand in mine. "I'll find you. I want to say hello to Pop."

"Sure." He squeezed my hand.

I leaned down to Min. "Let's both spend a little time with our dads, okay?"

"And I want to go to the apple tree you climbed on," she added.

I imagined Min straddling one of the crooked branches up in the old tree, inching her way along it. Then I saw the branch break and my daughter tumble out, falling head first onto the hard ground. I can't keep her safe, I thought, my heart clutching then starting off again twice as fast. As hard as I try to protect her from harm, she'll be on the brink of disaster every minute. Anything can happen.

"Don't let her climb it," I told Jonathan, gripping his hand tightly. "It's too dangerous."

"It wasn't when you did it." He pulled his hand out of mine.

I looked hard at him. "No, I mean it. Don't let her leave the ground." He stared at me as if I were crazy. I felt crazy. Something was wrong with me, but I couldn't stop myself. "*Please*, Jonathan."

"It'll be okay, Catherine. Calm down. We'll see you later." He turned from me. I stared after him. Why didn't he understand? I myself didn't understand this sudden terror, but the feeling was real, and strong. Why couldn't he see that and accept it? Why did he always have to contradict me? As they moved away, Min turned back and waved.

My father was standing on the front steps with his hands in the pockets of his Bermuda shorts fiddling with some change. He rocked back and forth on the balls of his sneakered feet. I stood beside him, sipping my coffee, looking out at the hills across from us. The area bordering our land was part of a state park, so there was no danger of it ever being developed. We had an uninterrupted view of leafy green maples and elms, a field overgrown with grass turned beige from lack of rain, and the pure blue sky overhead. There was no breeze. I could feel a trickle of sweat drip down my side.

My father had never been a talkative man. We stood for a while in silence, listening to the call of a mourning dove. A chipmunk ran across the lawn. As our silence wore on, I became aware of how acutely I still wanted to be close to him. I hoped he would tell me something about himself that could be between us alone. Maybe he had made a small breakthrough at the pharmaceutical lab where he worked. I had always admired my father's intelligence and perseverance. For a time, I had hoped to grow up to be like him, until I discovered that I disagreed with almost everything he believed in. Maybe he would ask me about something I cared about, showing me that he knew what that might be. I drank my coffee and tried to think of how to start such a conversation.

"Have you seen the garden?" he asked, turning to me.

Gratitude flared up in me for this small invitation into his life. Perhaps this was a turning point. I remembered how attentively he had listened to Jonathan as they climbed the hill earlier.

"No, I'd love to. You know, we just got here last night, Pop," I reminded him playfully.

He stepped onto the grass and began walking around the side of the house. Left behind, I put my coffee cup down on the top step and ran after him. Then, annoyed with myself, I slowed down to a walk. I breathed in the sweet scent of the freshly mown grass, a smell I missed in Mill Valley.

My parents' garden was a special project that they had worked on together for the past fifteen years, when one by one we had started to leave home for college. During the week my mother kept it watered while my father commuted from Poughkeepsie to his lab in the city; on weekends they weeded and checked for pests. I remembered winter nights when they would pore over seed catalogues, discussing in meticulous detail the quality of various strains of beets and melons. They managed to produce most of the vegetables they ate over the summer, and my mother canned the remainder. They used raised beds and covered the plants with a light, semi-transparent cloth instead of spraying them.

I fingered a fat, wrinkled leaf from a plant that was heavy with both green and red tomatoes, held up by a stake tied to the stem. I could smell the soil and the thin, bitter odor of the plant itself. Reaching out, I pulled a ripe tomato from the stem and bit into it. Its sweet, acidic juice filled my mouth. I ate it greedily, the juice spilling onto my hand.

"We've been having them every night in salads," my father informed me. "The lettuce is ours too." He pointed it out several rows down, pale green beside a line of darker skinny plants.

"Onions?" I guessed, feeling absurdly hopeful.

He nodded. "And string beans, cucumbers, carrots, potatoes," he said, walking down the beds. He bent over and pulled the leaves of one bushy plant aside, inspecting, then checked the next plant over. Straightening, he said, "Come see the flowers," then turned and walked around the corner of the house toward the patio.

These were less well cared for, for some reason, growing in unruly clusters along the low stone wall that edged the patio. Most of them were wildflowers. It looked as though the soil hadn't been weeded all summer or the flowers cut back. That didn't seem to matter; the bed was a wild, beautiful profusion of color.

The night before, after Jonathan and I had climbed up to our room, weary and a little disoriented, I had been touched to find violet stonecrop and blue sweet William arranged in a vase on the bureau. My parents didn't usually pick their flowers for the house. I asked my father, "Was it you who put the flowers in our room?"

"Flowers? I think Nora was asking about vases after dinner."

My father pulled a few weeds and threw them on the grass behind him. I looked up at the house, shading my eyes from the sun. The dark red wood and white trim had faded and was peeling in places. "Time for a paint job," I said.

My father looked up, appraising the house. "Yes, I've been putting it off. Maybe I'll get Robert to help me with it this weekend. Or Jonathan, if he's looking for some good, solid physical labor."

"I could help you, Pop," I ventured.

He shook his head, still gazing up at the house thoughtfully. "I don't think so, Cathy. I want it done right."

I stared, stunned, at the side of his face. Then I was furious, thinking
that I would know how to paint houses and measure out foundations if
he had taught me along with Robert and Andy. But there was no point in
getting angry at him. He would only tell me he didn't appreciate my tone
of voice. It would never occur to him that he had hurt me. I said simply,
"I'd like to help you, Pop."

"Why don't you go take a swim with the others," my father suggested
as he stepped onto the patio and opened the screen door. "I've got some
things to take care of this morning."

After he had gone inside, I stood where I was, too dazed to move.
Then I wandered along the flowerbed and picked a small bouquet of orange marigolds for Min. I am thirty-one years old, I reminded myself. I
have a husband and a daughter and a full life independent of my father.
But at that moment I couldn't make them real to myself. There was only
me and my father, and he was implacable. Walking back past the vegetable garden, I rolled the ruffled petals of the marigolds against my cheek,
breathing in the flowers' sturdy scent.

I rounded the corner of the house and stopped. On the front lawn
Jonathan stood holding Min in his arms, her short legs hanging down
on either side of him, his hands making a seat beneath her bottom. Her
arms were draped around his neck. She put her face very close to his
as she spoke, her fine black hair brushing his forehead. It looked like
a lovers' private conversation. Immediately I felt excluded. Min never
confided in me, whispering in my ear. With me her declarations were
always blunt, straightforward. I drew back to watch my husband and my
daughter whispering on the lawn. Both of them were too absorbed in
each other to notice me anyway.

Eventually Min pulled her upper body back. She put one fist to her
mouth and extended the other one out and back to the first. "Bom, bom,
bom, bom," she sang.

"What instrument is that, Min?" Jonathan asked her.

Min ignored him and kept on playing, tilting her face up to the sky. Her hair fell away from her neck.

"What instrument are you playing, Min?" Jonathan jiggled her a little to get her attention.

"The *tu*ba."

"Nope. The trom*bone*."

Min wound her arms around her father's neck, singing her simple melody to him as though there was nobody else in the world.

"How does the trombone look, Min?" Jonathan asked her. Immediately her hands went up to imitate it again.

"And what does the tuba look like?"

"It's *big*," she answered.

"What does it sound like?" Silence. "Does it have a low sound?"

Min started singing in a high voice, smiling at her father.

"And what does a *trump*et sound like?" Jonathan persisted.

"Daddy, let's sing some more," Min said, pulling on Jonathan's beard, making him smile.

"Anything you want, sweetheart. You're my little girl."

"I love you best of all, Daddy." She hugged him tightly around the neck. Then they began singing, her high trombone voice and his low tuba voice in unison, bom, bom, bom, bom.

I turned away from them and walked around the side of the house again to the back door. I felt dizzy and afraid, my heart beating hard in my body. Jonathan had always been a very loving father to Min. He was the playful, indulgent parent, the one who came home from his office and provided the gift, the magic, the special surprise. Of course she would say she loved her father best. I was always with her, feeding and washing and caring for her. I was the one who made the rules, who told her no and sometimes made her angry. I knew I could be over-protective as a mother. I had no right to expect Min to return the passion I felt for her. But inside I felt ripped apart, shredded like a flimsy cloth torn in two.

I lived for her. I couldn't bear to think that anyone—even Jonathan—
might be closer to her than I was.

In the stream that ran at the bottom of the hill below the house, a series
of stepping stones crossed a calm pool of water. They were flat and fairly
evenly spaced, yet it only occurred to me for the first time as I walked
from one to the next that they had been put in place by hand, probably
by my grandfather or his father. The stream ran clear and wide and shallow, bounded by woods on both sides. As a teenager I had spent hours
sitting by its shore, watching the water move unhurriedly downstream. I
remembered admiring how it bent around rocks or fallen tree branches,
the way flames did but without burning them up. I had wanted to grow
into a life that was more like water and less like fire, where being near
others was soothing rather than searing. I remembered too finding the
stream's quiet gurgle a relief from the constant calling of human voices
up at the house. I would bring a book with me to read, propping myself
against the wide trunk of a tree.

On the far shore, I followed alongside the brook. Occasionally I
grazed past the underbrush, brambles scratching my legs. The sun was
now directly overhead, beating through the leafy trees, creating a dappled effect on the surface of the water. A mosquito hummed near my
head. The earth smelled cool and damp. I was trying to think of nothing, to empty myself of words and faces and feelings until all that remained was the sun's heat on my skin and the stream's constant babble
like chimes on a breezy day.

Small dark fish darted around in the water. I didn't know what they
were called. I crouched down to watch them flicking their tails, changing direction. I watched for a long time, then I stood and walked again.
Eventually I found the clearing on the other side of the stream where my
father wanted to build his guest house, marked by stakes in the ground
and a string running in a rectangle between them. I moved on, not thinking, just walking, listening, watching.

I was hungry when I climbed the hill back to the house. In the kitchen the dishes from lunch lay soaking in the sink. I wondered if my mother had made some disapproving remark about my absence when they sat down to eat. I wondered if they had missed me. The house was quiet; my parents were most likely resting in their room. I didn't know where everybody else was. They had probably driven off after lunch to play tennis at the club, bringing the children along as ballboys. I took a large bowl of potato salad out of the ice box and picked at it with a fork from the sink. There were a few bologna slices left from the kids' sandwiches. I unwrapped them from their waxed paper, put a little potato salad inside, rolled them up, and ate them. Then I went upstairs to change into my bathing suit.

Jonathan and Min and my niece and nephews were in the water when I arrived at the pool. The children were taking turns diving from the deep end and swimming underwater to the other side. Jonathan stood in the shallow end, crouched down, making shapes with his body for the children to swim through. I smiled, watching them, enjoying their enjoyment. Whatever it was I had been going through earlier had dissipated entirely, and I was relieved. All I had needed was a quiet walk.

"Hi," Jonathan said as I sat down on a folding lawn chair and arranged my towel, suntan lotion, and book beside me. "Where've you been? We looked for you. You disappeared."

"I'm sorry, Jonathan. I guess I needed some time alone." I unscrewed the top from the tube of Bain de Soleil, squeezed a dollop onto my palm, and began to rub it into my legs. "I went down to the stream." I was even starting to feel good, stretched out in the sun, not having to go anywhere. I had everything under control now.

Porter popped up from underwater, shaking the wet hair from his face like a puppy. "Betchya can't catch me!" he yelled, splashing Jonathan and ducking underwater again.

The other children shouted, "You're it! You're it!" and swam as hard as they could away from Jonathan, who splashed back to give them time, then dove after them. I took off my glasses to dab lotion on my cheeks and smooth it in, then leaned back, closing my eyes. Everything was all right.

Not long after, my sister Susie showed up at the pool with Robert and Nora. She wore baby-blue hot pants and a scoop-necked t-shirt, and her hair fell past her waist, all of which made her look even younger than she already was. She came over and crouched to kiss my cheek. "How are you?" she asked, her sunglasses mirroring my face in two dark ovals.

"Fine. Have you seen Mom? She expected you for breakfast this morning."

"Yeah." Susie grinned. "She's a trip. 'When you tell me you'll be here by ten, I expect you to be here by ten.'" Susie's imitation was perfect.

I had to admire my little sister. She truly didn't care what our parents thought of her. "How long are you here for?" I asked.

"The long weekend. I have a date Monday night."

"Oh? Someone serious?"

She laughed. "Nah. A friend. We just ball, he brings dope. Hey, where's Min?" she asked. "I haven't seen her for ages."

I nodded toward the pool, where my daughter swam clumsily but energetically after Trish, trying to tag her. Jonathan shepherded them toward the steps, then hoisted himself out of the water. He padded over the hot cement, dripping, to offer Susie a kiss. "Good to see you, Susie."

"You too, Jonathan."

Jonathan sat down with Robert and Nora on the grass, stretching out his legs and propping himself back on his elbows. Nora lit another cigarette. Her kids went running off back to the house, passing my father, who had appeared behind us and stood with his hands in his shorts' pockets, surveying us all. When Jonathan waved him over, my father pulled up a lawn chair beside him.

Susie sat down on the cement next to Min and helped her towel dry. "Do you remember me? I'm your Aunt Susie. I'm your mom's sister."

Min smiled at her shyly.

"I can tell you're going to be a strong swimmer, Min."

"How do you know?" Min asked, squinting up at her.

"Because you dig the water so much. You can already swim in the deep end."

"I can dive too. You want to see?" Min stood up, ready to jump back into the water.

"Yeah, but let me go in first. We have a rule here. It's the only one you should never break. Do you know what it is?"

"No."

"That's the first word. No children allowed in the pool alone. It's a good rule too, because we don't want you to get hurt." Susie stood up, took a few steps toward the water, and dove in.

My father leaned forward, frowning. "Susie!" he barked at my sister when her dark head reappeared above the water, the ends of her hair trailing on the surface. "What do you think you're doing? You're in shorts."

Susie floated on her back, fanning gently with her hands. Her nipples hardened beneath her light t-shirt. Embarrassed, I looked over at the others. Robert and Nora were pretending to have a conversation. Jonathan looked at my sister's breasts outlined behind the wet fabric of her shirt, then at my father. Min stood near the edge of the pool, watching me uncertainly, scratching her leg. I smiled at her. She turned back toward my sister.

"I forgot to bring my bathing suit, Pop, all right?" Susie let her legs drop, treading water. "I'm ready, Min. Let's see you dive."

But my father wouldn't let it go. "You could have borrowed a bathing suit from your sister or your mother. A t-shirt is not appropriate. As you well know."

"My God, Pop, I'm just swimming. Don't hit the panic button." Then she turned her head and said in a gentler voice, "Come on, Min. It's okay."

My father grunted and stood up, starting back to the house, his posture as upright as ever. Min looked quickly at me. I nodded at her encouragingly. "Go on."

I could never have spoken to my father the way Susie had, dismissing his concerns so easily, as if they didn't matter. Sometimes I felt Susie and I were from completely different generations. I had been raised in an era that stressed respect for one's parents, regular attendance at church, loyalty to one's government: deference to authority in general. My family was contented with its hard-earned affluence and wanted only to remain that way. During my childhood, politics rarely moved beyond the public debate; when I was in college, except for the first sit-ins in the South, civil disobedience was unnecessary, unthinkable. The best I could do was move far enough away in order to live as I wanted, work steadily toward social justice, and raise Min. But now even that wasn't enough. The nation was being torn apart by violence. In the spring, watching the nightly news, Jonathan and I had seen city after city erupt in riots and flames for weeks after King was killed. We were saddened, and not only by his death. It seemed to us the last hope for peaceful integration had been snuffed out; the Black Panthers would push their militant agenda now, and whites and blacks would be at each other's throats. And while the paper reported almost daily another anti-war protest on a college campus or in Washington, complete with arrests and injuries, the war in Vietnam dragged on. Two nights before coming east, we had stood horrified in front of the TV set watching the Chicago police bludgeon protesters in a haze of tear gas outside the Democratic National Convention. I envied those people their willingness to risk their lives, but I knew I wasn't one of them. I cared too much about the consequences of my actions. What was happening all over the country was exhilarating, and it was frightening, and it was significant, and without even trying Susie was part of it in a way I could never be. Watching my little sister stroke languidly through the water in her clothes, unconcerned, I felt cheated. I had been born years too early.

Min went to the deep end of the pool and backed up a few steps. Then she ran with her arms held out ahead of her and hurled herself into the water head first.

At dinner the conversation eventually turned to the assassinations earlier in the year. My parents didn't seem particularly interested; in fact, I felt they were almost relieved by the deaths of King and Kennedy, though they didn't say so. Jonathan was brilliant contending with them from his vast store of facts and his certainty. But it was clear by the end of the meal that he hadn't changed anyone's mind.

We moved into the large, comfortable living room, where my father poured us glasses of Drambuie from the bar. This had always been my favorite room in the house. It had a low wood beam ceiling and several window seats and sofas piled with throw pillows. The lamps cast a warm yellow light. We broke into smaller groups, Robert and Nora's children playing Parcheesi on the rug, the men smoking cigars in one corner, while Susie, Nora, my mother, and I sat near the fireplace. Min wanted to stay near me rather than play with the other children. She settled sleepily in my lap, her curled body warm and familiar. Nora opened her pocketbook and took out her cigarettes and silver lighter. She tapped out a cigarette, bent her head over the lighter's flame.

"Jonathan's very passionate about his beliefs, isn't he?" Nora asked me, blowing a stream of smoke into the air above her. "I mean, I care about civil rights and everything, but don't you think Dr. King was asking for too much?"

Susie looked at me and raised an eyebrow. I could tell Nora had been holding this thought inside her ever since the subject came up, but she had been afraid to express it at the dining table. She assumed that because my husband was out of earshot, she could voice it now.

"I'm the wrong person to ask," I told my sister-in-law. "I happen to agree with Jonathan. If white people in this country could get it through their heads that *equal* rights can never be 'too much,' then we might start to make some progress."

"I didn't mean to offend you, Catherine," Nora replied. "I was upset too when I heard he'd been shot. But most people thought he was getting hard to handle. He would have been assassinated at some point anyway. It was just a matter of when."

"Are you saying he deserved to die? He should have known when to shut up because whites were getting tired of the uppity nigger?"

"Oh, Catherine, you're being extreme," my mother said. She put her glass on the side table next to the sofa and crossed one leg over the other, smoothing the light material of her dress. I glanced down at Min. She was already asleep. "I think you and Nora are essentially in agreement," my mother continued. "You just have to realize that progress takes a long time. I don't think Negroes are ready for the changes King wanted for them. Maybe they themselves don't want to be brought forward so fast. They certainly aren't acting very responsibly with all the freedoms they've already been given."

Susie seemed distracted. She was going to be no help at all. "That's ridiculous," I began.

Susie interrupted. "Mom, what would you say if one weekend I brought a black boyfriend to visit?"

Our mother visibly stiffened. "Are you dating a Negro, Susan?"

"The term is 'black.'" Susie shrugged. "Not necessarily."

I stared at my sister. Was the lover she had mentioned to me earlier a black man?

"Well, what's the hassle?" Susie asked my mother. "There's already one minority person in the family."

"That's different," my mother said, looking away. "Min is Oriental. It's not the same thing at all."

I felt caught up short, as though someone had punched me in the stomach. "Why does everyone keep harping on Min's race?" I demanded, furious. "Why does anyone care? It's not important. Can't you see that?" *Can't you see, Andy? She belongs here. It doesn't matter what she looks like.*

The three of them stared at me. I stared back. I was so enraged I was barely aware of what I had said. My hand trembling, I finished off my drink and put the glass down on the arm of my chair. In her sleep, Min shifted a little. I held her to me securely.

"You're so uptight sometimes," Susie said after a silence.

"I am not," I insisted. "I get angry when defenseless people get picked on."

"You do always stick up for the underdog, don't you?" Susie commented, as if she had just understood this about me.

"Don't you?" I asked, and then I realized that Susie wasn't actually interested in political change. She simply ignored what she didn't like.

She shook her head. "No, not always. But you've got an argument for everything. The only person you never seemed to fight with was Andy. I don't know why not. He could be such a freak. Remember when he stole my diary? Maybe you were at Smith by then. He took it to school and read it to his friends. It took me months to forgive him."

I felt as if I couldn't breathe, as if a hand had gripped my heart and squeezed. I was afraid I might black out. I wanted to leave the room, but I couldn't move. I looked away from Susie. I didn't say anything.

"I remember," my mother chimed in, "how as a little girl you used to defend both Susie and Andy when you thought they were being unfairly punished." She turned to Nora. "I'll never forget when Andy brought home a few fish from the stream in a jar that he kept hidden in his room. When they died, Douglas was furious at Andy for bringing them into the house in the first place. Catherine argued with her father that Andy didn't know any better."

Astonished, I listened as though I didn't know this story. My mother had never been someone who reminisced about the past. She had always been impatient, telling us to put aside what was over and move ahead. It occurred to me that maybe Andy's death had changed her. I didn't know what to do with that possibility.

"How old was Andy?" Nora asked.

"Six or seven. You see, he had wanted a pet and his father wouldn't allow it. Catherine argued that it was Andy's way of solving the problem.

Now that the fish were dead, she told her father, he didn't have to make it worse by scolding Andy." She turned to me. "Although I think the word you used was 'berating.'"

As my mother spoke, I remembered Andy holding the jar of stagnant water, the fish floating unmoving on the surface. By the time my father had finished, Andy's mouth was trembling from trying to keep back tears. The painful tightness in my chest wasn't letting up. I blinked, slightly dizzy. I felt myself receding, so that I watched my mother and sister and sister-in-law sitting together in the warm, lighted room from a great distance.

I said, "I have to put Min to bed. It's getting late." I looked down at my daughter. Her mouth was beginning to fall open. I saw her stubby black eyelashes resting on the tender, slightly clammy skin of her cheeks. I felt a stab of sympathy for her, for the bewildered helplessness of children. I thought, *She's your niece. Why couldn't you see how beautiful she is?* I sat gazing at my sleeping child, feeling unreal, feverish, feeling so far away from that room that I could have been asleep myself.

"You never want to talk about him," Susie said. Startled, I looked up at her. Nora stubbed out her cigarette, stood up, and went to sit on the rug with her children, folding her legs beneath her. "Whenever I bring him up, you change the subject," Susie went on. "It's been four years. He was our brother. Can't we remember him together?"

I wanted to be able to talk with her, but how could we? No one in my family ever said what they felt. I could see how remembering Andy gave my family something back of him: the knowledge that he had once been part of their lives. Telling their affectionate little anecdotes gratified them. They could take comfort in each other's memories. But sharing memories of Andy was the last thing I wanted to do.

I rubbed my left temple. My headache was coming back. "I don't think about Andy," I told Susie. "There's no point. He's gone." She stared at me, her face changing. I hated her for pitying me. When had she ever offered me real concern?

I said, "Min, it's time for bed now. Let's go brush your teeth." I rested my hand on the top of her head, smoothing her glossy hair.

Min started and looked up at me. "But I'm not tired," she said.

I smiled. "Come on, let's say goodnight."

"Are you ready?" I asked Min from the doorway of her tiny bedroom. I put my palms to my temples and pressed. My headache had reinstated itself, full-blown. The light from the hall threw a rectangle of brightness into the unlit room. Min lay with the blanket and sheet thrown off, her sleeveless cotton nightgown twisted and crumpled beneath her.

"It's hot," Min said.

I crossed the room to push the single window up as far as it would go. "I'll leave the door open a little when I leave so you can have the cross breeze, okay?" She nodded. I sat down next to her on the edge of the bed.

"How many days until we go home, Mommy?"

"You're not having fun?" I asked, resting the backs of my fingers against her warm cheek for a moment.

I heard a creak behind me. Jonathan walked softly into the room and sat down on the other side of the bed across from me. We looked at each other briefly in the half dark.

"Hi, Daddy," Min said.

"Hi, sweetheart," he answered, bending over her.

"Will you tell me a story? One with you and me in it?"

He brushed her hair back from her forehead with his fingers. "Not tonight, Min. It's late. Maybe tomorrow. I'll give you a backrub instead."

"Okay."

Min turned onto her stomach and pulled up her nightgown. In the gloom of the room, the white sheets were startlingly bright beside her olive skin. Jonathan began to knead her shoulders, then rub her back. His hand looked huge against her small body. With his fingers spread out, his palm easily spanned the width of her torso. I had never seen him give her a backrub before; usually one or the other of us put her to bed alone.

Gently, Jonathan brushed his fingers down her spine and up again. He touched his daughter with so much tenderness it made my throat ache. I sat mutely by, watching. There was nothing for me to do.

When he was finished, Jonathan pulled down Min's nightgown and patted her back.

"Bear hug," he said.

"Rhinoceros hug," she mumbled against her pillow.

"Elephant hug."

"Whale hug." Almost asleep.

"King Kong hug."

"That's too big," she said, rousing briefly. "I'd get squished."

"No, you wouldn't," Jonathan said. "I would never squish you. You know that." She was smiling. She had everything she wanted.

He bent over and kissed her hair, then stood up. I kissed her too and followed him out of the room, leaving the door ajar.

A few steps down the hall I whispered, "Jonathan! I want to talk to you."

He turned back to me. "What about?"

"Not here. Let's go to our room."

"Can't it wait? Your father offered me brandy."

"Please. I need to talk to you." I didn't know why I was begging. My headache was worse.

He shrugged. "All right."

We passed the living room and climbed the stairs to my childhood bedroom, ducking our heads where the ceiling came down at a sharp diagonal.

In the room Jonathan closed the door and fell onto the bed, the springs squeaking, while I went over to the bureau and fumbled for the switch on the lamp. I opened the aspirin bottle and swallowed four of the little white pills. The weak lamplight threw long shadows over the floral pattern on the walls. I remembered my dream of trying to keep my head above water in the perpetual dark, and the fear that something would grab me from the deep and pull me down.

His hands behind his head, Jonathan looked ordinary and familiar. My throat ached again as I looked at him, because I was afraid.

"Why are you standing way over there? Come here," Jonathan suggested, patting the covers beside him.

It was what I had wanted to hear all day, but I couldn't move. "How long have you been giving Min backrubs?" I asked.

His eyebrows went up. "I don't know. A year or so?"

"You rub her back until she falls asleep?"

"Sometimes I make it a game. I spell words on her back and she guesses what they are. She draws a picture and I try to figure out what she's drawn."

"She rubs your back too?" I asked, startled. It seemed today I had stumbled on a whole treasure trove of secrets between them. I walked over and sat down on the edge of the bed, pressing my fingertips into my temples as hard as I could.

"Sure. She likes it. Unlike her mother," Jonathan said. I had always gotten bored after a few minutes of rubbing his back. "What's wrong, Catherine?" He sat up and kneaded my arm in a friendly way.

"Don't touch me," I said, shrugging him off. "Don't you think I could see how you were looking at Susie down at the pool? I don't care how provocative she was being—"

"You're the one who's being provocative," Jonathan interrupted me.

I turned on him. "Don't use my words against me, Jonathan." My rage had come unleashed. All I wanted was to decimate him, I didn't care how. "Just because you see things your way doesn't mean they're true."

"You are really out of whack, Catherine. You don't seriously think I lust after Susie, do you?"

"You did it right in front of me."

"Then you're as hidebound as your parents."

"I thought you liked my parents. My father wants to keep you in his pocket with the rest of his change. You're a good little man."

Instead of becoming angry, as I expected, Jonathan stroked his beard with one hand, watching me. "What's going on here? Are you jealous of my relationship with your parents?"

I screamed at him, "I am not jealous! Why can't you understand?" and suddenly I was making horrible, dry sobbing sounds from deep inside my chest, but I couldn't cry any tears. Something was wrong with me. I couldn't go on feeling this way. I realized that Jonathan was holding me, saying, "Shhhh, shhhh." Why couldn't he help me? Jonathan stroked my back. After a long time, I started to calm down.

Jonathan said, his voice near my ear, "I don't know why this happens between us, Cath. We never used to fight."

Something was wrong with me, and I didn't know what it was. Something that pulled at me and kept me apart. I needed Jonathan to understand so he could help me get back. But I had given up expecting him to. He said, "Shhhh, shhhh," and began to kiss my face, small kisses, gestures of good faith.

When he started to kiss my neck, I breathed, and it sounded like a sigh. Jonathan watched me as he took off my glasses. He loosened my hair from its ponytail. The heavy mass of it fell forward into my face. I touched the bristly hairs of his beard, and he smiled. "Don't do a thing," he said. "This is my show now." He pushed me back gently against the pillows and bent over me, kissing me.

When I closed my eyes, my headache was gone, and the long shadows on the wall were shut away. I gave myself over to Jonathan, as I had hundreds of times before. I didn't know what else to do. He was tender, as always. I loved how sexy he made me feel. But there was still something very wrong with me, and it made me afraid. I let Jonathan take me with him, holding him as close as any two people can get, frantic for more.

CHAPTER 3

Laura

Fall 1973

DURING HOMEROOM ON THE FIRST day of fifth grade, the girl sitting at the desk behind me whispered words I could barely hear: "menstruation . . . gynecologist . . . copulation . . ." I knew what the first word meant. I had learned it that summer from my friend Eleanor. Her older sister had shown her in the bathroom. The idea of it grossed me out, but I also wanted it to happen to me. I wanted anything that was grown-up. I couldn't wait to drink coffee, have ID cards, walk downtown by myself. Bleeding every month had the added bonus of being something boys couldn't do. They thought they were the best at everything. Menstruation was so private that my mother and sister had never said anything to me about it. (After I found out about menstruation from Eleanor, Claudia did tell me that the huge boxes our mother kept in the linen closet were called "sanitary napkins" and explained how they worked.)

It was my first day at that school. I didn't know anybody there. I sat at my new desk, too scared to listen to all the names the teacher was calling out. Those three big words I thought I'd heard stayed in my head. If the other two were anything like menstruation, then I wanted to learn them too. I turned around. The girl behind me was Oriental with long black hair and gold posts in her ears. Back home, I hadn't known anybody my age who had pierced ears. She was watching the teacher take roll. She didn't notice me looking at her. Confused, I turned forward again. Maybe I hadn't really heard anything. In front of me, most of the kids were doodling on their desks or passing notes to their friends. Then I heard the voice again, whispering close to my ear. "Cunnilingus . . ."

My family had moved to Mill Valley in August. Before that we lived in Middlebury, Vermont. On a snowy night in March, my parents called Jamie and Claudia and me together in the living room. Standing in front of us, my father told us that the college hadn't given him tenure. Claudia turned to me and said that meant he couldn't teach there anymore. My father said he had applied for other jobs and had been hired by the College of Marin. I listened carefully while he spoke, storing the new word "tenure." He sounded the way he always did when we were all together, like he was giving a lecture to his history class.

"Any questions?" he asked when he was finished.

"Why California?" my brother asked. Ever since Jamie had turned sixteen he sounded like he thought he was talking to the most retarded person in the world. He got up from the sofa, pulled the wire screen away from the fireplace, and jabbed at the burning logs with a poker.

My parents gave each other their look, then my father sat down in an armchair and crossed one leg over the other. "Well, for one thing, I'm fond of it. You'll remember I was stationed in Oakland before I was shipped out to Japan during the war. That's the Korean War, not World War II," he said to me. I glared at him. Of course I knew which war he meant. He had told us his stories about the Occupation millions of times. My father was older than the parents of other kids my age. Sometimes I worried because he didn't seem to remember the things he had already said. "The Bay Area is terrific," he told us. "You'll all love it."

For a long time the damp wood hissed in the fire. Nobody looked at anybody else. Why weren't Jamie or Claudia saying anything? Then I realized they had already guessed. They had probably even talked about it together. That meant I was the only one who was surprised by our father's news. I felt scared, like during a thunderstorm when the lightning was very bright and the thunder sounded like we were being blown up.

I couldn't keep still. "What about Eleanor and Mary? How will I see them?"

"You won't, Laura," my mother said. "Where we're going is very far away. You'll have to say goodbye to them." I wished I hadn't said anything. My mother was in one of her bad moods. "You just have to get used to it," she said. "We'll probably never come back to this godforsaken town." She crossed her legs, just like my father, and twirled a finger in her short curled hair. "Don't worry, sweetie, you'll make new friends right away." She said that gently, like she was being comforting.

I stared at her. I didn't feel better. I felt worse. "Why?" I asked. "Why do we have to leave?" Then I started to cry. I thought about the soda fountain my mother took me to sometimes after school where she ordered a brownie à la mode and I ordered a vanilla milkshake and bounced on the seat in the booth. I thought about sledding down the wide hills of the campus (except lately Jamie wouldn't take me). And I thought about our attic, full of old boxes and furniture, where Eleanor and Mary and I went to play "Mission: Impossible." I wiped my nose on my sleeve.

Claudia looked like she wanted to cry too. She was just a year younger than Jamie, but she cried a lot, especially at the movies. My mother rubbed her foot against the head of the bearskin rug where Jamie was sitting. Under his breath, Jamie said to me, "You're such a baby." He poked at the logs some more, sending sparks up the flue. My father cleared his throat.

"We have to go to California, Laura, because no one will give me a job here. I have to work. I have to bring home the bacon for all of you, right? Right?" He tilted his head, trying to catch my eye. I nodded. I wiped my nose on my other sleeve.

"Laura, for God's sake," my mother said, frowning at me.

"We all have to pitch in and help make this move as easy as possible," my father went on. "Will you do that for me?" I nodded again. I felt bad for my father. He stayed at the college late. Sometimes he didn't come home until after I was in bed. Now after all his hard work they didn't want him. It was unfair. Maybe his job in California would be better. But I still didn't want to go.

"Good, so that's settled," my father said, clapping his hands on his knees. "Why don't we all go bowling?"

"I hate bowling," Jamie said. He threw the poker into the fire, stood up, and left the house, slamming the door shut behind him.

I wanted to follow Jamie, but I wouldn't dare slam the door. I liked him best when we were alone. He explained things to me, like why Mary was sometimes mean to me (because she was jealous I was friends with Eleanor). The poker lay half sticking out of the flames. I was afraid it might melt like the Wicked Witch of the West. If I ran through the snow after Jamie, he'd just tell me to go back to the house.

Claudia said, "We're still going to Mackinac in June like always, aren't we?"

My mother crouched in front of the fire and fished out the poker with the long tongs. "Of course we are," she answered.

"Is it true it never snows in California?" I asked my father. "Will we get to wear shorts every day?"

That first day at my new school, I waited for the bell to ring for recess. It wasn't hard to find the girl who sat behind me. For one thing, nobody else in the class was Oriental (though there were two dark-skinned boys I guessed were Mexican). For another thing, she didn't run outside onto the blacktop with the rest of the kids, where they yelled and jostled each other and broke into groups to play kickball and hopscotch. I wished I knew how to join them. The homeroom teacher had told the class that I was new from Vermont, but nobody had said hi to me. They already had their friends that they hadn't seen all summer. So far, I didn't like this school at all. In my school back home there had been fewer kids in my class, and the teacher came around to our desks to help us. I watched the

other kids through the wide back windows chasing each other and sharing secrets in twos and threes by the chain-link fence, imagining myself
out there with them. I would be the fastest runner, the one everybody
wanted on their team. I wondered if in California they knew how to play
dodgeball. That was my favorite game, even if I wasn't that good at it.

When I looked back around the empty classroom, even our teacher
had left. At the side of the room, the girl who sat behind me climbed
onto a window seat that had yellow and orange cushions. She settled into
one corner, putting all the pillows behind her against the wall. Then she
opened up a book and laid it on her bent knees. It looked like a grown-up
book, heavy with a hard cover. She turned a page. The sun glinted on her
dark hair. She didn't seem to care if I stayed or left.

The classroom looked huge with nobody else there, and it was quiet
too. I didn't like being alone in the middle of it. I stood up and went to
the window seat, threading my way between the desks. She didn't look
at me even when I pulled myself up and sat cross-legged facing her. I
watched her eyes moving back and forth. She really was reading. I could
never sit still long enough to get very far in a book. Anything I had to do
sitting down made me fidget. I was afraid something important might
happen somewhere else and I wouldn't be there for it.

"What are you reading?" I asked her.

"*Small Changes*," she said without looking up. Her eyes kept moving
across and back. She turned another page.

"What's that?" I asked.

She raised her head. I saw from the way she looked straight into my
eyes that she didn't think I was dumb for asking. "It's a novel by Marge
Piercy. My mom's CR group read it."

"Oh," I said, even more lost but not wanting to say so. "Well, what's
it about?"

"My mom says it's about women who liberate themselves from the
patriarchy and have all kinds of relationships. She says it's a life-changing
story. So far it's kind of boring."

"I'd probably like it," I said, trying to memorize her description for later. I leaned forward and rested my forearms on my knees, hoping to hear more.

We watched each other for a few seconds. I could hear the shouts and laughter of the kids playing outside, but I didn't look away. Then she looked down at her book. "Maybe you would."

She opened the book to a page where the spine had been broken and passed it over. She pointed to a short paragraph. I read, "She became aware his impotence had vanished when still lying beside her he guided his penis gently between her labia and slowly began to slide into her. She tried to say no, but she could not speak. She shook her head wildly and tried to push him back, but he held her with the full strength of his hands and arms until he was buried in her with his legs scissored about hers."

I could feel my face turning red. It made me uncomfortable reading this sexy scene in front of this girl. She might see how interested I was. I didn't know what "labia" was, but I could guess. I started to read it again.

"There's another good part on page seventy-four, if you want to look," she told me.

Surprised, I raised my head. Her face looked hopeful and a little pink. Right then I saw we were just the same. She was curious too.

"Where'd you get this?" I asked.

"It's my mom's."

Her mother must have lent it to her, or else she had stolen it from her mother's bookshelves. Either way, I was amazed.

"Does this have those words you were whispering?" I asked.

"Nobody uses those words in novels." She sounded just like Jamie. "My mom has this other book, *Our Bodies, Ourselves*. It even has pictures of women giving birth and stuff. Of course, you can always look in the dictionary."

"Oh, well, yeah." Actually, I hadn't thought of that. I'd seen a large dictionary lying open on a stand in the school library. I could look up all the bad words I wanted without anybody knowing what I was doing.

Maybe this girl would come with me and help with the spellings. Maybe we would find some words even she didn't know. "What's your name?" I handed back her book.

"Min. That's M-I-N. It's a Korean name, but I'm not Korean. I was adopted." She riffled the pages of her book with her thumb.

I didn't know what to say, so I said, "I'm Laura."

"I know."

I didn't know what to say to that, either. We watched each other, while the clock on the wall ticked loudly and I heard a boy outside yell, "Hey, pea-brain, over here!"

"Do you want to play Scissors, Paper, Stone?" I asked.

"Okay," she answered, a huge smile on her face. I'd never made anybody so happy just by asking them to play a game before. She scooted closer and sat cross-legged too and put out her fist.

"One, two, three, go!" I counted. She had paper, I had scissors.

"I won," I said, and I wetted my two scissors fingers on my tongue and slapped her hand hard.

"Hey! What'd you do that for?" Min pulled her hand back to her chest, covering it with her other hand.

"It's how you play," I answered.

"It hurts," Min said.

"Well, yeah, if you lose."

"Are you making this up?" she asked me.

"No. Me and my friends played all the time. Isn't that how you play?"

"No."

My mother had warned me that people in California were different from the rest of us. "Okay," I said, "here's how it goes. If it's paper and stone, you slap the other person's hand with your whole hand." I slapped her hand. "If it's stone and scissors, you punch them on the shoulder."

"Don't show me," Min commanded.

I dropped my hand and waited, starting to feel scared. Now she wouldn't like me. Min was frowning, thinking hard. I wondered how you could play the game differently. With Mary and Eleanor and me, we played to hurt each other. That was part of what made us friends.

"Well," she said, "can you play it the way we play it here?"

I nodded. I was sure if I said no, she wouldn't talk to me anymore.

"Okay. Let's start," she said. We held up our fists. "One, two, three, shoot."

We had the exact same thing as before, scissors and paper. I grinned at her. She didn't notice.

She said, "Okay, now you open your scissors and put my paper in between." Min moved the side of her hand against the tips of my fingers. I parted them, and she moved her hand right in. "Now cut." I tried to close and open my two fingers around her hand. It felt like chewing with my fingers instead of with my teeth. It made me tense, the way I got when I was in the front during a dodgeball game and I had to be extra alert. I looked up at Min. Her head was bowed and her hair was falling in her face. I couldn't tell if her eyes were closed or not.

We started over. This time I had stone and she had paper. She covered my fist with her open hand and held on to it. "See?" she asked, looking up. "Paper wraps stone. That's how it's supposed to go."

"Are you making this up?" I asked her. She smiled. I was teasing, but I also didn't really see the point of playing this way. It seemed silly. But I wasn't bored.

Her hand over mine was very warm. Her fingers were long and thin, and she didn't have chewed fingernails like I did. I wanted to put my other hand over hers, and her other one over mine, and my bottom one over hers, stacking our hands, changing the game. But I pulled my fist away.

I pointed at the book in her lap. "So is that a dirty book?"

She smiled, just a little. "No."

"Then why did you take off the paper cover?"

"So I wouldn't mess it up. All the other girls are passing around *Are You There God? It's Me, Margaret.* Have you read that?"

I shook my head. "No, but I want to."

"Well, I can lend it to you. You'd probably like it. She moves to a new town too."

"Can I also borrow *Small Changes* when you're finished with it?" I asked.

Min grinned, looking into my eyes again. I grinned happily back. We were going to be friends, I knew it. Here I was, sitting with a girl named Min near a mountain called Tamalpais in a state where palm trees grew all over the place. Everything was new, and for the first time since we had moved I was excited, even about coming back to school the next day. I remembered Eleanor and Mary, wondering if I was being disloyal. I'd written each of them every week since we had cried saying goodbye, but I'd only gotten one letter from Eleanor. I imagined them going to Mary's house to play together after their first day of school. Missing them made me want this new friend even more.

The school bell rang. The rest of the class lined up outside and started coming back into the room, still talking and laughing. Min jumped down off the bench, taking her book. I watched her, wanting to talk with her about everything. I wanted to make pretend ID cards with her and play "Mission: Impossible." Her black hair was almost as long as mine. She walked to her desk and stuffed the book in her backpack. She didn't speak to anybody else. Seeing that, I felt sorry for her, and I also felt glad. Her calmness amazed me. When she sat down, I remembered the games I had watched the other kids playing at the beginning of recess. I looked outside the big windows. Near the playground area, two boys kicked a red gym ball back and forth between them.

CHAPTER 4

Laura
Winter 1976

"BAND-AID SLOWED YOU IN HISTORY. I bet you'll get a grape."

The note had fallen to the bottom of my locker between my sneakers. It was written in green fountain pen ink on a torn-off piece of lined notebook paper and had been folded several times into a small, thick square. Every time I found one, which was at least once a day, was like discovering a pastel-colored Easter egg or a chocolate bunny wrapped in foil, hidden in the grass. Except these prizes were meant for me alone. The notes were from Min, written in our code. Getting a note from her and writing back felt like having a second, separate friend that no one else knew about. We had most of our classes together, ate lunch together, hung out in front of the school together waiting for her mom to pick her up (except for the afternoons I stayed late for basketball practice), and talked on the phone almost every night. Even so, when I found a note from Min in my locker, I was as thrilled as if it had been a boy who had written me.

"Band-Aid" was our code word for Nick, a boy in our seventh-grade class we both had started to like in the fall. Of all the guys, we mentioned him the most (Nick: cut: Band-Aid). "Slow" meant "watch" (watch: time: slow). A "grape" was a date (fig was too obvious). We had words for kissing, boys, having a crush, all the bases, individual boys and teachers we thought were cute, various body parts, even three different positions of

61

intercourse. It was Min's idea to include the positions, but we hardly ever used those words.

It was my idea to make up the code. The year before, a kid I never liked anyway had intercepted a note I was passing to Min during geography. It said, "Don't look now but Mrs. Garibaldi's cleavage is showing." For the whole rest of the day, he and his friends kept following me and Min around, calling, "Cleavage!" I could have died. I kept wishing for a huge earthquake so the building would fall down and we wouldn't have to go to school anymore. I tried pretending I didn't hear them, which was what Jamie and Claudia did sometimes when I wanted them to play with me. It wasn't helping to get rid of those boys. Min got so sick of them that she turned around in the hall and shouted, "Shut up, you morons!" They found that really hysterical.

After that, there was no way I was going to get caught saying or writing anything the other kids could tease me for. Especially since Min and I had started to have a lot to say about the guys at school. Min didn't seem to care who knew what we were talking about. But she got into it, thinking up translations that were easy to remember. We stopped passing notes during classes.

At my locker, I unzipped my plastic pencil case. I slipped Min's note next to several others beside my collection of colored pens. Then I rummaged in my backpack for my small notepad, ripped out a page, and took out my purple, light green, and pink pens. Alternating colors for each letter, I wrote, "And finally eat dessert? I doubt it. Only in my oasis." "Dessert" meant a kiss (kiss: chocolate: dessert). "Oasis" stood for fantasy (fantasy: mirage: oasis). At the bottom in orange ink I drew a big smiley face with one raised eyebrow, our version of a lewd expression. Then I folded up the note into a paper airplane, walked down the hall, and squeezed it between the slats of Min's locker.

It was lunch period. Even with staggered hours, the cafeteria was crowded with yelling kids. The boys usually sat in large groups eating food from each other's tray, making fun of each other, and looking around to see if anyone was watching. The girls sat two or four together, whispering about makeup and movie stars and pretending not to notice the boys. In the food line, I pushed my tray along the metal bars and filled it with chicken potpie, succotash, milk, and an ice cream sandwich, my favorite dessert. Then I headed toward a table by one of the windows where Min was already eating. She was reading, her book open on the table beside her tray. In the middle of the din in that room she looked totally peaceful, like she was at home by herself and nobody was sitting next to her jostling her elbow. I envied the way she shut out the world, content with the one inside her head or on the page she was reading. My brother Jamie said I was a follower. He said I wanted too much from other people, and I depended on them more than I should. I knew I hoped for a lot, but I didn't see how that made me too trusting. I thought I was the opposite.

Min had saved the seat across from her with her sweater. "Hi," I said, putting down my tray. I handed the sweater back and slid into the empty chair. Next to us, some eighth-grade girls complained about a math test they'd just gotten back. Min grinned at me and closed her book.

I moved my fork around in the succotash, dividing the mushy lima beans from the sweet corn. Min pushed her lunch tray away from her. She gathered her long black hair in both hands behind her head like a ponytail and then let it fall. She folded her forearms against the edge of the table. Today she was wearing pearl earrings. I liked the white glow of them against her skin. The summer before, I had asked my mother if I could get my ears pierced. She had told me that I would be deforming myself, that only gypsies and Africans pierced their bodies. She said those holes would be there forever, even if I decided I didn't want them anymore. I had seen pictures in *Life* magazine of African women whose ear lobes hung to their shoulders with holes in them you could put your hand through. Did my mother think that was what I meant? I tried again. I told her five girls in my class had had their ears pierced in the last year, and Min had had hers pierced when she was seven. My mother said

Min was spoiled. Her parents gave her everything she wanted because she probably would have starved to death in China or whatever country she came from if they hadn't adopted her. I started to tell my mother that Min wasn't spoiled, but as soon as I opened my mouth she yelled at me for not listening to her the first time: I could not have pierced ears. I turned away, my throat aching and my eyes watering, and stomped down the hall to my room. I didn't care anymore about piercing my ears. My mother was mean and unfair. And she didn't know anything about Min.

I broke the crust of the potpie with my fork and let the steam escape. "Do you know about Diana's party?" Min asked. I stared at her. She looked gleeful, almost triumphant. I was the one always listening in on conversations, trying to find out about everything that happened at the school. Min hardly ever heard about anything that I didn't already know. I hadn't thought she cared.

"What party?" I asked. In the clamor of the cafeteria I had to raise my voice to be heard.

"Diana's parents are going away for Friday night and leaving her and her older sister alone in the house. So she's having a party, and the whole class is invited." I'd been to some birthday parties, but neither of us had ever been asked to the smaller make-out parties that I heard about sometimes in the girls' bathroom. Mostly they played "Spin the Bottle" and "Two Minutes in the Closet." If the whole class was invited, then it would be more of a dance, but with no grown-ups around. I hoped there would still be "Spin the Bottle." Min leaned forward against her crossed forearms like she was trying to hold in her excitement. "I bet Band-Aid will be there." She lowered her voice. "He likes you, Laura, I can tell."

Privately, I thought so too. I had felt Nick's gaze on me earlier that morning in history class, and at other times too. We had even begun to talk to each other, when Min wasn't around, in the afternoons after basketball practice. He was on the boys' JV team. So while I was running around one half of the gym learning to dribble and pass and shoot with the girls, Nick was doing the same thing at the other end with the boys.

I'd heard he was their best player. Sometimes, afterwards, I'd see him hanging out with a bunch of his friends, usually skateboarding around the almost-empty parking lot beside the gym. We'd started walking home together for the four blocks before I turned off toward my house. After a while I figured out that he was waiting for me. My fantasies about him were starting to come true.

I hadn't told Min any of this. For one thing, I was afraid of jinxing it. Mostly I didn't really believe anything would ever happen between Nick and me. He was too cool, too popular, too good-looking to want me to be his girlfriend. Every girl in the class had a crush on him. And I really liked him. But I didn't know what to say to him. When I was around him I forgot all the advice my mother was always giving Claudia and me about how to get a guy, except "Play hard to get." I thought he could see how much I wished he would ask me out, and that was sure to scare him away. The problem was, I wanted him to more than like me. I wanted him to love me, heart and soul.

"Do you think so?" I asked, taking a bite of chicken potpie. It was still too hot. I opened my mouth, breathing the hot air out while waving cool air inside. Min handed me my carton of milk, and I drank half of it. "I don't know," I said after swallowing. "He seems to like Caroline a lot. He's always talking to her before homeroom."

Min thought about this. "That's true. But wouldn't it be great if he did like you? God, those blue eyes . . ."

We were silent, remembering his blue eyes. At night in my bed I imagined Nick standing with his arms around me, his blond hair slightly tousled, his beautiful blue eyes brimming with love as he brought his face close to mine to kiss me for the first time. His lips would be gentle and soft. He would tell me how much he cherished me, like the David Cassidy song I listened to on my record player all the time. He would say he wanted to be with me forever. Lying alone in the dark, I could feel the safety of his arms embracing me. I could feel my own heart filling with love and the happiness of being loved. Sometimes I wanted that so much

I couldn't keep from crying. The ache inside made me even lonelier, my tears trickling down onto the sheets as I lay curled on my side clutching my pillow.

"Get one for me!" a girl's voice nearby called out, startling me. I swallowed, my throat raw. Min had closed her eyes. I couldn't look at her dreamy face. I knew I should tell her Nick and I walked partway home together, but I was scared she would feel left out. And that would mess up everything. I wanted to keep the little piece of him I already had.

I studied the other kids eating their lunches. I went from one to the next, trying to imagine their surprise seeing me in the school halls holding hands with Nick. The pleasure of it made me smile.

Then I saw Nick's face. He was looking right at me. In the middle of the cafeteria, surrounded by all the other girls, he was watching me with his electric blue gaze. When our eyes met he smiled, a big, open grin. I couldn't believe how cute he was. I wished I was sitting with him, his arm around me, his lips against my hair like a couple in a movie. I immediately looked away. My heart was going a million miles a minute.

I glanced at Min. She was still in her fantasy world, her eyes shut, her mouth partly open. I could still feel how the side of his body would press against mine because we were sitting so close. I shivered, getting goosebumps. Under the table I ground the sole of my shoe into the top of Min's sneaker. She opened her eyes, surprised.

"I'm going to ask my mom if I can spend Friday night at your house. I'm not going to even mention the party."

"Okay." Min drank some of my milk from the carton.

"Let's go," I said. I started to stack our plates, sliding my tray under hers. I wanted to look at Nick again. "I can barely think in here."

"You haven't eaten your ice cream sandwich."

"I'm not hungry."

"What's wrong?" she asked, reaching for it.

"Come on," I answered, pushing back my chair. I knew Nick was still watching me. I had to get out of that room as fast as possible. I carried our trays over to the kitchen and shoved them through the window opening. I headed toward the exit, the whole time trying not to turn my head in his direction. Min was waiting for me in the hall.

She had tied her sweater around her waist and stuck her book inside it, like a sword. She tore the paper wrapping from the top half of the ice cream sandwich.

I stared at her, panicking. "You're not allowed to take food out of the cafeteria."

"Band-Aid slowed you leaving," she said casually, as if reporting something as uninteresting as the weather. Then she closed her teeth over the chocolate wafer and the creamy, cold vanilla filling. My mouth watered. My stomach was still too jittery to eat.

Besides the code, there was another secret side to my friendship with Min. It had started about six weeks before, when Min was staying overnight at my house. We were talking, as usual, about boys. We lay on our sides, watching each other across the space between the beds. Her face was silvery from the street light outside the window. We had just discovered we both had a crush on our art teacher, Mr. Ketchum. We called him Ketchup. All the kids did. Min immediately came up with the code name "after-dinner mint" (ketchup: condiment: after-dinner mint).

"You know what it is?" Min asked. "That makes him sexy?"

I had no idea. Mr. Ketchum was almost bald, and he was old, probably in his forties. There was nothing at all cute about him.

Min said, "It's his bulge."

"Ewww!" I yelped, then remembered my parents downstairs and clapped my hand over my mouth. The last time Min and I had made too much noise, because we couldn't stop laughing, my father had stormed up the stairs and into the room to remind us that they had guests over and would we pipe down and go to sleep. After he left, Min, furious, said in a not-very-quiet voice that we could hear them laughing downstairs just as easily and wasn't she a guest too?

"His *bulge*," Min repeated, drawing it out to tease me, so that the word itself grew and strained at the seams. Now I was giggling (quietly), trying to picture Mr. Ketchum with his round, shiny head, his short legs, and the bulge in his jeans. Min was right. It was definitely there, like it was inviting us to touch, even push against it. I didn't think about what was actually inside his pants. I didn't want to ruin the shivery feeling I was having. I liked the hint of what lay underneath his denim jeans without having to worry about the gross and nauseating object itself.

"It's very ... prominent, isn't it?" I asked, and we both burst into giggles.

Min pulled her pillow from beneath her head and hugged it. "Sometimes," Min confided, "I watch to see if it moves."

"What, like a mouse trying to get out?" This set us off again. I covered my mouth with both hands, trying to keep quiet.

"No, no," Min answered, catching her breath. "Like a hopping frog."

"Ribbit," I croaked in my deepest voice, which sounded more like a hiccup and sent us off into another round of giggles.

Then Min sat up and pushed down her covers. Her sudden movement spooked me. She got up from her bed. I thought she had to go to the bathroom, but she stood above me in her long nightgown. "Move over," she whispered. I did, and she got into my bed with me, pulling the blankets up to our necks. I was still giddy, no longer laughing but feeling tingly. Now her face was in shadow. Our knees bumped together, and I could feel Min's foot touching mine. It was nice having her right next to me, not halfway across the room.

She asked, "What would you do if Ketchup wanted you to touch him there?" Her voice was low and hypnotizing. I felt her hand touching the thick cotton of my nightgown over my pubic area, where I had started to sprout a lot of curly hair. Min's favorite game that we played at sleepovers was asking these questions, but she had never cuddled up like this before. We just asked and answered from our separate beds. What would you do if Johnnie put his arm around you? Would you let Nick French you? Would you let Matthew feel you up? We had to tell the truth. Mostly I said I wouldn't, and Min said she would. I wondered if she would in real life. I wanted to have a boyfriend and I wanted to kiss him, but that was different from letting a boy do whatever he wanted without knowing how much he liked me. Min's hand moved gently, stroking downward over my slight mound of flesh, like she was petting the animal she had discovered there. I liked the simple, soothing motion. I wanted her to do it over my whole body.

"I'd touch him. But only through his clothes, not naked."

She was silent, still stroking. Maybe she'd forgotten she was doing it.

"What about you?" I asked.

"Naked," she said, her voice drowsy. I realized my eyes were closed. She said, "I'd want to feel his skin. I'd want to find out how that froggy jumps."

I smiled at the image in my head, which at the moment didn't seem that gross, just silly. If I ever got to go out with a boy, some day he might ask me to touch the front of his pants. I tried to imagine Nick with Mr. Ketchum's bulge. I would do it if we were going steady.

I reached down and brought Min's hand away from my nightgown. I was starting to feel again that I wanted more than I could ever hope for. To have a boyfriend. To be held all night. To be adored. Someday, to get married and have a family of my own.

I asked, "Would you put your arm around me?" I kept my eyes shut tight.

"'Course, Laura-lee." I felt her breath on my face. Taking her hand from mine, she put it around my back, inching closer. I wondered if she thought we were still playing the game. But her body was warm, and I felt better. We fell asleep that way.

The next time Min spent the night, a week later, she climbed into my bed right away. This time I put my arm around her too. We smiled at each other, and I saw that she was already so comfortable, she was half-asleep.

My mother had taken us to a movie that afternoon. At the end, the man and the woman finally confessed they loved each other and made out for a long time. We could see how they opened their mouths wide, practically biting each other. Once the man's tongue darted out like an eel between the lips of the woman. I could barely watch with my mother sitting next to me, but I couldn't look away either. This was how grown-ups kissed. I was afraid I wouldn't know how. I wanted to be good at it when a boy French kissed me.

Min must have felt the same way, because after we'd gone over that make-out scene for a while, she said, "We could try it."

"What?" I asked, my heart beating fast and hard, like I'd been out on the basketball court.

"Kissing," she said. When I didn't say anything, she went on, "So we'll know what to do."

I could feel every place where Min and I were touching like there were bugs crawling there. But if I moved away, Min would know I was scared and she wouldn't offer again. I kept myself very still, not even breathing. "Okay," I said.

A few days before that, Nick had smiled at me for the first time ever when I came out the back door of the school still sweaty from practice. He had such a cute smile, I grinned back not even thinking about it. I was in seventh heaven. I couldn't wait to get home and call Min. He was with a couple of his teammates on the lawn, sprawled out on his side. It was a rare warm January day, and we were all still in our t-shirts and gym shorts. He took a puff from a cigarette. I thought only the bad kids who hated school smoked. At first it bothered me. Then I decided it was kind of cool. As I walked across the parking lot toward the road, he flicked his cigarette butt on the sidewalk, stood up, gave a little wave to his team-mates, and bounded up to me. His friends made teasing noises, calling his name with a little lilt. It turned out he lived nearby too, so we walked together for a few blocks. We didn't say much. I was too nervous, and he seemed moody. At home afterwards I kept remembering his bangs hanging over his eyes and the awkward way he'd leaned on his elbow on the lawn. He wasn't really any cooler or more mature than the other boys. My heart kept filling up thinking of him. Somehow I never did get around to telling Min. Nothing had really happened. I didn't know if he liked me or anything.

Next to Min in the dark, I felt disoriented. I had kept that walk with Nick a secret from her, something I never thought I'd do. Now I felt strange for liking the idea of kissing her when it was Nick I fantasized about. I closed my eyes. I wanted to know what it was like. It might be years before I'd ever get to kiss a boy. I opened my eyes. "What do we do?" I asked her.

"Just kiss me, dummy." Her voice was mean and affectionate at the same time.

I thought of something. "Maybe it's different with girls than with boys. Maybe this won't really help—"

I saw her shadowed face move closer on the pillow and felt her mouth land on mine, a little off-center. Her lips were soft and open slightly. Mine were tense and partly open because she'd caught me in mid-sentence. We pressed our mouths together while I held my breath, hoping she wasn't going to want to try French kissing. Then I remembered the movie. I had to learn to kiss like that. Nick was probably an expert.

I pulled away, our lips peeling apart.

"Maybe we should move our mouths around more," I said. Min nodded, silent. I wanted to crack a joke. Min and I were never this quiet together.

On our second try we were like two fish opening and closing our mouths against each other, but at the wrong time. Min started laughing, her lips still attached to mine. I imagined Nick laughing at how I kissed.

I pulled away again. "It's not funny," I said. "Do you want to kiss like that when it's the real thing?"

Min wiggled her other arm, the one on the side she was lying on, underneath my neck, clasping both hands behind me. She snuggled closer to me, so that our chests and more of our legs touched. I could smell her breath, minty from toothpaste. I could feel the hard buds of her nipples on her flat chest even through both our nightgowns. My own breasts had grown in the last year to the size of tomatoes. Now they were pressed against Min, molded to her shape. I wondered what it would be like to be pressed against her without our nightgowns on. I rolled quickly onto my back. She kept her arms around me.

"Okay, let's be serious," Min said in a mock-stern voice.

I realized she was answering my question, that only a few seconds had passed since I'd asked it. She pushed up on one elbow and leaned down and kissed me again, closing her eyes and parting her lips. Her hair fell against my cheek. It was weird how naturally she did it this time, pressing her mouth softly against mine, peeling her lips away, then bringing them down again in a slightly different place. She was kissing me like she meant it, the way Nick did in my fantasies. I almost wanted to stop. We were girls. We were just friends, not boyfriend and girlfriend. Then she sighed, a blissful sound. I opened my eyes.

She stopped kissing me, but she stayed above me, her hair falling around her face. Her eyes were too dark for me to see clearly. I wonder what she could see in mine.

"Okay?" she asked in a normal voice. Then I figured it out. She'd been pretending. Her confidence, her sighing were part of our practicing. When I nodded, she brought her head down again. I tried to relax and keep my jaw slack. I felt the tip of her tongue against my lips. I felt my mouth open and her wet tongue inside and my tongue moving to meet it. Her tongue was pleasantly warm. Lazily, we slipped and slid over and around each other. It was like playing, teasing each other, laughing. It was its own kind of code. I was happy that Min and I were trying it. Now we shared another secret nobody else knew about.

After a while she sighed again. This time I ignored it. I was concentrating on the nice feeling of our tongues together, wondering if we were doing it right. In the movie they had been more frantic. Then Min's hand, the one that wasn't under me, moved along my shoulder and onto the front of my nightgown, over my breast. I froze. We were only going to kiss, nothing else. I was afraid she wasn't pretending anymore. Maybe she did mean it. Maybe she was a sex maniac.

"What are you doing?" I asked, pushing her away, hard.

She lay next to me, her breathing rough. She didn't speak. I thought she might be about to cry. Immediately I felt terrible for hurting her feelings. I knew she wasn't a pervert. She was just curious, like me.

I wanted back the comfort of her arms around me. I turned on my side and put my arm across her stomach. She was pretending to be asleep, her eyes closed and her breathing deep. But after a while she turned on her side too and put her arm around me. I snuggled in closer.

Since then we'd practiced kissing almost every week, when one of us spent the night at the other's house. We didn't mention her touching my breast, and she never did it again. In the same bed, we'd talk, then kiss, then fall asleep, our arms around each other. I thought maybe now I might be ready to move on to boys.

The afternoon of the day Min told me about Diana's party, I stayed late as usual for basketball. It was after five and getting dark by the time our coach let us out of there. I called goodbye as my teammates climbed into their mothers' cars. I was hoping to see Nick on my walk home, but it was still lightly raining and nobody was hanging out around the school. It had been raining a lot for February. I hadn't run into him there for over a week. I breathed in the wet, tarry smell of the road, feeling sorry for myself.

When I had walked a couple of blocks, I heard a rolling noise and looked back, hoping it was Nick on his skateboard. It was. I was thrilled. He rumbled past me, pushing off the road with his sneaker a few times, then wheeled around and stopped right in front of me, blocking my way.

"Fancy meeting you here," he said. Even though the dusk made everything gray, his eyes were a greenish-blue.

"Yeah," I said, feeling shy standing so close to him. I watched as he flipped the skateboard up on its end with his high-top and caught its edge. He was good.

We started walking. "How was practice?" he asked.

I made a face. "Not that great. Debra kept running into me, like tackling me, and knocking the ball out of my hands, but when I hit her in the face with my elbow by accident, I was taken out of the game."

"That sucks. Well, if it'll make you feel any better, last week I fell right on my butt jumping for a rebound. Hurt like hell."

"You?"

He nodded, smiling. I liked him for being able to admit he'd messed up, knowing I would now have a picture in my head of him landing clumsily under the hoop.

"Do you like basketball?" I asked.

"Sure. I'm good at it. Why?"

"I don't know if I'm very good. But I want to be." I tried to think out what I was trying to say. "When I have the ball, it's like I've got the world in my hands. The worst thing is for somebody to take it away from me. But the best thing is when I know what to do and I can do it. No, it's when I can do it without even thinking about it. That's heaven. I've never told anybody that," I added, afraid I had been talking too much.

"You're intense," he said. His head was tilted away from me. I didn't know if intense was good or bad.

After a while, he asked, "Are you going to Diana's party?"

I stared down at the pavement in front of my feet, my heart pounding. I knew he was invited to a lot of "Spin the Bottle" parties. If we played "Spin the Bottle," would I let Nick French kiss me in front of everybody else? I wanted to be able to kiss him without even thinking about it. I could feel my face heating up.

"I don't know." It was true, but I sounded like a dope. My answer was the kind of thing my mom would approve of, what she called "being coy."

He said, "Well, I am, and I hope you'll go too."

"This is my street," I said, starting off to the left away from him. "Bye."

He flashed me a little wave, but he looked baffled. The whole rest of the way home I cursed myself out for not telling him I would be there.

When Min and I walked into my house after school the next afternoon, my mother was in the kitchen on the phone. As we kicked off our shoes in the front hall, I could hear her voice rising and falling, though not the words. I thought it was a positive sign. Talking on the phone with her friends usually put her in a good mood. Min and I left our bookbags on the floor and quietly went into the kitchen. I was starving for something sweet.

My mother was sitting on a stool at the breakfast bar, hunched over, one hand rubbing her forehead. She'd had her monthly perm that day. Her light-brown hair was tightly curled around her head and touched up with blonde highlights. She didn't seem to hear us until after we were in the room. Then, startled, she turned around and frowned at us. With one hand still holding the receiver to her ear, she picked up the phone, stood up, and took it into the laundry room, kicking the door closed behind her.

"What was that about?" Min asked. From the way she said it, I could tell she was insulted.

I shrugged. Jamie said our mother was crazy. He said he'd seen pills in her bathroom cabinet to prove it. The two of them could never get along anymore. He had just turned eighteen, and he was always reminding her he was legally an adult. He liked to stay out late with his greasy-haired friends. He wouldn't even call if he wasn't home by his old curfew. I didn't see what was so thrilling about driving around all night, which was what he told me they did when I asked. Personally, I wasn't sure why our mother was the way she was. But I felt sort of glad when I heard them yelling at each other. At least then I knew it wasn't just me she hated.

I opened the refrigerator door and handed Min a Dutch Apple yogurt and got a Cherry one for myself. She pulled two spoons out of the silverware drawer. We sat at the bar, twisting our feet between the rungs of the stools, and pried the cardboard disk from inside the lid to add to our collections. I had every kind except Prune Whip, which made me sick just thinking of it. Now I was working on collecting extras. Kids traded them at school. I told Min about my father's stack of beer coasters that he'd collected before he met my mother, when he was in college and then in the army and traveling a lot. He had a story to go along with every coaster. Claudia and Jamie and I used to shuffle through them, smelling their faintly malty odor and picking the ones with the maidens and lions to make up our own stories about.

There was a noise from behind the laundry room door like something heavy being dropped on the cement floor. "Why should I believe you anymore?" I heard my mother yell. I hated the hysterical whine of her voice, like a record being played too fast. Min and I stopped eating our yogurt and listened, not moving, our eyes on each other. Who was she talking to? A friend of hers? My brother? The whole house was silent, waiting for something to happen. "Fine, then, if that's what you want to do." I heard the receiver slam down in its cradle. Then it sounded like she was pounding on the top of the dryer with her fists. The sound made me flinch.

Min said, "Hey," and reached out to touch my arm. I couldn't look at her. If I did, I'd start to cry.

"Sorry," I said. I stirred my yogurt. I had been hungry a few minutes ago.

"Don't apologize," Min answered, and from the way she said it I knew she meant not just for my jumpiness but for my mother too. My face felt like it was slowly burning up. I wished I *could* burn up, all of me, into nothing but ashes. It didn't matter that Min had seen my mother like this before. Right then I despised my mother. I hated Min a little bit too. Her mother would never embarrass her. The laundry room door opened.

"That was your father," my mother said, walking back across the kitchen with the phone, kicking the slack cord in front of her. "He won't be home for dinner tonight." The phone as she dropped it on the counter top gave out a muted ring.

"Again?" I asked. It seemed like at least once a week now my father had to stay late at the college where he taught. Sometimes it was because he needed the quiet to grade papers, sometimes it was to hear a speaker on campus or go to a faculty meeting. I asked, "Why couldn't he grade papers here? We can all be quiet. I have homework."

My mother stared at me for a second, then opened the breadbox and ate the last two donuts. Min and I looked at each other, and she puffed out her cheeks. I didn't think my mom's weight was funny. Still chewing, my mother went to the refrigerator and pulled out broccoli and a mound of hamburger wrapped in plastic. She got a bag of French fries out of the freezer. "Are you staying for dinner, Min?" she asked, not very nicely. "I guess there's enough food now with only four of us. It shouldn't go to waste."

"Uh, no, I can't," Min answered. "My parents expect me home tonight." She scraped around the bottom of her yogurt container, gathering the last spoonful. At her house her father and mother never fought, at least not in front of me. Min said she heard them sometimes, late at night when she was in bed. She said her mother could get really quiet and not even answer when Min or her father said something to her. I thought Catherine was nice. I had never heard of a mom who wanted her daughter's friends to call her by her first name. She would sit down and listen when I went to her with my problems at school or when my own mother was being really mean. I liked Min's father mostly because he made me laugh. And he loved Min so much that it hurt to watch them sometimes, kidding around. He was always giving her a hug or resting his hand on her shoulder. I wished he'd do that with me. When my father gave me pocket money, he might touch the top of my head, fluffing my hair like I was a little kid.

"Mom, can I make the hamburger patties?" I asked. I liked shaping them into a ball, then smushing them flat. She was pulling the cutting board down from its rack and clearing counter space near the stove.

"Don't eat the raw meat, you'll get sick. Here's salt and pepper. Shall we put in an onion?"

"Yeah."

She took one out of the wire basket hanging near the window. Her anger seemed to be leaking away. I got up and walked past Min, around the breakfast bar to the sink. Over the splash of running water, I said, "Mom, I've got something to ask you."

Behind me, my mother asked, "What's that?" Slowly, I lathered my hands with soap, washing each finger carefully.

"Well, Diana Sykes, in my class?" It wasn't what I had expected to say. There was no response, just the rhythmic thunk of her knife against the cutting board. "Well, she's having a party this weekend, and I was wondering if I could go." I had lost my nerve. Why couldn't I learn to lie to my mother?

"Who else will be there?"

"The whole class is invited."

"Will there be boys?"

I turned around, my hands dripping wet, and reached for the dish-towel on the counter. "Of course, Mom, it's the whole class." Because my mother had her back to Min and me, I made a face, crossing my eyes. Min smiled.

My mother put down her knife and turned to me, one hand on her hip. "Is this one of those kissing parties? Everyone groping each other in the dark?"

I stared at her. I couldn't think of anything to say. How did she know? It was like she had read my thoughts. Then I stammered, "I don't know. I've never been to one before."

"No."

"What?"

"I said no. You can't go." She turned back to hacking up the onion.

"But Mom—" I began.

"It's just a party," Min interrupted, sounding really earnest, like she went to these parties all the time. "Just a bunch of kids getting together, drinking soda and eating chips and talking to each other. Maybe there'll be some dancing."

My mother turned on her. "Listen, young lady, I know what happens at these parties. Don't you dare tell me any different. You two want to run off and fool around with those boys the first chance you get. And those boys will take advantage of you. I've told Laura that a million times. My answer is no."

All my mother's anger had rushed up to her face, turning it beet red. Every time she got mad I was afraid she was going to have a heart attack or something. I unwrapped the plastic and dug my hands into the hamburger meat. Then I had the awful thought that she had read our notes to each other and somehow decoded them. How else could she have found out what would be happening at the party? How else could she know how much I wanted to be kissed? I would die if my mother found out everything that Min and I talked about. I frantically tried to remember where I had hidden those tightly folded pieces of paper in my room. From now on, I would have to throw them away as soon as I'd read them.

Behind me, Min said, "You never let Laura do anything." I froze, my hands greasy from holding blobs of hamburger. She didn't know what a mistake she was making, talking back. If I kept very still, maybe it would be like I wasn't there at all.

"Min, you've overstayed your welcome." My mother's voice was a high whine again. I wished Min would go home too. Her being there hadn't helped anything.

"It's normal to go to parties." Min had raised her voice. "We know those boys from school. You're just too old to remember."

"Min," my mother said in a suddenly low, threatening tone. She turned around, her knife still in her hand.

"Okay, I'm leaving." Hearing Min scrape back her chair, I still couldn't turn around. The front door closed. I wondered if Min would ever come to my house again. I'd never heard her sound scared before.

My mother turned to me. "Are you going to make the hamburgers, Laura?"

I convinced my mother to let me stay overnight at Min's house on Friday night, telling her the party was Saturday, so we got to go anyway. We spent over an hour getting ready. I couldn't decide whether to wear my cream-colored shirt with the V-neck and long sleeves or my purple t-shirt with the cartoon of an old-fashioned telephone on the front. I was afraid I would spill on the lighter one, but I always wore the purple one.

"No, wear the first one," Min said as I stood on the edge of the bathtub and leaned to the left to see myself in the mirror over the sink. I pulled the telephone shirt over my head for the second time, wishing I had asked Claudia before she went out if I could borrow one of hers. "It's older, more sophisticated," Min added. "And it looks nice with those pants."

I looked down at my white bra, my stocky torso, the flare at the hem of my green cotton pants, and my pale feet. My hair fell forward over my face, and I flicked it behind my ears, impatient. I didn't like my body. For so long I had waited to be grown up, old enough to make decisions for myself. Now that I was almost a teenager, practically an adult, even my own body wasn't mine anymore. I'd started getting my period two months before, but after the excitement of the first time, all it boiled down to was stained underwear and having to wear a bulky pad between my legs for five whole days. Min handed me the cream shirt. I put it on and looked down again, then in the mirror. I felt fat and lumpy. I would never get used to having breasts.

"Yeah, you look great," Min said, and she meant it. If she thought so, maybe Nick would too. She pulled me down from the bathtub by my arm. "Come on, we're already late."

"Wait, I want to put on eye makeup."

"Oh God." She made a face. "Okay." She sat down sideways on the closed toilet lid, pulled her knees up to her chest, and leaned back against the wall. "Tell me when you're ready to go," she said, closing her eyes.

Min had decided what she was going to wear days before. She had on blue jeans, a black sleeveless shirt, and her blue Adidas. She looked like she was part of a rock and roll band. I tried to remember if there were any bands with women in them. I didn't think so. Her black hair fell straight down either side of her face to her waist. Her lips gleamed with lipgloss, but otherwise she wasn't wearing any makeup. I'd asked if she wanted to use some of mine, but she'd said no, she didn't see why she should get all gooped up just to see the same old bozos she'd been in classes with all week. I thought that was the point. It was a chance for us to be somebody different, even if it was only for a night.

I had already curled my hair earlier. I leaned close to the mirror and brushed dark brown mascara onto my upper lashes, then the lower ones. I got some on my cheek and had to wipe it off with cold cream. I tried to pick the little clumps off, getting brown streaks on my fingers. With a little spongy wand I put on green eyeshadow. I stood back and examined my reflection. Would Nick like it? I glanced over at Min, wanting to ask her. She was watching me and smiling like she approved. I smiled too and looked away. I was blushing.

It had started to rain while we were eating dinner. Min's mom offered to drop us off. In the car I was too jittery to say much. Catherine asked Min to call her by ten so she could pick us up. I sat in the back seat, chewing on the ends of my hair and wishing I had brought a sweater. Outside the rain-spotted windows, redwoods loomed on either side of the narrow road. Diana lived a ways out of town, in the foothills of Mount Tam. I could smell wood smoke from some of the houses we passed. Out there, a lot of them were homemade, not much more than cabins hammered together, with rooms added on and VW Bugs in the dirt driveways.

We knew we were close when we heard the rock and roll. Catherine drove slowly up the winding driveway covered with pine needles.

The house looked small from the outside, hidden beneath the trees, its brown-stained wood making it seem part of the hillside. "What's that music?" I asked Min. It made me want to dance.

"'Brown Sugar.' The Rolling Stones."

"Oh." The records I listened to were more folk music: Joni Mitchell, Harry Chapin, Bread. I liked the love songs best. Catherine pulled over into a ditch and turned to Min in the passenger seat, letting the engine idle.

"Have fun," she said as she and Min hugged. I was already turning the door handle when she said, "Here, Laura, give me a hug too." I slid back over and we grabbed each other, the front seat between us. Not only was she letting Min go to this party, she was driving her to it. I wished she was my mother. She squeezed my shoulder. "You look very nice," she said. Min and I scrambled out of the car.

We ran to the front door, trying not to get rained on. "Are you nervous?" I asked Min before we went in.

"Maybe."

We grinned at each other.

"You go first," she said.

In the living room, all the furniture had been pushed against the walls. The only light was from the hall. Nobody was in the middle of the large, darkened room dancing to the cranked-up music. About twenty kids sat around the edges, on the couches and chairs, drinking soda and not talking much. Some of them were smoking cigarettes. I looked carefully, but none of them was Nick. Some I didn't know at all from the other section of the class. I realized that all the girls were sitting on one side and all the boys were sitting on the other. Suddenly I was depressed. Maybe nothing was going to happen after all.

While Min threw her sweatshirt into the coat closet, I asked Joey where the drinks were. He was talking to Ron and just pointed his thumb behind him like he was hitching. In the kitchen, Diana stood with her best friend Melissa near a big picnic chest on the floor filled with ice and sodas. Diana was tall and had beautiful, long chestnut hair. I knew her somewhat from having had classes together over the past three years. She was nice for a girl who was so popular.

"Hi," she said when she saw me, "want some?" She held up her ginger ale. I'd seen some of the girls with pink cans of Tab. I couldn't decide which I wanted.

"Where is everybody?" Min asked, bending down and grabbing a Tab.

"Their parents wouldn't let them come," Melissa said. "Like, why would they ask their *parents?*"

"Well, maybe they couldn't get a ride otherwise," I said.

Melissa rolled her eyes. I decided on ginger ale. I didn't know why Melissa didn't like me. I started to move away.

"What do you have to spike it with?" Min asked.

"Now that you mention it . . ." Diana said. I could see she admired Min a little more. I felt stupid. I hadn't even guessed there might be liquor at this party. "Vodka," Diana answered. "Are you game?"

"Sure."

Min followed Diana into a back room. Melissa and I ignored each other. I realized that most of the kids there were the ones who got in trouble at school. Maybe we shouldn't have come. I doubted Min would like the vodka. I'd tasted my father's gin and tonic the summer before. It was medicinal and bitter, and when I made a face, everybody laughed.

When Min got back we wandered into the living room. I kept looking around for Nick, scared that I might see him and scared that he wouldn't come. There was space on one of the couches, and we squeezed in and sat there, sipping from our cans. The music had changed to "Dream Weaver." I knew the words from listening to the radio and sang along. Still nobody got up to dance, though now there was a couple sitting on the floor in the corner making out. In the dimness I couldn't tell who they were.

Min leaned over. "I wonder if Band-Aid's going to show up," she yelled over the music.

I almost said, "He told me he would," but stopped myself in time. It was weird not telling her everything. But I couldn't. Even if Nick arrived, he might not talk to me.

"Yeah, I wonder," I yelled back.

I was glad Min was there with me. Sitting around in somebody's unlit living room wasn't what I had expected. I thought there would be dancing, people talking to each other, maybe card games or something so we could all get to know each other better. I would have liked a birthday party, with its chocolate cake and unwrapping of presents, more than this.

"Let's look around," I said. "There's nothing happening here."

We went upstairs. The light was on in one of the bedrooms at the top. Eight kids were sitting on the floor in a circle. A girl and a boy were crawling past each other, changing places. Diana held a Coke bottle in her lap. Min grinned at me. I started to get nervous.

As soon as we came in, they all stopped talking and gaped at us like they'd been caught by their parents stealing money. One of the boys said, "No way, I'm not playing with *them*!" Karen, sitting next to him, slapped his knee lightly, giggling. Her laughter hurt even more than what he'd said.

Diana looked down at the Coke bottle, then leaned forward and placed it on its side in the middle of the circle. "Sorry," she said, looking like she really was, "we've got the same number of girls and boys. We can't add two more girls."

"Come on," I muttered to Min, plucking at the back of her shirt. I started to leave the room.

"Can we watch?" Min asked them.

All I wanted to do was get out of there. But I turned back. Now instead of staring up at us, they were all looking at each other or picking at their sneaker laces. A few of the girls shrugged.

"I guess so," Diana said. There were a couple of nods.

"This isn't a spectator sport," the same boy protested.

"What difference does it make?" Min asked. "You're all going to be watching each other."

"Let's start," Karen said, impatient.

"Close the door," another boy said. I pushed it shut behind me, which cut the volume of the music. I could feel the bass through the floor under my feet.

We sat above them on the canopy bed. Min lay on her stomach with her head in her hands, like she was watching TV in her living room. Her hair fell all around her, landing like a flouncy skirt. The only way I could tell her feelings had been hurt too was because she was extra calm and focused on the game, like she didn't notice she had been left out. I wished for the millionth time I could be more like her. I couldn't get comfortable. Finally I sat back against the pillows, holding one of them against my chest. Outside the window, the rain had stopped.

It seemed like they'd all played before. There was no hesitation, once the bottle stopped spinning. The boy or girl would lean forward on hands and knees and kiss the person of the opposite sex closest to the bottle's open neck. The kiss was either fast or slow. Sometimes the others commented, rating the kiss. There were no tongues involved that I could see. A couple of times a boy looked down the shirt of the girl leaning toward him. I held my pillow closer against me.

Min, lying on the bed in front of me, watched everything carefully like she was studying for a class. Under her black shirt, her torso moved up and down as she breathed. Once, I noticed the muscles of her behind clenching and then relaxing.

I was getting restless. Unlike Min, I couldn't pay attention. Too much was going on inside me. Something in my chest kept pulling tighter, like it was tied up with string.

Leaning forward, I whispered to Min, "I'm bored, I'm going downstairs." She turned her head toward me. I thought she looked worried, but she turned back to the game before I could be sure. I quietly edged off the bed and left the room, closing the door behind me.

On the landing I was alone for the first time since I'd entered the house. Down the stairs I saw kids moving across the hall between the living room and the kitchen, laughing, drinking from their soda cans. A boy crossed to the living room with his arm around a girl's shoulders. The music had changed. There was a slow song playing, another one I didn't know. It sounded like the Rolling Stones again. A girl needed to be free, and the singer was saying goodbye. I stood at the top of the stairs with my arms wrapped around myself and swayed slowly. The song made me sad. I didn't want to be free if it meant being lonely. I was afraid I would be dancing by myself at the top of the stairs forever.

I had to go to the bathroom. I turned around and began looking, trying a couple of locked doors before I found it around the corner. I turned on the light and turned the lock in the doorknob. After I was done, I washed my hands, looking in the mirror. In the harsh light, my face looked blotchy. My mascara had smeared under my right eye. I turned on the hot water and splashed my face, trying to scrub off the makeup. The eyeshadow went, but the mascara smeared worse, making me look like a raccoon. Panicked, I looked inside the medicine cabinet. Luckily there was a jar of Ponds cold cream. I swabbed some out with a crumpled-up wad of toilet paper, scoured around my eyes, then washed it all off. I felt so dumb. I had worn that makeup because of Nick, and he wasn't even there.

The fast music was back on when I opened the bathroom door. I went out and stood on the landing again, trying to decide where to go. I didn't really want to go downstairs just to watch everybody dancing when I had nobody to dance with, but I didn't feel like watching more of Spin the Bottle either. Suddenly I felt hands grabbing my sides, hard, tickling me. I yelped, pushing them away and turning around.

It was Nick, grinning. "Hey, where've you been?" he asked, standing back. He was wearing a mock turtleneck with wide green and yellow stripes. His hair was falling in his eyes as usual and his thick eyelashes and pinkened cheeks made him look young and really adorable. His eyes were darker than usual, a royal blue. Three of his friends and Caroline and her friend Stacy came out of the room behind him and stampeded past us down the stairs.

"Where've *you* been?" I asked, then realized I sounded like my mother when Jamie came home late. I was so relieved to see Nick, I wanted to put my arms around him and burst into tears. I couldn't stop grinning.

"Looking for you," he answered. I knew it wasn't true, but I was flattered anyway. "You look very pretty tonight. Do you want to dance?"

I nodded. We went downstairs and into the dark living room. Now the cleared floor was full of kids moving to the music. Nick pushed ahead of me into the crowd and found us a little space near one corner of the room. He turned around and grinned at me, then started to dance. It was another song I didn't know, but I didn't care. Dancing was a way to lose myself, like I was hurling myself away. At school dances I was usually asked to dance by the nerdiest guys, if I was asked at all. When I didn't turn them down, I held myself back dancing because I didn't want them to follow me around. Dancing with Nick, I threw myself into the music, trying to become it.

I watched Nick out of the corner of my eye. His dancing was jerky and uncoordinated. He kept taking the same steps back and forth. Looking around the room, I compared him to the other guys. There was only one who knew how to dance. I wondered why that was true when all the girls were good at it.

I looked up at Nick's face. He had been watching me too. He leaned closer. "You're a great dancer," he yelled into my ear.

I was glad it was dark in the room. My face was heating up. "Thank you," I yelled back, pleased. We danced some more, through another song, and I tried not to feel self-conscious. I wanted to let the music take me wherever it was going.

When the second song ended, Nick wiped his forehead with his shirtsleeve. "It's really hot in here. Do you want to go outside and get some air?"

Suddenly I got scared. Outside we'd be alone. He'd probably want to go off into the woods. I didn't want anything to happen that I couldn't control. I smiled. "Let's keep dancing for now," I said.

We danced another fast dance, and then Diana changed the record and announced to the room that this would be the last song and then everybody could help her clean up. There was a chorus of groans, particularly from the boys. Nick and I exchanged smiles and stood together, waiting for the music to start again. He stuffed his hands in his pockets, then pulled them out, hooking his thumbs in his belt loops. I kept my arms folded across my chest. I looked around the room. One couple near us was just standing there kissing. It was Caroline and a guy named Alex. Min had had a crush on him in the beginning of the year. I'd have to remember to tell her when I saw her.

The first single notes of "Stairway to Heaven" came on. I almost swooned. I had always wanted to dance to that song. Every time it came on the radio or was played at a school dance, it sent shivers through me. I hoped Nick wouldn't decide he had to get a drink right then. I looked at him. I didn't care that my face showed so obviously what I wanted.

He was saying something to a friend of his sitting on the arm of one of the couches, using little hand gestures I didn't recognize. They grinned at each other, and then he turned toward me and, without asking, without even really looking at me, brought his arms up around me. I put my hands on his back. His shirt was damp. We were almost the same height. He smelled of cigarettes and something sweet that reminded me of my father's aftershave. He started to sway, and I followed him, our feet barely moving as we turned in a slow circle. We were sticking to each other from perspiration. I let the side of my head rest against his and closed my eyes, smiling. I could hardly believe I was finally in his arms.

After a while his hand slowly moved across my back, gripping me tighter. Nick was holding me, he really liked me. I had never been so happy. I gripped him tighter too, trying to keep my sweaty hands from slipping off his shirt. When his hand kept going I realized he was trying to feel the side of my breast. A cold shock went through me. Even my brain felt paralyzed. He couldn't reach and gave up. Then he inched one hand down my back and under my shirt, so that his palm was on the skin of my waist. His warm hand against my back felt comforting, but then it started to travel up toward my bra. This wasn't going the way I'd imagined. Maybe my mother was right about boys. I felt like he was trying to get away with something without my knowing.

Trying to be casual, I brought my arm from his back and pulled away to scratch my nose, making him take his hand off me and wait. I tucked my shirt in, then moved close to him again. He said into my ear, "You feel so good." I liked hearing that, but it made me nervous.

All I wanted was for this slow dance to go on forever. I wanted to stay in our little circle, swaying from one foot to the other, the bounds of the universe as wide as the reach of our arms. I had dreamed for so long of this moment, of being held tightly in the arms of a boy I could almost say I loved, a boy who wanted to be with me and not with somebody else.

The tempo of the song started to speed up, but we didn't. He kept one hand on my waist, where I could feel the grip of each finger and his thumb. As the music got more frenzied, I seemed to go into a trance. I wondered when I could start calling Nick my boyfriend. Did I have to wait until after he kissed me? I wondered when he would give me his ring or his chain necklace. He moved his head, then I felt cool air against my neck. It tickled. The breeze stopped, then it started again. I opened my eyes. Nick was blowing against my neck like an air conditioner.

I pulled my head back, loosening my hold a little, hoping he would stop. He said, "Took you long enough," and then he kissed me. His lips mashed into mine so hard it hurt. He pulled back, licked his lips, and then came at me again. This time his tongue pushed against my mouth. I kept my teeth clenched. He got my lips open and his tongue slid around the surface of my teeth. I suddenly was aware that his hand had found its way up the back of my shirt. My bare back was exposed to the whole

room. All around me the guitars were thrashing away, the music building up and up in a frenzy of instruments.

Nick pulled away. "What's wrong?" He asked it like he was concerned. There was something about the way his hair hung down over his
forehead that made my heart melt. I remembered that this was the same
Nick I walked home with, sharing basketball stories.

I said, "Slow down. You're going too fast."

He looked hurt, and I cursed myself for telling him outright. My
mother said it was all a game. You had to coax a boy into doing what you
wanted, while he tried the same thing with you. We were still moving,
not in circles anymore, just back and forth. He said, "I'm sorry. I guess
that's just my way."

He pulled his hand from under my shirt and wrapped his arms
around me again. He really did care about me. I put my cheek against
his. Then the music stopped. I held my breath. These were the last few
seconds I would have him with me like this, while the singer, a cappella,
sang the last line of the song.

There was silence in the room. For that moment I was perfectly happy.
Then somebody turned on the overhead lights. I blinked, surprised that
the walls were covered with a shiny silver wallpaper. Nick and I pulled
apart from each other. In the bright light, it was hard to look him in
the eye for some reason. As the other kids started talking and moving
around, Nick said, "Can I walk you home?"

I remembered suddenly how I had gotten there. On the dance floor,
I had completely forgotten about Min. I said, "Well, I'm staying at Min's
house tonight," for the first time wishing it wasn't true. Then I felt guilty.
I was a terrible friend.

"That's okay. I'll walk you both home."

"Her mother was going to pick us up. Let me check with her." I was
excited now. I didn't want to say goodnight to him. "I'll be right back," I
promised.

"I'll be here." He grinned at me, then turned to Caroline and Alex next to us. They were still kissing. "Hey, knock it off, you two," he said, rapping Alex on the arm with his knuckles. "The party's over."

I didn't have any idea what time it was. I started toward the hall to find Min upstairs and saw her a few yards away from where Nick and I had been dancing, near the door. She was leaning with one shoulder against the wall, her arms crossed, holding a ginger ale can in one hand. She looked bored and faintly amused and cool, more like somebody in a rock and roll band than ever, even if she was a girl. Seeing her made my skin feel prickly, like I had developed a sudden rash. I hadn't expected to see her there. She was watching everybody funnel back into their all-boy and all-girl groups as they left the room. I wondered if Min had come downstairs in time to see. I had slow-danced with Nick! I wondered what the whole class would be saying on Monday, and if I would be one of the people they talked about. I wanted them to be envious of me for once.

I touched Min on the shoulder. She turned her head, then pushed herself from the wall and flipped her hair behind her shoulder.

"Hi," she said. She was smiling, but not in her usual way when she was happy to see me.

"Min, about getting to your house—"

"I called my mother," she said. "She said we can walk back if we want."

"That's what I wanted to ask you. Nick wants to walk us home."

"I doubt it's *us* he wants to walk with," she said. She brought her can to her lips and finished what was inside, shaking the last drops out. I realized she'd seen me dancing with Nick after all. I thought she'd be happy for me. I would have been if she had danced with somebody. But not with Nick, I realized. He was different. I wondered how long I had been thinking of him as mine.

"How long have you been down here?" I asked her.

"A while."

I was thinking of the last song and my universe inside Nick's arms. "Did you see—"

"Yeah." She dropped the can on the floor and crushed it with her sneaker. I picked it up and threw it at the wastebasket in the corner, sinking it.

Then I remembered how Nick had pushed my shirt up my back and mashed his mouth against mine. For a minute or two I had forgotten. It hadn't all been perfect. I tried to imagine what we had looked like from where Min was standing. Instead I remembered how nice it felt when Min and I practiced. If we hadn't done that, would I have liked Nick's kissing more? Maybe something was wrong with me now. Maybe I had messed myself up somehow by kissing a girl.

We were silent. Then she said, "Mom's waiting for us at home. I don't want her to start worrying."

Outside, the ground was damp and the tall trees dripped water down on our heads. There was an almost-full moon high in the black sky. As we started down the winding road, Nick tried to whistle the opening bars of "Stairway to Heaven." I laughed. On the other side of me, Min pulled her sweatshirt over her head. She was walking unsteadily. I wondered how much of that vodka she had had. She kicked at the water in a puddle. "I'm siiinging in the rain, just siiii—"

"Shhhh," I said, afraid she would wake up the neighbors.

"It's not raining," Nick said at the same time. Min threw him a look like he was an idiot.

I shivered. "You cold?" Nick asked. He was wearing a varsity jacket. He put his arm around me, hugging me close to his side. I remembered Min's voice from the other bed in my room, all those times we had played our question game. "Would you let Nick put his arm around you? What would you do if he kissed you? If he tried to French kiss you?" They weren't what ifs anymore, they were real. I had never really believed Nick would ever put his arm around me. Now he had. We had already kissed. It was happening so fast.

"Warmer now?" he asked.

"Yes." I grinned up at him. I thought about putting my arm around his waist. Then I did it. We were a couple now, there was no doubt about it.

The three of us walked downhill for a while, turning onto wider roads as we got closer to town. Nick and Min talked about our history teacher and how easy the homework was. I thought it was hard, but I didn't say anything. An occasional car drove past, its headlights sweeping over us. The moon stayed ahead of us. Walking between my best friend and my new boyfriend, I had the amazing feeling that everything fit into its own place. I looked up at the glowing moon. We were only specks on a tiny planet in the middle of a whirling galaxy, but we were where we were supposed to be.

Nick pulled a pack of cigarettes from his jacket pocket. "Sorry," he said to me, removing his arm.

"Can I have one?" Min asked, leaning her head forward to look at him. I almost said, "You don't smoke," but didn't, not in front of Nick. We stopped on the sidewalk. Nick held out the pack and Min pulled a cigarette out. Nick lit his with a Bic lighter, then offered the flame to Min, holding it beneath the cigarette in her mouth. The tip glowed red in the dark. He dropped his hand, pocketing the lighter. She took the cigarette from her mouth, holding it between her first two fingers like it was natural to her, blew out smoke, and said, "Thanks." He nodded. I was amazed. Min seemed to be an old hand. Maybe she was and maybe she wasn't. Knowing Min, she could be smoking for the first time and pull it off so that nobody would ever know.

We continued walking. The two of them puffed away on either side of me. I tried not to cough. Nick slipped his hand in mine. It was warm and slightly damp.

"I really didn't know if you'd show up tonight," Nick said to me. "You were so shy the last time we talked after practice."

Inside I seized up. I had meant to tell Min about my walks with Nick when we got to her house.

Min said, "Laura shy? Ha!" I looked at her, surprised. She blew smoke into the air and tapped ash from the tip of her cigarette. She didn't look at me.

"Well, she may not be around *you*," Nick said, "but she hardly opens her mouth when she's around me."

"Oh, she opens her mouth around me," Min said.

I pinched her waist. There was hardly anything to grab hold of. She looked at me quickly, smiling. It wasn't funny. What if Nick figured out what she was talking about?

They went back to the subject of school, disagreeing about the character of Stella in the book we were reading in English class, *Great Expectations*. I was bored. They seemed to have a lot in common. I began to be afraid that Nick would start to like Min more than me. It was a strange, vicious fear I'd never felt before. Up to now, I had been winning our competition for Nick.

We reached her house and stopped on the sidewalk. Nick threw his cigarette out into the street sideways. Min's parents had left the outside light on. There was another light on upstairs. We stood in a little cluster. Nick was still holding my hand.

"Hey, Min," he said, sort of embarrassed, "get lost."

She stared at him, then turned and went into the house without saying goodbye. As soon as the door closed, I said, "What did you say that for?"

"I wasn't going to kiss you goodnight in front of her."

"Oh." Still, it seemed like he could have found a nicer way to tell her. He led me toward the brown-shingled siding of the house under the eave where it was darkest, then took my other hand. We stood face to face. I was still worrying about Min and him having so much in common.

"Nick, how come you decided you liked me? What if it was Min walking home after basketball, would you have started waiting for her?"

He made a face. "Min? No way. Not in a million years."

I was stung. "Why not? I think she's really pretty."

"With those slanty eyes? They give me the creeps."

I couldn't believe it. I liked Min's eyes. "You're kidding, right?"

"No." When I just stared at him he tried again. "She's Oriental, and that's putting it nicely."

"So?"

"So I don't think the races should mix. People should stick with their own kind."

Now I was getting angry. He was talking about my best friend. I pulled my hands out of his, crossing them over my chest. "Where'd you get that crazy idea?"

"Everybody knows that, Laura. Where've you been? On the moon?"

"Yeah, and you've been in some other solar system."

We were silent. None of this was making sense to me. The worst part was I didn't think I liked Nick very much anymore. "I don't get it," I said. "You seemed to like talking to Min tonight."

"That's different. I'll do a lot to spend more time with you. Anyway, why are we talking about her?" He put his arms around my shoulders, pulling me closer. I slid my hands around his waist without even thinking about it. "I had a nice time dancing with you tonight," he said. "I knew I'd break through your shyness, and I was right. You're a wild dancer."

Then he pushed me against the house and kissed me. He didn't waste any time with his tongue. I hadn't decided what I wanted to do, but my mouth opened anyway. He pushed his tongue inside, practically down my throat. Instead of gently playing with my tongue the way Min did, he ignored it completely. He kept jabbing at the inside of my mouth. It was like having a large wet fish thrashing around, one that tasted like cigarettes. I tried to pull away, but he only held me more tightly, grasping the back of my head. He had his other arm at my waist, holding me pinned between him and the house. I felt his hand pull at my shirt and slide up my side. He grabbed my breast over my bra, squeezing it like a sponge, then pushed underneath the bra with his fingers. I tried again to break free of him. He made a moaning noise in my mouth and ground his pelvis against me. My jaw was getting sore. I didn't know what to do. I had gone too far, and now I couldn't stop it. This boy I hardly knew was all over me, and I had no idea how to get away.

Finally he let me go, staggering back a little. He was breathing hard. "You really *are* wild," he said. He wiped his mouth with the back of his hand. Then he hitched up his pants, gave me a little wave, said "See you at school," and walked away. He emerged from the shadow of the house onto the moonlit sidewalk, walking the way I'd noticed most guys did. He bounced from one foot to the other, like he was happy.

In the dark, I practically tiptoed up the stairs. Now I didn't know how I should feel. I decided that the next time Nick and I made out, it would be better because we'd be more used to each other. He wouldn't go so berserk. As I passed Min's parents' room, I saw the door was ajar and a light on. I heard Catherine softly call out my name. She was sitting by herself in bed with a book propped up against the quilt over her knees. The covers on Min's father's side of the bed were rumpled. She took off her reading glasses as I came into the room.

"Did you lock the front door?" she asked almost in a whisper.

I nodded. She squinted at me, then put her reading glasses on the night table, unfolded her other pair, and put them on. She studied me again.

"How was the party?"

"It was okay."

She patted the edge of the bed by her legs. I sat down.

"Min seems to think you had a good time."

I could picture Min sitting in the same spot at the edge of the bed, talking to her mother, knowing I was outside with Nick. Sitting in her place, I realized if Nick had danced with Min, even danced one dance with her instead of asking me, I would have been totally destroyed. But she hadn't been talking to him for weeks, getting her hopes up. I said, like it might change something, "Well, I danced with Nick. Min has a crush on him too."

"Oh, Nick of the fabulous blue eyes."

I nodded. There didn't seem to be anything more to say.

After a while Catherine asked, "Did something happen that you didn't like?"

I looked up at her. How did she know that? The kindness in her face made me feel like crying. I could never have had a talk like this with my mother. Catherine's face was long and plain with a chin that jutted out like a rock at the edge of the waves, solid and dependable. I looked down again. My hair fell forward. I took a few strands and started picking at the ends.

"I don't know," I finally admitted. "It's like I love him and I hate him at the same time. He's not how I expected him to be."

"I know what that's like. Even when you know someone well they can disappoint you."

Right then, picturing Nick smiling at me made me feel sick. "I wanted him to kiss me, but not like he did."

"It was yucky?"

I looked up at her again. The expression on her face was so serious that I laughed, just a little. "Yeah. It was yucky."

She sighed. "Life's confusing, isn't it?" She reached forward and took my hair out of my hands, gently tucking it behind my shoulder.

Min's father came into the room. His high forehead and mustache always reminded me of Sonny from Sonny and Cher. I felt worn out. I got up from the bed.

"Hi, Laura," he said. He turned to Catherine. "She won't talk to me." I knew he meant Min. Then nobody spoke. I couldn't help feeling like he was blaming me.

"Waffles in the morning, does that sound okay?" Catherine asked.

"I love waffles," I answered. Min's father sat down on the bed, kicked off his slippers, and swung his feet under the covers. I hardly ever saw my father in his pajamas, and never in bed. Min's father turned on his bedside lamp and opened his own book. Catherine looked over at him like she was surprised, then turned off her light. I said goodnight, closing their door behind me.

In Min's room there was only the light of the moon to see by. Because she had only one bed, when I was over she slept on an air mattress on the floor. (Except when she got into the bed with me.) I stepped around the bundle of her body in the sleeping bag. On top of the blanket, in the middle of the bed, my bookbag was open. Tucked inside my nightgown was a piece of paper folded up into a small square. For a delighted second I thought it could be from Nick, but of course I knew it wasn't. I unfolded the note and read it in the silvery moonlight. She hadn't written in our code. The note said, "I don't want to practice kissing anymore. We're too old for notes too."

I missed Min then. Even though she was there in the same room, it was like she'd said goodbye. Now our friendship would become ordinary again. At the same time I was relieved, because what would be the point of making out with her when I had Nick? As I gathered everything together for my trip to the bathroom, I heard Min stir.

"Min?" I whispered. There was no answer. She was asleep. I went to the bathroom next door to brush my teeth.

A sound woke me up in the middle of the night. "Min?" I called softly, sitting up in bed. Her sleeping bag was empty. I pushed off my covers and went out to the bathroom. The door was closed. "Min?" I called, knocking quietly.

She didn't answer. I opened the door, and at first my eyes teared, blinded by the bright light. Then I saw her kneeling in front of the toilet. The seat was up. Some of her beautiful long hair had fallen forward into the bowl. She started to heave again, holding on to the edges. I knelt down next to her and gathered her hair in my hands, holding it back from her face as she threw up into the toilet. Spit and a yellowish mess slid down her chin. The stink was as strong as ammonia. I tore off some toilet paper with my free hand and wiped her chin clean. She didn't seem to know I was there as she knelt rocking a little on the bathroom mat, her eyes closed, taking deep breaths.

Then she said, her eyes still closed, "Why did you lie to me, Laura? Why didn't you tell me you had talked to Nick before tonight?"

"I don't know," I said, feeling helpless. What was it I'd thought I could have for myself, mine alone, by not telling her? Right then, Nick was a distant idea, the way he'd been in my fantasies.

"I don't care if you kiss him or let him feel you up or anything. Just tell me. Don't lie to me."

I wondered if that meant telling her why he would never go out with her. "Okay," I said.

She started to heave again. She gripped the sides of the toilet bowl, getting ready. Still holding her hair, I leaned forward with her. When she was done I wiped her mouth.

"Oh God," she said. "I don't think ginger ale and vodka are such a good combination." She took a deep breath, then another.

"Do you still like him?" I asked her. If she said yes, I wouldn't tell her about his thrusting tongue in my mouth or the rest of it. I didn't want to disappoint her.

"He's an asshole." She stated it as fact.

I didn't say anything. I felt attacked, the way I had when Nick had said he didn't like Min. It had been so great slow dancing with him, when he wasn't trying anything. I had let myself hope for a little while. Inside me, the part that wanted so much to be touched, to be held, blew out, like a gas flame turned down too low.

"He's a terrible kisser," I admitted.

She turned her head toward me. Her eyes were bloodshot. "How would you know?" But there was a tiny smile at the edges of her mouth.

I smiled too. "How *would* I know?" I asked.

CHAPTER 5

Min

Summer 1979

"IMPRESSIVE, MIN," MR. CONNOR SAID as he gave me my paper. It was eighth period English, minutes before the end of class. He paced the aisles between our desks and placed a paper in front of each one of us. For a moment I left mine face down without looking at it, letting the pleasure of his compliment wash through me. I had enjoyed comparing and contrasting "The Magi" by W. B. Yeats with "Journey of the Magi" by T. S. Eliot. I turned the paper over. On top was an A+ in bright red ink and the words "Very original and deftly written. Well done!" below the grade.

When the bell rang, I heard the halls flooding with students' voices. In the front of the room, Nick asked Mr. C. if there would be extra credit questions on the exam. We were in the final marking period of tenth grade, but I knew Nick was planning to apply only to Ivy League colleges and wanted to graduate at the top of the class. I didn't know what he was worried about. He would get in anywhere he wanted: in addition to being smarter than everyone else in our grade except me, he was wholesomely blond, a star basketball player, a member of the debate team, and Secretary of the Student Council. He was the most well-rounded person on the face of the earth. I liked to make him sweat, competing for first place with me, even though I knew I wouldn't be going to college. Since my parents' divorce two years before, my father had pretty much disappeared from my life, and my mother was barely making it on her own. That was another thing: Nick was rich. I had a shitload of reasons for hating his guts.

I stood up, while around me the others filed out, talking and laughing. A couple of girls said goodbye to me as they left. I watched them go, thinking how stupid feathered hair looked, then collected my books together as I listened to the shouting voices beyond the door.

When I was leaving, Mr. C. called out, "Hold on a minute, Min," so I waited by his desk while he finished answering Nick's questions. By the time he and Nick nodded goodbye and he turned to me, the room was empty.

"That was an excellent paper, Min, your best yet. I'm proud of you."

"Thanks, Mr. Connor."

"You probably know you're in the running for the English award. There's one more paper due for this class. Keep it up and the award is yours. That's off the record, by the way."

I grinned at him. Sophomores hardly ever won the English prize. I left the classroom on a total high.

In the hall, I almost collided with Nick, who was standing outside the door. I looked up at him, startled, then moved around him and walked away.

He kept up easily. "Think you're going to win it, don't you?"

"What were you doing, eavesdropping?"

"You should go back where you came from, gook. You know you don't belong here."

Blank silence. I stopped. "What did you say?"

Nick didn't even bother to look back as he walked away. I had been an idiot to believe that because I was grown up no one would use words like that against me anymore. It had been years since anyone had. I stood watching him go, waiting for something to happen. I wanted somebody to kill him. Then I felt a surge of energy race through my body. I had to move or I'd explode. "You cocksucking motherfucker," I heard myself yell. I ran down the hall after him and threw my armload of books at his back as hard as I could. They hit him and clattered to the floor.

Nick turned around and started to move toward me. I was suddenly aware of how tall he was and how solidly built. I stood my ground, shaking. His gaze shifted, moving beyond me. I knew he was bluffing. I didn't dare take my eyes off him.

"What in God's name is going on here?" a voice demanded.

I turned around. Mr. Connor was standing in his doorway down the hall.

Neither Nick nor I said a word. I crossed my arms and refused to speak at all. Mr. Connor looked from Nick to me and back, clearly frustrated.

"This behavior is childish. Fighting in the hall is beneath either of you. What's going on?" He waited, giving us another chance to explain ourselves. Then he said, "This had better be the end of it." I watched him go back into his classroom, feeling strangely sad. Even Mr. C. had no special authority, no real answers.

Nick left too. Alone, I gathered up my books from the floor. I couldn't make my hands stop shaking. I told myself I should have been on my guard with Nick; I couldn't let him get to me. Walking toward the other end of the building where my locker was, I ran the fingers of my free hand against the rough white wall. The tips began tingling, sending bursts of sensation down the nerves of my hand. It was a rush without lighting up. I used to create this energy feeling from the walls of my elementary school, too, which were made of the same drab cinder block. Back then, I liked to pretend I was a superhero recharging my super powers. I would use them to knock the other kids unconscious, just from the force that would emanate from my hands.

When I turned the corner, I found Laura sitting slouched against my locker, her arms resting on her upright knees, her long, honey-blonde hair in her face. She was just sitting there, without even a book, waiting for me in her gym shorts, t-shirt, new white socks, and cleats. This year

Laura had made it onto the girls' varsity soccer team. She'd been JV in tennis and basketball two years in a row. I stared at her legs, which had grown thick and muscled from practice. I loved her legs.

In the last month, I had become aware that I had a serious crush on Laura. It had been a gradual realization: a growing warmth in my chest whenever I saw her, an increasing attention to her clothes, the way she wore her hair from one day to the next. For six years she had been my best friend. Now I was discovering that she was beautiful. She tended to complain that she was too big, her hair too limp, her face too round, uninteresting. I thought differently. I thought her face was wonderful, expressive and alive. I thought about her all the time, though she didn't know it. Right now I wanted to run my hand along the smooth curve of her calf, which she shaved faithfully every week.

I sat down on the linoleum floor beside her. Laura looked up, and her smile made my heart tighten a little and then start beating harder. I kept my arms wrapped safely around my knees, uncertain what to think, how to act. Sometimes I desperately wanted her to know how I felt about her, and at the same time I knew I would die if she ever found out. I had started to watch myself carefully. Even sitting next to her like this felt like an honor. I had to rely on memory for the right way to act around her. I was forgetting what it felt like to be a friend.

"Where've you been?" Laura asked, slapping the back of her hand playfully against my jeans. When I didn't answer she asked, concerned, "Did you get your paper back?"

Normally, I would have bumped her arm with mine, then stayed leaning against her. I needed her warm skin against my arm grounding me. But now I was too scared to do it. The way I had come to feel around her wasn't going to help me. I realized I was still trembling.

I nodded. "Yeah. A+." The grade seemed trivial now.

Laura looked down. "That's great, Min. You must have worked hard on it."

"No, not really," I admitted. I didn't want to talk about the paper. I leaned back against the hard metal of the lockers. "Someone called me a gook."

I felt Laura get very still beside me. I didn't know what that meant, or what she would say. We had never had this conversation before. We had never had to.

"Who?"

"Nick. He said I should go back where I came from."

I had hated Nick ever since seventh grade, when he dated Laura a few times and then dumped her. She was devastated. He was the first boy she ever kissed. I remembered that we both had thought he was cute. In seventh grade, Nick had a lanky body and sandy blond hair that fell into his gorgeous blue eyes. He had been shorter then. Even while they were together, I used to put myself to sleep by masturbating as I fantasized about making out with him. How could I have thought about him so much? As I sat next to Laura on the cold linoleum tiles, the memory of wanting him to kiss me made me feel sick.

"Nick called you a gook?" Laura sounded as though she didn't believe me. I wondered if she still liked him and I had made a big mistake by telling her. I wished suddenly that she hadn't waited for me this afternoon.

"That's what I said."

She was frowning. Her face was turning pink, the way it did when she was angry or embarrassed. She shook her head. "He's such a jerk. He always was."

I shrugged. "They all are. So what's new?" I thought she'd agree. The handful of guys she'd gone out with since Nick had all dropped her after a few weeks.

Laura said nothing. She retied the laces on her right cleat. "Walk me to practice, okay? I'm late."

"Sure."

I was happy to change the subject. I stood up, got books for that night's homework out of my locker, and threw them into my knapsack before spinning the combination lock closed. Outside, the sun was bright, reflecting off the windows of the beige stucco buildings. I lit a cigarette as soon as we had pushed through the double doors and took a long, satisfying drag.

"Are you crazy?" Laura asked, looking behind her. We weren't allowed to smoke on school grounds. "Someone might see you."

"Like I give a shit," I said and stuffed my lighter back into the front pocket of my jeans. We ran down the steps and took the path down the hill to the gym. As we passed the girls' locker room on our way out toward the athletic fields, Laura said, "Eric Newell invited me to his party next weekend. Will you go with me?"

"Those parties suck, Laura."

"Come with me, Min," Laura pleaded. "It'll be fun. James and Devin will be there. I like Devin. He's a really nice guy. He doesn't try to show off in front of girls. I could definitely see losing it with him. I bet he's really gentle."

She waited for me to respond, but I had nothing to say. She'd had the chance to go all the way with three different guys in the last two years, but she'd stopped them at second base, saying she wasn't comfortable going further. I didn't get what she was waiting for.

"Do you know what James told me at lunch?" Laura asked, sounding happy. I stifled a flip response. I was already tuning her out. "That Devin grew up in Vermont. Can you believe it? I want to find out if he lived in Middlebury. Wouldn't it be great if he asked me out at the party?" She waved away the smoke from my cigarette. "Maybe I should ask him out. Min, do you think he'd be scared off if I asked him out?"

"Laura, I don't care," I burst out. "Why can't you shut up about boys for just one second?"

She did shut up. I could feel the hurt coming off her in waves, like heat. Then she said, stiffly, "Sorry to bore you. You never minded before."

"It wasn't the constant topic of conversation before."

I didn't really understand myself why I had lashed out at her. When Laura had started going out with boys, I liked to hear in detail about her dates: what he did, what she did, how it felt. But these days she just seemed obsessed, and about the most moronic things. It was as though there was nothing else she ever thought about except boys. It infuriated me.

I was aware of another reason for my flaring anger, one that I had been trying for a long time to ignore. The unspoken rule. None of the boys Laura and I liked—the blond ones, the all-American types—would ever ask me out. I was an Asian in a ninety-nine percent white town. Even though I had grown up going to the same stores, eating the same kinds of meals, watching the same TV shows, even though I had white parents just like them, I wasn't accepted as being the same as everybody else. For years at Old Mill, my classmates had called me "slant-eyes" and "Jap." The girls wouldn't let me join their games of hopscotch and cat's cradle and jacks. The boys were no better. A group of them used to ambush Roberto and Miguel outside after school, beating them up until they managed to scramble, bleeding and crying, away from the circle of legs. I used to overhear those boys bragging about it outside during recess while I sat reading a book. I started to store up my super powers by dragging my fingers along the school walls.

Since I'd been going to Tam High, I'd made a few friends I went to the movies and hung out downtown with. I had learned from watching the way they acted with me in public how to be what they expected: white at times, Asian at others. But when it came to dating, the policy of exclusion remained firmly in place. It didn't matter how I behaved or how much I fantasized about those fair-skinned, beautiful boys. As much as a guy might like me, I wasn't good enough to go out with. Maybe I was also angry at Laura for not being aware of this rule, or if she was aware of it, for not acknowledging it.

We had arrived at the chain-link fence at the edge of the baseball fields. The soccer field was beyond, with the Richardson Bay Bridge in the distance, a glimmer of water peeking out from beneath it. The rest of

Laura's team stood around in clumps, kicking balls back and forth. The coach, a woman who had taught my gymnastics class the year before, had taken one girl aside and was speaking to her intently, one arm around her shoulder, the other gesturing.

"Don't go yet," Laura said. She grabbed the horizontal metal pole at the top of the fence and walked her legs back, until she could lean into her stretch.

"Okay," I agreed, surprised at how happy her request made me. The muscles in her legs stood out, shifting as she moved. I was mesmerized.

"When do you think you'll get home tonight?" I asked her. I took a last drag from my cigarette and stamped it out on the pavement. Suddenly I couldn't watch her anymore as she lunged and extended, loosening up. The way I felt was frightening me again. There was nowhere I could go with it, no one I trusted enough not to use it against me.

"About six-thirty, maybe seven. Don't call till after eight. We should be finished eating by then."

I kept my eyes on the coach out in the field, pacing in her deliberate way, making her points to the girl she was with. I wished I was that girl; I wished that I had someone to put her arm around me and help me see my way through. The coach was a woman I had developed a minor obsession with the year before while she taught me the back walkover, spotting me again and again until I could do it on my own. The touch of her hand on my back as I arched my body over gave me confidence and a feeling of excitement low in my stomach. Watching her now as she walked with her soccer student in their private conference, I wondered if the rumors were true that she was a lesbian.

As soon as I thought that word, everything seemed to get very still and silent around me, as though the world had gone into slow motion. All my senses were magnified: I felt my vision was sharper; I could hear from greater distances. I was a lesbian. There was a name for my feelings. Just knowing that changed my whole life in an instant. Everything would unfold differently now. I was surprised that I hadn't figured it out before. Why hadn't I understood something that was so obvious?

Then my heart started beating so hard I was afraid it would seize up. I didn't want to be gay. I didn't want to be even more different than I already was. Lesbians were ugly women with hair on their faces. They hated men. They were unhappy. So I wasn't gay after all. I just had crushes sometimes on other girls. That seemed normal to me, nothing to jump to conclusions over. What about all the crushes on boys I'd had? From the time I became aware of sex, I'd thought about boys. What about the guys I still thought were cute? I even had a life-size poster of Mick Jagger up on my wall at home.

Trying to look calm, I took my cigarettes out of my pocket and lit another one. Laura finished her stretches. We stood together, heads down. Her new white socks were already dusty from our walk. I was too aware of her legs, the fresh green of the grass beyond the fence, my own body hardly able to stand still with everything inside me going off at once. Some of the girls on the team had seen us and called out to Laura.

"You'd better go practice," I said, nodding sideways toward her friends. "Why don't you call me when you're through with dinner?"

Behind the hair fallen over her face, Laura nodded. "Okay. But call me if it's getting late." She swept her hair behind her ear, then looked up at me. Her inviting brown eyes, her face close to mine made me dizzy with the urge to kiss her. I stepped back.

"I just don't want to piss off your mother if you're still at the table." Then I waved, some kind of dumb smile on my face, and walked away from her.

I bicycled home, pedaling fast, pushing myself. I wanted to feel the ache in my legs and nothing else. When I could be alone in my room I would let my discovery bubble up again, filling me. I would think it through, see what made sense. I arrived at the house sweaty and out of breath.

My mother was waiting for me in the kitchen. "I was just on the phone with your English teacher," she said as soon as I came in, slamming the back door behind me. "And don't slam the door, Min."

"I don't want to talk about it right now," I called back, taking the stairs two at a time. What had he told her? How much had he actually heard?

"I don't care what you want," she said, following after me. "He told me you hit a boy in your class."

"I threw books at him. There's a difference." In my room, I swung my knapsack off my shoulders and let it slide to the wood floor.

My mother caught up to me and turned me around, her hands on my shoulders startling me. "Don't act smart with me. I want to know what happened."

"Didn't Mr. Connor tell you?"

"He seemed to think your classmate was aggravating you in some way. He wanted me to tell you that if there's another incident, you'll forfeit your chance for the English award. Min, he likes you very much and doesn't want to see you go astray." I shrugged. My mother's hands rested heavier on my shoulders, as if they could cure me of shrugging. She had pulled back her hair with a barrette, but most of what used to be her bangs had escaped. She looked at me fixedly through her new reading glasses, which she had forgotten to take off. "I want to ask you up front. Was it about drugs?"

"*What?*" I pulled away from her, sat down on my bed, and started to pull off my high-tops. My mother made no sense to me sometimes. "Where did you get that idea?" Maybe she had found my nickel bag in one of my old rain-boots.

"Just answer me, Min."

I was struggling with a knotted shoelace. "No, it had nothing to do with drugs. He called me some names." I hadn't meant to tell her that, but I was angry and wanted to show her how off the mark she was.

"What did he call you?"

"Why does it matter?"

"Because you tried to hurt him. Min, what did he call you?"

The knot refused to loosen, and I was sick of picking at it. I gave up, reached over to my desk for my scissors, and cut the lace of my sneaker. I kicked the shoe off; it landed with a thud. Looking at it lying forlornly on its side, I said, "He called me a gook."

My mother didn't say anything. Then she sat down on the bed next to me. She seemed to be feeling something very strongly, struggling with it. Seeing her upset, I was instantly back in the shock and sting I had felt with Nick in the hallway, like being hit with pebbles and spattered with mud. But this time I wasn't completely alone. I was glad I had told her.

"Kids call each other names, Min," she said after a while. I stared at her, stunned, but she wasn't looking at me. "It's normal. My classmates called me Four-Eyes when I was in school. You just have to ignore them. It happens to everybody." My chest felt emptied out, hollow. I'd been stupid to think she had changed.

When I was growing up, she and my father had made a point of teaching me to be aware of the struggles of blacks in the US. She used to tell me that their fight for civil rights was different from the fight for recognition of any other minority group. She said none of us could understand the experience of being black no matter how closely we identified or worked with black people. Maybe it was true that no one could know what it was like for people different from themselves. But I thought she knew something of what I went through. She was my mother. She had raised me. Not only that, she had chosen to adopt me. Not from down the street, from Korea. Why wouldn't she admit what my life had been like here?

At least my father had never blurted out "No, no," and left the room when I told him how some kids had teased me at school. He had never gone off on some stranger on the street when they asked if I was related. The nights my father put me to bed, he couldn't tell me whether it would have been easier if I'd had Korean parents, if I'd grown up with them in Korea. But he had helped me feel better, just by listening, just by being there. Sitting with my mother, I missed my father sharply. After two years, I had almost gotten used to him not living with us anymore.

I looked down at my mother's lap, where one of her hands gripped the other. They were pale and useless hands. She said, "What that boy called you was wrong. But you shouldn't have struck out at him, Min. Violence won't solve anything."

I didn't agree, but I kept quiet.

"I want you to think about what you did," she went on. "I'm grounding you for the weekend."

"You're *grounding* me? But I was defending myself!"

"It doesn't matter. You know better."

"This is completely unfair!" I shouted at her. She flinched, but she didn't move. I stood, wanting to push her off my bed, kick her onto the floor. "Get out of here. Get the fuck out of my room!" I didn't understand anything anymore. The world was insane.

"Min, watch your mouth or I'll ground you next weekend too." I could barely restrain myself. How could she be so unfair? My mother stood up and smoothed down the back of her wraparound skirt. "I'm sorry, Min. It's for your own good."

"Get out!" I screamed.

After she had closed the door behind her, I cried for a long time, soaking my pillow. When it was over, I lay crumpled on my bed, feeling like something very small, something thrown away and worthless.

Every summer Laura went away for two months with her family. They went to Michigan to stay with her aunt and uncle who had a summerhouse on Mackinac Island. During these months we wrote long letters to each other in which we described the activities of each day, interlacing these meticulous descriptions with full paragraphs on how much we missed each other and wished we were in the same place. During that summer, I had to acknowledge that mine, at least, had become love let-

ters of a sort: to my eyes there was no mistaking how full of my longing
for her they were.

I was also becoming aware that part of my longing was for everything
she had: a family, a place to go, the freedom to spend the day sailing or
swimming or reading a book. Over that summer I wrote to Laura during
my breaks while I sat smoking a cigarette on the back steps of the ice
cream store in San Francisco where I worked. My mother, who had a job
as the bookkeeper at the local animal hospital, had informed me when
summer began that because her boss had to cut her salary, she couldn't
afford to give me an allowance anymore. I'd have to find a job if I wanted
to have any pocket money. When I asked her why she couldn't stop going
to therapy instead, she snapped that her therapy wasn't up for discussion.
She said money was tight and I would have to start contributing something of my own. It felt unfair, like every rule she made that summer. I
yelled at her that she was selfish, slammed the door behind me, and rode
my bike around in the rain, not really having anywhere to go.

I wrote Laura that after work I liked to walk around the city, climbing the hills and catching my breath at the top. Sometimes I explored
alone and sometimes with Alison, who was in college at San Francisco
State and worked with me behind the ice cream counter. I didn't tell
Laura that Alison had a girlfriend who sometimes stopped by the store,
and that they left me in charge while they went out back to make out. I
told Laura about the customers who came in to buy a cone or use the
bathroom: the tourists underdressed in shorts and t-shirts, the hippies
walking around barefoot, the groups of college students with the munch-
ies, the men reeking of alcohol who panhandled for change. I didn't tell
her I had begun looking for lesbians on the street, or that I liked the
confident way they walked and how they cut their hair. I didn't tell her I
was afraid to tell Alison about me because I'd never had a girlfriend. If
I was a lesbian, it was purely theoretical; I didn't have the experience of
sleeping with another girl to know for sure.

Laura wrote back long, chatty letters full of complaints about her parents, who fought nonstop when they were away from home, and about being grouped with her younger cousins while her sister and brother were treated like adults. Almost three weeks into her vacation, Laura wrote that she had started going out with a boy who was the brother of a cousin's friend.

"He's got curly light brown hair and freckles on his face and all over his arms," she wrote. "He's a year younger than us, so, you know, he's kind of awkward. He's really thoughtful and polite, though. He's the exact same height as me. I met him playing tennis. He's good. We play tennis almost every day. Oh, and I almost forgot! His name is Dave."

She wrote me in the usual detail about their dates, describing how his braces cut her lip the first time they made out, how he asked permission before he unclasped her bra and felt her up, and fully setting the scene the night his parents came home to find them in the dark, semi-clothed and wedged together on the living room couch. All his mother said was, "We're off to sleep. You just go on doing what you were doing" as they walked through to their bedroom, clicking off the light again before leaving the room.

I couldn't stand reading those letters. At each mention of Dave, my stomach would curdle. Every time Laura began an enthusiastic portrayal of an evening spent fooling around with her new boyfriend, I dreaded what I might stumble across, as though I had inadvertently entered a field planted with land mines. The scenery was pretty, but every step could mean getting blown to bits. It didn't help that all I was doing was scooping ice cream and walking a lot. Even if I had wanted to sleep with a boy, I wasn't meeting any that I considered mature and interesting enough to spend any time with. And I would probably never meet a girl who liked other girls who wasn't already involved. I kept waiting for the letter in which Laura would tell me that they had had sex. That would, I knew, send me over the edge. I didn't know if I'd be able to forgive her. It would hurt too much. For weeks my stomach roiled. I lost my appetite completely. It was turning out to be the worst summer of my entire life.

At night sometimes, when we were getting along, I hung out talking with my mother in the kitchen. She'd make us a pot of decaf coffee and we'd share work stories. When she asked if I'd heard from Laura I didn't tell her much. On the days I didn't work in San Francisco, I liked to take the long bike ride down to Muir Beach, zipping around the hairpin turns as the road descended through the redwoods and emerged into the sunlight again. On the damp beach I'd walk away from the dog walkers and picnicking families down to a more deserted area, then sit on top of a rock formation jutting out into the sea and, out of the wind, light up a joint. I preferred sitting on rocks where the spray of the crashing waves against the battered stone showered me lightly. I pretended I was a captain at sea valiantly standing at the wheel, calling orders to the crew as a storm raged around our great wooden sailing ship.

Toward the end of July, I had just arrived at the beach and was locking up my bike when I heard my name being called. It was Miguel from school. I didn't know him very well. Through Laura I knew he had had sex with several girls in our class, though I had never seen him with any of them in the halls or hanging out after school in the parking lot. Once, I'd overheard a girl in an adjacent bathroom stall tell her friend, "Well, he's not so bad for a wetback. You should try him once or twice." At the beach, he was standing with three other guys, none of whom I recognized, but he broke away from them and came over to talk. After a while he invited me to get high with them. The five of us walked down the beach and passed around a couple of joints. I didn't like his friends, who seemed mostly interested in comparing the improvements they'd made on their cars. I didn't get the sense that Miguel liked them much either. But I liked Miguel, who made me laugh and who made me feel sharp-witted. At school he played the strong, silent type, but I saw that wasn't him at all. Later that afternoon, he stored my bike in the trunk of his parents' car and drove me home.

We started hanging out together after that. We'd meet at the beach and climb out onto the rocks and get high, then sometimes drive to my house while my mother was still at work. In my room we'd listen to music and crack up at the lyrics, or have heavy talks about school, or fall asleep. I tried to recount our stuporous, hilarious conversations in my letters to Laura. She was disapproving in her return letters, upset that I was getting stoned so much and that Miguel and I drove around while high. In one, she reminded me that I was breaking the law. A page later she told me that she had given Dave her first hand job. She said the underside of his erect penis felt silky and warm, but basically the whole thing was weird. In my next letter, I ignored everything she had written and avoided mentioning Miguel altogether. It was a short letter.

The day Miguel and I had sex, neither of us expected it. We were lying on my bed listening to my new Supertramp record. We were too stoned to move, much less haul ourselves up and go anywhere. The music was turned up loud and seemed to emanate from everything: the furniture, the pines outside my window, Miguel himself. For a while I got very focused on watching his Adam's apple jump up and down in his throat, fascinated that it did this all on its own. Then I looked up at his face and realized it was because he was singing "Goodbye Stranger" in falsetto. I had the distinct sensation that someone was pushing my head up and forward, trying to get it to come off. I didn't know if I liked this.

The day was hot, and Miguel had taken off his shirt. I looked at his flat nipples on his bony chest, thinking there was something missing. When I realized what it was, I told him to turn over and began to draw letters on his back, making him guess what I had written. Other than my father's, I had never touched a male back before. Miguel's was hard where he had muscles, and soft everywhere else. I drew slowly, fascinated by the texture of his skin, the way it sank under my finger and yet didn't give way.

"B, R, E, A . . . Bread. Breath. Breakfast!"

"No!" I giggled. I wrote the next letter. A yeasty smell came from his skin. I bent my head over him to breathe it in. I was starting to feel excited touching him.

"S. Breas..."

"Let me finish," I said, and completed my word on his warm back. Watching my hand move over his body, I saw that his skin was only slightly darker than my own. For some reason this fact struck me as incredibly funny.

"Man, what are you laughing about?" he asked and rolled over to watch me, smiling. I was laughing so hard my stomach hurt. By the time I got myself under control, I had forgotten what had set me off in the first place.

In the silence that followed, we lay on our sides staring at each other, and I noticed for the first time how green his eyes were. My breathing had become ragged, and so had his. I looked at his half-open mouth. It occurred to me that Miguel wanted to sleep with me, and then it occurred to me that I wanted to sleep with him. Before touching him, I had never thought of Miguel sexually; he wasn't my type. He was as far from being a blond jock as I could imagine. But here we both were, and I was turned on. My mouth was parched. I was very high. I licked my lips, wishing I had thought to bring something in from the kitchen to drink. "Do you want to have sex with me?" I asked. I wasn't even nervous, just curious.

He reached out and touched my breast through my shirt, covering it with his palm. "I didn't think you wanted to. You never seemed interested."

"Like the other girls at school?"

"Shit." He looked away, embarrassed. "Maybe I'm kind of dense that way."

"No, you were reading me right." I wanted to put my hand in his thick, wavy black hair. Then I realized that I could. I stroked it back behind his ear. His hair was almost as long as mine and curled around like the earpiece to glasses. "Besides," I added, smiling, "Asian girls are much more subtle than white girls, you know. You could even say inscrutable."

The sides of his mouth pulled up. "Then what you need is a hot-blood-ed Chicano lover to spark your fires of passion." I rolled my eyes and we both burst into laughter again.

And then we fucked. We didn't spend a lot of time working up to it. He undressed, then took off my clothes, kneeling beside me, kissing the places he uncovered. Because I was high, each action seemed slowed down and deliberate. I could almost taste my own skin. When Miguel entered me, he rested on one elbow and guided his penis in with his own hand. It hurt; when I made a small grunting noise, he looked up at me, confused.

"I've never done this before," I told him apologetically.

He raised his eyebrows, then nodded and slowly pushed in farther. He stayed still inside me until I was used to him, propping himself above me and looking into my face for encouragement. "Okay," I said, a little breathlessly, not sure whether it really was.

He began fucking me in earnest. It was still uncomfortable, but I thought about how long I had been waiting to do this and now I was doing it. Then he shifted his position slightly, and the angle changed or something, because then I liked it, him filling up the space inside me like waves rushing in and the way it made me feel liquid and vast and sort of greedy. I wondered if I could come this way. I wondered why Laura always stopped short of fucking. Didn't she have any idea how good it would feel after all her experience of foreplay? Miguel increased his tem-po, his eyes closed, a look of concentration on his face. I was trying to catch my breath, wanting the slippery greedy feeling to last. When he came, silently but unmistakeably, I imagined Laura lying on her hot and sunny beach two thousand miles away as her freckled boyfriend slipped his hand into the bottom half of her bikini. Except the image changed, and it was my hand feeling the wetness there. I closed my eyes, concen-trating on the solidity of Miguel's body against mine.

Miguel lay on top of me, breathing hard, while I moved my hand across his back and smelled his ripe smell. I was still excited and a little afraid that he would fall asleep now. I was happy too, pleased with myself. I listened to the birds calling outside for what seemed like an hour before realizing that the record had ended. A trickle of fluid ran out of my body. I remembered that we hadn't used any birth control, but I was feeling far too diffuse to care. Miguel lifted his head and then rolled us both over so that I was on top. This took a little maneuvering on my twin bed. I propped myself up on my elbows and looked down at him.

"You didn't come, did you?" he asked. He pulled lightly on a fistful of my hair. I felt it fall, the edges grazing my chin.

I shook my head. "I didn't think I would."

"Do you want to now?"

"Sure."

"Come up here." He started to pull me up.

"Why? What are you going to do?"

"Just come up here, I'll show you. Hey, slowly, my pecker's still attached to me, you know. Okay, kneel over my face. Just sink down. Yeah, like that."

What he did felt so different from anything I had been able to do for myself that I knew I would never be able to describe it to Laura. I was aware of wetness, and coolness, and the pointed end of his tongue. When my legs started to tremble, I held on to the bedboard. In the end, the pressure he used was too hard, and then I was afraid I was smothering him, and then I couldn't think about him because I was coming and it was so much better than it had ever been alone.

Afterwards we lay unmoving on the bed, exactly as we had been an hour earlier except that we had no clothes on. I was lying on a large wet spot. I wondered what Laura would say now that I had finally gone and done it. I wondered if she'd be surprised. I was relieved. This proved I wasn't a lesbian after all. How could I be if sex with a guy was so easy and fun? Maybe all my feelings about Laura during the last months only meant that I was horny. I was glad that I didn't have to go through that anymore, channeling my frustration toward the person closest at hand. She and I could resume our old friendship, only now instead of talking about the boys we had crushes on, we would talk about the ones we were sleeping with. It wouldn't have to be me asking her questions all the time, or me trying to figure out when I could touch her so it would seem casual, like a friend would. I swallowed, drawing saliva into my dry mouth. For some reason, I felt disappointed. I realized the pot had worn off.

Miguel shifted beside me and opened his eyes. He moved his arm, resting it palm up on my stomach. I could smell sex and sweat mingled. "How's it going?" he asked.

"Fine."

"Fine?" He seemed amused. "In my book, that was great."

"It isn't always like that?"

He smiled, closed his eyes, then opened them. "Well, for one thing, not every girl lets me do what you just did."

"Really?" That had been my favorite part.

"No way. Girls can be real uptight."

I wondered why that was. Everything Miguel and I had done had felt great. I couldn't wait to do it the next day. Again, I felt a wash of relief. Then I looked at the clock and saw how late it was. My mother would be arriving home from work soon. We took turns in the shower, got dressed, and I hurried him out the door. After his car was out of sight, I went into the kitchen to find something to eat. By then I was starving.

That night, after my mother went to bed, I sat at the kitchen table, drinking the last of the coffee in the pot, and tried to write Laura. It was harder than I expected.

"Dear Laura," I finally wrote. "You'll never guess what happened today. Miguel and I DID IT. As you know, I really wasn't thinking about him that way. It just happened. And guess what? I liked it. A lot. Remember my favorite word, cunnilingus? He did that too. The whole thing seems like too much to tell you about in a letter, unless you really want me to. I wanted you to know right away. Write me soon. I miss you. Bunches of love, Min."

I read my letter over and over again, not liking it at all but not sure how to fix it. For some reason, I was afraid of sending it. I wasn't sure, really, how Laura would react. At the same time, I urgently wanted her to know. And she would hate me if I didn't tell her immediately. At least I hadn't told her I thought I was gay, only to take it back as soon as a boy touched me. I thought again of how horny I had been for so long. Then I thought of the afternoon with Miguel and grinned. In the end, I addressed the envelope, licked it closed, wrote S.W.A.K. across the back, and left it on the table for my mother to mail in the morning.

Laura didn't write back. I started waiting for the mail in the morning, but there was no envelope addressed to me in Laura's large, squared-off handwriting. At first I thought she hadn't gotten the letter; I thought maybe her mother had intercepted it. Then I realized that was ridiculous, that she had received the letter and she disapproved. Of all the things I'd done that she thought were wrong, sleeping with Miguel probably topped the list. I knew she had a set of requirements in her head about the first time. She thought it had to be with the right kind of guy, and you had to be going steady, and you had to lead up to it slowly. She was punishing me by not writing back. Realizing this was what had happened, I was furious. Laura had no right to judge me. I didn't have to follow anyone's rules. Rules were for fools. I didn't try writing her again. She would have to make the next move. But I still missed her.

The last weeks of summer were winding down. In the time we had left, Miguel and I would meet at my house while my mother worked and screw until I had to go in to San Francisco to my job. I was learning things from him I could never have gotten from books or my teachers. When Miguel stroked my breasts, and when he showed me how he liked his balls fondled, and when we watched each other masturbate, and when we took each other's fingers, tongues, nipples, and genitals into our mouths, I discovered that sex was more than fucking. It was more, even, than running the bases, progressing from point A to point Z. Sometimes it was much less than that. Sometimes it was holding still, and sometimes it wasn't even touching. I never knew exactly if Miguel felt this way, because at the end of everything we did, he wanted to come, wanted the waiting and the building frustration to resolve into a spurting orgasm. But I could remain waiting. I could stop and do something utterly different—go for a drive, scavenge in the kitchen, watch TV—and then come back to what we were doing and it would be as if we had never stopped. Or we could not come back, and I would take the feeling with me into the rest of the day or through the night. I liked that feeling of suspension. I liked the exhilaration of being aroused and not knowing when or if or why I would leave that state.

At the same time, I was slowly coming to the conclusion that I was a lesbian after all. Miguel would have been surprised to learn it during those days our sweating bodies ground themselves against each other, fierce in their pursuit of pleasure. He would have laughed at the suggestion as I kissed his back, slowly licking from end to end the indentation his spine made, then starting on the other side. But when I touched his flat chest, I wanted to cup rounded breasts; when I ran my hand over the front of his shorts, I became impatient with the blatant presence of his erection. The more familiar I became with his body, the more it startled me. The truth was I wished he were a woman.

For a while I reasoned with myself that I didn't really know whether it was a girl's body I craved, because I had never been with a girl, if I didn't count Laura's and my experimental kissing in seventh grade. And I didn't, exactly. It had been a stupid experiment, and Laura had been more anxious than curious, more interested in kissing Nick than in kissing for its own sake. Sometimes when we spent the night at the other's house, we put ourselves to sleep by touching ourselves simultaneously, under our separate bed covers, our hushed voices slowing down as we pretended to keep up the conversation. When we heard the other coming, we tried to come at the same time. This, too, had never struck me as a sexual interchange. It was something Laura and I occasionally did together. But as the summer weeks passed, I finally admitted to myself that when I gazed, aroused, at Miguel, it was Laura that I wanted to see, her skin I imagined touching. That didn't make me want to stop fucking him while she was gone.

A couple of days before I knew Laura would be getting back from Michigan, I sat with Miguel on my favorite rock, staring out at the flat gray ocean, which was mostly covered by mist. I was not in a talkative mood, and that seemed to suit him. We hadn't smoked any pot, but even so I felt myself shift into and out of the landscape around me; I was unsure if I was part of it or only watching it from a distance. The sea and the sky were almost the same color. The waves sprayed us as they broke on the rocks below. I smoked a cigarette. Eventually the fog lifted, and the sun fell warm on our faces. I shivered in the wind.

When Miguel put his arm around my shoulder, I was thinking of how soon I would see Laura's bright face again, of the grounding sensation I got when I leaned into her. I said, still looking out at the dark, choppy water, "Miguel, I think we should just be friends."

"Why?" He sounded surprised. And hurt.

Everything with him had been easy, natural, up to this moment. "Well, I've really liked being with you, and we have a lot of fun, but I just don't feel like I want to keep doing this."

"Why, are you embarrassed to be seen at school with me?" His tone was accusing.

"No," I said. And that wasn't why. But I also knew I was lying. Right then I hated myself, because I realized it was true that I didn't want to be seen as his girlfriend at school. I thought of Miguel exactly the way the kids in our class thought of me. I felt my face get hot, realizing the unspoken rules had insinuated their way inside me too. I despised Nick, the well-rounded, all-American asshole, but I wouldn't have been ashamed of him. Miguel took his arm away. I felt cold.

"I should have known you were just like the other girls," he said. "You never wanted to hang out downtown or even introduce me to your mom.

You never asked me to stay for dinner. You just wanted to keep me hidden, your dirty secret." He had my lighter in his hand and started flicking it on and off.

I was astonished. It had never occurred to me to tell my mother that I even knew Miguel. I was certain she would have forbidden me to spend time with any boy in the house alone, and lying was easier than trying to negotiate with her. Being with Miguel, I realized, had been a very separate part of my life. I had never asked him to meet me in the city either, or introduced him to Alison, or even talked about Laura. Most of the pieces of my life never overlapped. I wondered why this was. At the same time, it seemed absolutely necessary. Even the thought of doing it differently made me nervous. It occurred to me that I was a different person with everyone I knew. I couldn't risk changing that. I sat looking out over the roiling ocean made bright by the glare of the sun, and I squinted, my eyes stinging. But I couldn't blame the salt spray. And now I had cut myself off from Miguel, the only person who had any idea what it was like to live that way.

I said, "You can think whatever you want, but that's not the reason I want to break up."

"I thought you were happy." He flicked the lighter. "We're good together." Flick. The lighter's flame was barely visible.

I looked sideways at him. His face was sullen, angry. I liked him so much, I almost couldn't understand myself why it was so impossible for me to go on being with him. I just knew I couldn't. I wanted to be with girls. "We're good, but maybe we're not right together," I said. He wouldn't look at me. I tried again. "I really do still want to be friends."

"Who the fuck do you think you are?" He brought his arm back and threw my lighter as far as he could out into the water. I watched his face twist with the effort. I wanted to reach out and touch his cheek, but I had given up that right. I felt terrible.

He didn't speak to me the whole drive home.

Three days after Laura was supposed to get back, I still hadn't heard from her. I had assumed she would call me immediately, as she did every year.

I thought she'd want to get away from her family, and that now that she could see me face to face, either we would talk about whatever was bothering her or it would dissipate, like fog on a hot afternoon. As each day passed, I started jumping up for the phone whenever it rang, but it was never for me. My mother got exasperated and told me to just call Laura myself. But I couldn't, and I couldn't tell my mother why, and I couldn't even bike down to the beach and hang out on my favorite rock because I might see Miguel there.

By mid-morning of the fourth day I couldn't stand it any longer. It was one of my days off from work, and I was going nuts with restlessness. Every other thought was about Laura. I needed to hear her voice; I had to find out what was wrong, why she still wouldn't talk to me weeks after I had sent the letter. I tossed my book onto the bed and pulled on my high-tops. I grabbed my bike from the narrow front hall, wheeling it through the kitchen.

"What's the rush?" my mother called from the living room, where she was reading a history of the New Deal.

"I'm going to Laura's," I answered.

"Good. Give her my love."

By then I was out of the house and didn't answer. I remembered to turn back to catch the door before it closed just as it slammed shut. "Sorry!" I yelled over my shoulder, already coasting out onto the street as I swung my leg back over the bicycle seat.

The sun was hot and bright, and every shiny surface—cars, windows—reflected back into my eyes, dazzling me. Now that I was on my way to see Laura, I was happy. I put my face up to the sun and felt my hair fall away from my neck. I coasted down the road, past my old elementary school, and veered into the square downtown. A high wind pushed at the languidly waving fronds of the palm trees surrounding the depot. Then I stood and pumped the pedals until I got up some momentum on Miller, before swerving left across traffic to Laura's house. I swung the bike around in a wide circle on the empty road before letting it fall with a clatter in the driveway beside her mother's car.

Now that I was there, I thought maybe I shouldn't have come. I didn't want to run into her parents and have to make polite conversation. And what if Laura still refused to speak to me? I glanced at the sprawling house, all dark wood and glass, hoping to catch sight of her in a window. And if she did speak to me, would I tell her about myself? I heard birds, no human voices. I walked around to the back and climbed the steps to the large wooden deck. Laura was lying on her back on the bench built along the deck's perimeter. She was wearing a t-shirt and cut-offs, and her hair was loose, spilling off the edge of the bench. She was very brown from the sun. She looked wonderful. I stood still, watching her, thinking she might be asleep.

"Daddy?" she said, not moving or opening her eyes.

"No, it's me," I answered.

"Min! What are you doing here?" She sat up in one graceful motion, a huge grin on her face. She was happy to see me. My breath started coming faster, as though my bike race through town was finally catching up with me. I stood at the other end of the deck, light-headed with relief.

"You didn't call," I explained. Then I started walking toward her. As far as I was concerned, Laura and I were the only two people for miles around. But she didn't stand up, she didn't move in any way toward me. I sat down beside her on the bench's warm wooden slats and caught sight of the hot tub in the corner, covered and silent. That was what we needed.

I turned to her. "Laura, let's use the hot tub. I've never been in one before." The round wooden tub had been installed a few months earlier, before her family had left for Michigan. I couldn't imagine Laura sitting in a little circle with her brother and sister and parents, all of them naked in the steaming water and carrying on a conversation. The idea made me laugh, abruptly, the sound of my voice sharp and clear in the piney air.

"I don't really want to," Laura said. I turned back to her, surprised. She looked at me steadily, and I saw that she was angry at me. In another second, I realized, she might ask me to leave. And I would have to. But I also thought part of her wanted to get in the hot tub with me, and I wanted to win that side over.

"Please?" I asked. "Just think how great it will feel. We can just relax, it'll be nice. Please, Laura?"

The screen door creaked and Laura's mother leaned her head out. She was tan too, and had gained a lot of weight. "I thought I heard someone laughing. Hello, Min. Laura, I'm going out. Can you two entertain your-selves for an hour or so?"

While her mother was speaking, Laura had walked over to the hot tub. She turned on a switch on the other side. Underneath the plastic cover I could hear the water start to gurgle.

"Where are you going?" I asked Laura's mother.

She ignored me. "Don't forget to turn that off when you're finished, Laura."

"Do I ever forget?" Laura asked testily.

Laura's mother ignored that too. Laura slumped down cross-legged next to me. Her hair fell forward into her face. Her mother said, "Did you bring your bathing suit, Min?"

"Why?"

"For the hot tub, obviously." She nodded at it.

"You can borrow one of mine," Laura told me.

"Sweetie," her mother said, "for God's sake, don't pick at your split ends."

Laura dropped the ends of her hair that she had been examining. "Bye, Mom. Have a good time."

"All right, I'm going. Bye, girls." The screen door bumped shut behind her.

Laura pulled the short sleeves of her t-shirt up around her shoulders, stretched out her bare legs, and lay back down on the bench. I scoot-ed back a few feet to give her room and sat in the shade of the house's eave, arms around my knees, staring out at the trees in front of the high wooden fence that separated her house from the next one over. I had the uneasy feeling she was displaying herself for my benefit. I counted seven pots of rosemary and other herbs scattered around the deck. I wondered who had watered them while Laura's family was away. I wished I had brought my cigarettes. Out front, a car door slammed and the engine, after a false start, kicked into life.

"She spent the whole summer screaming at everyone," Laura said, "even about the tiniest things." I looked at her lying on the bench, eyes closed, and imagined leaning over to kiss her.

"You'd think my father was the biggest klutz around. And nobody did anything. They all acted like it was normal to be angry all the time."

I was having trouble concentrating on what Laura was saying. I was too intoxicated by the tranquil day and Laura stretched out half-undressed before me.

She said, "Going out with Dave was the only way I could get away from their arguing. But even that didn't help, it just got me in trouble."

She had never told me any of that in her letters. "What do you mean?"

Laura rolled onto her side, cradling her head in the crook of her arm. I could no longer see her face, just the slightly oily sheen of her burnished hair, her part dividing it neatly down the middle. "My parents weren't nearly as laid back about Dave and me as his parents were," she said. "You're lucky you have privacy, a place to go where no one will barge in on you."

I thought of my narrow bed, and for the first time I realized that I *had* been lucky. Where else could Miguel and I have gone, with his mother home with his youngest brother all day? It would have turned out very differently. I said, "That was because I didn't tell my mother about Miguel. There's no way she would have let me see him while she was at work. No fucking way. You're the only one who knows about him."

She seemed to consider that. Then she said, "Dave and I mostly fooled around outside. In the woods or on the beach. One time he got a wicked sunburn on his butt."

I laughed. Here we were, back in our friendship again, trading stories about boys, just as I had imagined it after the first time with Miguel. She was still curled away from me. I wanted to stroke her hair, let her know how much I cared about her.

Laura said, "I think my father is having an affair."

"Your father?" I was shocked. But I also believed it right away. I had always thought her father was attractive with his gray hair and arched eyebrows that made me feel he was daring me in some way. And he was almost never home.

Then Laura stood up abruptly. "Let's get in," she said. "I just want to be quiet for a while." She pulled the cover off the tub. I watched her carefully. Her father. The water bubbled gently, masking the steady drone of the pump. Laura went inside the house and came out carrying two large white bath towels and a glass of water. She seemed to have forgotten about the bathing suits, which was fine with me.

We stripped in the sun and hurriedly climbed over the rim of the tub to sink naked into the hot water. Though we were used to undressing in front of each other, over the past year Laura had grown self-conscious about her body. Knowing that made me a little nervous. I also felt the difference in my own body from having been with Miguel: how I enjoyed its suppleness, how easy being naked was. Submerged to our necks, sitting across from each other on the ledge that circled the tub, we leaned back, feigning nonchalance. Gradually I relaxed, enjoying the enclosing heat of the water and the breeze that fanned my face. I closed my eyes, listening to the silence interrupted occasionally by the whisper of car tires on the road out front. I felt my body expand as if it were slowly being filled with the water and the water was as wide as the ocean.

After a while I asked, "Why didn't you write me back?" I looked over at her, but she avoided my gaze. Her long hair trailed in the water.

"You know why," she said. "Miguel."

My anger was right there, rushing through me. "What, because Miguel's Chicano? That's bullshit, Laura, I can't believe—"

"No, Min, why would I care about that?" She gazed at me severely. "When I got your letter, it was like you were telling me you had moved to the moon."

"Why?" I asked, bewildered. "I wasn't the one who left. You have no idea how much I missed you, Laura. I spent most of the summer doing nothing and hating it. I was miserable waiting for you to come back."

"You weren't when you went all the way with Miguel." She waited. I was silent. It was true: for a few weeks I hadn't felt as lonely. Her face was getting red from the water's heat. "I felt like you had turned into someone else, Min. I felt like you had jumped into this other world of sex and pot. I couldn't understand what you were doing. I still can't."

"I was doing the same thing you were doing," I answered. Laura frowned. Underneath the water, my limbs stretched away from me. I lifted my foot, stirring the thick liquid heat. Then I stood up in the middle of the tub, leaned back slightly, and went under, dunking my head so that all of me was submerged. When I came up, Laura hadn't moved. I swept my wet hair off my face and sat back across from her.

"So you might as well tell me what happened." I could hear the attempt at indifference in Laura's voice.

"What do you want to know?" I asked, sounding equally unconcerned.

"You know, what he did, what it felt like."

"The first time, or after that?"

"Oh. The first time, I guess."

I smiled, remembering. "Well, I liked it, of course."

"Of course?" Laura sounded angry.

"Well, yeah," I answered, baffled. "Fucking is fun."

"How can you call the first time you made love 'fucking'?"

Here it was, the argument I had been anticipating for weeks. It was hard for us to look at each other. This time I glanced away. I looked up at the pine trees on the other side of the yard and at the blue sky. "Because it *was* fucking. We were high, and it seemed like a good idea. It wasn't anything romantic."

Laura stared at me, an expression in her eyes like a wince. "I can't believe you," she said. "You just gave it away, like that, in one afternoon? How could you let someone you don't even know very well touch you like that? You didn't even build up to it."

"Why should I? I've been waiting a long time."

"So have I," she replied heatedly.

"Yeah, but you never take the opportunities handed to you."

"That's because I'm not—" Abruptly, she stopped speaking, but I knew what she meant. She thought I was a slut, the kind of girl she wanted to be but couldn't let herself. That's what it was, I realized suddenly. She was angry at me because I didn't follow all the restrictions that were in her head keeping her back.

"Okay, start from the beginning. Did it hurt when he put himself in?"

"A little, at first. He stopped until I was ready."

"Did you bleed?"

"No."

"Did it feel weird inside you?" She made a face when she said this, scrunching up her nose.

I remembered her description of Dave's cock, how foreign it had seemed to her. I had never felt awkward with Miguel's penis, only tired of it eventually. "What do you mean by weird?" I asked.

"Okay, was he rough?" I looked at her blankly. "You know," she said, "did he pound into you?"

Why was she so scared of it? "No. Well, there were times, later, when we got kind of frenzied. But sometimes he hardly moved at all and took a long time. I liked it both ways."

"You did?"

We looked at each other, surprised. "Yeah," I said and laughed. I glanced down at her body refracted and wiggly below the water, then looked away.

"What kind of birth control did you use?"

"Nothing the first time. Later he used rubbers."

"Jesus, Min, what if you're pregnant?"

"Well, I'm not."

"But you could have been. That was really stupid."

I looked at her. I could feel my jaw tightening. I breathed in, then out. Bringing my hands up through the heated water, I rested them on the surface, then swept them, open-palmed, back and forth as they sank back down. I said, more coldly than I meant to, "You sound like your mother. Do you want me to tell you this or not?"

"Okay." Silence. She reached up with a dripping hand to push her hair behind her ear. "What about cunnilingus? You said he did that in your letter."

"I liked that the most of everything we did." I was smiling. I leaned my head back and closed my eyes, remembering. "Guys really love going down on girls, don't they? Miguel could stay down there for the longest time. I'd have to drag him back up." I opened my eyes halfway. "Well, I guess I don't have to tell you, you know what I'm talking about."

"Not really," Laura said in a voice I could barely hear.

I sat up. "Dave never went down on you? Didn't you do 69?"

"No. I wouldn't have let him go down on me even if he'd wanted to. But he didn't. He thought it was gross."

"Why?"

Laura merely looked at me disbelievingly and shook her head. I really didn't understand. All I ever thought about was getting my face between a girl's thighs. Underwater, Laura stretched out her legs. One of them touched one of mine. "Sorry," she said quickly, moving her leg away and sitting up straighter.

I was about to speak when Laura cleared her throat. "How come you keep talking about Miguel in the past tense? Aren't you still together?" She pushed herself up from the water and stretched out her arms along the side of the wooden tub.

I looked away from her, mostly because it was hard not to notice her round, sloping breasts just above water level. I reached over the rim of the tub to the switch behind me and turned on the jets, then sat in front of one. Beneath the water, its heavy spray hit the small of my back.

Laura apparently took my silence for assent. She asked, "Didn't you love each other?"

"Love?" I asked, trying to remember the surprising strength of my regret the day I broke up with Miguel. Instead I had an image of Laura's father with his pants down screwing one of his colleagues, or maybe it was a secretary, on the carpet of his office at Sonoma State, her skirt pushed up and her knees in the air on either side of him. My stomach lurched. I stared at Laura. Was this what she imagined too?

When I didn't say anything more, Laura said, "From what you've said, Miguel sounds really nice. I thought at first you were crossing another line, like with all your pot smoking and driving without a license and everything, and I thought you were choosing someone really bad to do it with. But he isn't, is he?" I shook my head. She gazed at me for a moment. "I don't know what's wrong with you, Min."

"Nothing's wrong with me."

"I don't mean it the way it sounded. I mean, he sounds so great. He could have been a real creep, for all you knew. If I had gone all the way with Dave—"

"Yeah, why didn't you?" I interrupted, anxious to change the subject.

"What?"

"Go all the way. With Dave."

"I didn't want to. It wasn't an obvious thing, the way I guess it was for you. I liked him a lot, he was really nice. I sort of wanted to, but not with him. I don't know," she drifted off. We were silent. I listened to the whoosh of the water jets and the dull roar of a far-off airplane. I moved away from the spray at my back. I was getting overheated and a little lightheaded. My body felt rubbery, far away.

"I don't want to be in competition with you," Laura finally said.

We stared at each other. Her face was pinched, as though she was about to cry.

"We're not in a race," I said.

"But now I feel like I have to keep up with you. I almost did it with Dave just because *you* had. I feel like I'm always trying to keep up."

"With me?" I asked, astonished. "But you're the one who's had boyfriends. Why would you feel competitive? I'm the one who's always waiting to hear what happened."

"Nothing ever happens, Min. I mean, it's never how I hope it will be. I always think it would be better if I could be more like you."

"But you want different things than I do."

"You think I know what I want? I don't. I don't know what's wrong with me. I want to lose it, but not with Dave. I mean, he's not somebody I'd want to marry or anything. He's nice, I like him, but that's all. I want more than that."

"Like what?" A small tendril of hope was unfurling inside me. Maybe Laura couldn't bring herself to have sex with boys because she didn't like them. Maybe she could like girls instead.

"I want it to be more than fumbling around. I want what you had with Miguel. Min, you have no idea how lucky you were. And I want . . ."

She closed her eyes and shook her head. Then she cupped her hands to splash her reddened face. The slope of her breasts moved as she leaned forward and gathered up the water. She lifted her arms and brought the water to her face. Trickles ran down her neck and over her round breasts, glinting for a second in the sunlight. I wanted to put my hands on her breasts and let the water run over my fingers. I wanted to touch Laura's breasts, and I wanted her to like it.

"What?" I said quietly, urgently.

"Well, I want to love him. I want to *be* loved."

Then Laura started to cry. She brought her hand up from the rim of the tub to cover her mouth, as though she could keep me from hearing the occasional sob that escaped her. I stood up and pushed through the water toward her, wanting to put my arms around her and hold her close against me. If I hugged her tight, stroking her half-wet hair, she might not keep herself back as she was now, her eyes squeezed shut to fend off the tears, her hand trying to smother all sound. But I realized as I reached out to touch her shoulder that we were both naked, and suddenly I didn't dare. I stood next to her, inches away, hoping she could feel my silent presence beside her.

Finally I said, my voice sounding odd to me, "I love you, Laura." I'd meant it as an offering, my attempt at giving comfort. But as the words became sound in the air between us, I realized it was my confession. I was shaking after I said it.

Laura wiped her cheeks with the palm of her hand. "I know, Min, and I love you too. But it's not enough. I mean *in* love."

I gripped the rim of the hot tub behind me with both hands, while inside my chest something that had been stretching out snapped back tightly, like a fist. My eyes filled, but I blinked the tears back before she could see them.

Laura pulled her hair back from her forehead with her hands. The skin around her eyes was swollen, and her face was blotchy from crying. She was still beautiful. She met my gaze and smiled, looking tired and at the same time gratified to see me still there.

"Thank you, though," she said. We stood in the bubbling water, helpless and half-smiling at each other, until she turned around and climbed out of the tub and covered herself with her towel.

Laura and I had only one class together in the fall of eleventh grade. In a way, I was relieved. After we had talked in the hot tub, an awkward tension settled over our friendship. What she had said about feeling she was in competition with me began to prove itself true; I could feel it not only in our comparing grades, but in the careful way we spoke of our other friendships, our families, and especially about boys. Sex hardly ever came up in our conversations anymore. When it did, it was in the abstract, something unconnected to our own bodies or to another person's. I never mentioned Miguel's name.

At school Laura and I still met between classes at her locker or mine. Sometimes, while we complained about our teachers and walked between buildings to our next class, Miguel would pass by. Each time I watched Laura stare at him as though she thought she was invisible and he couldn't see her doing it. Embarrassed, I would grab her by the arm and lead her off somewhere. I'd ask, "Are you listening to me?" to break her gaze and bring her attention, unfocused, a little lost, back to me. I could tell she was still trying to understand why I had slept with him and liked it while she continued to hold off, waiting for the right time, the perfect guy. She seemed to think that by scrutinizing Miguel she could discover some hidden trait in him that set him apart from other boys, some unknown quality that had made me respond to him over anyone else. Perhaps she was looking for something in him that she herself could respond to, if given the chance; something, I guessed, that was tender and thoughtful and safe. That wasn't what had turned me on about Miguel, but since our conversation in the hot tub, I had come to recognize a little better that what Laura wanted was also what frightened her. I didn't understand it, but I had begun to see it.

As for Miguel and me, he never directly caught my eye or acknowledged me. I had stopped hanging out at the beach, so we encountered each other only at school. He acted as though we barely knew each other, as though our lives had no point of intersection. Once he nearly knocked me over as he came careening out of the student center as I was going in for lunch. He put a hand on my arm to steady me.

"You okay?" he asked, and, seeing his face, I remembered the way he had looked at me after the first time we had had sex, when he was concerned that I hadn't had an orgasm. On either side of us, arriving students jostled by, in a hurry to eat. Someone bumped my arm with his knapsack and pushed on.

"Yeah, sure," I answered. I wanted to say more. "Listen, Miguel—"

"I've got to go. See you around." He moved away, unable to look at me for more than that one second. I had to admit to myself I was disappoint-

ed. I had hoped for some reason that during the school year we would re-
vive the easy rapport we had shared over the summer and develop a comfortable friendship, built from our past relationship and his continuing
desire for me. It appeared he'd gotten over that desire. There were days
when I found myself missing him. Not the sex so much, but his smile, and
the way our rowdy, stoned laughter had made me feel, for moments at a
time, no longer alone. On the other hand, I made no move toward reconciliation myself. I didn't even look at him with recognition when I saw
him in the crowded halls and on the sloping paths between classes. Something stopped me, and I acted as though we had never spoken beyond the
confines of the school. Yet I expected him to talk to me despite, or even
because of, the way I had treated him, and I was hurt that he didn't.

Near the end of September, Alison invited me to a David Bowie concert.
Flattered, I said yes and, not knowing his music, bought the new album
that afternoon. We went on a Saturday after work. We drove in her beat-
up Datsun to the Mission for a quick burrito, then across the Bay Bridge
with the rush-hour traffic to the Greek Theater in Berkeley. In the car I
rolled down my window and smoked a cigarette leaning back against the
door on my right, my left leg propped up on the seat, so that I was facing
Alison as she drove. Alison, like Laura, was blonde, but her hair was short
and messy, as though she never combed it. That day she was wearing jeans
and a soft-looking beige shirt and cowboy boots and two silver bracelets
on one wrist and her watch set in a thick leather band on the other. No
one at school ever looked that cool. I couldn't take my eyes off her.

　　She was telling me about a professor of hers at State who had come
on to her earlier that week. "The guy's in his fifties, at least. Like, I don't
think so, you know?" She glanced in her side mirror, accelerating as she
moved into the left lane to pass the car ahead of us.

　　I was confused. I had expected her to object to his gender, not his age.
But I took one last drag from my cigarette and said, "Yeah. There's a girl
in our class who's fucking our social studies teacher from ninth grade.

He's at least in his thirties. She thinks no one knows, but he's always goofy when he's around her." I flicked my cigarette butt out the window behind me.

She shook her head, grinning. "You can always tell," Alison said.

"What can you always tell?" I asked, thinking she was talking about older men.

She glanced at me. "You know, what other people want. Who they're attracted to."

I was silent. I picked at the torn threads around the knee of my jeans, feeling unaccountably sad.

"Don't you think?" Alison asked. I looked up. She was intent on the highway ahead, passing all the slower cars. The sun through her window lit up the hair that stood out from her head. When she shifted into fifth, her hand stayed wrapped around the gearshift for a moment before moving back onto the steering wheel. There was authority in that hand, and self-assurance. Feeling drawn to Alison felt odd after having been focused on Laura for so long. I was surprised at how effortless being attracted to her was, and I was even relieved; I could probably be interested in a lot of women simultaneously. At the same time, I knew I was giving up something that had been precious to me. I didn't know if I would feel anything close to the intensity of what I had felt about Laura ever again. I wasn't sad about it, exactly, but I was aware of a kind of wrenching or uprooting. The wind rushed through the car as we picked up speed. I felt paper-light, ready to blow away.

Alison glanced over at me. I said, "I guess you can tell, if you're looking."

My neck was getting stiff. I slid around in my seat and sat facing forward. Alison asked me to look through the cardboard box at my feet for *Diamond Dogs*. I flipped through the cassettes, found it, took it out of its case, and handed it to her. With one hand on the wheel, she popped the cassette into her tape player and cranked the volume up high. The bass reverberated under my feet. It was impossible to talk without shouting. I leaned my head back and let the music surround me from all four speakers, cocooning me. Except for conferring about directions, we drove in silence for the rest of the trip.

The Greek Theater was an outdoor concert hall set on a hill. Stone bleachers took up most of the area beyond the stage; higher up, the green grass of the hill provided extra seating. The concert had sold out, and by the time Alison and I arrived inside, the seats were filled but there were still patches of grass visible among the crowd of bodies. The hill looked like an unfinished quilt made up of spread blankets. We climbed up and found a spot near the center. Below us, the stage was set up with the band's instruments. I glanced around at the audience. A group of college kids to the right of us drank the beer they had smuggled in. People milled around, searching for faces they recognized. The sun was setting behind the hill we sat on, and the sky slowly leaked the dark ink of night onto the sky. I sprawled on the grass next to Alison and felt my skin tingle. I was waiting for the dark, wanting to be seduced by the music.

"What are you smiling about?" Alison asked, stretched out on her side, smiling herself.

"I don't know. I'm happy, I guess. What was that song about rock and roll we listened to in the car?"

She tilted her head back, gazing up at the promising sky. She started to sing. Her voice was lovely, high and clear, not at all what I had expected. She met my gaze.

"So, why didn't you invite your girlfriend instead of me?" I asked, opting for the direct approach to a question I had been wondering about since Alison first mentioned the concert.

"Oh, she hates David Bowie."

"Alison, come on."

She looked away for a moment, as if considering other responses. "Truthfully?" she asked. I nodded, but she wasn't looking at me. "It's pretty much over between us. It has been for a long time. I don't know why I've been hanging on." She looked down and pulled a blade of grass out of the ground, then pulled up another. I wondered why I hadn't known, seen the signs, whatever they were. All I had seen was that Alison had a girlfriend and I didn't.

She glanced up at me. "I guess that means I'm single again. Single young lesbian on the loose."

"So am I," I said, holding her gaze. Telling her was as easy as when I had asked Miguel to sleep with me.

"I know," Alison said lightly.

I stared at her. "No way. How did you know?"

"I just did."

"What, do I have 'lesbian' written across my forehead?"

She smiled. "Not exactly. But it's obvious."

"How?" I felt strange, exposed. Had something changed about me over the last few months? Would she have said the same thing a year ago, before I knew myself? Was it something only other lesbians could see? Had my mother guessed? Had Laura?

Alison said, "I told you, you can always tell what people want."

"Always?" I asked. Then I realized that her recognizing my desire was a good thing. I didn't have to hide it.

She reached across the space between us and slowly brushed her fingers over my hair. "When you're looking," she said.

Then she sat up and gazed down at the stage. "When's this show going to start?" she asked. It was already half an hour after the warm-up band was supposed to play, and there was still no sign of life on the stage.

I sat up too. "Let's rock and roll!" I shouted into the night air above me. One of the girls in the group to our right stared at me. She looked away when I glared back.

A week after the concert, I told my mother I would be working an evening shift so she would let me spend Saturday night in Alison's dorm room. It rained the entire day. After work Alison and I sat in a movie holding hands. I had never had that anticipatory time with Miguel, feeling excited by and also fearful of what would happen later. And it wasn't only fear of being sexual with Alison, it was a fear of what crossing that line would mean for me. As we watched the screen, I was aware that I was making a decision, and that what I chose would change me forever: how I lived, what I thought, who I was. I didn't know what I meant by that, but my trembling told me it was true. I breathed in deeply, held Alison's hand more tightly. I was ready for change.

When we arrived back in her dorm room, our pants and shoes soaked from the rain, I stood near the door while Alison shook out her umbrella and propped it in a corner to dry, then pulled shut the drapes and cleared books and clothes off her single bed. I looked around, surprised her room was so small, noticing the photographs of women on her walls. Somehow this first time mattered more to me than it had with Miguel; what Alison thought of me mattered more. And though I'd had a crash course in sex with a guy only a couple of months before, I was afraid it wouldn't help me. Alison came over and tugged on my hand. "Come on," she said, smiling. "Let's get out of these wet clothes."

It was not as easy as it had been with Miguel. We couldn't get in synch, get a rhythm going, so that while she was trying to kiss my ear, I was intent on unbuttoning her jeans. We tussled for a while, and then we stopped and looked at each other and started laughing. I saw that she was nervous too, and the relief of understanding this made me relax a little. We lay back on the bed and made out, stopping every now and then to pull back and smile at each other, touching the other's face or hair. Alison's hair was lighter in color than Laura's, her face more defined. I ran a finger along her cheekbone, down her jawline. She caught my finger with her teeth, then kissed me again. I wondered if this was all that was going to happen between us, and I wondered if that would be all right with me. I didn't know.

Eventually I started again to take off her clothes. She helped me with mine, and then she rolled on top of me, and we kept on kissing. The way she lay on me was uncomfortable, her hip bones digging into mine and her body heavier than I would have thought for someone as thin as

Alison was. Her smothering weight on me made me uneasy. Maybe she wasn't a very good lover. Maybe we'd be incompatible in other ways too. I remembered Laura telling me she wanted sex to be more than fumbling around, how lucky I had been with Miguel. I wondered if this was what she had meant. Maybe sex wasn't always easy. Always fun. But it was at the moment of doubt that Laura closed off, shut down, before she knew anything yet.

I shifted beneath Alison, rolling her half off me. If she noticed, she didn't seem to care. As we kissed, I moved my hands down her back, along her waist, her thigh. She moaned; my breathing quickened. We were beginning to match up. I loved how her skin felt, warm and dry and smooth, and the sheer luxuriousness of the feeling of her full body against mine made my eyes close with pleasure. This was what I had been waiting for.

I was very excited when Alison put her hand between my legs. With my eyes closed, I thought it would feel the way it had when Miguel did it. In fact, it didn't feel very different—his fingers, though bigger, were deft, as hers were—but it *was* different, because I knew it was her: her woman's fingers and breath and consciousness accompanying me where I was going. I wanted to give her instructions—a little further down, harder—but I knew there would be another time for that, and I didn't need much help. I heard her whisper, "Oh, baby," as I started to come, mildly, a small bubble of pleasure bursting.

It was later, when I did the same for Alison, that I felt something inside me click into place, like the last piece of a jigsaw puzzle that I had been working on for many years. Sliding my fingers into the slick wetness between her legs was beyond pleasure; it was a homecoming, to a place I hadn't known existed. I felt I had been born just to experience this moment, my fingers swimming in the juice of this woman, slipping over the folds and pouches of her flesh. I found her clitoris, hard beneath the skin like a pit inside fruit. I found the contracting, steady beat inside her. Startled, I said, "Oh!" out loud and stopped moving. I wanted to cry. Or laugh. Or tell her that I loved her. I opened my eyes and looked down at Alison's flushed face, her bright eyes looking back at me, a little puzzled. "You're beautiful," I said. I started to slide my fingers against her again and watched her eyelids sink slowly closed.

The next morning was clear and warm, and I invited Alison out to Mill Valley for the first time. I had been thinking a lot, since my breakup with Miguel, about the ways I kept the people in my life apart. I wanted to introduce Alison to my mother, not as my girlfriend—not yet, at least—but as my friend. We had breakfast at a Greek restaurant in the Sunset, taking our trays upstairs to the outdoor garden. On the drive up, I told Alison about my adoption, because I didn't want her to be surprised and say something stupid. By the time we arrived it was after noon. The house was empty. There was a note on the kitchen table from my mother saying that she had gone to brunch with two friends and would be back sometime that afternoon.

I started to show Alison around the house, but we couldn't keep our hands off each other and only got as far as the living room. We were standing in the middle of the room making out when I thought I heard the back door click shut. It was hard to pull myself away from Alison's mouth. I looked up. My mother stood in the entrance to the room.

"What are you doing?" she asked hesitantly. Alison and I quickly stepped back from each other. I couldn't tell if she had actually seen us kissing. Frantic, I tried to reconstruct the last few seconds in my mind. Her gaze moved from Alison to me. In the middle of my panic, I saw that she was carrying a sweater and her purse over her arm, and her hair was pinned up at the back of her head.

Then she focused on me, as though she finally recognized me, and her face changed, becoming angry. "What the hell do you think you're doing?" She didn't move but simply stood there, blocking the door.

I buttoned up the top buttons of my shirt, trying to think, but no thoughts would come to me. I remained silent.

Alison said, "Maybe I should go," more to me than to my mother. I stared at Alison for a moment, hoping she would understand that I wanted her to stay.

"No, you're not leaving this house," my mother shot back at her. "I don't even know who you are. Neither of you is going anywhere until you tell me what is going on here."

"I was going to tell you—" I began.

"You were going to tell me? You were going to tell me? What were you going to tell me? When? I hardly see you as it is."

"Well, that's as much your fault as it is mine," I countered.

"Don't talk back to me like that, Min."

Again I said nothing. Alison folded her arms across her chest and watched my mother warily. All three of us stood there, not moving, not saying anything, absolutely at a loss.

"Look," Alison said at last, moving toward the door, "this is really none of my business, and I think my being here just makes it worse. Um, I guess I can't say it was nice to meet you, but, you know, I hope we'll meet again sometime." She stood in front of my mother, waiting for her to move out of the doorway. She was several inches taller than me, about my mother's height. My mother looked at Alison for a long moment. Finally she stepped aside and let Alison pass. In the hallway, Alison turned around and looked at me. "Call me," she said.

After the door shut, my mother came into the room, circling around me as if she were afraid of touching me. She fell into her overstuffed armchair and covered her forehead with her hand, closing her eyes. "It's bad enough that you've been lying to me and running around behind my back," she said tiredly. "But this. I can't think of anything worse you could have done to me."

Now that she had lost the momentum of her indignation, I could listen to what she was saying. My dismay at being caught turned angry.

I said, "I could have done to *you*? What you saw was between Alison and me. It wasn't about you."

My mother looked up sharply. "In my house? Knowing I was coming home? I think that was a pretty clear message you were trying to send me."

I had to consider that. Why *had* we started kissing, knowing she could arrive home any moment? Confused, I wondered if my mother was right. Had I wanted to provoke her, upset her? Then I rejected the idea. Alison and I had just become lovers the night before. All I wanted to do was touch her. Even inside my own house, I had forgotten all about my mother. But the doubt lingered. I pushed it aside.

"There's no message, Mom. I'll tell you when I have something to say to you."

She laughed joylessly, shaking her head at me. "You don't even know what you feel. I think you're angry at me, Min. Very angry. For adopting you. For divorcing your father. For being a mother who sets limits for your own good. You're furious, and you're getting back at me with the thing that will hurt me the most. And it's working."

I moved closer to her chair, stood over her. I could feel the energy of my rage surge up in me, desperate for a way out. I yelled, "I wasn't trying to hurt you, Mom. This has nothing to do with you. I like girls. That's what we're talking about. I like Alison. A lot."

My mother sat through my tirade looking fixedly ahead of her, as if she were trying to concentrate on something else so that she wouldn't have to listen to me. "Are you finished?" she said.

"No. If you want to get angry at me for lying to you or whatever you think I've been doing, go ahead. I invited Alison up here today so you could meet her. I thought you'd be glad to know I have a new friend." She opened her mouth and started to respond. "Let me finish. I'm sorry you walked in on us, because I wanted to tell you that I'm a lesbian sometime soon, when we could have time to talk about it. I think you would have reacted differently if you had found out differently." I backed up a step, as though releasing her from a spell I had cast over her. "That's all I have to say for now."

She pushed herself out of her chair, and I was afraid for a second that she was going to come at me, maybe even hit me. Then I realized she wanted the advantage of height. She said, a hand on her hip, "How could you think I would be glad to meet a girl like that, who's obviously such a bad influence on you?" I started to protest but she held up a hand. "Now let *me* finish. You are not a lesbian, Min. You probably think you're in love with that girl, but let me tell you, you're not. This is a phase you're going through. You'll get over it."

"I think all that therapy you've had is making you crazy," I burst out.

"Don't talk back to me!" she lashed back. "Your anger is out of control. Partly it's your age. You're blindly acting out. Some day you'll look back at your behavior with this girl, and with me, and you'll be ashamed. I think you should consider seeing a therapist, Min. I really do." She sat back down in her chair, apparently exhausted.

"This is totally fucked up," I said. I had started to pace the room, but there was too much furniture to take long strides. I stood behind the rocking chair and held on to its two posts. I could have thrown it across the room just then. "You're not listening to me, Mom. This is not a phase. This is who I am. Of course I'm angry at you. You refuse to believe what I'm telling you."

"I refuse to believe it because it's not true!" my mother yelled at me.

"Yes it is!" I yelled back, ready to cry from frustration.

"And I will not allow you to see that girl again," she continued as if she hadn't heard me.

"How are you going to stop me?"

The pins holding up her hair had loosened, and her hair was falling down to her shoulders. She reached up and impatiently pulled them all out. "You will not see that girl while you are living in this house, is that clear?" she asked, stressing each word.

"Fine. Then I'm moving out."

"You are *not* moving out."

"You wanted me to learn to be more independent, remember?"

"Min, you're not going anywhere," she said tiredly. She didn't believe me.

"Watch me."

I turned and walked out of the room, grabbed my bike from its place in the hall. My mother tried to catch up with me, calling my name. I let the door slam in her face.

I rode away as fast as I could, mindless and seething with fury. After a while I began to notice I was on a road leading out of town, and I kept going. I thought I would eventually find a phone by the side of the road or in the next town, and I would call Alison and ask if I could stay with her. Then I remembered that Alison was probably still driving back to the city and wouldn't be home yet. I thought of Laura next and made a U-turn. But at her house no one answered my knock, and when I tried the back door, it was locked. "Where the fuck are you, Laura?" I shouted at the house. There was no response, only the whispering of the leaves in the surrounding trees. I looked around the deck and saw the covered hot tub in the corner. I was tired, sweaty, on the edge of tears. It would be so easy to lift off the cover and slip into the warm water inside. It would be like wrapping the water around me like a blanket or the embrace of human arms. I could think of nothing I'd rather do. But I knew that in the end Laura's whole family would come home and find me there, and they'd make a scene, and I'd have to explain what had happened, and her parents would send me back home to work out my problems. I wasn't willing to bear anymore alone. I needed Laura to get into that tub.

I picked up my bike from the driveway and pedaled slowly back toward the square, hoping Alison had reached her dorm by now.

That night in Alison's single bed, with only the soft light of a candle on her desk, we finished what we had started earlier in my mother's living room. I wouldn't let her try to make me come; I knew it would be useless. All I really wanted was to be touched and held. I had recounted word for word what my mother and I had said to each other. Alison had agreed that I should stay with her in her dorm room until we could figure out what to do next. I didn't want to think about that yet.

Alison rolled onto her side facing me and propped her head up on her arm. She passed her hand lightly over my sweating body, feeling my ribs and hipbones through the skin, shaping her fingers to the curve of my shoulder. I loved the way hands could travel the planes of the body, covering it, stimulating or soothing it. I loved how the merest brush of Alison's fingertips against my face felt like communion. I closed my eyes and breathed deeply. I moved my head slightly, nestling my cheek into her warm palm. When I exhaled, I could feel the tightness in my chest creak loose and settle, like sand spilling to the bottom of a dune.

Alison said, "I love the texture of your skin. It's so soft. Do all Asian women have such soft skin?"

I looked up at her, thinking she was joking. She was waiting for my answer. I caught her hand, held it away from me.

"No, just the adopted ones," I said.

She shot me a bewildered look. I ignored it and pushed her onto her back, not gently. Holding her down, I straddled her thighs, leaned over, and bit her pink nipple, scraping my teeth over its hard, wrinkled skin.

When Alison and I woke up the next morning, we both realized I should go back. At least until I had a plan. But as the bus crossed the bridge and I sat looking out at the parched brown grasses of the Marin Headlands, I knew I would stay once I got home. I wasn't ready to find my own place, or transfer to another school, or live in another city from my friends. How would I pay rent? My mother wouldn't help me; she didn't want me to leave. As for seeing Alison, I would work it out.

I was late getting to school. I smoked a cigarette sitting on the terrace wall by the entrance while I waited for the bell to ring for the mid-morning break. The day was overcast and windy. A few cars passed by. Nobody was out on the street.

Inside, as the hall flooded with students, I pushed through to my
locker to get rid of my knapsack. Laura was there, waiting for me. She
looked extremely pretty, her long blonde hair French braided and hanging in a thick rope behind her head. She also looked upset.

"What's wrong?" I asked, walking up to her.

She turned towards me and grabbed my arm. "Min! God, I was so
worried. I went over to your house yesterday afternoon."

"Shit. Let's go outside and talk."

We went back out and sat on the wide tiled steps. A few other kids
were standing around. One guy started pushing another, trying to start
a fight. We had fifteen minutes until the next class started.

"Okay," I said, turning to Laura. "What happened?"

"Well, I went over to see if you were home. Your mother—"

"Wait. What time was this?"

"I don't know. About three." I nodded and she continued. "Your mother was in the kitchen. She was on the phone. When she saw it was me,
she hung up and invited me in and asked if I had seen you. She made a
pot of coffee and we sat at the kitchen table and talked for a long time."

"About me? What did she tell you?"

"Well, not much. She said you'd been arguing, but she didn't say what
about. I didn't want to pry or anything. We talked about how hard it is
between mothers and daughters sometimes. I told her about the problems I've been having with my mom. She seemed really interested, and
she helped me look at some of it from my mother's point of view. You
know, your mom is really cool."

I snorted and shook my head. "Yeah, well, she's not that cool. She
can't handle reality."

"You're so hard on her, Min."

I knew her talk with my mother was important to Laura. The whole
time we had been friends, my mother had acted as a kind of second
mother to her, almost a sister. Often while she was over at my house,
Laura would wander into whatever room my mother was in and hang out

with her for a while. I could hear them laughing. Sometimes I got angry because Laura was *my* friend.

"She deserves it," I said, and the frustration I had felt with my mother the day before rose up in me, catching in my throat. "I'll tell you the reason we fought yesterday. I've started seeing someone. My mother found out about it."

Laura's face changed, and I remembered why we had stopped talking about sex. She looked away as if that could hide what she was feeling. "So soon?" she said.

"Well, it's not that quick. I think it's been building up for a while."

She nodded, then she was silent. Then, "Who is he? Do I know him?"

"That's the part my mother didn't like. It's not a guy. It's Alison."

"Alison," she repeated, dully. "Your friend at work."

"Right."

Laura still wouldn't look at me. She seemed to have stopped breathing. "You never—" she began, then stopped. I was afraid she wouldn't accept it either, just like my mother. She looked down at her hands, which were clasped very tightly together. "Have you made love yet?"

I almost smiled at her choice of words but inside me something was twisting around like a towel being wrung dry. I finally understood what she had meant about having to keep up with me. Even the language we each used about sex was different. "Yes, we're sleeping together. It only started about a week ago," I added.

She looked up at me, her head cocked, squinting as though I was casting a bright light. "Does this mean you're a lesbian?" The bell in the clock tower started its hourly chime: we had five minutes before the beginning of class.

I nodded.

A long silence. "I guess you'll spend a lot of time with Alison now."

"Probably."

"When will I ever see you?" she asked.

I realized in that moment just how much my life had changed. I would never again be able to have everything the way it had been for so long. I felt afraid. Unlike two nights before, when I had anticipated sex with Alison with excitement as well as fear, I saw now there would be losses. They had already begun.

Laura and I stared at each other. The future loomed ahead, completely unknown. I could see in her face that she was thinking the same thing. I looked around. No one else was still outside but us.

CHAPTER 6

Min

Spring 1982

THE ENVELOPE WAS LIGHT BLUE and smelled faintly of honeysuckle. I put it up to my nose, inhaling. It was addressed to me in a woman's round, loopy handwriting. I flipped the metal door in the bank of mailboxes closed and ran up the stairs to my apartment. As far as I could remember, I didn't know anyone who used scents. For a moment I wondered if it could be a card from one of the women I'd been flirting with during the last few months. I thought I could guess which one.

Inside, I threw my keys and knapsack on the kitchen table. As soon as I turned the envelope over and saw my father's name on the back, still in the woman's handwriting, I knew exactly what it contained: an invitation to his wedding. The sweet odor of honeysuckle was nauseating. I said "Shit" out loud and threw the envelope down on the floor as though it had burned my hand.

Trembling, I leafed through the rest of the mail. There was only one other thing for me, a flyer from an Asian-American women's group that kept sending me notices about upcoming events because I had called once to ask about their meetings. I balled it up and threw it at the trash can. I had been trying to work up the nerve to go for weeks, but right then, looking for a sense of community felt beside the point. The crushed paper hit the side and fell onto the floor.

I knew I had to open it eventually. I left the bills and Henry's mail on the kitchen table. Picking up the blue envelope from the floor, I went out to the back porch where I sat on the rickety stairs overlooking the yard two flights down. I pulled a pack of Benson & Hedges and my lighter from my denim jacket and lit a cigarette. I'd been telling myself I would stop smoking by the time I turned eighteen, but my birthday had been half a year before. Now the deadline was when I became a certified massage practitioner. I had a little more than a month left, and I was down to half a pack a day.

As I pulled the smoke down into my lungs and then let it escape through my open mouth, a calm spread over me. I could feel my heart slow in my chest and a tranquility similar to a warm, comforting hand on my shoulder. Of course, I would have preferred someone's actual arm around me. I thought of Laura, out of habit, and then I thought of Jane, a woman I had met one night a couple of months before at Clementina's and slept with sometimes. It was nice to have a night of friendly sex occasionally with someone who didn't need anything from me the next morning. I inhaled another luscious lungful of smoke and wondered why I had wanted to quit. In the fenced-off yard below me, Clara, one of the dykes living on the first floor, was kneeling over the small patch of vegetable garden she was trying to get going. Since she'd moved in the month before, I'd been coming onto her whenever possible, with minimal success. We had taken a walk together, but she hadn't accepted my suggestion afterwards that we go up to my apartment for something to drink. While I smoked, I admired the curve of her ass in her fuschia drawstring pants and hoped she wouldn't notice me. I was in no mood to talk, much less flirt. I was imagining untying her pants and tugging them down past her hips when she looked up and waved, calling my name. I waved back briefly, looked away, took another drag.

My gaze wandered over to our next-door neighbors' backyard. Strung between two posts, clean laundry hung limply in the windless air. The city, or what I could see of it—rooftops, telephone poles and electric wires, laurel and fir trees, glimpses into open windows—struck me as more hushed than usual under the gray sky, as if waiting for something to happen: the wail of a police siren, a ground tremor, causing everything to set off again at some slightly different, unknown pace. I blew my last comforting lungful of smoke into the air, watching it drift and disappear, then stubbed the butt out in the tuna can I kept by the door. The invitation lay next to me on the chipped white paint of the top step. I stared at it for a few seconds and then, telling myself I was being stupid, I grabbed it and tore open the side of the envelope.

The invitation itself was simple, a card with raised lettering setting out the date, time, and place, and an RSVP card and envelope. I stared at the embossed words, my father's name paired with that of a woman I had met twice. Angela was his boss at the environmental non-profit where he was Director of Development. She wore dark suits in an office where everyone else was in khakis or jeans. She was thirty-one, closer to my age than to his. She could have once been my babysitter. At the bottom of the invitation my father had scrawled, "We hope you'll celebrate with us."

We. The word reverberated oddly inside me, a harsh clanging. I wanted another cigarette. Fingering the pack in my jacket pocket, I reread his sentence several times. Who was this "we"? Why didn't he just say "Angela and I" to avoid confusion? When he'd lived at home he had said "we" and meant him and my mother, or the three of us. In his occasional letters since he had left, five years before, I was used to reading "we" as me and him. I knew I could unfold my father's letters and trace the evolution of his relationship with this woman, but those scant pages couldn't help me make the leap to this other, outside "we." He had kicked open the battered circle in which I still imagined the three of us and walked out, collapsing it. Staring down at the card and his short, simple sentence, I saw for the first time that what he and my mother and I had been together was nothing. It was over and done with. Our family was simply the easily assembled pieces of a toy: the orphan daughter brought over from another country, the parents making vows they wouldn't keep—everyone fitting into their assigned slot until someone decided he wanted to try something new and broke the cheap plastic toy apart.

I had lit another cigarette without even noticing. I sat hunched over, my forearms on my knees, puffing away. What made him my father? Or my mother my mother? The adoption papers they had signed a few months after I was born? My childhood memories? Our relationship now? I didn't remember my birth parents; as far as I was concerned, they had never existed. If I went back to Korea, I would know no one there. Nothing would be recognizable. These were the parents I had lived with my whole life, the parents I loved. But if they could get divorced, if he could remarry, what made my bond with either of them permanent? Documents were useless. My mother kept her divorce decree in a safe deposit box right next to my adoption papers and the revoked marriage license. If my parents' feelings for each other could change, they could also stop loving me. How else could he have moved so far away, to San Diego? Why else would he work so much that I hardly ever saw him face to face? Sitting on the porch steps, watching Clara in the darkening yard below brush the dirt off her hands, gather her tools, and head inside, I tried to list the ways he had remained my father. He had paid child support. He was paying for massage school. He called me a couple of times a year. I couldn't think of anything more.

I smashed my cigarette out in the bottom of the tuna can. I wanted to grind it into my own flesh, feel its searing heat. I breathed out abruptly, breathed in again. At the massage school we had been learning to use our breath as a way to ground ourselves, sinking our energy down into the center of our pelvis where it could take root and keep us from getting carried away by negative feelings. When we were first asked to do this, I thought it was bullshit. Yet I was already breathing deeply, my body softening as it did only when I was in bed with someone else.

Now I breathed the late afternoon air slowly, drawing in from the backyard trees a tangy scent like rust. I couldn't get that grounded feeling. Maybe I was trying too hard. Somewhere in the street out front I heard a car honking. A light went on in the house next door and a man crossed from one side of the window to the other. He was home. Where was I? Even if I admitted to wanting it, there was no home to go to. Not my first home. Not my second. Now I shared an apartment with a Chinese-American man who was a bass player in a local band when he wasn't studying medicine. Answering his ad looking for a student, preferably someone neat, responsible, and Asian, I had felt like a fraud on every count. Before my interview, I had been most afraid he'd make references to Asian culture I wouldn't pick up on. As it turned out, Henry was easy to live with, but we had almost nothing in common.

How would I even recognize home now?

Natalie both fascinated and terrified me. She was a black woman in my class at the massage school, one of three other minority people in a group of twenty-five. The other two were Japanese. In the beginning I had avoided speaking to all three of them. I had hardly been able to look the Japanese women in the eye. One day when the class split up to practice strokes for the neck and shoulders, Natalie looked at me expectantly. I couldn't refuse. She lay on the table, and when I raised her head and rolled it slowly to the side, surprised at how much it weighed, she asked me, "Why do you hang out with white people all the time? Why don't you talk to your sisters?"

At first I was pissed. What right did she have to tell me what to do? But as I slid my oiled palm down the length of her neck, working the sternocleidomastoid with my thumb, I also felt let in. She breathed deeply, and I could feel the muscle under my thumb soften just a little. It was a revelation to me: I could create change in another person's body; I could help them to feel better. I had thought up to then I was learning bodywork for my own enjoyment. My realization gave me a rush of power and of something else. Gratitude. It softened me as well, let me think again about what she had said.

We exchanged a lot of information about ourselves that afternoon. She told me she was biracial: half white. I told her that I felt white, until somebody made a comment that reminded me I was not, and somebody always did. I told her that a couple of ex-lovers had said they considered me white, as though they were paying me the highest compliment. I felt hopeful, talking to her. I went home that evening and called the group she had told me about. Then I got freaked out and fell asleep for ten hours. After the day she questioned my alliances, I returned to avoiding Natalie. I was aware of her silent condemnation during our classes, only to be surprised when she caught my eye and grinned. She had a beautiful smile.

One night a couple of weeks after I received my father's wedding invitation, I went to Maud's with my ex-lover Alison and some of her friends, all white, and Natalie was there, playing pool with some of her friends, all black. I wasn't surprised to see her; I'd been wondering since before she'd approached me in class if she was a dyke. We smiled and nodded to each other, and I followed my crowd further back into the large room. They all wanted to sit at the bar drinking and scoping out the girls. With Natalie there, I felt even more self-conscious than I usually did at the clubs. For a while, Alison and I stood together at the far end of the bar with our beers. The music was loud and the room was stuffy and hazy with smoke. Alison shouted the story of how she had met her current lover, who was sitting three stools down from us, and I grinned and asked increasingly personal questions. I kept lighting up cigarettes and looking over toward the pool game, wondering which of those women was Natalie's lover. I assumed she had a lover. Once, while Alison was admitting out loud that she thought she was falling in love, I caught Natalie's eye, and she lifted her brows at me. I knew exactly what she meant: why are you hanging out with those white girls? But she wasn't making it any easier for me to cross the slowly filling dance floor between us to join her and her friends.

Besides, I wasn't white, but I wasn't black either. What made her think her crowd was "my people" more than my friends were?

When Alison rejoined her girlfriend, I pushed my way through the women milling around and stood in line for the bathroom. After peeing, I looked at myself critically in the mirror as I washed my hands. Was I attractive? It wasn't a question I had bothered with in a long time. When I looked at myself, the first thing I always focused on was my ears, which I thought stuck out too far, and the mole that had appeared a couple of years before on my temple. My hair was fairly short, cut to about the level of my chin. My face was flushed and slightly oily. I had never liked the soft roundness of my face much, but I was proud of my clear skin and wide, outgoing mouth. Many of the women I had slept with had told me they loved my mouth, which was so much fuller than their own. Natalie had full lips too, and tight, kinky hair, and large, liquid-brown eyes. She had probably never been in a white woman's bed, whereas all my women lovers had been white. Studying myself in the mirror, I had no idea what, if anything, Natalie might be attracted to in me. I took a breath and turned to leave the cramped little room.

When I emerged, I pushed through to the pool table, where Natalie and her friends had just finished a second game and were ceding the cues to another group of women. The noise of people shouting over the thudding music disoriented me. I went to the clubs to meet women, but I disliked the crowds pressing in and the jarring motion of dancing separate from my partners. The booming, mindless songs often gave me headaches. I was much more suited to silence.

As I approached, Natalie, who was yelling into the ear of one of her friends, saw me and grinned. I noticed for the first time how endearingly she dipped her head before speaking, as though she were bashful, though I guessed it had more to do with being tall. I stood in front of them as she finished whatever she was saying.

Her friend turned to look at her, and they both burst out laughing. Then Natalie introduced me to Tracy, and we shook hands, and Natalie said she needed some air, would we walk with her? Tracy wanted a beer, but I said I'd go outside with her.

The cool night air was a relief. Behind the ivy-covered wall, the muffled music seemed a world away. Across the street, I could make out cans of paint arranged in pyramids in the window display of a darkened hardware store. I lit a cigarette. We started walking toward the Haight. I felt a little awkward, uncertain. I was extremely aware of her height, her arm near mine, of our steps gradually falling into synch. I realized I knew nothing at all about this woman.

We walked for a block in silence and then I said, "Can I ask you a question?"

Natalie looked at me and grinned as if she knew what it was going to be. "Sure."

"Do you ever sleep with white women?" Only after I had asked did it occur to me that she might be offended by the suggestion.

Natalie laughed, and, fascinated, I watched her head tilt back. "Not if I can help it!"

"But you're half white," I said.

"So?"

"Aren't you rejecting a part of yourself?"

"No, I'm rejecting white women." She waited, and when I didn't say anything, she said, "Do I have to explain it to you?"

"No." But I was amazed that without white women she apparently had a large enough community of people in whom she found herself. "I went to that group you told me about," I said.

"Finally." She glanced down at me, and I saw from the sly, self-mocking curl of her smile that she was flirting with me. "And?" she prompted.

I grinned back, feeling more sure of myself, more at ease in my body as I strode beside her down Haight Street. We passed the Double Rainbow where I used to work with Alison.

"I didn't make any great discovery," I admitted, feeling I had failed somehow, as I had felt while I waited for the meeting to be over. I hadn't passed this simple test of Asian-American identification. "I tried to. There were about ten women. They all seemed to have known each other for years. I tend to have a hard time with groups, being the outsider."

We passed the free medical clinic and Reckless Records and the head shop where I had bought my bong that same summer I was scooping ice cream. "They seemed to be in the middle of a fight about whether to become more politically active or whether to continue to be a social group. I didn't say a word the entire meeting. I wasn't even that interested, to tell you the truth. Their concerns were foreign to me. I'm not into making a statement, and I'm not looking for a group to go on picnics with." I saw Natalie's frown. "No, they do other stuff, but that's what it felt like." One woman had talked about her parents' continual insistence that she marry a man who was also Korean. Another woman complained that her favorite dim sum restaurant had closed, causing the whole room to burst out laughing. I sat, bewildered, looking at each of their faces in turn and feeling despair.

"Were there any lesbians?" Natalie asked.

"Two." I couldn't tell her that they had turned me off the most with their ridiculous multisyllabic rhetoric. One of them had asked me after the meeting if I'd like to go out with a few of them for a late snack. Though I was grateful for the invitation, I knew I would have to force myself to sit through it. I told her thanks, maybe next time, but I hadn't gone back. "They didn't impress me particularly."

"You didn't give them a chance."

Natalie knew them, I realized then. Maybe she had even told her friends to expect me. I felt my face get hot. At least I hadn't been rude.

"I guess I connect with people better individually."

She looked thoughtful. "I wonder if there are any support groups for people adopted from other countries."

"No," I said, cutting her off. "I don't need a support group."

"But meeting other Asian adoptees—"

"No," I repeated. The idea terrified me. What if I met them and I still couldn't recognize myself?

"Hmmm. Well, when you're ready, I could help you look."

I glanced up at Natalie and was aware again of her height, her thick eyelashes, the scoop of her bent neck. Her hair, cut so short she was almost bald, made the shape of her head more prominent. I wanted to put my hand in her hair, feel her scalp beneath my fingers. I wasn't used to her style of kindness.

"I'll answer your earlier question, if you want," she offered. I nodded. On the side of an apartment building someone had spray-painted, "Be the bomb you throw." We walked down the hill toward Divisadero.

"I may be half white, but I was raised by a black mother. White women were raised white." She said it flatly, her voice dismissive.

"I was raised white too," I reminded her, bristling. "In a sense, I'm more white than you are."

"Yeah, you definitely are." She laughed. I wondered what she was thinking of and if I would recognize it in myself. I could feel my jealousy snaking through me: her parents, black and white, reflected who she was.

She went on, "I realized in college that I had to choose, one way or another. Not how I was perceived, because other people would take care of that for me. But how I lived inside that perception. And, more importantly, what the world looked like from where *I* stood."

We were meandering toward Fillmore by then, passing bars with darkened windows lit only by neon beer signs and a café from which a surge of voices and the bitter odor of coffee emanated. Diagonally across from a corner health food store was a storefront with "Meat Market" on its awning. The gate that had been rolled down in front of its windows was covered with graffiti. A mix of people was out on the street—heading up to the clubs on Haight, out late buying food from the health food store, waiting around. It was an odd part of town, bordered by the projects on one side and peeling stately old Victorians on the other. We stopped in front of a display of fruit in baskets. I liked the energy and light on that block. It was a border, and it was coming into its own.

Natalie said she lived nearby. I walked with her to her building. Standing on the steps, she said, "You don't have to choose anything. That's a choice too. But you can't reject your choices until you know what they are." She bent down and kissed me lightly. I followed her upstairs.

I whipped out the long cord behind me to untangle it, taking the phone to my room and closing the door. Sitting on my bed, the pillows propping me up, I settled in for the conversation. I was ready to savor every brief minute.

"It was beautiful here today," he said. "Not a cloud in the sky."

I heard my father's voice three, maybe four times a year, but I still knew it inside and out. Closing my eyes, it was possible to pretend that we were walking down a trail on Mount Tam and he was holding my hand, pointing out wildflowers and telling me their names. He'd always been proud of how quickly I learned. Sometimes I would make up silly pretend names just to tease him. Bananaberry bush. Skyhighflower. He'd giggle with me, squeezing my hand.

"So are you coming to the wedding?"

I opened my eyes. The small lamp by my bed cast a shadow against the far wall. I could hear Henry in the kitchen singing "Born in the USA" with the radio as he washed the dishes.

"I guess so," I said. I had put the wedding out of my head since I'd received the invitation three weeks before. "Do you want me to be there?"

"Of course, Min. Didn't we send an invitation? Aren't I calling you?"

I flinched at the "we." For a brief moment I felt stupid, as though I hadn't remembered the name of a simple lupine. Then I was angry. How was I supposed to know what he wanted from me now, after all these years when he'd made no effort to see me? I didn't count his money for the train to visit him a total of three times in five years as "effort." I had initiated every trip, willing to give up days of school and to lie to my mother in order to work around his busy schedule.

"Maybe you feel you have to," I answered.

"Min, sweetheart, what's this all about? You're my daughter. I love you. Of course I want you to be at my wedding. Angie and I want to see more of you from now on. I will admit it's odd asking my grown-up child to watch me get married." The idea seemed to strike him as amusing, but it only made me sad.

"I'm not technically your child," I reminded him. I couldn't keep myself from trying to hurt him.

"Yes, you are," he responded angrily. "Don't do that to yourself. Remember when you would tell me about what one or another of your classmates called you, when I gave you a backrub before you went to sleep? Remember what I said to you then?"

I remembered the clean smell of the sheets, the faint rustling of Bingo, my parakeet, beneath the cloth draping his cage in the corner, my father's warm hand on my back. His touch had made the outside world shrink away to where it couldn't hurt me. Those long backrubs had been my resting place, the only time I felt what it was to be myself. When being me was easy. Clasping my hands around my knees, listening to my father's voice hundreds of miles away, I thought of my life now. I wondered for the first time if I was actually in search of just one thing: those murmured conferences, the comfort of his firm touch, my certainty of receiving such simple care again, the next night.

I couldn't answer right away. "You said they were just repeating what they heard their parents say."

"And?" he prompted.

"You knew who I was. I was your little girl." I could hear him saying it, in memory.

Now he said nothing. I listened to the crackle of static on the phone line, that slight, tenuous thread of communication.

"Dad?" I asked. "Are you happy being with Angela?"

"Yes, I am. We're very happy."

"Why weren't you happy with Mom?"

"Did she tell you that? I think she was the one who was unhappy with me."

"But you left."

Silence. "I had to, Min." I wished he would say more. I hadn't known they were fighting that much when he moved out. My mother still refused to talk about it.

"What about me?" I asked, hating myself for asking. "Why didn't you take me?"

"Sweetheart, I wanted to, believe me." He stopped speaking, and I thought for a second that the line had gone dead. "But you were settled at home, you had school, your whole life. Besides, it's hard for fathers to get custody of their kids."

"Did you even try?"

Again, the static between us crackled in my ear. I realized this would be my last opportunity to approach the subject with him. I wanted to understand what had gone wrong between them, and why he had allowed himself to drift out of my range. I knew what I wanted to hear—how he had tried to fight in court, how my mother had refused to let him visit me. Even before he spoke I knew my version wasn't true.

"It wouldn't have made a difference," he said quietly. "I had to leave you behind. I had to make a new life for myself. I couldn't be near you but not with you."

"Why not?" It came out as a squeak. I closed my eyes, squeezing them tight. I didn't want him to know I was crying. I heard him take a breath, like a hiccup. Now he wouldn't even answer me.

"There's a full moon tonight. Can you see it?" he asked after a while.

I looked up through my window, the receiver slipping. I caught it with one hand and brought it back up to my ear. Of course the sky was dark, the moon nowhere near that distorting square of glass.

"Yes," I said, wiping my nose with the back of my hand. A few months before he had left, during my spring break in eighth grade, he'd found an old book about stars up high in the living room bookcase. We went outside every night for a week and learned the constellations, memorizing their shapes in the sky. I still remembered them all, but in the city I could never see them.

"Will you be there, Min?" he asked.

"Are you asking for my blessing?" I was only half joking.

"No. I'm asking for your presence at my wedding."

I considered it seriously for the first time. I dreaded going, but I was afraid he might disappear entirely if I didn't. "Can I bring someone?"

"You mean Beth?" I had told him about Beth during our last conversation in December, two girlfriends previous.

"I don't know yet."

His voice changed, became more decisive. "I'll welcome anyone you choose to bring. So, can I count on you?"

What was the point of refusing? "Yes."

"That's my girl. We can talk more when you arrive. Listen, Angie's got dinner almost ready. I'll talk to you soon. Bear hug."

"Elephant hug," I answered without thinking.

"Whale hug."

How could whales hug without arms? It was a stupid game we had played. Into the lingering silence, he said, "Goodnight, Min." I waited. I listened to the dial tone for at least a minute before hanging up. Then I realized what his hiccups were. He had been crying too.

The next weekend I ate lunch with my mother at Café Picaro, surrounded by students loudly arguing Marxist theory and men and women drinking red wine together and blowing clouds of smoke into the air above their heads. I had managed to grab a table by the window. Across the street, a matinee was letting out at the Roxie; people wandered into the sunlight, put their hands up or pulled sunglasses from their pockets, and set off down the street. Three plump, white-haired women walked by carrying heavy shopping bags. This was my neighborhood, the land of family-owned taquerias, used appliance stores, and a few dyke-owned businesses: the Artemis Café, Old Wives Tales Bookstore, Amelia's.

I turned my attention back to my mother, who was picking at her spinach salad. She was telling me about the NOW meeting she'd just come from. We were having our monthly lunch out. We'd agreed to do this when I found a place to live, even though I still came home with my dirty laundry and let her feed me once in a while. Often, being in each other's company was still difficult for both of us. I felt sometimes as though we had known each other in some long-past, dimly remembered life. BC: Before I Came Out. It didn't matter that we had continued to live in the same house while I finished high school. It did help a little that she had been glad to have me home, and I had been relieved to be home. We had learned not to ask too much of each other. Our conversations had settled into a safe exchange of selected information. Since I'd moved out, talking to my mother was both easier and harder.

"How's your job?" she asked, pushing her frizzy hair back from her face with one hand as she fed herself a bite of spinach leaves with the other. I had often wondered why she didn't either wear her hair tied back or cut it short. It always seemed to be getting in her way.

I shrugged, looked down at my lasagna. "It's okay. I got a raise." I was a stocker at a natural foods wholesaler.

"That's great."

"It's not big," I added. I didn't want her to stop helping me with the rent.

"And massage school?"

"I'm almost through. I gave my first full-body massage two nights ago. I was nervous at first, but really the only hard part was getting from one area of the body to the next. You don't want to do it suddenly. The massage itself was like painting. You have all these colors to work with in whatever combination you want. The guy I worked on loved it."

We had set up tables all over the room, half of us working on the oth-er half, then switching. Receiving first, I'd been surprised by the extent to which I was aware of my partner's fear as I lay listening to the hum of other people's conversations. He would touch one area briefly, then lift his hands away from my body, dropping them down again suddenly in a completely different place to try a new stroke. He moved tentatively around the table, uncertain where to go next. He splashed dribbles of oil on me without noticing. With my eyes closed, I listened to him breath-ing, fast, through his mouth. I was confused by his discomfort, bewil-dered by why he would pursue massage if he was so ill at ease being in physical contact with another person's body. I loved the slide of my oiled palms over warm skin, pressing deep with my thumbs along the length of the trapezius or gastrocnemius. On him there wasn't much muscle to get hold of, so I concentrated on simple relaxation. I was careful about draping him, and conscious of watching his face and his hands for any reaction to the depth or quality of my touch. Ultimately, I lost track of time. By the end, when I quietly told him that I was done, I was exhil-arated. I had never worked at anything before that made me feel such satisfaction. The sound of my voice startled him; he was so relaxed he had fallen asleep.

My mother was looking at me with the hint of a smile on her face. I noticed the fine lines of exhaustion around her eyes and the huddle of her shoulders. "Maybe you'd like a massage sometime," I offered. "It's a nice way to take time out for an hour. And I could use the practice."

"Oh, no." She pushed her glasses further up her nose with one finger. "I don't think I could take off all my clothes and lie down naked like that."

"You're covered with a sheet. And you could leave on your underwear if you wanted."

"No, no. It seems like such a vulnerable thing to do."

"It is." I was smiling. Massage, I was discovering, was a way for me to connect with another person in a way that I most likely never could have in the context of our daily life. It brought our interaction immediately to the level of the body, where everyone was the same, and everyone was unique. "Maybe it would be easier if you went to a stranger."

"I don't know, I think that would be worse." She looked slightly apologetic.

When I had scraped up the last of the tomato sauce, I pushed my plate away. "Mom, there's something you should know."

She looked up. "You have a new girlfriend." She said it resignedly, as though she were only confirming the inevitable. A few months before, she had complained that it seemed like every time we spoke I was seeing someone new. I made it a point to inform her about most of my girlfriends, those that lasted for more than a few nights. That was all; I just let her know, as part of the conversation. She never asked for any details, or even a name. But I refused to allow her to completely ignore how my sexuality shaped my day-to-day life.

"Well, actually, I am kind of seeing someone new, but that's not what I was going to tell you."

"What, then?"

I hesitated, not sure how to phrase it. I didn't know what my mother would feel, but I wasn't eager to make it worse by rubbing it in somehow. "Dad's getting remarried."

There was another long silence. I watched my mother's face carefully, but she kept her eyes lowered as she picked up her sweating glass of Diet Coke with lemon and drank from it. I was aware of the ceaseless clink of silverware. A man's voice laughed and boomed out, "That's Gerald for you." A bead of condensation ran down the side of my mother's glass, colliding with her index finger. She put her drink down on the table carefully. She said, "When's the wedding?"

"Next month." I wasn't going to tell her anything she hadn't asked. I'd already decided that.

"Have you met her?"

"Yes."

"Do you like her?" My mother looked up, her eyes meeting mine.

I hadn't expected that question. "Not really," I answered. My mother smiled. "She's a lot younger than him, which is weird. Very serious about her work. Uptight. I don't get why he likes her."

"Well," she said, and she let out air as if she had been holding her breath. "Are you going?"

I looked down, traced a scratch in the table with my fingernail. "I don't know. He says he wants me to."

"Oh, I think you should go. You'll be sorry later not to have been part of it if you don't. It's an important event."

"Why? They're already living together."

She leaned forward, her arms folded on the table, and for a moment I thought she was going to answer, give me a lecture about my duty as a daughter and all that shit. Instead she repeated, "I think you should go. A wedding is a time of promise, of committing to one's best intentions. I wish I were going to see you get married one day."

"Mom," I warned. Why couldn't she get over it? She'd been a member of PFLAG for more than a year, talking to other parents of gay children. As much as I considered her a meeting junkie, I had been relieved that she was going somewhere else to educate herself and get support for her feelings about my lesbianism. It had been a big step for her at the time, and it helped lift some of the tension between us. But not all.

She put up a hand. "Wait. I wouldn't care if it were to a woman. I think marriage is an important institution."

"That is not what you meant. Gay people can't marry. You want me to end up with a man."

"No, Min. But I do want to see you in a committed and happy long-term relationship."

"Why? Who says I'm not happy the way I am?"

"Are you?"

I glanced out the window. From the opposite sidewalk, a woman wearing a leather jacket ran across the street. As she approached the door of the café, our eyes met. We both smiled, then looked away. I loved the possibility inherent in that smile. I loved walking around the city constantly aware of the women around me, feeling my own appeal to other lesbians. I loved being free to act on my desire every time. I didn't think my mother wanted to know this. I said, "I can't see Dad's marriage lasting very long."

She brought her hands up under her glasses and rubbed her eyes. Behind her, a line had formed at the door. "Let's go," I urged. "There are people waiting for tables." As we squeezed out the door past the standing line, I saw the woman in the leather jacket, who shot me another little smile.

Outside, we stood in the busy street. I took my sunglasses from where they hung at the front of my t-shirt and put them on. My mother squinted, holding her hand over her glasses to shade her eyes. It seemed to me that every time we had these lunches there was this moment, at the end, of emerging into the too-bright daylight, as though we had spent the last hour or two tunneling through the rocky earth, digging our separate paths in each other's direction. I had no idea if we were getting any nearer, if we would ever meet in the middle.

"Well," she said, "I wish your father all the luck in the world. I have to admit I'm curious about this woman he's marrying," she added. "But I won't ask you anything you don't want to talk about."

I shrugged. "I don't mind. I don't know that much. We're not in touch that often."

"Oh." She bit her lip, released it. "I didn't know that."

What did she think, I saw him every weekend? What had she imagined would happen once they divorced?

The day I saw Laura on her spring vacation, she wanted to spend the afternoon by the ocean, which she had missed while stuck all winter in the middle of Ohio. We walked barefoot near the water, the chilly waves lapping at our feet, leaving small pools in our footprints behind us. In the wind, wisps of Laura's long hair pulled free of her braid and blew in her

face. We watched people throw sticks into the frigid water for their dogs
and the dogs happily crash into the waves to retrieve them. We walked
down toward the Cliff House, hoping to see the seals on their rock sun-
ning themselves. Since she'd started at Kenyon the fall before, I had seen
Laura only a couple of times, on her Christmas break, before her parents
had whisked her off for a vacation on St. John. After all those months
apart, we seemed to have everything to say to each other and yet nothing.
Our friendship was intact, but it had suffered some kind of stroke in the
interim, resulting in a barely noticeable paralysis. I wondered, not for the
first time, if we had anything in common anymore.

I told her about massage school and my father's remarriage. I didn't
say much about the women I'd slept with that year, knowing she would
accuse me of being promiscuous. Turning back, with the Pacific coast
stretching south as far as we could see, Laura informed me that she had
finally lost her virginity. I was relieved by this news, and then I wondered
why she hadn't told me earlier. How long had it been since we had shared
the physical details of our sex lives? I missed that side of our friendship.
So I asked for a description of her first time, just as she had prompted
me so long ago. But the truth was I wasn't much interested, especially
after she described how he left his Jockey shorts on until the last minute,
pulling them back up again as soon as he was finished. "Do you think
that's strange?" she asked me. I said I thought it was, but on the other
hand, how would I know since I'd only gone to bed with one guy? Then
she changed the subject, and I let her.

Now it was late afternoon and we were in Golden Gate Park, slowly
making our way back toward the center of the city. The sun was at our
backs, sending our shadows shooting out ahead of us over the grassy field
we were walking through. On either side of us the fir trees let diagonal
shafts of golden light pour between them like streams of water through
the spread fingers of a cupped hand. I hardly ever came out to the ocean
or the park. I wondered why not; it was so beautiful. Laura and I walked
through a grove of redwoods, and I inhaled their piney scent mixed with

the rich odor of damp earth and was glad for the first time that day that I was with her. I turned to Laura and asked if she'd come to my father's wedding with me.

"Me?" she asked. I wondered who else she expected me to invite.

"Yeah, you. He always liked you, Laura. And it would be a lot easier for me if you were there with me."

"Are you nervous about going?" she asked.

"I just can't imagine it at all," I said. "I don't know what to expect. I need some moral support."

Laura turned her face toward me and grinned. Suddenly it was the two of us again, best friends, inseparable.

"When is it?" she asked.

I named the date in May.

She thought, then shook her head. "I can't. I've still got exams then."

I was surprised by how hurt I was. Somehow I had assumed she would go without thinking about it. I hadn't considered that she might have other commitments.

"Can't you take them earlier?" I asked anyway.

She looked at me skeptically.

"Okay," I said. The breeze off the ocean had picked up. The sun was going down. I saw the square pink dome of the De Young Museum among the trees in the distance.

It was almost dark when, on Irving Street looking for a Japanese restaurant I'd heard about, we ran into Natalie coming out of a lingerie store with a shopping bag. Since the night at Maud's that I'd gone home with her, we had slept together only a few times, always during the day. Ana, the woman she had been living with for seven years, had gotten home from visiting her parents to learn that Natalie had started up with me, and it had pissed her off. This wasn't the first time she'd cheated, Natalie told me. I didn't want to get in the middle, but Natalie insisted it would be okay if we kept it light and discreet. I never called her at home. I was glad of the limitations. I knew I could fall hard for her, and not in a good way. When we talked, I always found myself in the position of disciple, and I was uncomfortable with how completely she relished her role as my teacher. I wasn't willing to get attached to someone who assumed she knew me better than I knew myself.

On Irving Street, lit by the bright neon colors of early evening, Natalie seemed taller than ever. When she moved, she chimed with long silver earrings and bracelets on both arms. Seeing her out of context, in a neighborhood neither of us ever went, I was incredibly aroused.

"Min!" Natalie walked up to me and stopped inches away, her arm almost touching mine, her face glowing with her wonderful smile. I was suddenly acutely conscious of Laura beside me. I hadn't mentioned Natalie to her, and I had only spoken briefly of Laura to Natalie. I stood back slightly and gestured to Laura, trying to create a circle for the three of us. I said, "Natalie, I want you to meet my friend Laura. Laura, this is Natalie."

Laura smiled and said, "Hi," raising her hand from her side to shake Natalie's.

Natalie glanced at her and then away. "Min, I gave my first paid massage today!" she said, touching my arm. "Forty bucks. I'm celebrating." She dipped her head down at the bag she was carrying.

I saw how Laura's face moved from discomfort to curiosity and warmth at being introduced to a kind of bewildered shock. Natalie kept talking as though we were in a room alone. I didn't know what to do. So I did the easiest thing. I let Natalie tell me about her massage while Laura stood by. Finally I mentioned that Laura and I needed to get something to eat.

"Yeah, all right," she said. Then she bent down and kissed me, tongue and all. I meant to stop her, uncomfortable with Laura right there, but my body responded without my thinking about it. I felt the pulse in her neck under my hand. Then I pulled away.

"I'll call you," Natalie said and sauntered away down the street, her earrings swinging. I watched two men and a woman stare at her as they passed. She had not acknowledged Laura's presence once. I was furious with her. And I wanted to be walking down the street beside her.

"I'm sorry," I said, turning to Laura.

Laura kept her gaze trained down the street. "Well, I don't appreciate having to watch you make out. It seems like I'm always being reminded how easy it is for you."

I was mystified. "How easy *what* is for me? Kissing?"

She turned her face toward me; her eyes were accusing. "Being sexual. Finding someone to sleep with."

I could feel my head move back, away from her. "Wait a minute, Laura. Where is this coming from?"

She gestured with her head down the street, and we started walking. When I looked over at her, she seemed to be concentrating, her face angry and intent. "It's always been that way, Min. It's just not usually so obvious." I could hear how she was struggling for the words. I waited, biting down on my need to defend myself. "You assume that if you're attracted to someone, you'll have sex with them. And you usually do. You don't worry about whether the other person's attracted to you or whether it's a good idea in the long run or whether you have anything in common."

It was true; when I felt attracted to another woman, I was helpless to it. I loved the sexual force that brought two people so intimately into each other's orbit, even briefly. It was impossible to resist, like gravity.

Laura went on, "Maybe that person isn't available. I never expect that anything will happen just because I'm interested. I think it's kind of presumptuous, actually."

I was listening to Laura carefully. I didn't disagree with anything she had said. But I felt strangely removed from her emotion. What did she want me to do? We were different; I attracted lovers more easily than she did. I didn't feel as rejected when we broke up. I didn't need as much from other people as she seemed to. For a moment I felt guilty, but there was nothing I could do.

"What about this guy you're with now, Ethan?" I asked. "What about Nick and Devin and Al?" I added, referring to guys she'd gone out with when we were in school. I knew I had to be careful with her, but I kept going. "Guys have always liked you, Laura. You're pretty and you're fun to be with and you're sexy too. I was jealous of you all the way back in junior high because you had boobs and I didn't." She smiled, looking down at the sidewalk. We stopped at a corner to wait for the light. I took a breath. "But you don't let guys in. You keep yourself hidden. You don't put out the energy that you're available. Sexually, and emotionally too." I wanted her to understand what I meant, but at the same time I knew there was a point beyond which she would stop hearing what I was telling her.

The stoplight changed, and I started to cross. Laura didn't follow. I went back to where she stood, her hands in the pockets of her painters pants, staring at the white pedestrian lines on the street.

I stood in front of her, trying to coax her to look up. "Have I hurt your feelings?"

"Not exactly."

Right then, I felt how much I loved Laura—not in the passionate, hungry way I had three years before, just loved her, pure and simple. I didn't often feel this forceful welling up of affection for another person. It was almost painful.

I pulled her arm, freeing her hand, took it in my own and led her across the street. "I'm sorry," I said. "The last thing I want to do is hurt you. But I thought you needed to hear it."

She shifted her hand in mine for a better fit, and I thought that in tenth grade I would have been ecstatic if she'd held my hand. Back then I would have misinterpreted the gesture, wanting so much for our intertwined fingers to mean more than they actually did.

"I'm not sure I know what you mean," she told me. "I don't know how to be any more open than I am."

I squeezed her hand. It wasn't as though I could teach her any technique. On the street, people passing glanced down at our linked hands and looked away. I smiled at them anyway.

I said, "I think you're *very* open, at least with me. But I've known you for a long time. It's hard for you to trust that a stranger could really like you. Especially when you're attracted and want to establish something that might last. Am I right?" I wasn't sure; she had already accused me of being presumptuous.

"Yes," Laura said reluctantly. She stopped, pulling my hand, in front of a restaurant. "This is it."

It was impossible to see inside. Paper screens were set in all the windows. Behind them a warm yellow light invited us in. I was ravenous. I said to Laura, who was studying the menu, "You have a lot of integrity, Laura. And a good heart. Someone will recognize that."

"You think so?"

I took my hand from hers and put both my arms around her shoulders, holding her close. She held me too, swaying slightly from side to side. My cheek against her hair, I realized I was smiling. "I know so," I said.

Surely there was one other person in the world who would love Laura the way I did.

Natalie brought her head up to mine and kissed me, her mouth tasting of my own wetness.

"Mmm, you taste good," I said.

"I thought so too."

Her breath was warm and slightly sweet. The fingers of one hand still inside me, she held me while another shudder rippled up my spine. I could feel the lazy grin on my face. My entire body was in a state of suspended animation. I was glad I hadn't let my annoyance with Natalie's behavior on the street stop me from sleeping with her again. Laura, in my position, probably would have refused to speak to her. Maybe if Laura let go of her scruples once in a while, she'd have better luck with guys. I immediately regretted the thought, knowing it was unfair.

"Do you need to go home soon?" I asked. I craned my neck around to look at the clock. 10:07 p.m. Natalie had told Ana she was going to the movies with a friend. I wondered if Ana had believed her. Through the wall, in the other bedroom, I could hear Henry and his girlfriend Karen giggling.

"Yeah, but not right away." Slowly, Natalie eased her hand out, pressing a sweaty thigh between my legs. I shivered, though I wasn't cold. She was good at keeping contact, at not leaving a part of the body where she had been without warning. She would do well as a massage practitioner. She licked each finger, closing her eyes as she did it.

"So tell me something," she said. "You've been talking about your dad's wedding every time we get together. How come you didn't ask me to go along?"

"Would you have gone?" I asked, astonished. It seemed pretty clear to me that our relationship didn't extend to weekends away together. But I hadn't even considered asking her.

She ignored my question. "I'm your lover, right?" she asked.

I nodded.

"The only one you've got at the moment, hmmm?"

Again I nodded. Jane didn't count.

"Are you afraid to show up with a woman lover? A black woman?" She was looking down at me searchingly, waiting to see what I would say.

I took her sticky hand in mine, clutching it against the pillow above my head. "Do you want me to ask you just because you're my black lesbian lover? Do you want to go so you can make a statement? I don't." I released her hand and rolled us both over onto our sides.

"No," she said, frowning, which made me want to kiss the rumpled furrow between her brows. "I'm not interested in whether your father and all his white friends can deal with me, I'm interested in whether you can deal with me. How are you going to present yourself in that world? Why do you want to play it safe?"

I propped my head up on one hand. Why did she think she knew what was best for me? "I can't play it safe, Natalie. Most of those people won't even know who I am or why I'm there. I asked Laura to go because she's my best friend."

Natalie rolled her eyes and lay on her back, pulling a pillow under her head.

I was tired of this bullshit. "Fuck it, Natalie, what's the problem? You don't like Laura because she's white?"

She looked at me hard. She didn't move, but I could see the shrug in her shoulders. "I have no reason to like her."

"You didn't give her a chance! She's my closest friend. Did you think that would change?"

Her gaze suddenly became remote, guarded, her eyes half hooded by her lids. She looked almost as disinterested as when she had met Laura.

I sat up, scrambling to the edge of the bed. "It's getting late. You should leave." I stood up, opened the creaky door, and left the room. Naked, I felt my way down the hall in the dark to the bathroom.

When I came back, Natalie was gone. I switched off my bedside lamp and lay in the dark, wide awake, still furious. Outside the window, the orange slice of the waning moon hovered behind a drift of clouds. I looked down at my body stretched out on the bed, silvered by moonlight. My legs were long and sturdy, my chest almost flat with two button nipples, my stomach taut above the bush of black curly hair. In the room next door, Karen moaned, then moaned again. There was a bump against the wall, then Henry said something I couldn't hear. Then, after a long silence, Karen's voice rose and called out in inarticulate syllables, wafting on a breeze of pleasure. Smiling, I touched myself, and soon I was calling out, quietly, too. Listening to another woman come always made me happy.

I went to my father's wedding alone. I took the train down the coast to San Diego and arrived the night before in time for the rehearsal dinner at the bride's parents' house. Most of the guests were my father's and Angela's friends or from Angela's family; the only person I knew, vaguely, was a friend of my father's from his old job in San Francisco who now worked in LA. I didn't recognize him when he said my name and shook my hand. After he identified himself, he said, "Isn't this wonderful? I've never seen your father looking so happy." I merely stared at him. Didn't I want him to be happy? At that moment I wished I hadn't come. It could only get worse. My father's friend asked me a few questions about myself which I answered in monosyllables. When he saw I wasn't going to help him out, he wandered away in search of a drink. Even though I had stopped smoking, I bummed a cigarette from a woman sitting on a couch petting the dog.

That night Dad never left Angela's side. I barely got a chance to hug him hello before his attention was pulled away by someone else, and Angela and I were left standing together, face to face. She still wore suits, but perhaps in honor of the occasion this one was a peach color. Her pearls nicely set off the tone of her skin around her clavicle.

"Well," she said brightly. I looked up at her face. Why would my father want to marry someone like her? I couldn't figure it out. "I'm so glad you could come, Min. I hope you'll visit us more in the future. I really want to get to know you better. You know, you're always welcome in our house."

"You could come visit me," I suggested, thinking that maybe with her influence I could finally get Dad up to San Francisco.

"That's nice of you, Min, but we're awfully busy. We're not taking our honeymoon until the fall, when things at work ease up a little." She seemed proud of this. She gulped from her drink, something that smelled like floor wax. "Oh God, do you think anyone's enjoying this party? How's the massage business going?"

"I graduated a few weeks ago, so I'm certified now."

"It sounds like a fun thing to do, taking a course for a few months. You'll probably make tons."

"I really don't care about the money," I said.

"Listen," Angela said, laying a hand on my shoulder confidingly, "if you decide you want to go to college after all, I have some very well-placed connections. You'll have no trouble getting in." I realized as she spoke that her working for a non-profit had nothing to do with wanting to save the environment. I remembered one of my father's letters in which he wrote that Angela had gotten her MBA from Harvard immediately after college. She looked around the room appraisingly. She turned to my father to whisper quickly into his ear, and then she hustled him off to take care of some problem that needed fixing. The woman he had been speaking with and I smiled helplessly at each other, and she shook her head and turned away.

It was worse the next morning, when the caterers had to be directed and the putting up of the decorations overseen. I tried to ask my father if we'd have any time to talk alone, and, distracted, he smoothed down his moustache with one knuckle while watching the serving tables being unfolded and said maybe the next day, before I left. Then he excused himself and walked off to supervise where the tables were supposed to go. I kept telling myself I couldn't expect his full attention today of all days.

The wedding was held outside, in the afternoon, in a huge garden behind an old mansion of a hotel that overlooked the ocean. The ceremony itself took place at a corner bower where the trellises were woven with white silk ribbons and two huge palm trees presided overhead. My father looked spare and nervous and surprisingly handsome in his tux. Angela carried baby's breath and wore a simple, long white dress. Over her newly wavy hair she had a headdress with a train. She let it trail behind her on the grass, and, at the altar, turned to gather it up, letting it fall in a heap beside her. Seeing her face as she turned, her wide-set eyes and delicate, pointed chin, I found myself thinking that if she weren't marrying my father I might have asked her out myself. She turned back to the minister, and I tried to concentrate on the ceremony. All around me people were smiling. I heard a woman whisper to her husband, "They wrote the vows themselves. Isn't it moving?" I realized there were very few single people there, and no children. Just a lot of straight couples, mostly married, all white, there to welcome the happy couple into the fold. I missed Laura, wishing she had been able to come with me. Then I realized that some day I'd have to go to *her* wedding. She wanted this particular brand of acceptance, this social approval. She thought being married sealed the commitment. I was boiling hot in the silk tunic and loose pants my father's check had allowed me to buy. A man in front of me shifted and blocked my view. I stood on tiptoe, craning to see over his shoulder. I couldn't even hear my father and Angela exchange their vows. The light wind from the ocean blew away their words.

The reception was a complete farce. I stood waiting a long time in line to be received by the wedding party, which was only my father and Angela and his best man and her bridesmaid. My father had tears in his eyes after he hugged me, but I didn't know what they meant. Was he glad, in the end, that I was there? Was he that happy to be married again, to someone other than my mother? He introduced me as his daughter to the couple in front of me and the man behind me. They all looked at me, astonished, and the woman said she didn't know he had a daughter. Angela hugged me too, an exuberant embrace during which I felt her breasts through her wedding dress, soft and ample. Afterwards, I went directly to the drinks table and asked the sandy-haired surfer boy in a suit standing behind it for a Scotch on the rocks. I'd never had Scotch before—I'd discovered long ago that I didn't react well to hard liquor—but it was a drink I remembered all the adults having at my grandparents' house in Rhinebeck.

The garden had a series of walks, and down every one vases had been placed, full of fresh-cut gladioli and lilies. Tables with white linen cloths and table settings were arranged every few yards so that people could move around and eat where they wanted. In the center of the garden a band had set up in front of a large area inlaid with blue and green tiles. I walked around for a while, testing myself on the names of the shrubbery while gulping the stinging scotch. Then the first notes of a big band tune started up. I went back to the drinks table to get another Scotch before helping myself to food.

I found a seat at a table with two older couples. One of the men I was sitting next to, portly with long steel-gray hair, turned out to be Angela's uncle. His name was Morris, his wife's was Jill. I was surprised when he turned his full attention to me, ignoring the conversation Jill was in the middle of with the other couple, who hadn't bothered to introduce themselves.

"This must be kind of tough for you," he said. "Your parents got divorced five years ago, didn't they?"

"Yeah. Sometimes I still can't believe it."

"I can imagine. On our side of the family, we're happy for Angie. She's over thirty already, and Jonathan's a terrific guy. But it's more complicated for you."

"Yeah, well. I don't know Angela. Maybe she's great for him. I hardly see him since he left. I don't know much about his life. The truth is I feel like I've lost him completely." I felt tears brim over. I wiped my cheeks with my fist, furious with myself. The Scotch was already affecting me.

Morris watched me, his bushy gray eyebrows pulled together. "I don't know if this will help you. I've gotten to know Jonathan a bit over the last two years. When we get together, he always talks about you. He misses you, very much. It sounds like you were extremely close. He told me once that when your mother and he agreed the marriage was over, he realized he couldn't face living nearby. It would have been too painful to be a part-time father, picking you up every other weekend, hoping all the gifts he gave you might make up for his not being at home. For him it was all or nothing. Don't think less of him for that." He paused. My tears kept spilling over. "I'm sorry, maybe I shouldn't have said anything." He pulled a handkerchief from his jacket pocket and handed it to me.

I took it, dabbing my face. I saw Jill glance at me worriedly. I smiled at her, folding the handkerchief.

"We were just talking about Acapulco," she said to Morris and me. Unwillingly, I let myself be pulled into this stream of conversation. I had no appetite, but I kept drinking.

As the sun went down, bathing the tall palm trees in an orange-pink glow, floodlights came on and the catering staff went from table to table lighting candles in clear glass lanterns. The ocean breeze felt good against my clammy skin. It seemed as if the approaching night made the salt air more pungent, and I breathed it in deeply, relaxing in spite of myself. I liked the luxury of this setting. I might never be in a place this nice again. I wondered how much the evening had cost and who had paid for it. When the bandleader made an announcement, we all turned to watch my father dance with his new bride. It was a slow song, maybe a waltz. He took her hand and put his other hand around her waist, looking into her face tenderly. I stood up and went to refill my drink.

When I came back, the other couple sat at the table by themselves, bickering. I looked for Morris and Jill and saw them on the dance floor. The woman at the table was fussing with her husband's lapels. He seemed to be explaining to her how she should have ironed his suit at the hotel. I sat down across from them, sipping my Scotch and watching Jill and Morris do what I imagined to be the foxtrot, though I wasn't sure where this impression came from. They didn't have much style, but they were enjoying themselves enormously. I grinned. The woman stood and tried to pull her husband up with her. "Come along, darling, I want to dance," she coaxed. They disappeared into the throng.

I had lost sight of Morris and his wife, as well as of my father and Angela. At the other tables that I could see, people chatted in groups, some angled excitedly toward each other, others leaning expansively back in their chairs, holding forth. No one else was alone. The candles on the tables had an odd halo. I was getting drunk.

I sat back and gulped the last of my drink and wished I had gotten someone in San Francisco to come with me. Natalie would have been an excellent choice, if I hadn't driven her away. We could have walked around holding hands and made out in the arbor where my father had kissed his new wife. We could have made out on the dance floor. These straight white people all needed a little shaking up. I looked around at the women at the other tables, considering which one I would ask to dance. I would take her hand and lead her to the dance floor. The night wasn't over yet. I stood up to get myself another drink.

I turned over, and the late sun woke me up. I moved my head and groaned. I had a massive headache. I could hardly open my eyes; they felt dry and swollen. My mouth was parched too. My empty stomach roiled uneasily. I tried to go back to sleep but after a while gave up and opened my eyes. I didn't recognize the room I was in. It was a hotel room but not mine. Underneath the light blanket, I discovered I was wearing a man's undershirt. My silk tunic and pants were draped over a chair near the bathroom, ruined by large water stains. I realized I must have thrown up on myself, at least once. I wondered who had tried to soak it out.

I couldn't remember anything about the night before. I had a vague memory—or had it been a dream?—of my father yelling at me, his face red with anger, while I shivered in the wind. I was sure about having sat with Morris and Jill at dinner. After that there was nothing; I couldn't bring it back. Concentrating only made my headache worse.

I was splashing water on my face in the bathroom when the hotel room door opened and Morris looked in. He entered the room when he saw the empty bed and then stopped when he noticed me standing, my hands and face dripping, in front of the sink.

"Oops, sorry. I wanted to check on you. Jill has gone out for a little while and left me in charge." He shrugged and grinned, as though no one should attempt such a reckless act. I liked him.

"Is this your shirt?" I asked, plucking at the front of my makeshift nightwear.

"Yes," he said, averting his eyes. I couldn't tell if he was embarrassed to have lent me his undershirt or to see me wearing it. I crossed the room and sat back in bed, pulling the covers up. He relaxed visibly and sat down on the edge of the chair where my ruined tunic was draped.

"How are you feeling?" he asked.

"Like someone ran over me with a convoy of trucks. Do you have any aspirin?"

He looked confused for a moment, then put up his index finger. "Jill does. It may take me a moment to find it. I'll be back." He hefted himself up and left the room, leaving the door ajar behind him.

I lay back against the pillows, trying to ignore the slow heaving in my stomach and instead concentrate the pain in my head into one small area. There was a knock at the door. "Still here," I called, expecting Morris.

It was my father. He was wearing shorts and a polo shirt and sandals, and his eyes had large circles under them. He didn't look particularly happy for a newlywed.

"Hi," he said from the open door. "Can I come in?"

"Sure," I said, sweeping my arm before me, indicating that he should make himself at home. He approached and sat at the edge of the bed beside me. Briefly, I wondered how long it had been since he last did that, when he would come in to say goodnight and give me my backrub before I went to sleep. The truth was he had stopped some time before he actually left, somewhere around sixth or seventh grade. My father sat hunched over, his arms crossed. He appeared to be thinking hard. Maybe he had a hangover too.

Finally he looked up at me. "You don't feel so hot, do you?"

I shook my head, and pain shot through my skull.

"Well," he said, "Angie would probably be pleased."

I sat up straighter. "What do you mean? Why? Did I say something offensive to her last night?" Angela seemed like the type who got easily upset.

"You don't remember what you did?" He looked disbelieving.

I was careful not to shake my head again. "No. After about seven or eight o'clock last night, I draw a complete blank."

He looked away from me. I realized his unhappy expression was a look of disapproval, almost distaste. I began to be alarmed.

"Dad, what happened?" I asked.

He put one hand up to his moustache, tracing each side with his thumb and forefinger. This was difficult for him, I could tell. "You made a pass at Angie."

"I did?" A part of me was pleased. What shocking behavior of mine had they interpreted as a come-on? "What, you mean I asked her to dance and she couldn't take it?"

He frowned. "No, Min, she was flattered that you asked her to dance. I mean after the dance you invited her up to your hotel room. Then you tried to kiss her. In front of everyone."

Could I have done that? The thudding in my head wouldn't stop. I knew the answer was yes.

He still wouldn't look at me. "Min, I'm sorry to have to say this, but you brought it on yourself. I don't think you should come down to see us for a while. Angie doesn't forgive easily once someone's on her shit list."

"But, Dad, I was drunk. I didn't know what I was doing." I winced. Where the fuck was Morris with the aspirin? I couldn't have this conversation while my head was splitting apart.

He sighed and put his hands flat on his knees, hoisting himself up to a standing position. He was like a boss firing an employee, not like a father who supposedly adored his only child. "There's nothing else to say." He was looking at me now, his hands casually stuffed into his shorts pockets. "You embarrassed me and you hurt me. Not to mention Angie."

I couldn't stand the way he was gazing at me, as though I was some foreign object like a large insect he had found among the clothes in his suitcase. I put my hands up to the sides of my head, trying to hold it together. I was almost in tears from the pain. "I can't defend myself, Dad."

"You're right. It's indefensible." I remembered the times I'd gotten in trouble as a kid by dumping out and hiding the contents of his wallet, or demanding more candy, more time to play on the swings, more stories at bedtime, testing the limits of his love. It was in his saying yes or no, consistently and constantly defining the boundaries of our relationship, that I knew he wouldn't disappear. All or nothing, Morris had said. He almost looked like the father I remembered, but not quite. He turned and left the room.

I thought I might be sick again. Beneath my skull the pain was relentless. I had blown it. I had gone and fucked it all up. I had lost him in one single night. We would never be close, we wouldn't even be comfortable in each other's presence again, and it was my fault. If it hadn't been for the steady drumming inside my head, I would have screamed as loud as I could until somebody came running to shut me up.

PART TWO

1985

He comes to me like a mouth
speaking from under several inches of water.
I can no longer understand what he is saying.
He has become one
who never belonged among us, someone
it is useless to think about or remember.

—GALWAY KINNELL

Weeks ago, I said, I want to be only happy
with you, and you said, There are always other
feelings.

—HONOR MOORE

To survive the Borderlands
You must live sin fronteras
be a crossroads.

—GLORIA ANZALDÚA

CHAPTER 7

Min

Summer 1985

I FOLD THE SHEET DOWN across her hips, tucking it between her buttocks and the table. Her stomach is like a bowl of dough, rising gently as she breathes. Her breasts lie flat on either side of her chest. Her skin is dappled by sunlight falling through the trees outside the long, open windows. I pour almond-scented oil into my palm. I glance at her face. Her eyes are closed, her head is tilted slightly away from me. Her eyebrows are drawn together; the ridge between them looks like a frown. Her skin is pale for a white woman, as though she never goes out in the sun. She has dark circles beneath her eyes. I'm not sure if they have always been there. Her frizzy hair has silver threads now, but it's the way it springs off her head that I'm fascinated by. Why did I never notice these things when I was young? I rub my hands together, warming the oil. I bring them slowly to her stomach, resting them side by side on her soft, pinkish-white skin, then press in deeper. Other people have told me how powerful it must be to give massages to the woman whose body you came from. Well, I wasn't born from this body. But it's true she is my mother.

With the flat of my palms I begin a circular rocking that grows to a wider stirring motion, hand over hand. There are four distinct layers of muscle in the belly; I was tested on them in massage school when I graduated three years ago. In my mother, I can feel each sheaf of muscle as it holds itself hard against me. Most days I feel no change, but today

something is different. Her stomach is like a balloon deflating, letting
my hands sink further down.

Behind me in the kitchen, the refrigerator begins a low hum. I can
hear the clock too, but I don't need it to know I've been working for about
an hour. The shapes of sunlight through the leaves flicker on the woven
cotton rug, on the windowsill. I look up. My hands continue their easy
dance. Outside, the bay leaves, with the June sun shining through them,
are bright green, translucent, imbued with settled calm. A wind picks
up; they flutter, softly rustling. The sky beyond, what little I can see, is
a deep blue. Blue, green, white walls, the burgundy of the sheet beneath
which my mother lies. The weight of my hands, following her body's lead.

Two months ago, my mother asked me to give her these weekly massages, thinking they might ease her chronic headaches and the churning
in her stomach that is new and she says is getting worse. She said she felt
comfortable with me. She said she was reluctant to receive a massage for
the first time from someone she had never met. I was gratified. I wanted
a chance to move beyond my brief visits home, our monthly lunches out
sitting on opposite sides of a table. I was tired of all our talking. And I
wanted to be able to give her something without seeming to offer it. We
agreed on a fee and a time. Both of us were relieved, I think, to establish
the boundaries of a professional relationship.

The first thing I discovered was that her skin was touch-starved. At
the end of her third massage, she told me that she wished she could lie
beneath my hands for days at a time. That was a big admission for my
mother, to want that kind of extravagance for herself. Even with Lloyd,
her new "beau" as she calls him, she seems physically wary. She doesn't
touch him in my presence, not for comfort or out of affection, much less
desire. When she confided to me her craving for—as she sees it—the
luxury of received touch, it was the first time I had any clue my massage
was helping her.

But she couldn't tolerate the weight of my hands pressing beyond
the surface of her skin, even on her back where most people ask for the

deepest work. I like to begin there with long, firm strokes, then go in deeper, gathering the muscles between my hands, then press my thumbs along them. If there has still been no release, I will use the bony point of my elbow, guiding it carefully with my other hand to avoid the fragile vertebrae. My mother would hold her breath even before the petrissage, hunching her shoulders as though she were protecting herself from harm.

It isn't often a client resists so forcefully, or rather the client's body; my mother wasn't aware she was pulling away from me until I told her. Most of my clients are relieved when I focus on their areas of discomfort, marveling that I can zero in on their pain right away. Those places are easy to find even without asking. It's like running your fingers over a topographical map: you can't miss the mountains. My clients might say, "That's sore there, can you tell?" while I'm working on a muscle that's as intractable as an iron rod. My mother's entire body was like a suit of armor, not highly muscled but hard and unmoving nevertheless. Those first weeks, I was careful to ask her how she liked the pressure I was using as I varied my depth, trying to find a way in. I worried there was something I was doing that hurt her. I kept asking her to breathe, then reminding her that breath is not forced, it is allowed. She said the massages felt wonderful, while I became frustrated by the stillness with which she held her body. I could feel no change, no softening, under my hands. I thought I was wasting my time, and I wished she had asked some highly recommended stranger from Marin County to work on her instead of having me drive all the way up from the city.

But now I know her body, its subtle messages and miniscule movements. I can feel its limits, and I don't try to push past them. Watching her face and listening to her breath, I can alter the depth of my touch without asking. Whatever makes her shoulders sore, her head ache, I know now I am the means of relief, not the cause. Maybe it was merely coming back, staying with her because she wanted it, that allowed me to shift my expectations. And she, for her part, has less need to keep me out.

This, too, happens at the level of the body. In our speaking life, we have never been in such accord.

As I knead my mother's stomach, smooth it, and then work gently in under her ribs where I encounter tightness like a clenched fist in everyone I massage, I can almost feel the insistent pressure of my fingers just below my own heart. Suddenly, my body longs to be touched. I breathe in, filling my lungs with air. A moment later, my mother takes a deep, slow breath. It raises her ribcage, making more room for me underneath. I hold my fingers still beneath the bone—I can usually tell when she has had enough—and I look at her face. For the first time I see a liquid glimmer between her closed eyelids. In the whole of my life with her, almost twenty-two years, I have never seen my mother cry. She clamps her face down against her tears, as if she believes her determination can make her feelings disappear. I've wondered for a long time if she might be depressed. She doesn't tell me how she's feeling. That's one of the places we still don't go. I know she can get anxious, that small setbacks can seem like catastrophes. But something else is going on now, something more. I wonder if she knows what has brought up her tears. And if she knows, will she ever tell me? Or is it enough to be able to acknowledge it to herself?

I back off, retreating to her belly, circling with the flat of my hands. She breathes in again, then lets her breath float out. I am not imagining this; her lashes are wet. A rare tenderness for her washes through me. I don't need to know her reason. I can feel tears prick my eyes too. I look away, out the window, at the leafy shade of the laurel bay covering us, sheltering us. Perhaps I should be concerned about her, but instead I feel that something good has just occurred.

I finish with long strokes across her thighs up over her hips to the center of her abdomen, then I reach both hands around her waist until they meet beneath her spine. This is hard for me to do from the side of the table, off balance. I have to rely solely on the strength of my arms and hands. But I do it occasionally, waiting, waiting, then sliding my hands up and around, because my mother has told me it feels like being held, and because I have learned how important it is to connect the back and front, binding the body together.

Sometimes with my clients, I work up along the sternum to the muscles of the chest above the breasts. I look for as many ways to touch whole lengths of the body, to bring sensation from one area to another. Women usually come to be massaged because of an ache in their back or difficulty turning their head, some one reason that they want me to make disappear. They have no idea until the acute pain is relieved that they hurt somewhere else or that a part of their body feels nothing at all. Sometimes they become aware that their physical body is holding emotional pain. The trauma may have been stored for years. I wasn't trained to be a therapist or to make diagnoses, but I do know how to listen, to remain present with my clients as the new area is discovered and the change slowly takes place. I try to connect for them the body's map, to show them through touch that they are not made up of separate pieces.

Today, however, I sense my mother's continued resistance in the area around her chest: heart and breasts and muscles for holding. So I slide one hand to her hip and place the other flat on the opposite shoulder, pushing my hands apart for a gentle stretch. I learned that this balances a person's energy, but I like it simply to break the symmetry of the massage, to suggest a different kind. Then I do the same on the other side. A trickle of sweat tickles beneath my armpit. Last, I rest my hands firmly on her abdomen, rocking slightly, then gently lift them off.

Drawing the sheet up over her chest, covering her crescent breasts, the vulnerable place between them, I am reminded of last night, bending over Madeleine's naked body. I ran my fingers along the valley between her breasts before taking each nipple, one by one, into my mouth. For a moment, I am disoriented, lost between the present and the past. I blink, pouring oil into my hand. Then I take hold of my mother's wrist beneath the sheet and ease her arm out and spread the oil up one side and back down the other. I enjoy my memories of sex, almost as much as I enjoy having it. Madeleine is a new lover, a friend of an ex. She's moving to New York at the end of the summer to start graduate school, which gives our relationship a little extra kick, a bittersweet edge because there's no future together to look forward to or wrangle about. It doesn't matter whether I like her. Last night, when I felt Madeleine's nipple thicken under my tongue, I slid my palm down her body again, across her round hips, then pressed harder, kneading the skin of her buttocks.

I've lost my focus. Yet my hands go on, sure of their terrain. Does my mother sense some change in me, that I have left her momentarily? I look at her face as I knead the fleshy underside of her arm. The frown between her eyebrows is gone. Do my memories pull me inside them, altering the character of my touch? Can she sense my remembered desire? She is completely still. I don't know what that means.

Sex comes up sometimes between my clients and me. I notice the change in their breathing, in their bodies, or occasionally in mine. A couple of women have wanted to act on their arousal, and so we've talked about it as I continued working on them, careful not to change the quality or the pace of my strokes. I've told them the way they feel is a natural response to being touched, and as we've talked my hands on their bodies have been firm and unambiguous. More often with clients, nothing needs to be said. Somehow, they discover on their own that the pleasure of being touched is its own reward.

But this is different: it is a question of attention. I could give a full-body massage blindfolded, but could I give one without full consciousness, my mind on something other than the woman lying before me on the table? I have had massages from bodyworkers who seemed impatient, in a hurry to finish and move on to the next client in a string of clients booked one after the other. I have had massages from people whose main interest was to talk about themselves. One woman repeated the same motion on the arch of my foot for far longer than was necessary, apparently immobilized by her thoughts. But I didn't know *what* she was thinking; her sadness or glee or lust or rage wasn't communicated to me through her hands. Only that she was not with me. I do feel caring. When I'm receiving bodywork from my friend with whom I trade, I feel more focused on. She works in response to my body's particular needs. There is a gentleness that lets me know I am loved. I wonder if my mother can feel that from me.

Since I began working on her, other bodyworkers have told me they would be uncomfortable massaging their parents. They are afraid of feeling aroused or of their parent being turned on. Friends have asked me, Don't you forget sometimes that the body you are touching is your mother's and not Madeleine's?—or Lynn's or Annabeth's or whoever I'm seeing at the time. Laura asks me this. Ever since she came home from Kenyon last month, newly graduated and set free, she has been very curious about my massage practice. Last week she asked how I, of all people, can possibly touch another person without it becoming sexual. I was pissed off by her almost hostile tone. But I rose to the challenge. Find out for yourself, I said, knowing I couldn't make her understand with words that there are many kinds of touch. Each person's body is a different size, color, shape, proportion. I never get confused about who is under my hands.

Last weekend I gave Laura her first massage. I expected her to be shy about her body, a little afraid to be touched, like my mother. She surprised me. She draped herself on the table as though she'd been receiving bodywork for years. Then she surprised me again. As I worked the knots in her rhomboids and across the fibers of her chunky calves, I felt her body sink into that place of near-mindless relaxation. I was happy to be giving Laura this gift I knew she received as one. I was glad she would now know exactly what I did for work and that I did it well. Then I became aware of her longing. For me. She was attracted to me. I wouldn't have picked up on it during one of our walks in the city, but her body made it obvious. And it wasn't the massage itself that was turning her on; I can tell the difference. She wanted me to touch her as a lover.

I freaked out. I faltered for a moment, forgetting which direction I was moving in. Then I pulled back into myself. I ignored the tension building in the room. I worked steadily, professionally. I hoped she would stay quiet and take her feelings away with her. But I couldn't help my body's response: her desire aroused me. It wasn't until after I was finished, washing my hands in the bathroom, that I realized I hadn't convinced Laura of anything.

My mother snores loudly. Startled, I flinch. I have been in another place completely. Unusual for me. She opens her eyes and gazes groggily up at me. I am working on her other arm now, my weight shifting from foot to foot, my hips swinging slightly. At least my body goes on. I haven't stayed in one area repeating the same stroke.

"I fell asleep," my mother says. "Sorry."

"Don't apologize. It's your massage."

"I missed it. Did you do my other arm already?"

I nod. "You didn't miss it. The body remembers."

She closes her eyes. I can't tell whether she believes me. *My* body remembers everything: how it felt to yearn for Laura in tenth grade, even before I understood that my desire would change my life. How it felt to climb out of her parents' hot tub after realizing Laura couldn't love me back the same way. Those memories seem very distant to me now. My adolescent attraction to Laura was plowed under a long time ago. I don't want to dredge up those old feelings; they belong to another time and a younger, isolated me. I am no longer that girl. I am the woman whose body remembers how it felt to find myself at last in Alison's bed, and then Gina's, and then Amber's, to discover that the world was much larger than high school and there were other women I could be close to besides Laura.

I rest my mother's elbow on the table and bring her palm up to face me. With my thumbs, I work in circles. I concentrate on the broad pad of thenar muscles below her thumb, then move up the lumbricals in the channel between each finger bone. I feel an ache in my own palms and wrists. I am clenching. One by one I shake out each hand, the way my mother used to shake down the thermometer. I lower her palm and, starting with her pinkie, wrap each finger inside my fist and pull, gently, until the finger slips out. I move her hand up and down, small movements, then side to side. The wrist is made up of eight separate bones. In my well-worn anatomy text, they look like pebbles, the small, pitted kind I sometimes find on Ocean Beach glistening in the wake of a wave. The kind I hold in my pants pocket while I walk, my fingers ceaselessly moving over its surface. My hands are always restless.

Another thing about Laura: she's straight. I've been flirted with by straight women, and I end up feeling like an experiment, a dare they've set themselves, a story they can take back to their boyfriends. I can't open myself to her again only to have her back out. And if we did happen to get involved, what then? There's a reason I don't sleep with straight women, the ones who want to go through with it. I have no interest in bringing Laura out. And maybe she'd decide she wanted to be with men after all. I'm not looking to be her coach, her advisor. She should have already gotten their help at college.

Why is it so hard for me to stay focused? When I have finished with my mother's arm, I try to shake it side to side, holding her wrist as though ringing a bell. My mother has retrieved some part of herself, some control or necessary attempt at it; her arm hangs awkwardly, tightly hinged. For a moment I am impatient. *Relax*, I want to command her. Then I smile to myself, remembering saying exactly that when I was first certified, until an early client told me, "You can't force it, you know." And then it struck me as funny: as though the body's softening can be demanded by someone else. The only answer is to bring the client's awareness to the fact that they are holding themselves back, tightening up.

Gently I take my mother's elbow with my free hand and rotate it, moving her arm, her shoulder so that she can feel the freer motion. Again, I wonder if she has sensed my annoyance, if my touch changed. I breathe. I close my eyes for a moment, intent on my own movement, the slide of my muscles in my arms, my back. I keep my legs slightly bent. She will never know how much the practice of massage has forced me to grow up. As I knead the deltoids in her shoulder, I watch her face in repose. It is a different face from when we began, brighter, less tired, almost smiling. I lean into my strokes, gathering my strength. We both have worked hard to be here today.

The light outside has changed. It's weaker, more orange, almost red. It slants through the bay laurel and eucalyptus trees out back in focused beams rather than in a shower of generous daylight. The shadows in the room have crept along the floor; now silhouettes of leaves tremble against my mother's armchair and the white wall. Already I recognize darkness in the light. I can see how the planet is a ball of night but for the sun's bounce of brightness. Shadows are usually perceived as the spaces not filled by the light, but it is the sun's rays that seem to me to caulk up the flood of darkness. This is the time, in the late afternoon, I see how day is merely a shadow of light.

Still holding her arm aloft, I slide my hand down to my mother's shoulder, up her neck to the base of her skull, then back again. My fingers drag along the trapezius muscle, a chronically knotted clump beneath the skin. She makes a small noise, one I know is of pleasure, release. I repeat the action, slower this time, a little deeper, wanting to extend her moments of enjoyment that happen below the level of her skin. Then I place her arm back on the table at her side, rest my hand on top of her hand. Hers is pale and a little chapped despite the oil, the knuckles bony. My hand over hers looks small and dark and entirely at home. For a moment I feel humbled by her presence lying trustingly before me.

This is why I love massage: these minutes, sometimes hours of stopped time, the movement of sunlight in windows, the arrival of breath, the body's slow, sure knowledge of its work. Here there is always the possibility of one's own self, allowed into being. I could dance this way forever.

I lift the edge of the sheet and cover her arm and shoulder. I move to the end of the table, by her head. I take a long breath, let it out, watch the sheet over her chest rise and fall. My mother's eyelids flutter but remain shut. She knows where I am going. She is waiting for the long pull and stretch of her neck, the steady pressure of my fingers beneath the ridge of her skull. I lift my hands and begin.

CHAPTER 8

Catherine

Summer 1985

CHANGE SEEMS TO HAVE A way of sneaking up from behind. You might get what you were looking for, only to find it's not exactly what you want. I wanted freedom. I wanted to be an explorer, someone uncompromising and very brave. I wanted to engage with the world on my own terms. I wanted to leave everyone else behind.

I'm nearly fifty. Half a century. It's not that old. Even so, I have a hard time remembering that I still have responsibilities. I run a used bookstore in Fairfax. I pay rent for the top half of a small, funky house on a hillside above the town. I am treasurer of the local chapter of NOW. I date a man named Lloyd a couple of times a week. I am Min's mother.

Always that. Especially that. She will be twenty-two in October. She has been an adult for several years now. She is everything I wished to be. Yet increasingly I worry that I wasn't a good mother. Certainly nothing I've done turned out the way I originally thought it would. Have I been too hard on her? Have I given her the guidance she needs? Did I love her enough? Too much? Could I have done better?

I never thought much about marriage and family life when I was a child and making plans for the future. Or, rather, I studiously ignored them. Now it seems that Min will probably never have her own children, even adopted ones. She's young, but she has shown no sign of attachment to anyone, besides me and Laura. I try to let her find her own way. I try to be the parent I never had. But I want to tell her not to turn away from the unexpected. Maybe she'll have to make compromises, risk being wrong. I want her to succeed where I failed. About my own life, I can't stop feeling—I don't know why—regret.

These days I wake up early. I don't mind. I reach for my glasses and lean back to watch the world take on color outside my windows. I like the way the long gray-green leaves of the eucalyptus trees lean and flutter in the wind or hold still in the first grip of sunshine. I feel okay in the morning, when I haven't woken up from nightmares. No headaches yet, no upset stomach. There are reasons I feel old.

I've begun to dream about Laura. I dream I'm looking for something I've misplaced, and I search everywhere. Sometimes I'm in my apartment, sometimes in the house in Mill Valley that Jonathan and Min and I lived in, sometimes in my parents' house in Rhinebeck. I search with the growing panic that I used to feel when I was married, knowing something was wrong and having no idea how to fix it. If I am aware in the dream of what I'm looking for, I always forget when I wake up. When I've turned everything upside down and I can't think where else to look, I turn around to find Laura standing beside me, waiting for me to recognize her. In the dream she turns out to be my daughter, the daughter I had forgotten about until now. We have a tearful reunion, full of long, fierce hugs. I am filled with relief, and more than that, joy that my family is complete at last. Then I wake up. After the first moments of disappointment that it isn't true, I am appalled. In the dreams Min doesn't exist.

I love my daughter. I know it makes no difference to me that Min is adopted. I know Min is my child. I have had to prove it time and again. When Min and Laura were children and the three of us would go out together, it was Laura that strangers assumed was my daughter, even though she looked nothing like me. My hair is dark, much closer to Min's black hair than Laura's straw blonde. Mine is curly, theirs is straight. Laura didn't resemble me in the least. And Min already shared some of my mannerisms; we were becoming more alike as each year passed. What was wrong with those people that they couldn't see that? And when I corrected them, how dare they answer with, "Well, you can see how I'd make that mistake."

I know who my daughter is. I dread these dreams in which she has no part. I wake up sweating, asking myself, Why can't I remember? What was the thing I was looking for that I lost?

This morning the same thing happens. I wake up disappointed that it was only a dream, that my joy isn't real. And then I feel guilty, and my sweat turns cold. I am an unworthy mother.

I throw off the down comforter and dress quickly. The sun is peeking over the hill when I slide the glass door closed and hurry down the deck stairs to where the Rabbit is parked on the side of the narrow road. The car starts on the third try. I drive into town, where everything is quiet, and pull onto Sir Francis Drake toward Point Reyes. I want to get to the beach before anyone else arrives.

My driving is automatic, instinctive, even on the steep, winding roads. I don't want to think. When I arrive, I slip off my Birkenstocks, reach for my sweatshirt on the back seat, lock the car, and follow the path down to the beach. There's someone with his dog much farther down, taking a morning jog. I keep walking, straight to the water. It's numbingly cold, and I feel the shock to my skin and then relief, the way I do putting ice on a sprained ankle. I stand letting the water lap at my feet. The wet sand buries my toes. I watch the waves build and break and roll back into the sea. I listen to their roar and hiss. I wonder if they would take me with them, or would they only spit me back out.

I remember the beach of my earliest memories, on Long Island where my parents used to bring Robert and me in the summer, before Andy and Susie were born. I remember holding my mother's hand as I considered the height of the waves, and I remember being afraid.

I look down the beach at the distant cliffs, their craggy faces unmoved by the smash of the sea. I realize, surprised, that this is the beach Andy and I walked on the last evening of his visit. I haven't been here since. We walked on this beach, and we fought. I couldn't forgive him for refusing to accept Min as my daughter. And then he died, in Maine, drowned by the sea.

Goddamn you, Andy, you're wrong. Min is not a foreigner, not someone on loan for a while. She is more my family than anyone. Why won't you see it?

I am so tired. I stand, staring out, feeling as numb as my feet in the ocean. If he were alive, he would be in his mid-forties. What kind of person would he have become? I can't imagine him. My memories of him seem dusty, put away. I rarely think of him. He's been gone too long.

I am mesmerized by the ocean, the way I am by flames in a fireplace. The waves roar and they whisper. They rush toward me, tumbling over themselves, and they slip away. I shudder. Then I remember what day it is. Andy died twenty-one years ago today.

It's almost as long as he was alive.

The next morning I sleep late. As far as I know, I didn't dream at all. I feel well-rested. I lie in bed for awhile, then drive into town to do my laundry, reading the *Chronicle* and sipping take-out coffee on a bench outside while I wait. When I return, Min and Laura have already arrived, tracking sand into my three small rooms and spilling stones and shells from their pockets onto the kitchen table. They sit together exactly as they did in fifth grade, when they first discovered each other, arranging their bits of the sea into swirling designs, calling me in to look when they are done. A month ago they discovered a cache of sand dollars washed up onto the beach. They harvested the ones that were still intact and came to show me, bearing dozens of them in the lap of their shirts as offerings. I saw how bright their faces were with the adventure of it, as though no one but the two of them had ever had such luck. At the time I thought they were breathless from the wind, giddy from the sun and salt air. It's been so long since the mere presence of another person moved me, lifting me up.

I make apple pancakes. The three of us sit on wobbly plastic chairs out on the deck, our plates in our laps. I'm not very hungry, so I watch

as they dig in. Min has piled extra dollops of stewed apples on top of her
pancakes, then drenched it all with maple syrup. She chews slowly, with
her eyes closed. Laura eats hunched over her plate, as though hoarding
treasure. As always, her long, sun-lightened hair obscures her face, until
she sweeps it behind her ear with her hand. It stays tucked there for a moment, then falls forward again. I can't help smiling, watching her. The sun
warms my shoulders. The neighbors' cat slips through the fence to prowl
through the tall grass in the garden below. I sip black coffee, content.

All summer, watching the two girls together, I have seen their ponder-
ing gazes when the other is turned away, how near they stand together; I
have heard the edge of excitement behind every word they speak. Their
long friendship has broken open, and something new is spilling out.
When they visit me, they talk between themselves incessantly, leaning
into each other. Or, as they used to do before Min became a lesbian and
Laura went to college, they flop down, one's head in the other's lap, sprawling happily on my living room couch. I am sure they don't have a sexual
relationship. Min would never compromise their friendship. And Laura,
from everything she has told me, loves men. This is instead a summer of
held breath, a season of suspense. I'm relieved, actually, that Min is carrying on this harmless flirtation rather than jumping into bed with some
woman she might meet at the dance clubs Laura says they've been going
to. Sitting in my faded armchair by the window in the living room, or out
here on the deck underneath the sun, my eyes keep returning to the girls,
to the crackling of energy between them even when they're not touching.
They are a vortex, a black hole, a light pulling in every nearby moth.

I remember what it's like. I never felt that excitement with another
girl, but with boys—with Jonathan—I remember. I felt alive then, vigorous and powerful and full of my own daring. I think it's different when
you're young, no matter how much experience you've had: the world is
still an unfamiliar place. You discover your own allure with almost everyone you meet. Even repetition has its nuances, its exquisite variations.
By the time you're middle-aged, like me, those encounters tend to be

dismaying. They lose their intensity, and you discover that can be a relief. Hope for the future takes too much out of you.

Min slumps in her chair, sliding her bottom forward and stretching out her legs. She rests her empty plate on her stomach.

"Mom, before I forget, it turns out I'm not going to be able to give you your massage for a few weeks. Laura and I are driving her friend's car across the country."

I am so unprepared for this that I assume at first she's joking. It's not at all funny. I blink. She can't go. I am used to having her nearby, within reach on the phone, a mere hour's drive away. But I see from her face that she is serious. She thinks nothing of going off with Laura and leaving me alone.

My heart has started thumping fast, the way it does when I am afraid. I sip my coffee. My hand shakes. "Thanks for giving me advance warning," I say.

Min frowns and looks away.

Laura says, "We didn't know ourselves until a couple of days ago. It's a fluke kind of thing. A friend of mine from Kenyon drove out here and got food poisoning, and someone has to drive her car back."

"What about your roommate?" I ask Min.

"His name's Henry, Mom. You never remember." She glares at me, then says, "He wants me to send postcards."

"What about your clients?" I'm having difficulty adjusting to her news. How can it be so easy to pick up and leave her life, everyone in it?

"I'm letting them know. Mom, the only times I've ever been out of California were when we visited your parents in Poughkeepsie. I was a kid then."

"It wasn't Poughkeepsie, it was Rhinebeck."

"Okay, Rhinebeck, who fucking cares? You—"

"I do, Min," I snap back, "and don't use that language around me."

"Shit, you sound like some throwback to the fifties. I'm going on a trip across the country. You could at least be excited for me."

Laura is watching us, bewildered. I try to take a breath from the bottom of my diaphragm, the way Min has shown me during the massages. It's an effort. "I *am* excited for you, Min. I am. It's just sudden." My stomach isn't feeling so great. I lean back, stretching out the way she has. The chair threatens to fall over backwards, so I give up.

In the air in front of me I see a speeding car veer off a highway and jolt into a ditch, rolling over and over. The vision is so real I wonder if it is a premonition. It fills me with pure, ice-cold fear. "What if you have an accident?" I demand of Min. "What if you lose control of the car and crash?" I can see the wreckage of the car strewn across the empty highway, fields of wheat like ocean waves stretching into the distance. I can picture clearly two bodies trapped inside the overturned car, crushed and bleeding. I shudder. "Don't go, Min. For my sake, please don't go."

"Mom, we're not going to have an accident. We're going to have fun."

Min is wearing overalls with the cuffs rolled up to below her knees, and a nondescript pullover shirt she probably found in a thrift store. Her hair's too short: it sticks up from the top of her head and bristles at the back of her neck. With so little hair, Min's face looks narrower than I think of it. Her eyebrows seem thicker, her cheekbones more prominent. She's pretty, my daughter, though unfortunately I can't take any credit for that. I focus on Min's face, committing it to memory. I want to be prepared. "You've never been far away from me before. I'm afraid for you, Min. I'm afraid you won't come back."

She stares at me. Out of the corner of my eye I see Laura shift uncomfortably. Min says, "Mom, I don't think this is about me. I don't know what it is, but it's too intense to be about me."

I shake my head. "Yes, it is, Min." I want her to understand, even though I'm not sure I do. "I promise you, it is."

Instead of answering, Min leans forward, propelling herself to her feet. "Do you want more?" she asks Laura. She stands holding her own plate, all her weight on one hip, her palm out. How can I know what another mother would do? I don't want to let her go. She takes Laura's plate and leaves us, sliding the screen door wider open with her sneaker.

I force my gaze away from the door. I look around the deck, thinking I should cut back the wisteria. The lavender needs watering too.

"Catherine," Laura says, "I'd love to meet Lloyd one of these days. How about inviting him over sometime when we're here?"

"Lloyd?" I have no idea why she is asking. "What have I ever said about him?"

"Not very much," Laura admits. "Min talks about him sometimes. The long-haired animal doctor. She's curious."

"Otherwise known as a vet. I used to work for him. What's she curious about, whether we're having a relationship?"

Laura pushes her hair behind her ears again, then sweeps it all back and piles it on top of her head, holding it there for my assessment. It makes her look older, but I don't like it as a hairstyle. I scrunch up my face and shake my head, and she grins and lets it fall past her shoulders. "No, Min knows you have sex with him. I mean . . . you know, she figured . . ." She stops, her face turning a slow vermillion.

I raise my hand, waving her uncertainty away. "It's okay, she happens to be right."

Laura looks relieved. She nods slightly, contemplating me while pretending not to. It's one of those moments I've become more frequently aware of, when two people are having a conversation but what they're noticing as they listen to each other is something very different. I think Laura is trying to imagine me as a sexual person. I bite my lip, wanting to smile. Her best friend's mother. After my divorce from Jonathan, she met only one of the handful of men I've dated, and I'm sure he didn't inspire fantasies of torrid sex.

"Anything else you want to know?" I ask. It's a beautiful day, and she's so easy to be with.

"Yeah, there is. Do you think he might be the love of your life?"

She's so earnest, it's a little painful. I remember some of the boys she has confided in me about. My old therapist would say she needs to work through her pattern of choosing selfish men. But does she really believe everyone will find Mr. Right? "I don't think I'm going to have a love of my life," I tell her gently, but I can see from the way her eyebrows pull together that it's not what she wants to hear.

"Well, what about Jonathan?"

I can't lie to her. "Jonathan and I were very compatible for a while, but that's a different thing. At least it is in my experience."

"Maybe you've already met the love of your life," Laura says. "Maybe you're just not letting him in."

I hear the scrape of the screen door sliding shut. Min returns with their full plates. Laura smiles up at Min, and her hand brushes Min's as if by accident. Min grins back. What does the love of your life mean, exactly? Perhaps it's simply the person in your life you end up loving the most. If so, she's right here, sitting down cross-legged, wedging her sneakers between the arms of her chair. And for Laura?

"So when are we going to meet Lloyd?" Laura asks me, cutting up her stack of pancakes.

I turn to contemplate the garden with its overgrown hydrangea bushes, the lantana and jade plants running wild, the unpruned lemon tree in the corner by the fence. I've been meaning to do something about the garden. Somehow I never get around to it. Instead I sit on the deck, dragging my chair around to where the sun is and reading the books I take home from the bookstore. I get up when my coffee cup needs refilling or the light fades. I can see that the garden was well-tended once; someone put a lot of work into choosing these bushes, these flowers, nourishing them as they grew. Even now, left alone, the plants thrive in their straggly way.

What I am witnessing is simple: the girls are courting each other, after so long a time apart. They are once again getting used to being central in each other's lives. They are re-establishing their roles as best friends. There were times when Laura was at college that I felt I was the bridge between them, reporting to my daughter the news from Laura's letters, writing back to Laura when I had lunch in the city with Min, keeping their interest up. I have no doubt that nothing will come of this flirtation.

They are merely infatuated again, as they were when they first met in elementary school, many years ago now.

There is something else. I don't want them to bring sex into my house as casually as they spill the shells they find on the beach. Min thinks the way I feel about sex is old-fashioned. I think it's a private thing, clearly bounded. I don't flaunt my relationship, such as it is, with Lloyd. I don't have him here the mornings they arrive for brunch, or when Min comes to give me my massage. She has only met him twice, both times in town: once he was outside the animal hospital crouching on the pavement in front of a Doberman, its head between his hands; the other time he was coming out of the Good Earth, grocery bags in his arms. Even if his hands had been free, he wouldn't have touched me then, asserting his claim on me.

I can't imagine Lloyd sitting here with the three of us. But I answer Laura, "Whenever you like. He wants to meet you. Both of you," I add, but when I look at her, Min is savoring her pancakes, chewing slowly, eyes closed.

It was Jonathan who first noticed the sheen of buried sensuality on the girls' friendship, when they were in sixth or seventh grade. "Don't you think Min and her friend Laura are a little in love with each other?" he asked one night as we lay in bed, not touching but still talking, like kids in separate bunk beds at sleepaway camp, or like my child and her friend in the room down the hall. "The way they get giggly, and look at each other, and the cryptic references they make," he added. "As though they're trying to impress each other."

I lay staring at the rain trickling down the skylight above our bed, listening to its rataplan on our roof. I thought about what he had said, but by then I was having trouble trusting that what he said was what he meant. Or rather, I had become uncertain of my own ability to translate his meaning. "I don't know," I said, "I think that's normal for children their age."

"I didn't say it wasn't normal, Catherine, I was merely remarking on it."
His voice came from somewhere beside me, as if not attached to a person
at all. *Did* he think it was normal? Why was he paying so much attention
to the two girls? What was he trying to tell me about us? I turned my
head and looked at the cardboard Calder mobile revolving over the door.
I watched the shadowy silhouette of a triangle with rounded corners as it
waned to a thin line and waxed to two dimensions again.

"Neither of them has a lot of friends," I said after a moment. "I like
Laura. I'm glad they found each other."

"So am I." His voice had a plaintiveness to it, as though he was hurt
and trying to cover it up. I felt sorry then and wanted to reach out to
touch him, but the space between us felt too vast. "That's all I meant to
say," he added.

"You could have just said it."

"There are different ways of communicating things, Catherine. Language is a versatile tool. It can convey many layers of meaning while appearing to be one thing, or it can put forth one very fundamental idea
while appearing to be complex. I was trying to explore the quality of their
friendship, not dissect it."

I was silent. I didn't believe him. Jonathan called language a tool, but
he used it like a weapon. I had once loved that very intelligent and agile
quality about him. We were still at a point of trying to understand what
was going wrong with us, and I thought there must be clear rules that we
could follow. Jonathan didn't see it that way. I had grown tired of trying
to pin him down.

Min opens her eyes, puts down her fork. "So, Mom, about this trip. Henry's moving in with his girlfriend and I can't look for a roommate until I
get back. Could you help me cover the rent until I find someone?"

I wish she hadn't brought up the trip again. My fear is there on the
edge of my consciousness, hovering. I feel as though at any moment I
might startle us all by losing control of myself. Fleetingly, I wonder if

she'll choose an Asian roommate again. "Min, I don't know. I don't have a lot of extra money right now. When will you get back?"

She shrugs. "Whenever. We'll see how long the drive takes."

"My friend Nancy wants the car back in Washington as soon as possible," Laura adds.

"Well," I say, knowing I'm stating the obvious, "the sooner you get back, the sooner you can find a roommate. But while you're there, why don't you look up your aunt Susie? She lives in DC now. I know she'd love to see you."

"Mom, I don't know her." Min and Laura exchange a look.

"You don't remember her from the time we visited in 1968?"

"No."

The panic is getting worse. "Min, would you at least call me at regular intervals on this trip?"

She lowers her head, spears the last bit of pancake, but she doesn't eat it right away.

"*I* will," Laura says. Min looks up at her, frowning. "If you don't want to," she adds.

"I've got to check in at the store," I say, glancing at my watch without reading it. "Don't forget your pebbles, they're still on the kitchen table."

After the girls leave, I pile the dishes in the sink and gather my keys and purse. Last winter I hired a high school student, a young man named Mark, to unpack and shelve boxes of books from estate auctions and to mind the store for a few hours in the afternoons and all day on Saturdays. Most weekends I go in anyway. I like talking to my customers, and I like handling all those secondhand books, dog-eared and well-worn as they are.

By the time I'm out on the deck again, I realize I am thinking about Min. She has been my daughter for more than twenty-one years. In all that time I have been truly afraid of losing her only once, when I discovered her with that woman in my living room in Mill Valley. For a day and a half I was terrified she would disappear from my life altogether, that her anger would make her think she didn't care, or that I didn't. More than anything, I want to never allow that to happen again.

At the bottom of the stairs, I lean against the fence and look at the garden. It's not much, just some overgrown bushes gone wild in a yard. But I want it to be beautiful some day. Laura sees this. She has offered more than once to help me weed and trim. Min couldn't care less. "Mom, it's fine the way it is," she told me the last time she and Laura were here, when we ventured outside after a rain shower. She leaned over a tangled bush of wild roses, burying her face in their blossoms and breathing in to make her point. She straightened up, a fluid rolling motion like an unfurling, something she learned to do at massage school. "Actually, it's gorgeous," she added, her face wet from the rain. Then she opened her eyes.

But I want to impose order. I look at those roses, at the creeping vines and shaggy bushes, and know it can be my hand that shapes them. I want the edges to be neat, the design to be clear. I want to know that their particular beauty, their exuberant flowering, the direction of their growth, are all due to me. But I don't have the energy to start.

Two or three times, while I've been in the garden calculating the work I know lies ahead, Laura has come to stand by my side and survey the wreckage with me. She has told me what she envisions. I've listened quietly, taking it in. I find Laura's presence comforting. I have never felt this way about Min. Min has been a blessing in my life. She has been the object of my fiercest love, my deepest joy. She can be perceptive, sensitive, gentle, and rather brutally honest, but she has never been reassuring. She is someone to rely on, yes, but not to rest with. Even when she massages me, patiently rubbing my neck, my temples to help my headaches, I can never fully give myself into her hands. Maybe that's normal. At least I try to believe it is. Maybe a mother must always be alert, keeping an eye out, even when her daughter is almost twenty-two.

The garden will have to wait for another day.

CHAPTER 9

Laura

Summer 1985

MIN PUNCHES THE TAPE OFF. "Thank God," I say, trying to make it sound like a joke. I'm sick of David Bowie.

On every side of us, Utah's flat terrain stretches out, dry and reddish brown. The road is laid down in the middle of it like a dark, shimmering ribbon. In the far distance, spots of green tease us. They're the first hint of vegetation we've seen since leaving California, not counting the scrawny trees in the national park we spent last night in. I can feel the dust in my throat. I move my hand away from Min's leg. I shift my feet, pushing candy wrappers, books, and a pair of sandals to the side, and find the water bottle. The hot air blows around us, making loose papers and open food bags flutter noisily. After a long swallow, I pass the water to Min. She smiles at me and reaches across for the bottle. I love her smile. I love everything about her.

"I'll feed it to you," I offer, moving the bottle to her lips.

Min shakes her head, and the plastic rim scrapes lightly against her cheek. "Just give it to me," she says, frowning, grabbing the bottle away from me. What did I do? She swallows in large gulps, tipping the bottle back each time. I reach out to wipe a trickle of sweat from the back of her neck, then rub the same place, where I know she gets stiff from driving. Now that we're finally lovers, I don't want to stop touching her.

She returns the bottle. "Just hand it to me when I'm driving," she says. I screw the cap back on. I was only trying to help. It wouldn't kill her to appreciate me a little. I toss the bottle on top of the bag of gorp by my feet. I look out the window, but the landscape hasn't changed. I'm still thirsty.

So far, we've avoided the cities, stopping in towns that are just one street and at truck stops. Min likes the sense of being alone in this empty countryside. She says that with no people around she can see that the deserts are full of life. She likes coming over a small hill and discovering new stretches of sagebrush or an occasional rock formation. She says even the cracks running through the parched earth are gorgeous. I think the land is flat and endless and dull. It doesn't give anything back. I'm restless to see architecture. At night, the lights of a city reassure me far more than the thousand bright stars in the sky. But I've been happy to stay clear of the bigger towns because I want to have her all to myself.

Last night, using our single flashlight, we figured out how to spread our sleeping bags flat, one on top of the other, and zip them together. We got in and stayed on our separate sides. Inside the tent was completely dark. With Min only inches away, I was wide awake. Zipping together the sleeping bags had been her idea. Lying near her, I was afraid that something might happen, and I was terrified that it wouldn't. All summer she had been ignoring my hints, but I thought there was an energy between us. I wasn't sure. I'd been burned too often with guys, when it turned out that our mutual attraction was all in my head. With Min I was even more unsure. The boundaries of her relationships confused me. There seemed to be some kind of sexual attraction with everybody she knew.

Eventually I got up the nerve to reach out and touch her face. My hand fumbled a little before finding her cheek because I couldn't see. "Are you asleep?" I asked.

"No," she answered. "Are you?"

I smiled. "I can't," I said. I took my hand away. I could hear her body sliding around on the sleeping bag's nylon shell as she tried to find a comfortable position. I couldn't tell if she was restless and wide awake for the same reason I was. I thought, Why won't she make the first move? She's the lesbian.

Somewhere outside the tent, a bird called out. The hard ground beneath me dug into my side. As far as I knew, Min and I were in the only part of eastern Nevada that had lakes, full-grown trees, and birds. We were miles away from any other people. This thought both frightened me and gave me courage.

"I want to kiss you," I whispered into the dark.

At first Min didn't say anything, and I thought she might have fallen asleep after all. Then "Okay" came drifting back from the darkness on her side of the sleeping bag, sounding just as scared as I was.

"Well, where are you?" I asked, reaching out a tentative hand and making contact with her shoulder.

She caught my hand in hers and pulled me closer. We put our arms around each other. Because I couldn't see her anyway, I closed my eyes. We brushed our faces together. I kissed her cheek. Then I kissed the corner of her mouth. The darkness made everything easier. She pressed her mouth against mine, hard, so that I could feel the bone of her jaw behind the flesh, and then she eased back. I felt her tongue against my lips, opening them. I remembered we had done this once before, in seventh grade. But that had been when we were boy-crazy and didn't count. As we kissed last night, I felt I was in freefall, like I had walked off a cliff. I thought, amazed, How did this happen?

I was a little afraid of lying on top of her. I was used to men, who were bigger than me, and heftier, harder to reach around and hold with both my arms. On the hard ground, with only the tent floor and one of the sleeping bags to cushion us, we touched each other carefully. Now and then we asked permission. It only occurred to me after it was over and we were lying quietly together that this is what lovers do when they care about each other. The enjoyment is in pursuing the other's pleasure, not only your own. The men I had been with had been oblivious, but I'd always assumed there was something wrong with me for wanting more.

Eventually, Min unzipped and pushed away the top sleeping bag, then lay on her stomach, her head between my legs. At first I felt self-conscious and wanted to pull her back up. I was surprised when I came. It made me feel even more exposed. I reached down for her and she held me, covering me. Her face was wet. I shuddered, clinging to her.

"Thank you," I said.

"For what?" Min asked.

"What you just did. Nobody ever did that before."

She lifted her head from my shoulder. "You're kidding."

"No," I said, relieved that she couldn't see my face. "Actually, you're the first person I ever had an orgasm with." I was ashamed to admit that, but I wanted her to know how much it mattered to me. Before Min, I had had sex with exactly three men. One of those relationships had lasted almost a year, but as much as I had loved him, it had never quite felt like making love. Not one of them had done what Min had just done for me. My first lover said he didn't like the smell, and I never asked again. Min seemed to enjoy it. Maybe, some day in the far future, I would learn to receive that gift from her without such awed gratitude, like it was something everyday—even expected. I was in love with Min, I realized, holding her tight against me. I had always wondered why our friendship felt more like a long-term love affair to me than any relationship I had with a man. But I never could have put it into words. I understood too why Min had never fallen in love with even one of all the women she's been with. In a way, we had been together all along. I didn't want to ever let her go. I gripped her tighter, wanting to cry. Maybe after about ten years of being lovers I would start to take her for granted. But I doubted it.

As we approach it, Salt Lake City looks like any other American city. We drive past farms, a few factories. The land starts to get crowded with houses. Even the city is absolutely flat, like the rest of the state. There's

no obvious downtown, no hub of skyscrapers. There are no clear landmarks of any kind, no easy ways to get our bearings. Except for the lake.
The sun looms over the horizon to our left, a big orange disk spreading
rose and lilac across the sky. The lake mirrors the colors exactly.

For almost three days, driving through Nevada and Utah, we haven't
passed one lake or river. Earlier today we saw, way off in the distance, a
long stretch of land that glittered a dull white. At first we guessed it was
something left over from a nuclear testing site. I checked the map and
read "Sevier Lake (Dry)." Until then, we hadn't thought about the salt
lakes at all. We tried to imagine the kind of desert heat and centuries of
time it would have taken to evaporate that huge a body of water, leaving
only the salt behind, like ashes after a fire. Now that we're here in the city,
Min wants to go down to the shore of the Great Salt Lake and watch the
sun set over the water. I would love to see the sunset with Min. I would
stand with my arms around her and watch her face change in as many
ways as the sky. But I don't think it's a good idea. It's past six already, and
Neil, my father's friend, is expecting us to arrive at his house for dinner.

We get lost only once, turning right instead of left, but we figure it out
after a few blocks. We pass a mall, restaurants, what we assume are office
buildings. It's Friday, and people are still leaving work. Otherwise, the
streets are mostly empty. A few large families with young kids wander toward the mall, and a group of teenagers is hanging out together. The traffic is light too. We're the only car I can see with the windows rolled down.

"It's really deserted," I say.

"It's really white," Min says.

She drives slowly, squinting at the street signs. At first I think she
means the buildings, which are all gray and white and beige. Then I realize she means the people, and I almost say, surprised, "What did you
expect?" but I don't. Until she mentioned it, I hadn't noticed. What I'm
struck by is how Middle America everybody looks, how bland. I see only
one boy wearing a baseball cap, and it's not bright purple with yellow
zigzags, the fabric hand-woven in Guatemala, like Min's. The women

all have long, styled hair. They wear dresses or pleated pants, even in the heat. Nobody is wearing Birkenstocks or baggy men's boxers or labrys earrings like Min's, much less four in one ear plus an earcuff. Even I, in khaki shorts and sneakers, look more like the teenaged boys than the women. We drive through, not saying a word.

As we head into the suburbs on the other side of town, Min sees a Dairy Queen and gets so excited that I can't turn her down this time. I check my watch. We'll only take fifteen minutes. Inside, a crew of children is having a birthday party at the front tables, blowing their noise-makers in each other's faces and pulling down the streamers. I smile at them, remembering picnics and bowling parties back in Middlebury when I was little. A few of them crane their necks as we walk past, peering at us. One of them points. I tell myself he probably wants Min's colorful baseball cap. We order and walk with our ice cream to a booth in the back. But it's hard to ignore the father and son duo. The son, who is maybe eight or nine, is dressed in jeans, boots, a plaid shirt, and a Stetson, exactly like his father. I would be amused, or amazed, and gawk right back at them, but the hardness in their eyes as they check out Min, who is leading the way to our booth, scares me. They hate her without even knowing her. Even the little boy. I feel a shiver at the back of my neck.

When we sit down, Min is smirking. "What a trip. Like father, like son, huh?" She pulls off her purple cap. Her spiky hair is damp with sweat and a few clumps lie plastered to her skin. She rubs her temples, pushing the hair off her forehead, then starts in on her hot fudge sundae.

I push my dish of raspberry frozen yogurt away. "Didn't you see how they were looking at you? How can you ignore that?"

Min sucks in her lower lip and slowly edges her spoon through her dessert. Then she holds the plastic spoon out to me. On it is the maraschino cherry, peeking out from a blanket of fudge sauce. I love maraschino cherries. I put my mouth over it and pull slowly away, savoring the mix of impossibly sweet flavors on my tongue. I don't even realize I've closed my eyes until I open them and see Min's face. The lust in her eyes is just as startling as the cowboy and his son's bare loathing. I have never been sure of anybody's attraction to me. I've never known for certain that I am desirable just from a look. I need to be told, or shown. But what I see when Min gazes at me over her white plastic spoon is unmistakable. I feel the muscles between my legs tighten. Behind me, I know they are still staring. I look down at the table.

After we've eaten for a while in silence, I say, "You didn't answer me."

"Shit." Min jams her spoon into the mound of ice cream she is eating from and leaves it there. I can't tell if she's angry at me or something else. She leans back, stretching, her hands clasped above her head. Her t-shirt reads, "Love is Just a Four-Letter Word." An ex-lover gave it to her. She has cut out the neck and the sleeves. She brings her arms down again. "What do you want me to do, Laura? What do you fucking expect me to do?" Her voice is louder than I'd like.

"Well," I begin, knowing I am about to make her angrier, but feeling I have to say it. "Maybe you could wear regular earrings, and just one in each ear. Maybe you could dress a little differently."

"You think that will change something?"

"I don't know. It might. At least you wouldn't be advertising yourself."

"As what?"

"You know, as a lesbian."

A muscle in her jaw twitches. She closes her eyes, takes a deep breath, and lets it out. She opens her eyes. She says, "Look at me, Laura. Dress me in anything you want. What do you see?"

I look at her boy's hair, at the salamander tattooed on her wrist. She's got her arms stretched out along the top of the blue plastic seat like she owns it and she's ready to fight anybody who says she doesn't. She hasn't done one thing to make herself look pretty. It's like I'm seeing her for the first time. I love her more than anything. It shouldn't matter what other people think.

When I don't answer, she says, "What you see is a dyke. An Asian dyke." I think she wants to hurt me with the blunt ugliness of the word.

My frozen yogurt is a raspberry puddle half filling the cup. I stir it around while I try to let what she has said sink in. My heart is beating hard. I know that what is happening right now is important. I can't mess it up.

I take her hand and hold it resting on the table. I know everybody in the place must be watching. "You're right. I know you're right." I look only at her, but it's an effort not to glance around. "I'm sorry I asked you to hide who you are. You don't want to. I understand that."

"I *can't* hide who I am," she says, very quietly and very carefully.

I feel her start to pull her hand away. I grip it tighter. "You can't hide that you're Asian," I offer. Personally, I doubt her race has anything to do with the hatred I saw coming from the father-son pair three booths behind me. They've probably never even seen any Asians before.

"I can't hide that I'm a lesbian either," Min says.

I think she can. Not that she necessarily should, but I think it is possible. She takes her hand from mine. I look into her deep, black eyes, and I don't recognize her in them. I feel afraid.

"Come on," I say. "Let's get out of here."

The sun has dipped below the houses across the street, throwing long shadows across the lawn, when Min and I pull into the semicircular driveway in front of Neil's house. Two sprinklers whisper on the grass. I wish I could lie below their spray, the weight of the earth at my back.

We're almost an hour later than I told Neil we'd be. Maybe we should have called. He's probably pissed at us for keeping them waiting. I cut the engine, and we sit inside the car, staring up at the white stone house. The pink sky is reflected in the rows of black-shuttered windows. There are dormer windows on the third floor, and a porch around the side. Flower beds border the house. The front door looks like oak, with stained-glass panels flanking it. I remember my father saying that Neil and Olivia had their house built. It dwarfs the other ranch houses on the street, making them look shabby.

Despite our stop at the Dairy Queen, I can't break the rhythm of the drive. We could still be on our two-lane highway, mile after mile of parched, empty land rushing by. I feel the road rolling away beneath the car's tires.

"It's so white," I say, meaning the house, and I look over, expecting Min to smile. The car's engine whirrs inside me, a low hum, a vibration.

"It's so big," she says, staring.

I reach out and take her hand. I know she'd rather stay in an anonymous motel or in our tent in the desert than spend an evening with unknown friends of my father. The promise of a real bed doesn't lure her the way it does me. I grin at her. Looking at Min today, I feel like a totally new person. We're meant to be together. How come we never figured that out before now?

She leans over to kiss me. I pretend I don't know what she's doing. I lean away, pulling my hand from hers, and start to open my door. I'm afraid we'll be seen from one of the rose-tinted windows. We're a couple now, but I don't want Neil and his wife to know that.

"We should tell them we're here," I say. Then I realize Min doesn't care if they find out about our relationship. She doesn't know them and will probably never see them again. She has no reason to act like we're still just friends. But after our scene at the Dairy Queen, I don't dare ask anything else of her.

"Do we have to go up and knock?" Min asks. I don't think she's teasing me. She really doesn't know.

"Let's find out," I answer. I push my car door all the way open and stand up, dizzy.

A man in shorts and an alligator shirt comes around the side of the house, striding barefoot over the lawn. He's carrying a pair of steel brush cutters that dangle open, carelessly, in his left hand.

I hear Min say under her breath, "The upper classes play at being useful." Frowning, I glance back at her over the car roof. Neil is our host. He's my father's friend. She should be grateful that he's offered his home to us.

"Hello, hello!" he calls out. He has round wire-rimmed glasses and stormy-blue eyes. His wavy hair is reddish-brown and beginning to gray around the temples. He's handsome, in a boyish way. I like him immediately.

He stops in front of me, smiling widely, and shakes my hand. He's tall, over six feet, and both his height and the firm grip of his hand around mine steady me, bringing me off the road to solid ground. I grin back. He covers my hand with both of his, welcoming me to Salt Lake City. "Did you get lost downtown?" he asks, his eyes amused, already forgiving me for being late. His eyelashes are reddish too, almost gold.

"We took a few wrong turns," I say. I can't stop grinning at him. When he lets go of my hand I feel cast off. Behind me the passenger door slams. I turn toward Min and introduce them. They say hello in a muted way. I'm kind of glad he isn't instantly into her. She doesn't seem curious about him at all.

I've never met Neil before. But I feel I know him because of the stories my father used to tell about their college days. They would get into long debates at dinner in the cafeteria, arguing philosophy and political science long after their classmates had gone off to the libraries to study. They would go to dances at the women's colleges and make a play for the same girls. All this seemed boring when my father told it, and I would wonder if all guys were that competitive. But as Neil asks Min what he can carry in for us, I can see how that rivalry would seem exciting to my father, seducing him.

Of all his stories, the one I remember best he told only once, after we moved to Mill Valley. Neil and my father were taking the final exam for a class on the British Romantic poets, a class my father was struggling in. As the time wound down, my father realized this would be the first exam he would fail. He saw that Neil was hunched over, working steadily away. When the two hours were up and the proctor started collecting blue books, Neil reached over and took my father's exam, leaving his own on my father's desk. My father watched Neil erase and write something in on the cover. He looked down at Neil's blue book and saw his own name. He got an A on the exam, raising his average to a B. My father had never forgotten that. I was amazed nobody had seen, or if they had, that they hadn't turned Neil in.

Min and I haul our knapsacks out of the car and follow Neil into his house. Dropping the brush cutters on the front hall carpet, he closes the heavy front door behind us. Min stares up at the chandelier, looking around her like she's entered a cathedral. Putting a hand on each of our shoulders, Neil steers us past the polished mahogany staircase back through the dining room to the kitchen. I like the relaxed contact of his hand and my feeling that all the decisions will be taken care of by somebody else for a while. In the kitchen, everything is in its place or put away, the surfaces all wiped clean. In the center, a large butcher block table takes up half the room. A woman stands on the other side, cutting up tomatoes and yellow peppers. I can't tell if she's his wife or the cook.

"Our wayward travelers have arrived," Neil announces as we come into the room. He strides over to the table and pops a tomato wedge into his mouth.

The woman's bobbed hair is almost totally gray, and her face looks pinched, like she is constantly turning over something worrisome in her mind. She wipes her hands on her apron, comes around the table, and shakes our hands, first mine, then Min's. I realize this is Olivia, Neil's wife. She smiles like it doesn't come easily to her. I feel sorry for Neil.

"We thought you'd ended up in the wrong state," she says, looking over the top of her glasses at us.

"It just took us longer than we expected," I reply.

"Did you have a good drive?"

I remember David Bowie's weird wailing songs and the road that never seemed to get anywhere and Min's moodiness. But I tell them about the evaporated lake we glimpsed earlier this morning. I look at Neil and describe the huge purple desert plains dotted with low clumps of brush that stretched across Nevada, broken only by occasional small mountain ranges. I make it all sound beautiful. When I finally run out of steam, Olivia asks if we came across from California on Route 50, and did we see Temple Square on our way through the city. I look around at Min. She's standing behind me slightly. Why is she being so quiet?

Olivia moves closer to her husband and tucks her hands around his arm. "We were going to start dinner without you, so this is perfect timing, isn't it, Neil?"

He's smiling, like he's proud of having produced us out of thin air. "I guess I should get the steaks on the grill," he says, moving away from Olivia without looking at her. "It's the cook's night off." He slips behind me, resting his hand on my back as he moves toward the door. I can't help that I feel special, singled out.

After Neil leaves the room, the three of us are at a loss for words. It's like the electricity's been cut and all the lights and appliances have shut off. "Well," Olivia says after an awkward silence, her face pinching in again, "I'm sure you two girls would like to put down those packs and freshen up a little. I'll show you where you'll be staying. It used to be my daughter Katie's room. I mostly use it as a sewing room now." She seems to be annoyed with us. I'm beginning to get the sense she's that way all the time.

Olivia leads us up the carpeted stairs and to the back of the house. The room has two twin beds with matching white bedspreads. Arranged on top of the bookcase and the bureau is her daughter's childhood collection of dolls. Beneath one window on a table, the sewing machine sits among swatches of fabric and spools of thread.

Min pulls her knapsack from her shoulder, dumps it on the nearest bed, and wanders over to the other window to look out. She has shown no sign of interest in either Neil or Olivia. I'm embarrassed that she isn't even attempting to be polite, appreciative. "Thank you," I say to Olivia, hoping to make up for Min's obvious lack of manners. "It's really nice of you to let us stay here tonight."

"Oh, don't be silly. Neil and your father go back a long way. Of course you're welcome to stay with us any time."

"Thank you," I say again. I'm at the end of my own repertoire of social skills.

"Well, come down when you're ready," Olivia says, turning. She closes the door softly behind her.

Once I'm sure she's gone back downstairs, I go to the window and put my arms around Min from behind, pressing my body against the back of hers. I rest my lips against the nape of her neck. She brings her arms up and closes her hands over mine. I feel the car's idling whirr inside me finally slow and stop. When I'm with Min, I don't have to look around for landmarks to know where I am.

I stretch forward and kiss her warm cheek. I say, "I love holding you. I want to hold you forever." She doesn't say anything. She hasn't said much since we left the Dairy Queen. "Are you still mad at me?" I ask.

She smiles and squeezes my hands, then lets go and pulls me around to stand beside her at the window. "Look," she says, pointing. The yard behind the house is immense, bordered by more beautifully laid-out flowerbeds. In the gray light of dusk, I can still see the vibrant pinks and reds and yellows. A swing set and a shed are half-hidden in a grove of trees. Below us, on the lawn, Neil is standing over the smoking grill, poking at a slab of steak with a long barbeque fork. Tongues of flame rise around it. I watch Neil, feeling a small, secret thrill because he doesn't know I'm up here watching him. He's put on loafers, and he's humming to himself.

After a while I say, "The flowers are wonderful. Which one of them do you think is the gardener? I vote for Olivia."

Min turns to me. "Come on, Laura. She doesn't do the real work. They hire someone."

"How do you know?"

"You think Olivia gets her fingernails dirty? She just snips them and arranges them in a vase. Anyway, it's too professional-looking. Look at how the hedges are trimmed."

For the first time since I've known her, I feel like Min thinks I'm stupid. I wonder why she became my lover in the first place if she thinks so little of me. I almost ask her, but I'm not feeling confident about what she might say.

"Anyway, I like them, don't you?" I ask. "At least him. She's pretty much a cold fish."

"She's lonely."

I stare at Min. Where did she get that idea?

"Let's take a shower," I say. I've got to get out of my dusty clothes.

"Why don't the two of you stay an extra day?" Neil asks at the dining room table. There is candlelight and engraved silverware, and after three days of fast food, the steak tastes so good I could cry. We've been talking about the founding of Salt Lake City. Mostly Neil has been talking. I've been watching his face in the glow of the candles, and for a split second I wonder how it would feel if he kissed me. "Tomorrow we could show you the sights," he continues, "the Beehive House, the Mormon Temple, anything else you're interested in. You can stay here tomorrow night and get an early start the next day."

"I'd love to," I say without thinking, and then I remember that it's not my decision alone. I look over at Min. She's busy eating her salad.

Olivia puts a hand on Neil's where it lies on the table. "We have golf with Ted and Thelma tomorrow, remember?" Her voice has that hard, warning edge in it, just like my mother's. I don't like her.

Neil moves his hand, almost flicking hers off, and reaches for his glass of wine. "We can do that any time."

I look at Min again, wishing she would look up, join the conversation, help me. The thing is, I'm interested in seeing the city. In the car, I've been reading about Brigham Young and the Mormons. The AAA guidebook says Utah didn't become a state until 1896, less than a hundred years ago, when the Church of the Latter Day Saints abolished polygamy. I remember the dried-out lake we saw and realize how short a time a century really is. The division into states, even the presence of people, doesn't affect the land itself. That's why I think it's boring. You can travel an entire day and be in a different state by nightfall, but the geography is still the same. Min is entranced by the vast landscapes that stay unchanged for centuries. The mountains and deserts are too big to go away. But it's the people I want to hear about, how they managed to survive the harshness of the land and the weather.

"We'll have to think about it," I tell Neil. "Thank you."

"I'm a very good tour guide," he says, smiling at me. "You would enjoy it."

"I'm sure I would," I answer, smiling back. I really want to hang out for a day, take it easy. "I like historical stuff. Maybe I get it from my father."

Olivia offers me more salad, saying there's more of everything if we're still hungry. I scoop a second helping of steak and pan-roasted potatoes onto my plate and then pass the serving dish to Min. When our eyes meet, I try to communicate my need for her help, but I don't know if she gets it.

Neil leans forward and pours more wine into my half-full glass, then refills his own. "Did your father ever tell you about his visit to us in Japan?" he asks me, pushing his chair away from the table and hooking an arm around a chair post.

"No," I say. The only thing I know about Neil from after college is that he went to law school and married Olivia. My father was an army officer in Japan in the early '50s, before he went back to school and became a history professor, but he's never mentioned that he saw Neil there.

"We saw him in '51 or '52, during the Korean War. '52, wasn't it, Olivia?" She nods, but he's not paying attention to her. His eyes are squinting into the past. He's like my father, feeling his way back there, searching for the memories that will trigger his story.

"It was after the peace treaty was signed, at the tail end of the Occupation," Neil continues. "As I remember it, your father was stationed in Japan a year before I was, to replace somebody on his MG team."

"Yeah, he was an education officer," I say, remembering my father's stories of visiting rural schools, where he set up their classes and made sure the children were fed. He would visit houses where the women washed the men's clothes in separate washtubs from their own and dried them on separate bamboo poles. In the countryside where he was, the Japanese children were always clustering around the American soldiers begging for food and attention. And the adults stayed out of sight because they still were terrified of the enemy. I used to imagine those children racing up to my father's Jeep while their parents hid inside their houses. I wondered what the parents and the children thought of each other. Of all the stories about his past my father used to tell, to me those were the saddest.

"What does MG stand for?" Min asks.

"Military Government," Neil answers. "The MG teams moved in right after the war ended to help clean up, demilitarize the country, and steer the Japanese toward democracy."

"Sounds like brainwashing to me," Min says as if to herself and goes back to eating her steak. Why is she being so difficult? If she's going to speak at all, I wish she'd say something helpful.

After a short silence, Neil goes on. "When I was there, I was involved in a number of court cases defending American soldiers. Your father took a short leave and stayed with us during one particular case. It was a big victory. I thought he might have told you about it."

"No, he never did."

"Well, the fellow was a private, stationed out in the Yamagata prefecture. Min, you're not Japanese, are you?" From this angle I can't see his eyes behind the reflecting surfaces of his glasses.

Min puts her fork down. "No, I'm American."

"Of course you are," Neil says, impatient. "I meant your country of origin." All three of us are looking at Min expectantly.

She stares back at Neil, her mouth set in a hard, unyielding line.

I know Min hates being asked this question, in all its variations. But I can't stand the silence hanging in the air. Why won't she just answer him and get it over with? I open my mouth. "Min's Korean," I volunteer, my voice too loud.

"Ah. It was *your* people who pushed the Americans and the Japanese into an alliance by starting a civil war. Interesting turn of events."

"It wasn't a civil war, Neil," Olivia says, gathering our dishes. "Korea was a formerly occupied country split in two by the Americans and the Soviets." He doesn't respond. When she stands up to take the dishes into the kitchen, I want to ask if I can help, but I think it would be rude to interrupt Neil.

"Anyway, the incident in question took place one night when my client was standing guard at his base. It was late at night and he'd been drinking. A young Japanese woman wandered in. Apparently this happened all the time. Many of their men had been killed in the war." Olivia returns with a cut-glass bowl filled with something chocolaty-looking. I'm half-distracted wondering if it's a pudding or a mousse. I hate pudding.

"So this woman spoke to him, but, of course, all she knew was Japanese and all he knew was English. He gestured that he didn't understand, he gestured for her to leave. He was on sentry duty. It was against his orders to allow women on the base."

I glance at Min, who is sitting back with her arms crossed. She's staring at Neil like she despises him. I wish I could reach out and unfold her arms, hold her hand in mine, soften her. Olivia passes me a small bowl of dessert. It's pudding. I take a bite. I smile at her. Then I realize I'll have to eat it all.

"The woman wouldn't go. She pulled at his uniform, repeating the same phrases, and of course he still didn't understand. But he thought he knew what she wanted. It was what they all wanted. He walked with her down the road. When they got to a field he laid her down and had sexual intercourse with her. He was surprised as hell when he was charged with rape. Her family took it to court."

"He was surprised?" I blurt out.

"Sure. The Japanese all knew that the Americans were girl-crazy. Those girls loved the attention. In any case, we won."

"How?" Min asks flatly, challenging him. She's still glaring. Then I realize she guessed the end of his story a while ago.

Neil moves his head to look at Min. His whole face is soft with fondness for his memory. He pulls his chair up close to the table.

"My winning argument was that a civilized society cannot convict a man of rape who had no idea he was raping anyone." He says it gently, with finality, then sips from his wine glass. The candlelight from the table gives his face a sheen like sweat.

"Civilized, shit. You let a rapist walk," Min says.

"It was my job," he reminds her.

"Did you think he was innocent?"

He shrugs. "She did nothing to stop him."

"That's not an answer."

"At no time did she make him feel that what he was doing was wrong."

I can't stand this. Their antagonism is making me really anxious. I want to help Min make him understand, but I don't want to offend Neil. He's been very generous to us. I don't say anything.

Min takes a deep, slow breath, then says, "Think about it from the woman's point of view. Her country had lost a war and was being basically ruled by the occupying army. She was in a deserted area with a man who was obviously stronger than her. She needed his help in some way. He didn't speak her language, and he wasn't trying to understand anymore what she was saying. You lived in Japan, you know the constraints of the culture. Particularly on women. If he didn't mean to rape her, then why didn't he make sure it was what she wanted?"

"The woman wasn't unwilling," Neil says. He says it extra patiently, like he's getting tired of this conversation.

"She wasn't willing," Min counters. "That's the point. Why would anyone want to fuck someone who isn't interested?"

"You're feisty," Neil says, grinning like he's delighted. He leans forward and rests his arms on the table. "Maybe he thought she'd like it." His eyes never leave Min's face. In the dim candlelight, I notice how the golden hue of her skin makes her look darker than him. I feel sick.

Min pushes her chair back with a scraping sound and stands up. "I don't have to take this shit," she tells him. "Excuse me," she says to Olivia. I realize I've forgotten about Olivia. Without even glancing at me, Min walks out of the room.

I panic, watching her leave. Where is she going? Doesn't she understand the position she's putting me in? I would never walk out like this, if we were with her friends or whatever, leaving her to apologize. No matter how unhappy I was, I just wouldn't.

I look back at Neil and Olivia, more alone than I ever could be out there in the empty desert. Olivia looks upset, which makes me feel terrible. Neil's still watching the door Min left by, his mouth curling. "She's something," he says to me. "She's got cheek."

The front door slams shut. All of a sudden I hate Neil. I wish I had taken Min's side. I want to say something withering, but I have no idea what it would be. I am still his guest. He's still my father's friend. I look down at my empty pudding bowl.

"So, Laura, what are your plans now that you're out in the real world?" Neil asks. Olivia looks over at me like she's also interested in hearing the answer.

At first I think he means this trip across the country, then realize he's talking about after college. "Well, I'm thinking of teaching PE. Maybe at a girls' high school, like a boarding school or something. I was on the varsity soccer and basketball teams at Kenyon. And I've taken a lot of classes."

"Oh? What kinds of classes?" Olivia asks. I look at the two of them, sitting at the dinner table talking to me like they're a normal married couple taking a healthy interest in their friend's daughter's future and her companion hasn't just fled the house, offended. I can't wait to get out of here.

"Physiology, education classes, motivational psychology, that kind of thing."

"And do you have a boyfriend?" she asks.

I freeze. What do I say? The love of my life is wandering around outside, and I don't even know how to find her. "No, no boyfriend. Not right now," I answer. I can't look at Neil at all.

"How are your parents?" he asks. His voice is concerned, fatherly.

"They're fine," I say, still not catching his eye. "Just the same." My father still has affairs with his students, I silently add. It makes perfect sense to me that he and Neil are friends.

Neil stands up and stretches, pushing his chest forward and his raised arms back. In his law office he must be used to being the one to end the meeting, standing up and ushering his clients to the door. Olivia begins to clear the table. In the candlelight her face is less severe, just older, tired.

"I guess I'll go upstairs now," I say, rising. "We're pretty beat from driving. Thanks for this great dinner." Olivia nods, half-smiling, and disappears into the kitchen.

Neil takes my hand, covering it with both of his. "We've enjoyed having you," he tells me. I look up at his boyish smile, his dark blue eyes behind his glasses. His gaze is riveting. I start to pull my hand away. Neil holds on. "I'll leave the front door unlocked for your, ah . . . *friend*," he says. Then he lets me go.

About an hour later I'm sitting hunched on one of the beds, still dressed, when I hear the door open. I jump up and meet her as she walks in. She looks exhausted.

"Where have you been?" I whisper, pissed off again. I've been watching the clock, worrying about her. She goes over to the closest bed and curls up on top of it. Immediately my anger is gone. I get on the bed with her, snuggling up against her back, my knees behind her knees. She turns over and lets me put my arms around her. A breeze comes in the screen window behind me.

It is still so new to be holding her, and I am very aware of her slight body and the way her hands feel resting on me. Thin strips of moonlight between the blinds reflect onto the wall. We look at each other. She's so beautiful. I feel a little shock, like pain, near my heart.

"Where did you go?" I ask, gently this time.

"Just around. This town is dead. I felt like a freak."

"We'll leave in the morning," I promise her. I realize part of me was afraid she might hitch a ride back to San Francisco. I touch the side of her neck, stroking just under her hairline.

"Laura," Min says, but she doesn't finish.

I stop caressing her. She's never hesitant. "What?"

"Why did you flirt with him?"

"I wasn't flirting with him!"

"You were. You were attracted to him."

We are so close I can feel her breath on my face. I want to look away. I remember getting out of the car, how his hands around mine made me feel wanted. I couldn't stop grinning up at him. "Well, yeah, so? He's kind of cute for his age, so what? Nothing was going to happen." Doesn't she know I'm committed to her for the long haul?

She just looks at me. After a little while she says, "I knew you didn't want them to know about us. I was trying to be the way you wanted me to be. He's *your* family's friend."

I close my eyes, feeling horrible. I should have trusted Min more. But I did. I trusted her not to leave the table in the middle of dinner.

"He knew anyway," I tell her.

"That was obvious."

I open my eyes. It was? But I ask, "Do you think he saw us in the window when he was grilling the steak?" I felt so powerful, secretly watching him. Now I feel ashamed. I've been acting like a child, wanting all the attention. I say, "Min, you know, I don't hate men now just because we're together."

"Are we together?" she asks, like she doesn't know.

I look into her eyes, inches away. She's not kidding. My heart clutches. I'm afraid I might cry. "Aren't we?" I ask. "You were just upset that I liked Neil."

"I would be upset anyway. He's a creep. The fact is, you've got the world's worst taste in men." She smiles like it's a joke, but I'm hurt. I stop myself from saying something mean about *her* love life.

Min turns over onto her back. "I'm not sure what we are, Laura. You're my best friend. And now we've slept together. I don't know what that makes us."

"It makes us lovers. Doesn't it?" I put my hand on her flat stomach, underneath her shirt. Her skin is very warm. Almost absently, she moves her hand onto my arm, rubbing it lightly.

"For now."

"What do you mean, for now?" I'm getting angry again. "What do you think is going to happen?"

"We'll get back to San Francisco. We'll go back to our different lives."

"What does that have to do with anything?"

"For one thing, you've never been in an open relationship. I'm still seeing Madeleine. And, by the way—"

"Well, isn't Madeleine leaving for New York in a couple of weeks? You don't even like her." I can't believe Min would want to be involved with anyone else now that she's with me.

"We'll see what happens, Laura. I haven't been thinking about her."

"You don't miss her at all?"

"Why would I?"

Hearing that, I feel relieved. I decide it's not important to define our relationship tonight. Lying next to her, I'm starting to feel like I did in our tent, overwhelmed with longing. If I can let what's happening between us take its course, I know that everything will work out. It has to.

I slide my palm up to her breast and rub her nipple gently, back and forth. The soft skin crinkles into a tight little ball. Min closes her eyes. She rolls toward me again to kiss me.

After we've taken off our clothes, I tell her, "I'd like to do for you what you did for me last night." She is licking the side of my neck, long, slow strokes like a cat. They make me shiver. What I'm really doing is reminding her that I've never gone down on a woman before. I don't know what to do.

"Laura-lee," she whispers and lies back. I'm hoping that she's already so excited that whatever I do will feel good to her. I've known Min for over ten years. I'm very aware that this is her body, and that makes it harder. Once I'm down between her bent legs, I part her pubic hair and close my eyes. Hearing her moan, I stay where I am and keep doing what I'm doing. Last night I was completely silent, when I had the entire empty state of Nevada to make noise in. Down the hall from Neil and Olivia, Min's not afraid of being overheard. Listening to her, my fear starts to go too. I don't realize she has come until she sits up, reaching down to pull me up against her.

Lying on top of her, I am smiling, my face pushing against the side of her head. I feel giddy with success. I kiss her cheek near her ear. My lips come away wet. Another tear lands on my nose. I pull my head back, bring my hand from around her to wipe her face. Her eyes are squeezed closed. Putting my head down again, I hold her as tightly as I can. Maybe she didn't have an orgasm after all.

I wait as long as I can stand, then ask, "What's wrong?" I'm afraid she'll tell me I was doing it wrong. I know I can't compare to her other lovers.

Min swallows. "I'm so tired of having to answer those questions, hear those fucking lectures about 'my' country. As though I should know Korea's whole history, even take responsibility for it. I don't care about Korea. I was only born there."

"You're thinking of Neil's story," I say. "And the father and son at the Dairy Queen?" I add, because they are on my mind.

I feel her swallow again. "You have no idea how exhausting it is to carry your race around with you all the time, like a banner that people feel free to comment on. Or use for their own twisted reasons. It never goes away. You just don't know."

I bring my head up so I can see her face. "No," I say quietly, "I don't." I realize it is the first true thing I have said this evening. "I don't know what it's like, Min, but I want to. I wish there was something I could do to make it easier for you."

"Just keep holding me."

I tighten my arms around her. We lie on this stranger's bed, our two damp bodies pressed together. I wish I could go ahead in the world and clear the way before her. I think of the drive ahead of us, the states we will cross. As we near the East Coast, they will become more familiar to me as they grow more alien to Min. I think of Neil, and my blurting out, "She's Korean." If I can't make it easier for Min, at least I can try not to make it more difficult. I close my eyes. I inhale the clean scent of her hair.

"I love you so much, Min," I whisper.

I can't believe how much I love her.

Neither one of us sleeps very well. We get up early and decide to have breakfast on the road. The large house is silent as we carry our knapsacks down the carpeted stairs to the front door. Outside, the pale morning light is a little chilly. We throw our bags in the back of the car and look around us. Down the street, all the lawns are mowed. If there are children living here, their bicycles and toys have been brought inside. The houses are ugly, just because they are meant to look the same. A little regretful, I remember Brigham Young's Beehive House, the Tabernacle. I doubt I will ever come here again.

Min and I half-smile at each other, then turn to go back in the house to write Neil and Olivia a note thanking them for our stay. Olivia is standing in front of the open door in a light blue bathrobe, a pair of slippers on her feet.

"We didn't want to wake you," I say, my voice hushed in the still morning air. "We decided to get a lot of driving done today."

"Won't you have a cup of coffee at least?" she asks. I can't tell if she's being polite or if she really wants us to stay. I actually think she'd like the company.

I look at Min, tempted. She shakes her head. "No, we can't," she tells Olivia. I immediately want to apologize or at least soften Min's words with an explanation. But I step back. Min has said it. We're leaving.

Olivia nods and holds out both her hands to Min, who takes and squeezes them a long time, then lets them go. Olivia turns to me. "Please give my love to both your parents when you talk to them next," she says, hugging me. Smiling, I say I will. I don't mention Neil. I want to ask her why she stays with him, but I'm not sure I want to know the answer.

I hand Min the car keys, and we get in. I roll down my window to let out the stale air. Pulling out of the semicircular driveway, we wave to Olivia standing in front of her massive white house and drive away.

Hours later, we reach Yellowstone National Park. Much of it has been ravaged by a recent forest fire. On either side, we pass acres of black tree trunks sticking up into the sky, burnt free of leaves and branches. We decide to park and get out to take a walking tour of the hot springs. There are boardwalks and a railing to keep people from getting too close. The pools of bubbling water are beautiful and eerie, like jewels and like scabs both. We get whiffs of sulfur with the breeze. Steam floats off the surfaces. The flat ground surrounding the springs is crusted with minerals and small rocks. This could be the surface of the moon. The crowds push us along.

We get back in the car and keep driving north. Further down the road, the traffic slows. We wait in our idling car, wondering if there's been an accident up ahead. After a while, a man in a car going the other way tells us that a buffalo has gotten onto the road. As we drove in, I read to Min from the AAA guidebook about the bison. In this area, the national park is all that's left of the plains that used to be their home. The book said usually they stay away from the roads that wind through it. We wait some more, sweating in the baking heat.

The traffic is stop and go. Finally we see the buffalo up ahead, between the two lanes of stopped cars. Once it lumbers into sight, neither Min nor I say anything. I've seen the buffaloes in the paddocks at Golden Gate Park, but they've been far away. I'm amazed at how big this one is. It has heavy matted fur and a massive head. I love the hump on its back and the brown fur tufting down to its ankles like pants. I've never seen such a strange animal up close before. People are getting out of their cars to take pictures. They stand in front of it. They follow it. It doesn't stop walking. They touch its shaggy hide as though it is not huge and wild but something they own. It is approaching our car. I'm afraid to look into its black, tired eyes, of what mute helplessness I'll see there.

CHAPTER 10

Min

Fall 1985

I CLOSE THE DOOR TO the bedroom softly behind me, leaving my mother half-asleep on the table. I am in a tranquil state too: slowed down, satisfied. Today I worked on her pectoral muscles for the first time. I rested my palm on her sternum between her breasts, and her chest rose with her indrawn breath. When she released it, her whole body settled differently, as though relieved.

Humming, I wash my hands at the kitchen sink, then scrub at the oil bottle. I slowly become aware of the tune. It's a Joan Armatrading song: "I'm Lucky." I glance at the clock on the wall and begin setting the table. It's later than I thought.

The massage room door squeaks open. I listen to my mother's footsteps in the hall, the bathroom door closing. I lay forks on top of the folded paper napkins. I sing the words out loud, surprised that I remember them so well. Before long I hear the spray of falling water.

As I gather glasses from the cupboard, I can hear children playing, their voices loud with laughter, in someone's yard down the block. In the city alone there must be hundreds of people in their kitchens preparing midday meals, hundreds more in the streets on their way to spend time with family or friends. The shower water turns off. The apartment is silent except for the ticking of the clock. It is the silence of in-between time, the moment before everything starts off at a different pace, turning in another direction.

The downstairs door buzzer startles me. I close the cupboards and drawers and meet my mother in the hall clutching an oil-scented sheet to her chest, her hair wrapped in a towel.

"Don't let anyone in," she says, "I'm naked." Her shoulders slope away from her body as if ashamed. Without her glasses her eyes are squinting, half-blind.

"Go get dressed," I say, covering her shoulder with my hand as I squeeze by her. We move to the separate ends of the hall.

Downstairs, I open the front door, and there is Laura, haloed by surprisingly bright daylight on the street behind her. She steps up onto the doorjamb. I put my hands on either side of her face and start to kiss her. My eyes close at the taste of her mouth. I can never keep them open when I am touching someone in a way I want more of. She puts a hand on my side; in the other she is carrying something that bumps between us. I stroke the soft skin of her cheek. My tongue skims over her teeth, enters her wet mouth again, finds her tongue. Then she pulls her head away before the kiss has ended and steps back out of the entryway, out of my reach. Annoyed, I think she must be afraid that someone on the street might see her kissing another woman.

"Look, Min," she says excitedly, turning her head slightly to the side.

Then I see it. "Oh my god, you cut your hair."

It's gone. All her beautiful blonde hair that streamed down to her waist has disappeared. Laura's hair has been chopped bluntly at the back of her neck. She has it pulled back from her wide forehead and held in place by a brown velvet hairband. I loved her hair. The summer after tenth grade, I used to fantasize about Laura sweeping it across my body. I love to run my hand down the silky length of it when we're lying in bed. Now there's nothing left. She's gone and made herself into someone else. I feel breathless. Confused.

Between my thumb and forefinger I grip a few strands at the side of her head, sliding down them until they escape, much too soon, to rest against her cheek. Large gold crescent earrings sway against her neck in the strange new space where her hair used to be. She steps forward into the building, pushing against me and turning me with her. Gone is the gentle, shy way she approaches me, from the side fitting her hand to a curve of my body, slowly, like a sculptor. She's dressed differently too. Instead of her usual khakis or jeans, she's wearing a black scoop-necked sweater tucked into a red and brown printed floral skirt. The truth is she looks really great. She bends down to place the covered bowl of fruit salad she's carrying on the ratty carpet of the hallway. Leaning me back against the wall with her arms around my waist, she guides the door closed with one bunchy black suede boot. I suddenly feel scruffy in my bare feet, baggy pants, and the loose, faded sweatshirt that has fallen down over one shoulder. I've never cared before about how I look. Least of all with Laura.

I can't stop staring at her haircut, fascinated and horrified. My hand is at her head again, taking the hairband off. I run my palm down the short length of her hair, then hold it up to the newly chopped edges at her neck, pushing against their prickly bristles.

"What's wrong?" she asks, taking my hand from her hair and cradling it inside her own. "Don't you like it?"

"Why do you think something's wrong?"

"You look like you're about to cry."

"I do?"

She nods, her eyebrows drawn together.

We are silent a moment. We both watch my hand in hers turning in her grasp, my uncurling fingers opening her own, slipping between them, my thumb gently massaging her palm. Inside, I am whirling. Why do I feel so disappointed?

Then something catches, slowing me down. All the women I have slept with before Laura, I realize, have been androgynous and wiry and a little dangerous-looking, their faces not beautiful but unusual. I am drawn to women's faces that hint at something hidden behind them, some experience or knowledge I can't presume to know about. It finally occurs to me that what I was attracted to in those women was their acceptance of themselves as lesbians. Their identification as dykes showed in their faces. With each of them, I was drawn to my own kind.

Laura, on the other hand, looks even more like what she is—a straight woman—than she did before. She looks like someone I would never be with, like someone I wouldn't even know. It doesn't matter that she's sleeping with a woman. She will never be like me. She will never love me the way I loved her in high school, when what I felt was something I couldn't come back from. I know Laura will return to men one day. When she gets married and has kids with one of them, I'll take her children out on weekends and be their mother's wacky friend. It's not that scenario I mind. But I resent her assumption that in the meantime she can cultivate her straight look and still walk with me out into the world.

"Min," she says almost sharply, and I stop my hand's motion.

I can't look at her. I begin pulling Laura's black sweater from the waist of her skirt. I want to push it up to her neck, take her nipples in my mouth, one then the other, here at the foot of the stairs.

"Don't," she says, stopping my hand with her own. She pulls my body tight against hers. We stand unmoving, holding on, while my heart beats, and my breath expands and contracts in my ribcage, and a cool draft of air from beneath the door nips at my ankles.

"It looks . . ." I don't know what to say to her. "I liked the way you were before."

She drags my arms from around her, pulls the hairband from my hand and settles it back on her head. "Jesus, Min. These last few months being with you, it's like I finally got a chance to discover who I really am. I like my body now. I finally feel attractive. Are you saying I made a mistake by cutting my hair? I did it for me. I thought you'd appreciate that." Then she stoops to retrieve her fruit salad and runs up the stairs, her skirt fluttering behind her.

In the kitchen, my mother is putting her tuna casserole into the oven. She closes the oven door and turns around. "Laura, you look wonderful. When did you have your hair cut?"

"Yesterday," Laura answers, not looking at me as I come in to the room. She puts the fruit salad on the table and moves into my mother's embrace. My mother's hands around Laura's back are swathed in my roommate's large oven mitts, one that looks like the green head of an alligator, the other like a sheep with little cloth ears and button eyes sewn on. Of course my mother likes Laura's haircut. Was I supposed to lie to her? I start taking food from the refrigerator to the table. I've completely lost the feeling of satisfaction I had earlier. Their embrace goes on a long time.

"It's so good to see you, Catherine," Laura tells my mother, still hugging her. They break it off, grin at each other. Mom, after her massage and shower, looks ruddy and a little blissed out, the way I imagine saints look. Beatific. Her frizzy hair is still damp. I notice she's dressed up too, in tailored linen pants and a blouse.

"I wish you would come up to Fairfax and visit me sometime," she tells Laura, pulling off the oven mitts and pushing her glasses farther up on her nose. "With or without Min. I'd love to see you." She says it as though they're alone in the room.

"Okay, great, I'd like that," Laura answers. I can't tell if the enthusiasm in her voice is meant for me, to tell me that at least my mother appreciates her. "I'm visiting my parents next week. I could drop by afterwards."

I step around the two of them as they continue talking. Laura's neck is bare, beguiling. The haircut gives her face angles that I like. Cheekbones. I look away. What Laura doesn't understand is that she thinks she's in love with me only because we're sleeping together. If she were a lesbian, that would be the beginning of it, not the end. Laura has no idea what it means to put another woman first. To want a woman without needing to look around and check out where the men are. I wish we could be alone together. I take orange juice and milk from the refrigerator and put them on the table beside the butter and jam and lemon curd. The doorbell rings.

"Laura, could you start the coffee?" I ask as I leave the kitchen.

Margo is looking worriedly down the street when I open the door. "I think I'm blocking someone's driveway," she says. "I can't afford to get towed again."

"Why don't you put a note on the windshield saying you're here? Tell them you'll move it if they need you to."

"Smart cookie. Here." She hands me a warm paper bag full of fresh-baked crumpets from the shop on Irving. I use it to prop open the front door, then step onto the sidewalk in my bare feet. The bright autumn air is chilly, a relief from the stuffiness of my overheated apartment.

Margo plops herself down on the doorstep and pulls her knapsack off her back to rummage for a pen and paper. Margo carries her knapsack with her everywhere. She dreads being caught without her address book or her journal or her mace. She scribbles a note and hurries down the street with it, listing slightly because of her limp. The sun glints off her silver hair. I notice she's wearing the pinstriped vest I gave her with her usual jeans and Oxford shirt. I smile, watching her retreating back.

When we were together, two years ago, Margo began to want a committed, long-term relationship, despite our age difference. With her I almost wanted one too, but not enough. I remember telling her as we got dressed one morning that I wished we could have met in ten years, when I might be ready to settle down. I loved her fierce opinions, her wisdom, her straightforwardness, her open heart. I loved her huge collection of lesbian novels and her three dogs she kept well cared for and was obviously devoted to. When we did break up, she told me she needed to be out of touch for a while. I was surprised by how much I missed her during those weeks. In her absence I felt an ache that had never been there before. So when we did talk again, I worked hard at establishing a friendship. I think we're closer now than we would have been if we'd only been lovers or only friends. Margo agrees with me. She says that for lesbians it's often true. It was she who gave me the button I wear on my leather jacket: *An army of ex-lovers cannot fail.*

When Margo returns, she is panting. "Hey, babe," she says. Her embrace is vigorous and long. With my arms around her, I remember our bodies together: the force, the heat. I rub her back, feeling her spine beneath her clothes. There is still a spark of that desire between us now, a small reminder. I wonder what it will be like when Laura and I stop sleeping together. I know we won't resume our old, childhood connection; we outgrew that as soon as I let her kiss me in her flimsy tent in Nevada. The truth is we started to drift apart when I came out in eleventh grade. Maybe becoming lovers was the only way for us to find the friendship again.

Margo loosens her hold. Opening my eyes, I see a man and woman scowling at us as they pass by arm in arm on the sidewalk. I want to laugh at their disapproving faces. The sky is beginning to cloud over. Then the man says to the woman, "That's disgusting." Margo stiffens. I turn away and steer Margo inside the building, grabbing her knapsack and the crumpets. Without speaking, we climb the stairs to my apartment side by side.

Laura and my mother are leaning against the counter in the kitchen, deep into a conversation we have interrupted. They both look startled seeing us with our arms around each other's shoulders.

"Mom, this is Margo. Margo, Catherine." My mother holds out her hand a little uncertainly. Margo takes her arm from around me and shakes my mother's hand emphatically. "I'm so glad to finally meet you, Catherine."

I feel Laura's gaze on me, but when I look at her she glances away. I go to stand beside her, slide my arm around her waist. Her haircut gives her face more precision in profile, erasing the soft, fuzzy edges. She's more feminine now. No, that's not it. She was right: she's more aware of her attractiveness. I can't stop staring at her, drawn yet disturbed, trying to comprehend the transformation.

Laura bends her head toward me. "Why do you have to touch everybody so much?" she demands in a low voice, crossing her arms across her chest.

"Laura . . ."

We've been through this before. Now that we're lovers, she can't accept things about me that she took for granted when we were friends. After spending a night together, Laura will complain I don't have enough time for her, or she'll try to pull me back to bed when I have to go because I've got a massage client scheduled. She'll leave bewildered messages on the machine wondering where I am when I don't call her back for a few hours or a day, even though she knows I am working or with a friend. We argue a lot over what she sees as my inability to discriminate between clients and friends, between friends and lovers. She says these crossings-over of boundaries are confusing and in the end someone is bound to get hurt. We don't discuss non-monogamy anymore since I told her about a one-night stand, the only sexual encounter with another woman I've actually had since we got involved. Except for saying goodbye to Madeleine, of course. All along, I've made it clear that I'm not interested in a committed relationship. I've been completely open with Laura. But I feel her resentment, insistent, hovering over me, as if she is owed something. It infuriates me.

"Laura," I say, keeping my voice down, "when I'm with you, I'm with you. But I can't be with you all the time. Margo is a close friend."

"Would you ever sleep with her again?"

"Hey, Laura," Margo greets her, moving over to us. They've met only twice, once when Laura was home from college and wanted to meet my current girlfriend, and once this fall when Margo came for a massage and Laura was still in bed, refusing to leave.

Laura looks up and smiles. "Hi, Margo," she answers as though she is happy to see her.

They don't shake hands or touch in any way. Suddenly I am nervous that this gathering is going to bomb. I should never have brought Margo into the flux. She is too different from my mother and Laura, too provocative. That's of course one of the reasons I love her. I wanted the company of another lesbian at my brunch, someone who understands that need and accepts me utterly. I don't know if we will ever sleep together again. But I won't let Laura close down the possibility.

"Okay, we're all here," I say abruptly. "Let's eat. I can't wait any longer."

My mother shoos us toward the table so she can re-don the oven mitts and rescue her baking casserole. I think she wants to assert her role as my mom in front of my friends, even though I haven't lived in her home for four years. When she calls me now and then to offer me a meal or a day shopping for clothes, I realize she misses me. Thankfully, she is never as bad as the first month I moved out, right after graduation, when she called me every night checking that I had turned off the stove or locked the front door. The truth is sometimes I miss her too. At the table, she sets down the steaming dish in front of Margo and Laura with a small flourish. We all laugh.

I bring the crumpets and the coffee pot. We pour our drinks, pass food to one another, spread butter and lemon curd, and start eating. A feeble ray of sunshine falls on a corner of the table from the window behind Margo. I look at the three women sitting at my table. Now that we are eating, I realize what I've done. This is the first time I've deliberately brought people from different parts of my life together. It's terrifying. And it's exhilarating.

Margo, sitting across from me, looks up as she brings a spoonful of fruit salad to her mouth. "What?"

"I'm just glad you're here," I tell her. "All of you. It's nice." I know they're not so sure, but I don't care. Laura's smiling at me. I lean forward, reaching past the leg of the table, and put my hand over hers in her lap. She curls her fingers around mine.

"This *is* nice, Min," my mother says. "My generation doesn't seem to have potlucks anymore." She turns to Margo. "Do you know you're the first friend of Min's I've met? Besides Laura, who's an old friend of the family." She turns back to me. "You could have invited Margo up to Fairfax any time, you know. Or to one of our lunches here in the city. I would like to meet your friends. I always have."

As though a switch has been flipped, I am immediately irritated. I breathe in, then out. "Mom, don't forget you haven't been very happy about my 'friends.'" I squeeze Laura's hand and let it go.

My mother looks startled. "I didn't mean your girlfriends. Don't you have any plain and simple friends? What about heterosexual women? Or men?"

Men. I hardly ever think of men.

Laura says, "Of course Min has friends. I'm one." We all stare at her. Her face flares scarlet. "I mean, I've been her friend for a long time. I think I still am." She looks at me for help.

"You are," I say. "You're the one who insists that you're not."

My mother glances from Laura to me and shakes her head. "I think you lesbians make everything so complicated for yourselves." She raises her coffee cup, sips.

"Well, wait a minute, Catherine," Laura protests. "We're not all lesbians here."

She puts her coffee cup down. "I'm sorry, Laura. I just assumed, because you and Min . . ." She trails off. I hate the change in her tone, the sudden solicitousness.

"It's okay," Laura assures her, smiling. Margo and I exchange glances, looking away quickly. The sad thing is, compared to most of my friends' parents, my mother is a paragon of acceptance. At least she talks about it.

"So what *are* you?" Margo asks Laura, sounding curious. I smile a little. Margo is never merely curious.

"I don't know," Laura says simply. She sits back, spreading her hands on her lap. "Maybe bisexual? I don't really want to label myself."

Margo gazes at Laura impassively. "Uh huh." Margo has little tolerance for women who sleep with women but won't call themselves lesbians. Normally neither do I, but at the moment I'm more concerned that Margo might jump all over Laura about it. "Well," Margo continues, "when I came out in the '70s, we didn't have the luxury of tinkering with the definition of our sexuality. Either you were a lesbian or you weren't. I don't believe in bisexuality."

"I don't think it matters what you believe," Laura says, her voice shaking. She glances at me, then brings her attention back to Margo. "I just don't feel comfortable calling myself a lesbian. It doesn't feel true." She looks back at me. I wish I could feel more sympathetic.

"Look, it's actually very simple," Margo forges on, gesturing with the side of her flattened palm on the table, like she's cutting into it. "Lesbians are women who love other women. Do you love Min?"

Laura hesitates, darting a look at my mother, who keeps on eating with her eyes lowered. "Yes," Laura tells Margo. "I'm in love with Min."

Margo grins, shaking her head as if everything is resolved. But I stare at Laura, who's feeling so brave for declaring her love in public, and I think, *Now* you decide you're in love with me? I will always remember how completely alone I was when I fell in love with her back in high school. All she cared about then was boys. It was agony, and no one knew. No one will ever know.

"But I've never loved any other woman," Laura adds. "I don't think I ever will."

"Why not?" I ask, pushing my plate away from me and leaning my forearms on the table.

"Because I'm with you."

"What about when we break up?"

Laura stares at me.

"If we break up," I correct myself.

Laura shrugs.

"Okay, what about men?" Margo asks.

Laura turns to her, sitting up straighter. Her golden earrings sway back and forth below her small, exposed ears. I'd like to nibble on her earlobe. Whatever she says she feels about me, I am not in love with Laura. The risk is even greater now. What *about* men?

"I don't know," she answers Margo. "I've never had much luck with men. I don't know."

"Why can't you be sure?" Margo demands.

I would be a fool to fall in love.

I'm afraid Margo might launch into a speech about heterosexual privilege when my mother says, "You know, I was wrong about making things difficult for yourselves." She is pushing the remains of her helping of casserole around on her plate, absorbed. "I think your generation," she nods toward Laura and me, "has a harder time now because you don't have the rules we did. You don't know how to proceed. I think people to-day are much more interested in themselves, what they think they need at the moment, than they were in my time. There's a diminished sense of responsibility to others. Maybe you think you have more freedom, but it seems to me you flounder around a lot, reinventing the wheel."

Margo nods. "I agree with you, Catherine. I think there's been a real erosion of responsibility, even in the lesbian community. The women who are coming out now have no idea what a relationship looks like, what it requires."

"What do you mean? Because I've had a lot of girlfriends?" I ask, in-credulous.

Margo laughs. "No, honey, you're not the first dyke who's slept around." Laura visibly flinches at the word "dyke."

"Min," my mother answers me, "I'm not talking about you personally. I see it everywhere, a confounding inability to think about consequences before acting." I feel Laura's gaze on me. When I turn to her, she has that sad-eyed yearning look on her face. I hate it.

Margo has unobtrusively gotten up to retrieve the coffee pot from where it's warming. She pours us all fresh cups and pours orange juice for herself. I look up at her and smile.

She sits back down. "What I wanted to say earlier when you, Catherine, were saying lesbians have a complicated life, is that I think by being lesbians, we create our own kind of freedom. We're forced to. Even now when being a lesbian is a little easier. Definitely back in the '70s."

"How do you mean?" Laura asks.

"How do I mean," Margo muses. She takes a breath. "When I came out to my family, my father disowned me. I haven't seen my parents in twelve years. That's fucked up, but it's very liberating too. I don't have to worry about going home for the holidays. I'm free to make my own rituals that are meaningful to me. Being a lesbian means we can cut out lots of shit, like dealing with men and feeling pressured to get married and have children, because already what's important has changed. Straight people think we're being defensive, but we're not. Coming out is such a terrifying and exhilarating step to take that all the other life decisions that follow are just not going to seem as huge."

"Is it really so difficult?" my mother asks. "Min didn't seem to have any trouble. I think I would have been more open if I'd seen she was having a hard time."

"Uh huh," Margo says. "You mean you would've been concerned because there was something wrong with her."

"No! That's not what I meant." My mother looks at Margo, who's smiling, enjoying teasing her. Mom softens. "Well, okay, yes. If she had struggled with accepting it, I wouldn't have felt she had become almost another person."

Margo leans back, satisfied. "Honey, it's just as I thought. Mothers never change. They can't understand why their daughters aren't exactly like them."

Margo and my mother gaze at each other appreciatively. I catch Laura's eye. I raise my eyebrows twice briefly, suggestively. She laughs out loud.

"Does anyone want more to eat?" I ask. My mother shakes her head, drinks her coffee. I start to collect the empty plates.

"No, let me," Laura says, pushing my hands away.

"I almost forgot." Margo bends down to her knapsack on the floor beside her chair, unzips it, and brings out a package in gift wrapping. "Happy belated birthday."

"I told you I didn't want a present," I say, pleased and, more than that, embarrassed. She slides it across the table to me in her impatient way. Beneath the blue and white paper is a book of poems, Judy Grahn's *The Work of a Common Woman*. Laura comes back to the table, pulls her chair closer to mine, smooths her skirt beneath her as she sits.

"Thank you," I say, looking up at Margo, my hand on the book's cover. I am moved. The summer we were lovers, she read me several of these poems, just read without commenting on them. I remember the lines, *my lover's teeth are white geese flying above me, my lover's muscles are rope ladders under my hands.* Margo always kept the book by her bed, within easy reach.

I don't agree with Margo that coming out is the hardest thing a lesbian will ever do. For me, by the time I knew I was a dyke, I knew there were people like me. I had other women to identify with almost from the beginning. I remember how much I admired Alison's style, her assuredness, and I learned from her, and from all the others. My mother is right: it was easy to acknowledge my lesbianism. That was where I could recognize myself in the world around me.

A couple of weeks ago Laura showed me a newspaper article about white parents in Minnesota who send their adopted Korean children to culture camp for a week every summer. The reporter was beside herself with admiration for the American parents who pack off their foreign-born adopted kids to go experience their original culture. For one

entire week a year. Seven whole days. Reading the article, I was disgust-
ed. What can a child really take in over seven days when it is absent
from her life the other fifty-one weeks of the year? How does it become
"her" culture? If there had been a camp when I was little, and if both my
parents had agreed it was important for me to go, a big if, what could I
possibly have been able to take away with me that was mine?

I tried to imagine how straight parents might try to give their young
lesbian daughter "her" culture, which no straight parent would consider
doing in the first place. A rainbow flag and evenings at Sweet Honey
in the Rock and Ferron concerts? It made me laugh, and Laura didn't
understand what I found so funny. Lesbian culture is being with other
lesbians, acknowledging what is true for us, talking about things straight
people don't even think about and, as Margo said, not having to talk
about the things they do. I watch Laura lean forward against the table,
her arms cradled at her stomach. She is speaking intently. I wonder suddenly if maybe the real point of Korean culture camp isn't learning the
country's history and eating the spicy foods but living for that one week
a year among other adopted Korean children, forging their own culture.
If I could have taken that week of being with others like me into the rest
of the year, maybe I wouldn't have felt so alone.

I look up, becoming aware again of the kitchen with its cold floor
under my feet and its yellow walls and the weak shaft of sunlight like
another presence in the room. ". . . is true," Laura is saying. "My parents
are pressuring me to go to grad school and become a professional. They
don't even care so much about a professional what. I love sports, but I'm
not sure if I want to coach. Why do I have to decide right away? I really
don't know what I want to do."

"What are you doing now?" Margo asks.

"Temping. Actually, I'm not working right now," Laura answers apologetically.

Margo nods, her eyes on Laura. "You're lucky you can do that," she
says. There's no irony or judgment in her voice.

Mom shifts in her chair. "Margo, go back a minute. Don't you think you're being extreme not talking to your parents for so long? Do you actually think it's better to be cut off from them?" I stare at her. What's she talking about? She sees her parents maybe once every five years.

"*They* forbid *me* to set foot in the house." Margo is silent a minute, the side of her hand sawing the edge of the table. "I do talk to my mother on the phone a few times a year," she says quietly. I think of my father, then shake the thought off. "No," Margo continues, "I'm not saying lesbians are better off without their parents."

My mother smiles slightly.

"When I came out," Margo goes on, "it was 1973, and the lesbians and gay men I knew were either closeted or had been thrown out of the house. Frankly, I never imagined that one day I'd be sitting here with you and Min at the same table, a mother and her out lesbian daughter."

My mother smiles at me, her face glowing, the way it does at the end of a massage, and for the moment I am proud of us. I say to Margo, "It wasn't easy. It took a long time."

"I know, babe," Margo says gently. "And maybe your parents," she nods at Laura, "will accept your choices and maybe they won't."

"They know about Min," Laura says quickly, even though nobody has asked her.

"You told them?" I ask, surprised. She never mentioned it to me.

"Well, I think they know. It's pretty obvious from what I say about you. We haven't actually discussed it—"

"Why not?"

"There's no need to. They know. If they haven't figured it out, it's because they don't want to know."

"Doesn't that bother you?" I ask. "That your parents don't want to know who you're involved with?"

"It's not a big deal," Laura insists, her voice rising. "They haven't known about most of my boyfriends. What difference does it make?"

"Well, for one thing, they've known me a long time. For another, you say you love me. It seems pretty deceptive for all of you to pretend we're just friends."

"We don't pretend, Min, we just don't talk about it."

"That's the same thing."

"That's *not* the same thing! How come when you're telling me how you live your life, there are these subtle distinctions, all these ways that conflicting things are true at the same time, but when I tell you what I'm doing, you tell me I'm wrong?"

"Because—"

I fall silent. She's right. I think she's hiding, afraid to stand up to her parents. She's justifying the fact that she cares more about what they'll think if she tells them about me than what I'll think if she doesn't.

"You are *so* classic." Margo draws out the word, grinning. "I've been watching lesbians argue about how to be out for years. Listening to the two of you, though, I realize how much the context has changed. Back in the '70s, we thought the future of the gay community was at stake. And it was. Back then we had a movement; we had several movements. I miss those days. We worked damn hard." My mother is watching Margo and nodding, smiling a little.

"Here in San Francisco?" I ask. I remember Alison's outbursts of rage the summer we worked together scooping ice cream. The winter before, Dan White had shot and killed Mayor Moscone and another Supervisor, Harvey Milk, who, Alison informed me, had been San Francisco's first openly gay elected official. I had vivid memories of my mother the next morning reading the paper at breakfast and freaking out that the mayor had been gunned down in City Hall. In May, White had gotten off with a lenient sentence because of his "twinkie" defense: he'd been on a sugar high. Furious, Alison had rioted with the rest of the gay community that night. I remember how her eyes gleamed when she described the police cars in front of City Hall going up in flames. That summer, I couldn't have cared less about the city's politics. In the middle of sleeping with Miguel and being in love with Laura, I didn't see what it had to do with me.

"No," Margo answers, "I was still in New York then. I tell you, it was an exciting time. It was scary too. I used to get handwritten notes in my mailbox that said, 'Kill dykes not babies.' My phone was tapped when I was involved in the gay rights bill rallies. Friends of mine were bashed. Some of them died. There were nights I was afraid to go home."

"Why didn't you call the police?" Laura asks.

Margo stares at her. "You have no idea what I'm talking about, do you? It was the cops we were most afraid of. They didn't care that people stoned us for handing out leaflets. We were the troublemakers, the lawbreakers. You've never taken the streets and faced down a line of cops in full riot gear. They weren't there to protect us."

"But you put yourself in that situation," Laura argues. "And then you make it sound like you were being heroic."

"We were trying to claim our lives."

In the sudden silence, Margo looks down. She swallows. I am mortified by Laura's ignorance, her obtuseness. But I also understand it. As much as I admire Margo's involvement in the gay rights movement, it seems removed from my own struggles, the choices I have made. Her head still lowered, Margo tells Laura, "You college types can be so arrogant."

My mother has been rubbing the bridge of her nose, pushing up her glasses with the back of her hand. She removes her glasses entirely, folds them closed, and places them on the table. She lays her hand on Margo's arm. I realize they could probably reminisce for hours about their political involvements. Without her glasses, my mother's face is more vulnerable, the lines of worry and middle age etched more deeply.

I say to Margo, "It *is* different now. I've never had the sense of community you had."

"Maybe you haven't looked. It's out there." Margo smiles at my mother, who smiles back and takes her hand from Margo's sleeve.

I want her to understand. "You've told me that when you came out, there were other lesbians who taught you how to be a lesbian, like how to talk to women in bars and who to watch out for. Where the bars *were*. The codes and the rules like keeping your fingernails trimmed. That's pretty obvious, I could figure out a lot of that for myself. But nobody ever *told* me. They looked out for you and you for them. I never got that."

My mother says, "That's what I was saying, remember?"

I ignore her. "Now there are more dance clubs, there are even bars where mostly dykes of color go, but I don't feel any more of a sense of belonging."

"I hate to admit this," Margo offers, "but AIDS is bringing the community back together again. The men and women both. That's the only good to come out of this whole damn mess. It's always when a crisis threatens us that we get mobilized."

All I feel thinking about AIDS is bored. I don't have any interest in working on a hotline or doing educational outreach or buying groceries for men who are bedridden. I am nothing like Margo. I can't imagine a community ready-made, pulling me in to work with them. I can only create my own constellation, one by one, each star at some distance from the others, myself in the middle.

I turn to Laura and rub the fabric of her skirt, my hand closing around her muscled thigh underneath. I'm getting used to her haircut. She is gazing at me, her eyebrows pulled together. "I think you have a lot of community, Min. How can you say you don't?"

"That's what it looks like to you, you're on the outside."

Her mouth twitches. She looks away, then tries again. "But isn't this community?" she asks, indicating the table with a sideways dip of her head, the four of us seated around it.

I have no idea why I suddenly want to cry.

My mother is the first to leave. We all huddle together in the hallway downstairs. Mom hugs us goodbye, even Margo. Laura stands beside me, her hand around my waist. I bend my head toward her and kiss her neck just behind her ear, where the skin is newly bare. I love the smell of her, clean and slightly sweet, like clover. I breathe in, my lips lingering there. Her dangling earring bumps against my cheek.

Laura pulls her head away slightly. She doesn't want me to nuzzle her in front of my mother and Margo. After three months, she still won't hold hands with me on the street. Even at Ocean Beach she walks fearfully, her fingers cupped stiffly around mine. She used to like holding my hand outside, back when we were "just friends." Now, whenever someone approaches us on the damp sand, she disentangles quickly, pulling her warm skin from mine.

But she wants me to commit to her forever. Every day she gazes at me with her sad hope and a stubborn, growing resentment.

Finally Mom leaves, waving from the street as we crowd around the front door. Margo leads the way upstairs and back into the apartment. "Your mother's so accepting of you," she says over her shoulder. "You're lucky."

I flip on the kitchen light. The yellow walls jump out, brighter than I remember them. I want to put on warm socks, but I'm too lazy to go find them.

"What do you mean? She was spouting homophobic comments the minute you guys showed up."

Margo turns on me. "What do you want, Min? At least she lets you come home."

We stare at each other. At least she lets me come home. Is that all I should hope for? I imagine Margo standing on the doorstep of her parents' house, but the door is closed, the house is empty. I imagine Margo walking on a dark city street, and when someone approaches, she raises her arm to shield her face. *My lover's teeth are white geese flying above me.* I accused her—her generation—of not looking out for me, of not being there to show the way. But I can ask of my mother much more than merely being willing to speak to me. And I can listen to Laura say she isn't lesbian without turning away. *My lover's muscles are rope ladders under my hands.*

I gather Margo into my arms like folds of cloth. "I'm sorry," I say into the starched collar of her shirt. I rub her back, and she lets out a breath, leaning into me.

Over her shoulder, I see Laura walking out of the room. "Laura," I call, and when she turns back, I hold out my arm to her, inviting her in.

CHAPTER 11

Catherine

Fall 1985

IN AN ALCOVE BETWEEN TWO bookcases near the front of the store, I sit on a low stool, hunched over a box of hardback books. I reach for the nearest one, its cover green with gold lettering, wipe it down with a damp rag, and put it into one of eight piles gathered like schoolchildren sitting for story time at my feet: fiction, history, poetry, art history, philosophy and religion, sociology, women's issues, and drama. The dust makes me sneeze every so often. The stacks of history and sociology are growing tallest, mostly because I assign titles there for lack of a better choice. By now my back hurts, and my sweatshirt is smeared with my own dirty fingerprints. No one has come into the store for half an hour. On the radio, Mozart's Symphony No. 40 in G Minor keeps me company.

Laura has promised to visit me this afternoon. It will be the first time I have seen her alone for more than a year. Since she graduated from Kenyon and moved back to San Francisco, she has always had Min with her. They are lovers now. When Min told me, over two months ago at the end of summer, my immediate reaction was: *of course*. They belong together. Their friendship has always contained an element of wooing. My second feeling, following fast on the heels of the first, was a mixture of dismay, discomfort, even anger. I thought, I hope they don't kiss in front of me. I thought, Now they're going to shut me out. These are feelings that still stir around inside me. I am happy that Laura is visiting me today, and I know that one reason is because I will have a chance to claim her back.

I pick up another book, blow the dust from the top edge of its compressed pages. Despite my sore back, I like the rhythmic monotony of this work. I like categorizing the books, escorting them properly labeled to their respective shelves. I like the dreamy time inside these four walls, as lasting and as irrelevant to the outside world as time is inside the pages of a novel. Surrounded by row upon row of books that other people have read, other people have handled, cherished, and perhaps reluctantly let go, I feel I'm among an extended family of parents and spouses and siblings who've come to live with me for a while before moving on to other homes, their future lives. I only wish I could live with people this way: inviting them into my life without conditions, allowing them to leave without the fear they will never come back.

I have been dreaming more about Laura. This week I've dreamt about her almost every night. She takes me by the hand to the ocean's edge, then vanishes. Or I search for something I have misplaced, and Laura comes to help me. Or I look for something missing and finally discover it is Laura, who is my daughter, my lost daughter. The daughter I gave birth to. Each time I've woken up from these dreams in the dark, sweating. Each time I've realized immediately that in the dream I forgot about Min; she didn't exist. That scares me. I don't know why it happens, and I am afraid of it. In the night I lie curled up at the edge of the bed, my sweat cold on my skin, willing myself to fall back asleep. In the mornings I am exhausted.

The little bell on the front door of the bookshop tinkles as the door creaks open. I swivel my body around and look up to see Laura clicking the door carefully shut behind her. On the other side of the front windows, a white pickup truck slowly drives down the street, while a young man and woman walking hand in hand past the store glance at the book display but do not stop. Laura's gaze moves from the tall bookshelves to the empty counter where the cash register sits to the poster on the wall behind it, a portrait of Emily Dickinson looking very proper and yet defiant. Then Laura's eyes shift as she sees me bent over my boxes with my rag in one hand and a hardbound book in the other. In the dim light it seems to take her a moment to recognize me. When she moves forward, my heart is dazzled by the light of her smile.

As soon as she grins at seeing me, I find myself inside my nighttime dreams of her. The feeling is exactly the same: *this* is my daughter; *this* is the child I have been missing all these years. It is as though I have never looked at her closely until now, when all the while the proof was in plain sight. The joy I feel is sharp, like the cold ache of ice cream in summer. For a second I experience a sense of completeness I haven't felt for many years and never expected to find again, though I have dreamed it. She approaches me, that radiant smile still on her face, her arms extending toward me. If she is saying anything, I cannot hear it. Somehow I get to my feet, move toward her. I haven't lost her. She is right here in front of me.

As soon as I feel the warm, living weight of Laura's body against mine, I remember Min, and I am overwhelmed by guilt. How can I wish for even one moment that Laura was my daughter, as though Min had never existed? How can I think of Laura as the daughter I would have had, when it is Min who has *been* my daughter for the past twenty-two years? Is it because Laura and I are more alike and see things in similar ways? My relationship with Laura is so much simpler, more relaxed than mine with Min that perhaps it is normal to feel that Laura could be related to me. Yet I am uneasy, almost afraid. I remember when the girls were growing up, strangers on the street used to assume it was Laura who was my daughter. Because she looked more like me than Min did. Because she was white too.

My limbs go cold. That's why she inhabits my dreams. I feel frozen by surprise, horrified by my own impulse. Laura is the daughter that Andy would have accepted. Because she is white. I can't believe I have this wish. I want the daughter that Andy would have loved.

At the thought of Andy, I begin to cry. I never cry. Even more alarming, I can't get myself to stop. I sob, half-hicupping, trying to swallow to keep down the huge balloon of sorrow that is suddenly swelling inside me. I feel Laura's surprise in the way her arms start to lift from my back, uncertain. Her head pulls away from where it was resting against my shoulder. Then she tightens her grip, holding me more firmly. One hand makes small rubbing motions up and down my back. This only makes me cry harder. I stand sobbing in Laura's arms, silently asking for Min's forgiveness.

I try to get a grip on myself, but I can't do it. Something long stopped up has been forced open in me. I am afraid I will never stop crying. I can't bear it that I am capable of denying my daughter, even for a moment. How can I possibly feel the same thing Andy did? I hated that it mattered to him that Min was Asian and so couldn't be, or even pass for, my biological child. As we walked silently back to the car, I could only feel how irrevocably I had become her mother. No one, I thought, not even Andy, could come between us.

Suddenly my despair is so great, I can hardly feel Laura's reassuring presence against me anymore. I couldn't hate Andy. And I couldn't forgive him. The balloon of pain spreading from my chest seems much larger than my fragile body's ability to hold it. I'm afraid I will burst apart. I hear a groan, like a tree sawed through starting to fall, and I realize it's me. I am still waiting for him. For twenty-one years I have not allowed myself to accept that Andy is dead. I need him alive too much, to set right what he put askew in me. He told me my daughter was too different to be mine. Then he died. I've been trying to prove him wrong ever since.

I let him come between us after all.

I am holding on to Laura now to keep from sliding away, carried off into a whirlwind of grief and regret. If I open my eyes, I am certain everything will be spinning around me; already my head seems to be floating somewhere above the rest of my body. All I can do is cry and hold on tight. Behind my closed lids, I can see Andy clearly: brown curly hair, straight long nose, generous face. He's still young, not even out of college. It's as if I was with him just yesterday. He is looking at the ground as I speak, his thick brows lowered in concentration. He starts to nod. He looks up at me, and his eyes change, becoming warmer, softer. He doesn't agree, but he understands my feelings. This is my memory of who he used to be, and this is my dream.

Finally the tears start to subside. I become aware of my trembling legs, my feet still standing on the firm floor, of the traffic sounds out on the street. My chest and throat feel sore, raw, but the sadness feels manageable now. As Laura pulls slowly away from me, I register with shock how separate her small body is from mine. And then she is Laura again, standing uncomfortably before me, and I am a woman puffy-eyed and snotty from crying. I have no idea how long it's been. I pull out a crumpled tissue from my jeans pocket and blow my nose. Laura plunges her hands into the pockets of her wool jacket and offers me another tissue. I blow into it too, then use the dry edges to wipe my cheeks and chin. I feel as if my face has swollen to twice its size. I feel as though there's still a reservoir of tears pooled inside me, deeper than I could ever dive.

"Thanks," I say, starting to hand back the tissue. Then I realize what I am doing and pocket it. Laura smiles at me. She has such a kind face, open and intelligent. Her newly shorn hair suits her. I look around and remember where we are. There are the tall shelves full of books, the racks of cards near the front, the bulletin board filled with notices of rooms for rent and jobs wanted, the radio playing a piece for horns I don't know. There are the cardboard boxes I was rummaging through, and the piles of books I have dusted and divided to be sold. The store is still empty, except for the two of us. If a customer came in while I was crying, I never knew it.

"Are you all right?" Laura asks me. She looks worried, as if at any moment I might launch into something else unforeseen.

It occurs to me that I have frightened her. And why shouldn't she be scared? I was afraid myself. I put my hand on her arm and try to smile reassuringly. "I will be. Why don't we go to my office in back? I could use some tea."

She nods, her gaze dropping away from mine.

At the front door I turn the lock and flip over the "Open" sign to "Closed." On the sidewalk outside, the wind scuttles a crumpled brown paper bag underneath a parked car. The sky is a uniform dark gray, threatening rain. I hope for a thunderstorm, crashingly loud and blindingly bright, but those are rare here on the West Coast. In Northern California there is no dramatic weather like back east, only the threat of earthquakes. There are no snowbound winters or dripping hot summers, only seasons of fog and rain. I miss the landscape I grew up in. I glance at my storefront display of books and make a mental note to change it tomorrow. It needs more fall colors, red and yellow to catch the eye.

In the tiny room I use as an office, I gesture at the desk chair, the only place to sit, and take the electric kettle to the bathroom. I'm glad there's no mirror in there; I don't want to know what I look like. A wave of exhaustion breaks over me. I take off my glasses, splash cold water on my face, and fill the kettle. When I return to my office, Laura is sitting down, looking idly at the overdue bills and notes to myself I have taped to the wall above the desk. She looks around at me guiltily as I enter the room.

"Oh, go ahead, snoop around," I tell her, plugging the kettle into the wall socket. "I don't have any secrets. Chamomile, Raspberry Zinger, or Earl Gray?"

"Raspberry Zinger. Thanks."

"I bought a package of Pepperidge Farm cookies for the occasion," I say, holding it up. "I remembered that you like them. How are your parents? Did you have lunch with them?" I crank open the small casement window, letting a cool breeze into the stuffy room.

"Oh, they're fine." She pauses, then says rather meekly, "Catherine? I don't mean to pry. I mean, it's probably none of my business. But about what just happened . . . did I do something?"

Surprised, I turn around. I'm dismayed by the look on her face. "No, no, please don't think that, Laura. It has nothing to do with you." What can I tell her that isn't a lie? "I was thinking about my brother."

"The one who lives in New York? I forget his name."

I shake my head, clearing off a corner of the desk to sit on. "No, my younger brother, Andy."

"Oh, the dead uncle."

I look at her sharply, and she smiles, apologetic. "That's what Min calls him."

"Not Uncle Andy? I always refer to him as her uncle Andy."

Laura shakes her head. "No. She said you hardly ever talk about him at all."

I look away. "No, I don't suppose I do," I answer. I remember walking with Andy, Min on my back, in the hills above the ocean, imagining our lives twenty years in the future. She doesn't even have my memories of him. He is a cipher to her, someone from my distant past she doesn't even know enough about to call by name. I close my eyes, squeezing the tears back. I will not cry again.

I take a breath. "Andy died a long time ago. He was your age, twenty-two. He went sailing with a couple of friends off the coast in Maine. The boat capsized. Only one of them survived."

"I'm sorry," Laura says, her voice subdued.

I look up. She is squinting at me, the skin around her eyes flinching as if she can feel a little bit of how painful his loss was to me. My throat aches. I swallow, and swallow again.

"Thank you," I answer her. It is all I can say; then I realize it's all that is needed.

Outside the window, the rain has started falling with a soft patter. Laura asks, "You were close, weren't you?"

I can't speak now, my throat is too constricted. I nod, staring at the silver handle on the bottom drawer of the filing cabinet. My head hurts. I close my eyes. Andy is there behind my eyelids, grinning at me as he walks into my arms, as alive as ever. *I miss you*, I want to tell him. If I let him be dead, I'm afraid he'll disappear, no longer even a memory I can keep close to me.

The tea kettle whistles, startling me away from Andy into the present.

"I'll get it," Laura says, jumping up from her chair. I lift my glasses and brush my hand against my wet cheeks.

Laura pours boiling water into two mugs and hands me one. I hold onto its warmth with both hands, blowing at the rising steam. The tea-bag floats at the surface.

We drink our raspberry tea in silence. Its sweet-sour taste on my tongue soothes me. The heat strokes my throat, warms my chest. It's very companionable sitting here with Laura in my little office, sipping tea.

"He was incredibly focused," I say. Laura turns her face slightly toward me so that I know she is listening. "Not so much when he was little. During the summer we'd go down to the stream and make up stories to play. But when he got older he'd lie on his stomach looking into the water while I read or sketched. He liked to observe things up close, like insects crawling from one blade of grass to the next. He always had a scientific side."

"What was he looking at in the water?" Laura asks. Her question surprises me. It is so specific, as if he is a real person to her.

"I don't know," I admit. "I assumed he was watching the fish swimming around the bottom, but maybe he was interested in the water's surface. Maybe he was listening. I always liked the quiet down there." I still remember it, the humid, still air, the call of birds above us, the trickle of the water. The last time I was in Rhinebeck, Min was about five. The stream was still the same, but I had become someone else. Now, perhaps, other children play in the water. My parents sold the house and moved to Florida six years ago, when my father retired. "I remember once lying in the grass looking up at the trees. There were only a couple of weeks left before I was leaving for college, and Andy had been mad at me all summer. I had spent most of my time with my friends from school, knowing I might not see them again, or if I did, that we might have all changed. Andy came and lay next to me under the trees. I told him about the countries I wanted to visit when I graduated. He had plans too for when he was old enough to travel by himself. I still remember the places he named. The coral reefs off Australia. The ruins of Pompeii. He was interested in everything at one point or another. I never knew what I wanted my future to look like. I just knew I wanted to get away from my family. Andy always had specific goals, even if they kept changing."

It is searing to remember, knowing Andy will never do these things. But I like speaking about my brother, sharing who he was with someone else, someone whose only connection to him is through what I tell her. "He was very disciplined," I continue. "He always followed through once he made up his mind. He was going to go to law school that fall. I don't think it was what he really wanted." I stop myself. This isn't right, what I am doing. I lift my tea to drink it, but the cup is empty. I set it on the desk beside me, pushing aside a stack of mail.

"Laura, I shouldn't be talking with you this way. I've never told any of this to Min."

"Why not?" Laura asks.

I hesitate. "Because if I talked about her uncle Andy, I'd have to tell her what happened during his last visit with me. It would be painful. For both of us."

Laura doesn't say anything. If it were Min I was having this conversation with, she'd be on me in a minute, pressing me to explain myself, asking for details, seeking out the words that wound. So often when we talk she expects me to say something that will offend her. Of course, she has every right to be sensitive, but her bristliness doesn't ease our conversations. I feel a breeze through the window. I glance out at the rain.

"I'm glad you came to visit me today," I say. Laura looks skeptical. "No, really, I know you couldn't tell from my breakdown out there, but it's nice to see you."

"I'm glad too," she says. "You know," she ducks her head down, "I used to be jealous of Min because she had you for a mother."

Immediately I have the feeling again of rightness—this *is* my daughter, she has been looking for me too—but weaker this time, as if it is washing away. I want it to go, yet I am sorry too.

"Oh, I think almost everyone wishes they had someone else's mother," I say, trying to diffuse her shyness and my undeniable pleasure. It sounds insensitive. I don't want to diminish her feelings. Or mine. But at the moment my affection for Laura has a bitter taste. "I'm flattered, Laura," I say carefully, adding, after a moment, "You're very important to me."

"I am?"

Does she really not know? I nod. Then I say, "Sometimes I think about when you and Min were younger, when you used to come over to the house all the time. A lot has changed since then."

A creeping pink tinges the clear, milky skin of Laura's face. I hadn't realized before that their sexual relationship embarrasses her, at least in relation to me. I was thinking of other, less recent changes: my divorce from Jonathan, Min's becoming a lesbian, her move to the city, Laura's years away at college. Perhaps they don't matter now. We've all come through relatively intact. Even Min and I. How did we do it? How did I change, accept her lesbianism? It wasn't just because of my desire not to do to her what Andy had done to me: deny the truth of her life. It was Min herself. She was my daughter.

Except for the light, rapid tapping of the rain on the trees outside the window, it's very quiet in the room. Even the radio out front is momentarily silent, before the soft drone of a man's voice announces the next piece. Laura's empty cup sits between her thighs. Intent, she circles her index finger along its rim, back and forth.

"Catherine, I was wondering . . . was it weird at Min's brunch when I said I was in love with her?" She looks up at me suddenly. I'm startled by her question, embarrassed.

"Well, truthfully? Yes."

She nods, glances down at her circling finger, moves her hand away from the mug.

"Do you think that's homophobic?" I ask. "Min would. But I have to add that when you said it, I wasn't exactly surprised." I pause. "I think, in a way, you and Min have been in love since fifth grade."

Laura flashes me a quick smile, shy again. "I don't know about that." But she seems pleased that I would think it.

"When I was younger," she continues, "I always felt that I could talk to you about anything. I knew you wouldn't blame me or tell me how stupid I was. You were really helpful to me."

I look at her closely. Her hair is short enough now that even with her head bent, it no longer falls forward, hiding her face. "You can still talk to me, Laura."

She hesitates. "I don't know who else I can go to about this. I'm sorry, I don't want to burden you or anything. The problem is that Min isn't in love with me back." This time she doesn't raise her head, as if she is admitting to a great failing within herself.

I need to tread carefully here. Anything I say could carry too much weight, and in the end it might prove useless, or worse. I wait.

"I feel like I've finally found the love that I've been looking for all my life. Like Dorothy at the end of *The Wizard of Oz*. Home was in my backyard all the time. I thought Min would feel the same way. Maybe it's not the same for her because she's had so many girlfriends already."

She looks up at me pleadingly, desperate for help. Does she think I can tell her something my daughter might have confided in me? Does she think my age and experience give me the power to stave off a breaking heart?

"Did Min tell you she doesn't love you?" I ask.

"Oh, she loves me, the same way she always has." Laura stresses the word "love" as if it no longer holds meaning for her. Not enough, apparently. "But she doesn't want to spend the rest of her life with me. I can't imagine myself alone anymore, without her. I sometimes look at her and

I'm afraid I'll split open from so much love. I worship her. The only thing I want in my life is to be with her."

"I see." I am humbled by Laura's bare passion, this force of nature tearing through the landscape of her daily life. I don't think I could say I was ever in love, not even with Jonathan. Since my marriage broke up, each successive relationship seems to have ebbed in intensity, waning to a pale sliver of devotion, to mere affection, until now I feel, with Lloyd, as if I'm with a friend, not a lover. And isn't this what I wanted? Like the bookstore, where all the titles are labeled, shelved in their proper place. Like what I want my garden to be: something pruned, held back, controlled. Something predictable, something known.

The rain has stopped. When I stand up I realize how tightly I have been holding myself. The muscles along the right side of my neck are rigid with pain.

"Why don't we go for a walk?" I suggest.

Before we leave, I tape a note to the front door for Mark, who works in the afternoons after school lets out, explaining why the store is closed. The brisk air has the clean, sweet after-rain smell I love. It helps dispel the claustrophobic atmosphere from inside the store. I turn to Laura, who has stuffed her hands in her jacket pockets, and I slip my arm through hers. She grins at me, that radiant smile. We set off down the street.

I am half-hoping we don't need to speak, that the walk itself will shake up and clarify something for Laura. I don't know how to help her. She said that in the past talking to me was useful, but back then her problems were containable, and they were separate from me. How can I advise her about my own daughter? Overhead the sky is brightening slightly. I steer us left, toward the edge of town and Deer Park, where there are trails leading up into the wooded hills.

"Catherine, does Min ever talk about me?" Laura asks.

I take a breath, telling myself that the least I can do for Laura is be honest with her. "Well, no, not really. She doesn't like to discuss her . . . involvements with me."

Laura nods thoughtfully, then says, "She's had so many lovers, I don't think I even know about them all. And she remembers their names, even the one-night stands. For me, this is all so new."

Who are all these women Min has been with? I somehow assumed that the six or so girlfriends she has rather summarily informed me of were all there were. I feel naive suddenly, and old, as though my own life has already gone past, insignificant. We enter the woods, walking side by side until the trail rises steeply and narrows to a washed-out gully. All around us, trees drip with rain. I am so relieved to be outside. What happened at the bookstore has faded a little, become tinged with unreality.

I suggest, "Maybe Min is afraid that once the novelty wears off, your feelings will change."

Laura nods. "She's always telling me she expects me to go back to men. How can I prove to her that's not true?" Laura falls silent, then says, "Besides, she *wants* my feelings to change. She says I'm too intense."

"*Min?*" I interrupt, then start to laugh. It's so ironic.

"Yeah, well . . ."

Seeing Laura's face, I stop laughing. "Min struggled with a lot of things while you were away at school. She may be confused about what she feels. Try to give her time."

"What if she never feels the same way I do?"

There's no sound here beneath the trees except for the squelch of our shoes on the soggy mulch of fallen bay leaves. I can't think of an answer.

After a while, Laura asks, "Do you think being adopted is hard for Min? I don't mean that she'd wish she had another mother," she adds quickly, glancing at me.

I smile, but her question makes me uneasy. "We adopted her as an infant. Her life has always been here." I'm speaking slowly. It's an effort, trying to find the truth. I've never given much thought to what her adoption might mean to Min. "Jonathan and I were always open about Min being adopted. Of course, we had to be, she's Korean." Abruptly, I stop speaking. The words Andy and I exchanged at Point Reyes hover nearby, perilous, just beyond my memory.

"There's that part of it too," Laura says.

"What?" I ask, not following her.

"Her being Korean. Racism."

"Yes, well, people are idiots." I hear the anger in my voice, feel it surge inside me. I remember how Andy looked as he stood on the beach that day, scuffing at the sand, unyielding. I couldn't even tell Jonathan about our argument that afternoon. I knew he would say Andy was immature and then tell me to forget about him.

Laura and I switch over to a wider trail. We're in the open now, surrounded by tall golden grasses and the view of hills, one folding back into the next.

"Laura . . ." This is a mistake, I warn myself. At the same time I am summoning my courage. Laura is not Jonathan. "What I said before about Andy's last visit to me?"

"Yes?" Does she sound afraid? Am I being unfair to Laura by unburdening myself? But I can't stop now. I don't want to.

"Andy visited Jonathan and me a few months after we adopted Min," I say. As I start to recount it, my memories wash up, like ocean waves smoothing out the sand. "I was so happy that week. I had everyone I loved with me." Laura smiles, encouraging. I look away, concentrating on what I have to say. "We fought the last day because he said he couldn't accept Min as my daughter. Not because she was adopted, exactly, but because she was Asian. She was too different from me. From us. He'd never talked like that before. All I knew was that he was rejecting my daughter because of how she looked. I was livid. And helpless. How could he not love her too?"

"Yes," Laura says softly. It feels like a hand on my back.

"None of what I said to him seemed to make any difference. After he left, we didn't have any contact with each other. Then he died that summer."

I stop speaking. I don't know how much she will comprehend about the position I was in.

"Oh," Laura breathes out, barely audible. As we walk, she reaches out and puts her arm around me. My eyes tear up again. I look over at her quickly, not really seeing her before I look away, back at the trail. I feel a rush of relief. She understands. I reach up and squeeze her hand on my shoulder. She lets go, stuffs her hands in her pockets.

"When he died, I lost any way to resolve it with him. How could I ever have told Min that her uncle disavowed her? And for something so basic to who she was? How could I do that to her?"

"You couldn't."

"Then why do I feel I've done something wrong?"

Laura frowns. "I think you did the best you could. What happened with your brother is over. It would only hurt Min to bring it up now. Maybe you need to be easier on yourself. I don't think you can control what other people say or do. Or think."

The sun, low over the hills, finally breaks through the clouds in gauzy strands of light. I stop to look at it, unwilling to admit to Laura that I need to rest. The entire sky is astounding, changing every moment, in shades of gray and silver and blue. On the edge of the trail, pennyroyal's tiny purple flower is blooming. I breathe in peppermint. There's another plant I don't know that smells like chamomile but probably isn't. I have the feeling that I've never actually smelled them before, and I've never seen so many gradations of color in the sky.

Three days later, Min arrives at my house, hauling her table in its teal carrying case from her car. I have been needing this massage ever since the afternoon I spent with Laura. It is clear to me now why I've had so many headaches and stomach cramps. It has been about Andy all this time. The headaches have gone, but I still feel a constant knotting in my stomach like a fist of fear pressed hard inside me. I don't know if this is something she can help me with.

We hug and chat a little, small talk about the traffic and a movie she and Laura saw last night. There are dark smudges under her eyes. She doesn't seem particularly happy. "You look tired," I say.

"I am. Laura and I stayed up late talking. We're having a hard time."

I don't want to get in the middle. It's her life, hers and Laura's. I can't protect them. Besides, Min isn't asking for my advice.

In the living room, I help her push the chairs and coffee table to the side. Then, as she sets up her table, unfolding the sheets and warming her oil bottle on the electric heater I plugged in half an hour ago, I prowl through my rooms in search of cash to pay her. I sit at the end of my bed, having forgotten what I am looking for. I realize I am nervous. I need to tell Min what I told Laura.

On the wall to my left is a framed photograph of Min, four years old in a grassy, wind-flattened field on Mount Tam. It's a photograph I love for her unselfconscious glee at being alive, at being her very self. She is wearing a t-shirt stitched with daisies that I had made for her, and strands of her chin-length hair blow across her eyes. Her mouth is wide open with laughter. She looks as if she might float away, she is so suffused with joy. That day we climbed to the top of the mountain up the rutted dirt paths, and when Min grew tired, Jonathan and I traded off carrying her. He let her sit on his shoulders, holding her by her ankles while she clasped his forehead where the hair was thinning. I carried her on my back, my hands grasping her legs, her arms around my neck. In the field where Jonathan took the photograph, we had stopped to share a Hershey's chocolate bar. We sat in the tall grass on the gentle slope of the field, looking out on the sun-dazzled city of San Francisco in the distance, trying to imagine what it had looked like when the Indians lived there. I remember the heat that day and Jonathan breaking off the softened sections of chocolate. He didn't divide the bar in thirds but handed the squares out one at a time, to make it last. I remember how much Min enjoyed receiving her small piece, letting it melt on her tongue, then reaching toward her father for more. When I stand up to look at the photograph closely, I see a smear of chocolate on Min's raised hand.

I think of Laura asking me for advice, Laura holding me while I sobbed. I told Laura things about my family that my own daughter doesn't know. Even though they affect her. *Our* family. I raise my fingertips to the glass as if to touch Min's gleeful four-year-old face. I want so much for Min. Most of all, I want her to be happy. I can't tell her now.

When I return to the living room, Min goes to wash her hands, closing the bathroom door behind her. For a moment I stand in front of the glass door looking out beyond the deck at the eucalyptus trees towering behind the garden. I never cut the flowers back or pruned the bushes as I hoped to do last summer. I turn away, take off my terrycloth bathrobe and my glasses, and get on the table to lie on my stomach, pulling the top sheet up above my shoulders, around my neck. I turn my face to the left. The laurel bay beyond the side window is a blur of green. I hear Min entering. She asks if I'm warm enough. She rests her hands on my back over the sheet, runs them down my legs, my arms. All this is ritual, formal and familiar, and right now I depend on it.

She begins. Head down in the face cradle, I keep my eyes open as long as I can, watching Min's bare feet move in and out of my range of vision. The oil is warm, comforting. As Min spreads it on my back and I feel the weight of her hands glide over my skin, my eyes close, heavy, but I don't fall asleep as I usually do. Instead, as though Min has flipped some switch inside me, I am plunged into long-forgotten memories so vivid I can hear and smell them. Andy consulting with me during one of my vacations from college about how he should ask out a girl at school that he liked. My excitement, even pride, when he called to tell me he'd gotten into Vanderbilt, his first choice. Ten years earlier, the bewildered look on his face when all the Christmas presents were opened and he realized our parents hadn't given him the one thing he'd asked for, a book on tropical fish. Tears leak from my eyes; my throat is raw, my stomach queasy. Everything feels sore. Min's fingers press into my back, push beneath a shoulder blade. Her touch is more penetrating than it has ever been. Neither of us speaks. If she knows I am crying, she gives no indication.

She picks up my foot by the ankle, lifts and shakes my whole leg, then lays it gently down again. She smoothes oil on my thigh, digs her fingers or knuckles, I can't tell which, into the flesh around my hipbone. It is excruciating in a way I've never felt and, oddly, I want more. I remember the never-ending plane trip east, the days waiting for Andy's body to wash up on shore, the funeral in the tiny chapel in Rhinebeck where my parents went to Sunday services. I remember the feeling that none of it was real, none of it made any sense. I had been waiting for a phone call or a letter from him for four months. When Min asks me to turn over, I realize that the small towel covering the face cradle is soaking wet. She hands me a tissue, then two more. I prop myself up on my elbows and blow my nose. I tell her I'm sorry. She says there's no reason for me to be. I can see that my tears don't frighten her; if anything, she is relieved.

I lie down on my back beneath the sheet. My body no longer feels part of me. It is in pieces, scattered about. Min is collecting them, pressing them back together. There is my skin, oiled and leathery, there are my arms and legs which stretch far away, and there is the inside of me, where pain resides. The air rushes loudly in my ears. I am here inside my head, nauseated. Min is down at my feet, cupping one in her hands like something newborn and fluttery. She tells me to breathe. I hear my bones creak. I think of the sound of a mast in high wind, the sail whipping, the boom swinging over, capsizing the boat. She presses the flat of her palm deep into my stomach, rocking. It feels like being gored; it feels deeply satisfying. Min pushes down, her hands sliding over my skin, then lets up. Under my ribs, around my hip bones, to the center of my abdomen. Down, around. Over and over. It feels as though she has reached the center of my being at last.

I push down the plunger of the coffee press, slowly forcing the freshly ground beans to the bottom of the glass container. Min comes into the kitchen, having folded up her massage table and gathered everything she came with. I take a mug from the cupboard, pour the coffee, hand it to Min. "Thanks," she says. It's the first time either of us has spoken since the massage ended. She turns and opens the ice box, gets the milk from the door.

I'm completely wrung out. Sitting down at the kitchen table, I cross my arms and run my hands over the sleeves of my bathrobe.

"Here, you should drink water," Min says, filling a glass at the sink and bringing it to me. "You'll get dehydrated."

I sip, then drain the glass. My body feels rearranged, weightless; when I got off the massage table I had trouble balancing to walk. Min won't mention my tears earlier under her hands. As a masseuse she has very clear boundaries, as my therapist used to put it. It is up to me to reveal what I want to. But the habit of silence is hard to break. I don't know where to begin, what words to use. I stand, refill my glass at the sink, sit again. Min spoons sugar into her mug, stirs it, sips her coffee.

"Min, I can't tell you how amazing I feel now."

She sits back and regards me, running a hand through her spiky hair. "You don't have to. I can see it in your face. It's brighter. It's totally different."

"I was crying for Andy, my brother," I say. Instantly she's alert, paying minute attention, though she hasn't moved. But where I start is not with the history of my relationship with Andy, or even with his death, but right in the middle of that afternoon on the beach. I recount everything we said, as well as I can remember it. *You've been acting like she's not a real person. Why didn't you adopt a white child who might look like you? She's my child, you have to accept Min someday. She's not part of you; you're born into family.*

"I'm sorry I never told you before, Min. I couldn't begin to talk about it with you, let alone think about it, because of his death." I am rushing my words, relieved at how easy telling her is after all. "I wanted to make it all come out okay somehow, make him not be dead, make him not feel the way he did. I wanted him to love you. I wish you had known him. He was dedicated, fun to be with, very affectionate. He would have loved you, I know he would have."

I am hopeful. Everything is changing again. There will be nothing held back between Min and me now. I should have done this a long time ago. I look at her, full of my passion and faith. She is frowning.

"You're full of shit, Mom. I'm sorry he died, but your brother was a fucking bigot."

For a moment I am stunned. This was not the reaction I was expecting. Then my old instincts rush in. "No. He wasn't, Min. That's the point. I guess I haven't conveyed who he was. He wasn't usually like that at all." Even after twenty-one years, I still protect him.

"He was that day. He didn't like me because I have yellow skin and slanted eyes. Right?"

I wince at her choice of words. Her anger burns away all decorum, and her willingness to hurt—to *be* hurt—makes me go on the defense. "He didn't know you. He was not a bigot. Not usually. I think he felt threatened by how much I loved you."

"And you're as bad as he was. Why are you defending him?"

"What? Of course I defend him. I don't condone how he felt. I was infuriated. I was screaming at him I was so angry."

"Why did you bother? Why didn't you just walk away?"

I am shocked into silence, made as stupid and speechless as I was on the beach with Andy. Finally I manage, "I *couldn't*, Min. He was my brother." It is the only explanation I have.

She stares at me, her face slowly turning a dusky rose. "Yeah? Well, then I guess he was right, wasn't he? Family is what you're born into." She says it with barely controlled fury, then scrapes her chair back and stands up, turning and striding toward the living room all in one motion. This time I know that if she leaves, she won't come back.

"Min." I say it sternly, a mother reprimanding her child, and she stops, blinking at me with a child's surprise. I soften my voice. "You're right." She watches me, her jaw hard. I am trying to tell the truth, but I am afraid that I might not say the right thing. I cannot count on the familial bond between us. "You're right. I thought I was defending you. I thought if he changed his mind, it would be all right. I *am* as bad as he was."

Min stands in the doorway half-poised to flee, her head down. I can tell she is hesitating, uncertain. For the first time, I see how much she relies on the immediacy of her feelings. She wants to act on her fury. She can't come back into the kitchen with me, not so soon. I watch her all the way across the room, and suddenly, I don't know why, I feel how deeply I have hurt her, not in telling her, but in the ways I have tried to shield her from him all her life. As though he was the only person who could wound her because of who she is. As though ignoring her race could make her white.

Min says, not moving from the doorway, "You know, you admit you're racist, and you assume that's enough. Mom, do you realize . . .?" She hesitates, then plunges on, rage fueling her. "I remember the first time other kids called me 'slant-eyes.' That was the day I came home from kindergarten and figured out that you and Dad didn't look like me either. You sat with me and told me the facts about my adoption, but you never said anything about why those kids were mean to me or whether I had a right to want them to stop. I thought you were scared of me. I thought I had done something wrong when you got pissed off at people on the street who were curious about me. For the longest time I tried . . ." She closes her eyes and turns her head away from me. I want to go to her, but I know she won't let me touch her.

"Min, I'm sorry. I really, really am. I never meant to hurt you. I didn't realize what I was doing. All I wanted was to protect you."

She is still facing away. "You think it's not obvious how much you and Laura get off on pretending to be mother and daughter?"

My breath catches. I had no idea I was so transparent. "Min." I try not to sound like I'm begging or demanding. "Please come back and sit down."

"No."

"Then listen to me. This is important. And I'm not trying to make excuses for myself. What happened with Andy was not a contest between the two of you. I was not rejecting you because I couldn't cut him off. I loved him." I'm crying again, something I've never done in front of her before today, but I simply wipe my face and keep talking, letting the tears come. "I can't defend how I acted, who I was. Who I am. If I had to do it over again, I couldn't do anything differently, even now. I can only tell you what I told Andy. I *chose* you for my daughter. I do it every day."

She is looking at me now. I wipe away more tears with the heel of my hand and look back at her steadily.

"I have to go," she says. She retreats into the living room, laces up her sneakers, pulls on her knapsack.

I stand in the kitchen doorway where she just was. She does not look at me. It's a very lonely feeling, having her leave like this. I don't know, in fact, if we will ever speak again. But I do know that I have to let her go, for the first time, really, and trust who we are to each other. That she is my daughter is the least of it.

She bends to put the carrying case strap over her shoulder and grabs the handle, then straightens, hauling the table off the floor. I slide open the door for her. "Bye," she says as if it just slipped out, and she steps out into a windy, sunlit day.

CHAPTER 12

Laura

Winter 1985

"HOW ABOUT 'JOYFUL, JOYFUL, WE adore thee . . . under a sheet,'" I say, switching from musicals to Christmas carols. Holiday songs have been playing for weeks in every store in the financial district. For the past three days, whenever I take a latte break from my temp job at Crocker Bank, there's a group of women singing in the lobby, trying to sound like angels.

"That's a good one," Min says, grinning. She pushes a ripple of bubbles toward me. I gather them in my dripping hands and place them carefully on my nipples, like pasties. She says, "How about 'We three kings of Orient are . . . under a sheet.'"

We both laugh. The bubbles slide off my breasts. Seeing that, Min can't stop laughing. We're actually having fun. I want it to last forever.

The bathtub is narrow and barely fits us both, but I like her legs on either side of me and her hands clasping my knees. Min is great at coming up with song titles. My favorite so far is "What do the simple folk do (under a sheet)?" The game itself was her idea. I remember that she was the one who thought up all the best code words in seventh grade too.

"Do you remember kissing me in junior high?" I ask.

"Of course," she answers, dribbling handfuls of hot water on my shoulders. I lean toward her so she can reach my back.

"I do too." I remember her long hair falling around me as she bent over to kiss me the first time. "It was nice. I think we were already having a relationship then. We just didn't know it." It's strange to me that the girl with long hair in my memory is the same person I'm sharing a bath with. Min starts to rub my shoulders where I'm sore from sitting in front of a computer all day. "I think we got imprinted on each other," I add.

"I don't. I think we were twelve years old and finding out what our bodies did. You have a romantic view of everything."

I feel stung. What's wrong with that? "You don't think our being together now has *anything* to do with what happened then?"

She shrugs. "We were fooling around. I know I was interested in finding out what it was like to be female and sexual." She leans back, her arms on either side of the tub rim.

Sometimes what I love about Min is exactly the thing that makes me nuts. I've never met anyone who's so stubbornly herself. "But didn't you like kissing me?" I ask. I miss her warm hands on my skin. I'd like to lean back too but the faucet's behind me.

She looks at me oddly, like I've forgotten something obvious. "Of course I did. Don't start reinterpreting the past, Laura."

"What do you mean? What's wrong?"

She shakes her head. "Nothing. I'm getting out, I've had enough." She stands and steps out of the deep, old-fashioned tub. I wish she would turn around and look at me. I wish she was always turned in my direction, that every look was for me alone. Is that so terrible a thing to want?

"Thanks for the neck rub," I say. "It really helped."

"Sure."

Min towels herself dry. I turn around, fill the tub with more hot water, and sink back down until only my head and knees are sticking out. I imagine slipping completely under, disappearing below the surface. Sometimes I feel like Min and I never became lovers at all and I'm still waiting for the moment when she will make a move.

I lift my hand from the water and catch hers, bringing it to my lips to kiss. She opens her palm against my cheek. I want her to tell me everything will work out. I want her to say anything. When she leaves the bathroom, the opened door lets in a cold rush of air.

The bubbles are almost all gone. Before getting out, I hold my breath and slide down along the length of the tub, dunking my whole head beneath the hot water. I stay down for several seconds, shutting off all outside distractions. I never used to feel lonely with Min. The closer we get, the less I am sure where she is. I put my hands up and scrub at my scalp, my short hair floating against my fingers like seaweed. I can hear only one thing down here, amplified through the water. It is the insistent, rhythmic call of my own heart.

When I pull the covers down and get into bed beside her, naked and sweaty from the bath, Min is reading, her book propped up on her stomach. It's a faded hardback with brittle pages, probably something from Catherine's bookstore. When I'm settled against her, she rests her hand on my thigh without looking up.

"What are you reading?" I ask sleepily. It's her cue to put the book aside and roll toward me or let me climb on top of her.

"*Orlando*," she answers, turning a page. I hear the slow sound of the paper scraping against her fingers. Maybe she's reading to the end of the paragraph. I wait a minute, then one more. It must be a long paragraph. I wish she would finish. I want her back. When I hear her turning another page, something lurches inside me. I reach up to take the book from her.

She holds it away from me, still reading. "Come on, I'm trying to read."

"But *I'm* here. You can read any time."

"This is really good. Give me a few more minutes."

I sit up, my face suddenly burning. The sick feeling in my stomach that I often feel when I'm with Min now becomes hard, like a lump of dough I've swallowed without chewing. I want to throw it up.

"I can't stand this anymore," I tell her. "You want to read more than you want to be with me. I can't believe I'm competing with a goddamn book."

Min looks up at me for the first time since I came into the room. "No, Laura, I don't care about the book more than you." She sounds bored, like she's tired of having to explain the same thing all over again. "Would you stop comparing yourself to everything you see? I can't stand it either." Then she puts the book down on the floor next to the futon. But it's too late. I can't stop myself.

"Before we were lovers, you never had a problem paying attention to me. Why are you so stingy with the time we're together now?"

"Before we were lovers, you never needed so much attention."

I can hear the fury in her voice. It makes me cringe. How can I change her anger into caring? How can I make her see what she's doing to us? I look into her face, willing her to remember me. She looks back, her jaw set. We stare at each other.

My eyes fill with tears. I blink them back. "Why won't you soften?" I ask. "Why won't you let me in?" I am sitting cross-legged. She is leaning back against the pillows. I can feel my whole body angling in toward hers, yearning. If she were a guy, I would start to cry and he would instantly change, become concerned. But Min is more complicated. If I cry, she will see that vulnerable side of me, but it won't make her love me more. It will only make her feel more burdened. It always does, sooner or later.

"Laura," Min begins. I watch her eyebrows pull together like looking at me hurts her. "I don't think this is going to work between us."

"What?"

She doesn't answer. She knows I heard her. I hold still, not breathing, hoping the moment will pass and when I move again there will not be this sharp, terrible pain and we will go on as before.

"Why now?" I ask, my voice barely audible. Now I am crying for real. It takes so little these days. Just a few angry words from Min and I lose it. "It was feeling so good to be with you. Why do you have to ruin it?"

She sits up and brings my face between her two hands to a few inches away from hers. The force of her fingers is hard against my cheeks. I imagine her crushing my skull between her hands. Yet her face has the same look of injury on it as before.

"Listen to me," she says. "You know this isn't working. We have to talk about it. Can we discuss this rationally, when we aren't in the middle of a fight?"

"Rationally?" I ask. "Since when were you into being rational?"

I feel a slight tremor in her hands on either side of my face. "Stop it, Laura. You're just making this harder. We have to talk. Otherwise we're just going to keep sniping at each other until there isn't anything left."

I imagine us, two piles of dust scattered on the floor. "You want to break up," I say. It comes out sounding like a question because there's a wince in it, the fear she will agree. The idea alone is unbearable. I have to find a way to distract her, stop her from making this mistake. I bite the inside of my mouth, trying to keep the greater pain at bay.

Min closes her eyes, then opens them and looks into mine. "I want to consider it. I can't keep going on like this. I'm not happy. Neither are you."

I pull back, out of the grip of her hands. I used to envy the way she could take pleasure, and give it too, without hesitation. But the other side is that she wants only the moments of bliss. She depends on her submersion in it. She seeks it out.

"Relationships aren't always about being happy, Min," I tell her. I am saying it for her sake, not for mine. "It's not about feeling good all the time. Sometimes it takes work."

"Yeah, but what we're doing isn't work. It's a war zone."

Suddenly I'm pissed off. "That's because you won't commit to being in it with me for the long haul. You're like a child, you're only interested while it's new. Then you get bored and go off to find somebody else to play with."

"Who I sleep with is my business, Laura. We agreed on that."

"How can you know how happy you would be with me when you're sleeping with other women? I hate this non-monogamy shit. I only agreed to it because I thought you'd see how stupid it is and get over it."

She's silent, looking down. "Actually, I haven't been sleeping with other women. Not recently. You've never understood, Laura. I don't want to go out fucking everyone in sight. Mostly I am happy with you. But I can't promise a commitment that I might not always want to keep."

"Why not?"

"Why can't you call yourself a lesbian?"

Silence again. It's not the same. If she loved me like I love her . . . What hurts most is over and over bumping into the wall that she's put up around her love.

"Besides," she says, "you had a choice. You didn't have to agree to an open relationship. You could have said no."

"And you would have broken up with me. What kind of a choice is that?" I shout at her. I remember her roommate and lower my voice. "You gave me a choice between two things I didn't want. All I could hope for was that you'd change. But you have to have everything your way."

"That's not true," she counters. "You're the one who wants too much." I feel tears filling my eyes again as she goes on. "You want to direct my whole life, decide who I can see and for how long. You have to know where I am every second of the day. I don't have the freedom to come back to you." She shakes her head. I can't tell if she's near tears too. "You can't stand that I might be close to anyone other than you."

"You can't be close to anyone, Min. You spread yourself too thin." The realization grows bright inside me, like the shade pulled off a lamp. "And it's me you're the most scared of. I think you're terrified that if we get too close, I'll disappear. Like your father. Like your birth parents. Even like your mother, who you think can't really love you because she loved her own brother first. If you love me too much, you might lose me. That's *your* problem. The sad thing is, you're willing to get rid of me this other way." I take in a huge gulp of air, out of breath. I have never thought this through before, not so clearly. Min stares at me. She is breathing hard too.

"You don't know what you're talking about." Her voice is low, furious. "You don't know me half as well as you think you do. Don't try to own me." She starts to get up off the bed. I grab her hand.

"I have to pee," she says coldly.

While she's gone, exhaustion hits me, making me a little dizzy. I drag my open hand over my face, like a washcloth, but the tiredness doesn't go away.

"This isn't getting us anywhere," I tell Min when she returns. I lie down on my back. I reach for Min to pull her to me. "I'm cold." She gets into the bed and covers us both with the blankets, tucking me in up to my neck. There is nothing playful about it tonight, or even tender, just matter of fact. The overhead light switch is on my side, but I don't want to move.

"I think maybe we're better off as friends," she says quietly.

This time I don't feel anything except a sense of futility. Maybe the end is inevitable. I say, "I don't think I can go back to being friends with you again."

"You don't?" she asks. I turn my head to look at her. Her eyes seem very black, very wet. It's the first time tonight I've been sure I have hurt her. I don't feel proud of my accomplishment.

"There's nothing in it for me, trying to be friends again. We've gone too far. I want to be your *lover*, Min. Don't you understand that?" I want to shake her. Has she never understood the price of this relationship before now?

She closes her eyes, takes a deep breath and lets it go. I can tell she is holding herself back from crying. I watch her, worried for her and at the same time staggered that all this time she has taken me for granted. Something inside me loosens and is set free, and like a leaf it is swept downstream.

I drag myself out of the tightly wrapped covers and reach up along the wall for the light switch, then bundle myself back up. "Min," I say in the dark, and I touch her arm. I feel her hand on my hip. We inch ourselves together. We hold each other until we fall asleep.

It's evening two days later, and I miss her. We don't have a plan to get together until tomorrow. Even though we talk on the phone every day, I hate not being with Min this long. I start to feel jumpy, nervous. It's no good trying to distract myself with my job or my few friends. I don't care about them. I run five miles every day, but it doesn't calm me down. Tonight I'm hanging out watching TV with my roommates, Sally and Denise. I know Min has massage appointments. While Denise and Sally laugh at the sitcom jokes, I can't help wondering what she is doing right at this moment. Is she thinking of me? Does she miss me too?

I decide to go out for a walk to clear my head. I wrap a cotton scarf around my neck, pull on my field coat, and head out. The street is awash in fog. Stoplights loom, red and green, disembodied. I walk over the hill toward the Castro, taking unfamiliar streets. Off to my right, the lights of Sutro Tower flash, warning planes away. The damp of the fog wets my cheeks. I keep walking, down tiny streets with houses painted so elaborately they remind me of the animals on the merry-go-round in the park, and up streets so steep they have steps carved into the sidewalk. On a corner somewhere near upper Market, I stop and look down at the lights of the city glowing in the white mist. The fog is thinner here, trailing off as it descends the hill. Out over the bay, lights outline the bridge. I'm surprised by the number of windows in the office buildings downtown that are still lit up. I wonder how many people are working late tonight. It's after nine.

From where I stand, the valley where Min lives looks far away. I can see the dark square of Dolores Park, three blocks from her house. I've tried to get her to play tennis there with me, offering to teach her. She says she's not interested. When I sometimes walk to Min's instead of taking the bus, I like to stop up here before the long trek down, measuring, in a way, the distance between her house and mine. I especially love looking out over San Francisco at night, when the city looks like a cluster of individual lights spread wide into a net. Their reassurance of civilization (other people, warm rooms) keeps away the encroaching darkness.

Min would love this view tonight. I push up the sleeve of my coat and hold my watch to the blaze of a streetlight. She should be finished with her last massage. It takes me some time to find a phone, several streets away. I'm excited now, thinking of Min trudging up the hill toward me, our standing together hand in hand with the city in a web of light at our feet.

Her phone rings once, again. A man passes me, muttering under his breath. The street is pretty deserted. I shift my weight from one foot to the other, willing her to pick up.

On the third ring, somebody answers. I hear laughter, then Min's voice. "Hello?" I can imagine her, happy, the bright, warm walls of her kitchen behind her.

"Hey. It's me."

"Hey, you." Her voice is low, intimate. That private tone always thrills me. "What's up?"

"I can see your neighborhood. I was hoping you'd come up and look at the fog with me, it's amazing."

"Mmm, I can't. I'm not finished here."

"I could call you back in a while."

"No, this isn't a good time. I'll give you a call tomorrow."

"Can't I call you later tonight?" I ask, annoyed that she's putting me off.

"I don't know if I'll be here. I'll call you tomorrow." I'm trying very hard not to jump to the conclusion that she wants to make love with somebody else tonight. The suspicion is so automatic, even I'm getting tired of it. She said she isn't sleeping with other women. I have to believe her. If I can trust her, she might be able to give me what I want.

"I love you," I say, wanting to hear it back.

"Me too," she answers and hangs up.

As soon as I hear the dial tone, I'm pissed. She can't treat me like this anymore. I'm sick of being pushed aside when it's convenient for her. I've had it with running to see her when she wants me and waiting around when she doesn't. I start walking down toward the Mission, my breath coming in short bursts. I have the feeling everything would still be in shades of gray even if there were no fog. I march down the streets, zig-zagging diagonally, homing in on Min's building.

I slow down a couple of blocks away, out of breath and sweating inside my lined coat. The streets are crowded now. There seems to be a bar on every corner. The fog has cleared too, sweeping back up the hill where it came from. What do I want to say to her, now that I'm here? Maybe she'll be glad to see me, and my fury will have nowhere to turn. Or maybe she has already left the apartment, and I'll have wasted my energy coming down here. I could go to the women's clubs she hangs out at and look for her there. Somebody whistles at me as I pass him on the street. I glare at him. I could call Min's friends, see if she's with one of them. Her building is in the middle of the next street. I try to stay focused, calm. Upstairs in the building I am passing, a party is going full blast, the rhythm of salsa drifting down from the windows. I don't know what I want from Min right now, what I can demand. I stay on the other side of the street, approaching slowly, stuck somewhere between anger and embarrassment.

I look up at the second floor. She's got the curtains pulled over her bedroom windows, but they are a light material. In the middle of the lit room, I can see a figure bending, straightening. Maybe Min is folding up her massage table now that her client has left. Adrenalin starts zipping around inside me again because I'm watching my lover up there, only a few dozen yards away. I always feel this rush of anticipation when I am about to see Min. I don't think that will ever stop.

As I'm crossing the street, I see another figure come into her room and move toward the first. The two of them meld into one deformed shape. I stop and stare as it moves first to the left, then out of my sight to the right, where I know the bed is. I close my eyes. I'm afraid I might throw up. Then some tidal wave slams down inside me, and I am crushed beneath it and then rolled and dragged along with it, the roar of its fury in my ears. Deafened, I stumble into the street, half-aware of searching through the garbage by the curb. I find an empty beer bottle and bend down to pick it up. The headlights of a car blind me as I turn around, then the car slides past. Everything is moving slowly. I look up at the lighted windows. At my very center I am a thin, white-hot wire, vibrating and razor-sharp. I bring my arm back and then forward, hurling the bottle, and the roar in my ears sounds like a scream of outrage as the bottle shatters the glass of one of her windows and the curtain billows back into the room and then settles again, peaceful. Somebody comes to the other window to look out. She holds the curtain against her bare breasts. It's Min. We stare at each other until I turn away. I think I hear her calling my name, but it's faint, an echo of a sound, washed away by the rushing of the sea in my head.

I can't stop crying. We haven't talked to each other for almost two weeks. I leak onto the pizza my roommates had delivered, or as I stand in line waiting for an ATM. Whether I'm sitting in my room alone or out walking or on a crowded streetcar, the tears are always sudden. I feel like I'm going crazy. It's worst lying awake at night, when the hours are the longest. I can't stop thinking about Min, going over and over the details of every fight we ever had, revising them in my head, trying to make it all come out differently.

The temp agency fired me a week ago. At Crocker I couldn't concentrate. Even stuff I already knew how to do flew out of my head as soon as I sat down at the computer. Then I didn't show up at the bank at all one morning. I couldn't even get out of bed to call in sick. I haven't told anybody I lost my job except Sally and Denise. I can't let my parents know. They'd go ballistic. I can't even tell them why I'm so upset, because they never knew about Min and me in the first place.

I try to keep busy. On sunny days I take the N-Judah out to the ocean and count each of the times Min and I walked there, setting our footprints in the sand as the sun went down into the ocean or was hidden by clouds or shared the sky with the moon rising over the windmill in the park. I walk through the Arboretum, torturing myself with memories of picnics and naps on the grass with our heads resting in each other's laps. Even the memories of our friendship are painful, because I can't ever have it back. I'm afraid to go to the women's clubs she took me to or anywhere near her house. On the streets sometimes in my neighborhood I think I see her. I start to follow, walking faster to catch up, calling out her name, but it's never her. That's when I feel my pathetic hope for even a glimpse of her, for the simple knowledge that she's still somewhere out there, nearby. There might still be a chance. I never make it home before I start crying again.

It has rained for the past three days in a row, but I've gone out anyway with my umbrella, setting off in any direction except toward the Mission, letting the cogs of my brain spin while my legs carry me to every corner of the city. I won't call her or go over to her house. She might refuse to speak to me. At the same time, I don't want to see her. I finally accept that she didn't want to share her life with me. She kept pulling herself away and going to other people. What that left between us would look to anybody else like friendship. Maybe that was enough for her. It's worthless to me.

That's not even it. I can't forgive her for being willing to let me go.

One afternoon I wander around North Beach in the rain, buying fresh ravioli and stopping in bookstores and postcard shops. I'm soaking wet from the waist down and sneezing, afraid that I might be catching a cold but not really caring that much. Finally, hungry, I shake out my umbrella and go into a café with a long pastry counter and tiny marble-topped tables. It's crowded, but I find a table in the back, near the bathroom. The café is overheated, its wide windows opaque with condensation. I strip off the layers (my jacket and sweater and sweatshirt), leaving on my t-shirt, piling them on the chair across from me. As I am waiting for somebody to come and take my order, I look around at the tourist families and the writers scribbling in their notebooks and the carefully made-up women sitting with the grayer, older men they may be married to, and I wonder what I'm doing here. Not just here in this café but in San Francisco, where in eight months I have not made a dent. Then a waiter comes, and I order cappuccino and a slice of cake called chocolate raspberry decadence, and he leaves me alone again with myself.

I don't know if I will ever talk to Min again. I don't know if I will ever see her. It seems to me most likely we will let this two-week silence lengthen into months, and then into years, until we have the awkward, half-ashamed sense that something we should have figured out how to finish has instead been ended for us. I know that I'm capable of letting this happen. Already our not speaking has taken on a life of its own. I am small in comparison and much less sure of myself. I try to imagine my life here without Min in it, but it is much too painful to think about for more than a second or two. The best I can do is think of an alternate life, one at graduate school or in another city. There, as I did at Kenyon, I might be able to reinvent myself.

The waiter brings my order. I plow through the cake, afraid of tasting it because enjoying its excessive flavors would remind me of Min. Even so, I remember her sitting across from me at a Dairy Queen in Salt Lake City last summer, offering me hot fudge and a maraschino cherry from her spoon. The muscles in my thighs clench, and I cover my face with my hand and try as hard as I can not to cry. The summer seems so long ago, out of reach. How did this chasm open up, which neither of us will cross? I know she blames me. She says I'm too dependent on her, too demanding. I'm starting to think she's right. I don't know how to be myself without her.

Maybe, years from now, I could manage to forget her, or at least put somebody else in the place she holds in my heart. But I know this is impossible. She has been too great a presence for too many years. She has left her indelible mark. She has changed me in irreversible ways. If

I ever love anybody else, it will be with the bittersweet awareness that everything I know about loving I learned from Min. She will always have her own corner inside me, whether or not I come to remember her with regret or affection or anger or a vague nostalgia.

Wishing I could pull off my wet sneakers and socks and dry my feet by the radiator along the wall, I push the empty plate away and take a sip of my cappuccino. Something has to shift, because I can't go on living like this. I consider my options. There aren't many that I can see. Sneezing, I pull my sweatshirt and sweater back on. The cappuccino has gotten cold in its cup. It's mostly froth anyway. I leave money on the table, grab my jacket and dripping umbrella, and walk back out into the rain. As I trudge up another hill, a cable car goes clacking past, its bell ringing. I watch it pass me, only half full. In the back, a man sitting with two children takes a picture of the tip of the TransAmerica Pyramid. I always felt like a tourist in this city. Min is the one who lives here.

I find a bus and then wait a long time for another bus to take me back to the Haight. Sitting next to the window, I watch the rain slide down the glass in long streaks and listen to the exhausted hissing of the bus's windshield wipers. It's almost dark by the time I get off, stepping down into a large puddle on the street. It's windier here, but the rain is starting to ease. I don't bother opening my umbrella. I glance inside the Achilles Heel, a bar my ex-boyfriend Al took me to when I turned eighteen. A few couples are in there now. I wonder what Al is up to these days. I turn off Haight. I still have to climb about five blocks uphill. By the time I reach my building and take out my keys to open the wrought-iron security gate, I have made a decision. I feel relieved, almost hopeful. There is something I can do. I will move to Washington, DC, where my friend Nancy lives and has been urging me to come since graduation.

Three days later, I'm lying in bed with the flu feeling very sorry for myself. Everything aches, and my head feels stuffed full of wet cotton. There are Kleenexes all over the floor. Sally and Denise were sweet this morning, bringing me herbal tea and toast with jam before they left. But I wasn't hungry. I've spent the day sleeping on and off, half-waking from weird dreams to roll over, looking for a more comfortable position, before I drop off again.

Now it's early evening and already dark out. I'm trying to decide whether to get out of bed and look in the kitchen for something to eat when the doorbell rings, a long, insistent buzz. My first thought is that it's Min. I can't help hoping. I throw off the covers, pull my bathrobe over my nightgown, and kneel on the floor to reach for my slippers under the bed. The bell rings again as I go out the apartment door, remembering to leave it unlocked behind me. I realize I must be feeling a little better if I'm able to pay attention to those kinds of details.

At the bottom of the stairs, I can see Min looking up at me from the street through the bars of the gate. Her face is open, questioning. I walk through the lobby toward her, trying to control my facial muscles. I don't even know myself if I want to laugh or cry or yell at her to go away. I really believed I would never see her again. Now that she is here in front of me, the moment seems unreal.

I open the heavy front door and stand there, looking down at her. Neither of us seems to know what to say.

"Can I talk to you?" she asks at last.

I feel a heaviness inside me, which I recognize as dread. I think I know why she is here, and I wish she had just stayed away. I don't want to go through the motions of breaking up. The processing, the wishing each other well, the leave-taking. Min likes to know she has done the right thing. She hates feeling guilty. I don't want everything to be tied up neatly for her, with no loose ends. But I nod. I prop the door open with a wedge of wood lying by the wall and come down the steps. Turning the knob and pushing open the gate, I say, "Let's sit in here." I don't want her coming up to my room. She nods. She climbs the steps, and I let the gate clang shut.

We sit side by side on the cold stone steps. She touches the material of my bathrobe without creating any pressure against my leg. "Are you going to sleep early tonight?" she asks.

"I'm sick," I say. I can't quite manage to look at her fully. Two women walk by and peer at us. I pull my nightgown further down over my legs.

"Are you taking echinacea and goldenseal?"

"No."

"I can recommend a good acupuncturist if you want."

"Why did you come over?" My voice sounds raspy. I try to clear my clotted throat.

She doesn't answer for a long time. I'm afraid that whatever she says, I won't believe it. Either that or it will hurt too much.

I say, "Min, I'm moving to DC." I hadn't meant to tell her, but I don't know how else to get to the point. Suddenly her face seems very close to mine. I can feel heat emanating from her body, but that might be my own fever.

"You are?" I see her literally swallow, a bulge in her throat moving up and then down, disappearing. I've always thought it was just an expression. "When are you leaving?" she asks.

I shrug. "As soon as I get better. By the end of the month."

Nancy is thrilled and promises I can stay with her as long as I need to. She says she wants to fix me up with a couple of guys she thinks I'd really like, but I've told her I don't want to start dating anyone right away. My parents think my decision is a great idea too. My father says there are terrific job opportunities in DC. All I want is to get out, start over.

Min nods, squinting. "So, you're practically gone. I guess it's pretty obvious why you'd want to leave."

I stare at her. "God, you are so presumptuous."

She looks down. "I don't mean to be. I was trying to say I respect your decision."

I can't believe we are having this conversation. It really is true, she's willing to let me go. For her, it's the easiest thing to do. I look down at my hands, one clasped inside the other. I don't want her to know I'm getting tearful. She's seen too much of that.

Min starts to speak, stops, is silent again. A guy from the building appears on the street in front of us, unlocking the gate. "Hi," he says, skirting around us as he climbs the stairs. Neither of us answers him.

"I wanted to tell you I miss you," Min says. I close my eyes as my heart squeezes tight. I wait for her to go on. "I've done very little these last couple of weeks but think of you, you know. No, I guess you wouldn't know." She laughs a little, nervously. Then she swallows again. I can hear it this time. "I've been a mess. Margo finally came over to yell at me. She made me step back and get a little perspective. You were right, what you said that night about my being afraid of losing you if we got too close. It's true. Of course understanding it doesn't make it go away."

I smile in spite of myself. My eyes are still closed. I am holding my breath.

She goes on, "I realized something else. There are consequences to loving someone, to her loving you. I mean responsibility, I think. Margo helped me see that it wasn't fair of me to tell you that I wanted to be with you and at the same time that I wanted to be able to see other women."

I am so grateful to be hearing this at last. At the same time, a small voice inside me flares up, accusingly. (That's what I was telling you all along.) I reach into the pocket of my bathrobe and take out a tissue. I blow my stuffed-up nose into it.

I say, "Margo had to tell you what you wanted?"

"I didn't know what I wanted, Laura. I'm still not positive. I've always trusted my feelings in the moment to guide me. I'm impulsive. That's not something I feel I need to apologize for." I look at her, then away. I'm still waiting. Then I feel ashamed of myself. I'm acting like I deserve her apology. When did I stop receiving her love as a gift?

Min says, "What I realize is that I have to make a decision one way or the other. To commit or to get out. Something that takes you into consideration too. Otherwise you'll do something like move to Washington."

She hasn't said what her decision is, and her missing me isn't enough for me to jump to a conclusion. I turn, shifting my whole body toward her. I feel calm. In a strange way, it doesn't matter what happens now.

"Laura," Min says abruptly, and I can tell that she's holding herself back from touching me, which would be the easy answer, the one she has always used. "I really miss you. I don't want you to move to Washington. I want you to stay here. With me."

I have no immediate response, for her or for myself. A lot has happened between us, maybe more than we know what to do with. She's not the only one who's scared.

I reach out and cover her hand that is lying in a loose fist on her leg with my own hand. "Do you remember when I met you the first day of fifth grade and we played Scissors, Paper, Stone?"

"Yeah, you hit me!"

"I didn't know any better. Those were the rules I'd learned."

Sitting with her now on the steps of my building, I hold her fist firmly, paper covering stone. Then I slide my fingers lightly over her knuckles, her fingers, feeling the smoothness of the skin and the shape of the bones underneath. It's hard, but I hold her gaze as my hand moves along hers. Her fingers open and spread, and mine slip along their sides. I touch her very lightly. Now I couldn't look away from her eyes if I tried. Then she turns her hand over, unhurriedly, never losing contact with mine. We rub our palms together, lightly. My fingers slide between hers. We clasp hands. I want to spend the rest of my life memorizing her face, knowing she could someday turn away.

Then I close my eyes and sneeze, and sneeze again.

"It's chilly out here," Min says. "You should be in bed." We let our hands pull apart, and we stand up. I brush off the back of my bathrobe. I am giddy, though I have no idea how much is exhilaration and how much is being sick. When I run up the last steps to the door and turn around, Min is standing where I left her.

"Aren't you coming up?" I ask, afraid I have misunderstood everything.

"Wait," she says. "I want to know something. If I hadn't come over and you had moved to Washington, would you at least have said goodbye?"

I panic, not sure what to tell her. Her slight smile drains away. She can see from my face what the answer is.

"Well," she says, bounding up the steps and putting her hand on my back. "That was close."

I push open the door, kicking the wedge out of the way. We go inside.

ACKNOWLEDGMENTS

I wrote *Scissors, Paper, Stone* during the second half of the 1990s, two decades before it is being published. In the intervening years I lost my notes and documentation related to the book, so the following acknowledgments are necessarily incomplete. In addition to those named, a number of people gave me valuable assistance along the way, for which I am genuinely grateful.

My appreciation to the Virginia Center for the Creative Arts, the Djerassi Resident Artists Program, and the Saltonstall Foundation Arts Colony for their gifts of uninterrupted time to write in beautiful parts of the country.

Thank you to Red Hen Press for such a streamlined and rewarding publishing experience. I am especially grateful to Tobi Harper for founding the Quill Prose Award.

Most of all, I thank my non-writer friends who read the full manuscript at various stages and gave illuminating feedback: Joy Cramer, Ruth Chapman, Pam Roman, and Pat Uribe-Lichty. Your support and encouragement helped me persevere.

BIOGRAPHICAL NOTE

MARTHA K. DAVIS is a writer, editor, and teacher living in San Diego. Her short stories and essays have appeared in *River Styx, Stone Canoe, The Gay & Lesbian Review, StoryQuarterly, CALYX,* and elsewhere. She received her MFA in fiction from Columbia University. Parts of *Scissors, Paper, Stone* were written during residencies at the Virginia Center for the Creative Arts and the Djerassi Resident Artists Program.

CPSIA information can be obtained
at www.ICGtesting.com
Printed in the USA
BVOW09s1602060318
509774BV00002B/2/P